W9-BUK-334

THE WORST
INTENTIONS

Alessandro Piperno

THE WORST INTENTIONS

*Translated from the Italian
by Ann Goldstein*

Europa
editions

Europa Editions
116 East 16th Street
New York, N.Y. 10003
www.europaeditions.com
info@europaeditions.com

This book is a work of fiction. Any references to historical events,
real people, or real locales are used fictitiously.

Copyright © 2005 by Arnoldo Mondadori Editore S.p.A., Milano
First Publication 2007 by Europa Editions

Translation by Ann Goldstein
Original Title: *Con le peggiori intenzioni*
Translation copyright © 2007 by Europa Editions

All rights reserved, including the right of reproduction
in whole or in part in any form

Library of Congress Cataloging in Publication Data is available
ISBN 978-1-933372-33-4

Piperno, Alessandro
The Worst Intentions

Book design by Emanuele Ragnisco
www.mekkanografici.com

Cover photo: Runabout Riva Superflorida 1957-1968,
with kind permission © Archivio Riva

Printed in Italy
Arti Grafiche La Moderna – Rome

CONTENTS

For my little Emanuela

THE WORST
INTENTIONS

When God gives you a gift,
he also gives you a whip and the whip is
meant for self-flagellation.

—TRUMAN CAPOTE

Céline recommended that the Jews
be exterminated like bacteria.
It's the doctor in him, I suppose.

—SAUL BELLOW

And the World Trade Center rising
at the southern rim, the towers siamesed
when you see them from this angle,
joined at the waist by a transit crane.

—DON DELILLO

PART 1
HOW THE SONNINOS LIVED

Bepy felt he had no escape, when, several hours after absorbing the diagnosis of a tumor in his bladder, he chose from the infinite number of chilling questions: Will I still be able to fuck a woman or is this it?

Although the problem might appear to be a pathological inversion of priorities, for him, in this extreme crisis, the specter of compromised masculinity was more terrifying than terror of the void: maybe because in his imagination impotence and death coincided, even though the second was preferable to the first, if only for the consolation of eternal absence . . . Or maybe the leap in the dark that had brought this successful man to bankruptcy had been too shocking not to make a dent in his emotional wholeness.

But why keep the tightrope walker of adulterous sex— advocate of deporting the gays of the world to an island "all their own"—from being utterly himself?

His seasoned and hypercompetitive dick was ready, for the last time, to shine in the glow of an old flame; Giorgia Di Porto, seamstress, not to mention semi-clandestine lover in times of plenty, was about to rend the darkness of Bepy Sonnino's last years.

Things between them had gone to hell the day Ada, Bepy's moody wife, with skin the color of sugared almonds, discovered the seventeen-year-old girl—sassy and stuck-up, like Catherine Spaak in *The Easy Life*—urinating on the mustache of her consort, as he drank the golden ammonia with the greediness of a suckling infant. The rest is an inevitable climax: Ada's horrified cry, the forced dismissal of the whore, and the compensatory purchase of a coral necklace from Buccellati, which did, in fact, celebrate the end of that dissolute relationship.

Sixteen years later.

Bepy, going into a boutique to buy yet another gift destined for yet another pupil, seeing the faded version of Giorgia coming toward him as head saleswoman, feels the unmistakable surge rising from his loins that almost fifty years ago made him a man.

And although that bright-orange blend of rouge, hair coloring, and nail polish is a superb allegory of autumn, although, to look at her, one would say she had spent the past twenty years trying to resemble more and more every day her own caricature, although the leather miniskirt and the leopard-print body stocking are not the right ingredients for a hefty girl at least five years past thirty, when she exclaims, "My dear Mr. Sonnino!" (and with what an obsequious tone! what a merciful lack of irony!), he can't resist.

Giorgia saves his life.

So he likes to think, inviting her for a walk. And while his hand hurries to hide the hole in his cashmere sleeve and his heart erupts in incandescent lava, Bepy prays to God that she doesn't ask for a ride, because in the small car he has now it would be revolting. And just then—before the spectacle of his own irrefutable poverty—Bepy Sonnino understands that he has betrayed the maxim that, in good and ill, has determined his life: Better to stink of shit than of poverty!—as he has repeated obsessively to himself every day for the past fifty years.

On the wave of this recognition of negligence, he spontaneously exhumes from the record book of memory one of the last weekends spent with Giorgia: how marvelous, parading along the seafront at Forte, in the light-blue Jaguar with the honeyed-walnut dashboard, as he shows off a teenage lover to a crowd of livid contemporaries!

Is there a privilege more masculine than rousing the envy of the world?

It's in the name of that envy that Bepy—signing overdrawn checks, defying the fury of bank directors, asking sons and daughters-in-law for loans he can be repay, but above all relying on his reputation as an inscrutable man, which has been carved into the imagination of the aging and formidably immature Giò (as he likes to call her, with the open "o," just as he used to)—courts her fiercely, and gets her to capitulate, one evening, winning the ultimate libertine wager. But just then, in the recurrences that mark the life of this man, always wavering between disaster and parody, the illness appears. And the only thing that Bepy can ask himself, engrossed in the eager curves of the pseudo-arousing body of Giò, is if he will still be able, after the possible surgery, to fuck her with ease.

If no one had reproached the naturalness with which Ada and Bepy Sonnino absorbed the trauma of the birth of an albino like my father and a nutcase like my uncle, everyone had expected from those masters of the art of underestimation a rapid adaptation to the financial collapse that, besides reducing them to poverty, had undermined the foundation of the solid bond between them.

And, in effect, the two of them had managed, when all was said and done, by alternating—in the ménage of their old age—methodical smiles of resentment with shouting matches that were literally epoch-making. Like, for example, the time he rushed home to announce, at the height of indignation, that he had seen Rabbi Perugia in the checkout line of a supermarket carrying two enormous, bright-colored boxes of panettone.

"Where is it written that a rabbi can't buy a panettone?"

"A rabbi should set an example . . ."

"Did it occur to you that it might be a kosher panettone?"

"Ada, I'm serious . . ."

"Find me a single rule—one!—that prohibits a Jew from buying a panettone."

"So then why not a crèche? Is it written somewhere that a Jew can't have a crèche?"

"So then tell me why you're so sure he was going to eat it?"

"You think he got it for to put on the mantlepiece?"

(It should be noted how the Sonninos Jewishly preferred the interrogative dimension to the typically Christian asseverative one.)

Or the day of the phone call from an employee of the cemetery informing us—before giving the news to the press, to arouse the usual trite indignation—that some hoodlum had not only disfigured the family tomb with painted swastikas but, still not satisfied, had stolen the mineralized remains of my great-grandfather, what was left of the venerable lawyer and music-lover Graziaddio Sonnino:

"Poor Papa!"

"It's ten years since you've been to see him . . ."

"You think that matters to him? He's dead."

Not to mention the times when Bepy let himself go in dreamlike paeans to the great artists of our century: his passion for contemporary art, which verged on idolatry, not only could temporarily break the chains of his skepticism but seemed to throw him into a sensual swoon incompatible with his all-too-well-publicized coolness.

"Tell me, Ada . . . if at this exact moment the great Picasso should appear . . . what would you say to him?" he asked dreamily.

"Bah, I'd probably ask for a loan!"

I have to confess that my favorite quarrel (maybe because I

have the honor of playing the role of the frightened nine-year-old witness) is the one where Ada and Bepy, returning home, find the very young and attractive Ukrainian maid with her hair wet and wearing Grandma's dressing gown.

"May I ask what the hell you're doing?"

"But signora, it was you who ordered me to wash every day."

"Are you making fun of me? I didn't mean wash yourself!"

It's here that Bepy, spurred by a pedantic form of gallantry, feels obliged to intervene:

"Well, Ada, we have to allow that your expression was rather ambiguous."

And who knows if that flow of cynicism, with which from time to time one annihilated the passions of the other, was not a way of putting off the serious discussion that—in half a century of marriage consecrated to mutual infidelity and the meticulous squandering of money—they hadn't had the stomach to confront.

Since any allusion had been forbidden, the curtain fell on that drama in progress even before it unfolded on the stage, as if the entire world had been drugged by the elixir of talc and lime cologne with which Bepy, after his morning shower, generously soaked his groin. Even the retro-fear of the Imponderable had been banished in that absurd family, with a few ritual exceptions: the anxieties that tortured Bepy in the middle of the night, as he waited for a telephone call from a public official who would report an automobile accident in which one of his sons had lost his life, news that would in a single blow transform the exemplary human doings of Bepy Sonnino & family into an inexpressible darkness of suffering. But at least he was spared this.

And yet you had to understand them!

Having swallowed, after a comfortable adolescence, the

dose of erotic frustration that is, after all, what the anti-Jewish laws of '38 were, and literally infected by the epidemic postwar joy, these Jews of bourgeois Rome had replaced—and how extemporaneously!—the terror of Benito Mussolini and Adolf Hitler with a mimetic veneration of Clark Gable and Elizabeth Taylor. It was as if that frightening, clownish pair of Fascist dictators had never existed, as if—in the hearts of all Italian Bepys—they had been buried along with the indistinguishable bodies of the hundreds of deported relatives: the mass of cousins, brothers- and sisters-in-law, sisters, mothers- and fathers-in-law and grandchildren whose remains by now would take up a couple of garbage bags, whom you were harshly forbidden to mention and whose end you were secretly ashamed of. Even more completely eliminated from the memory of their surviving relatives than from the face of the earth: as if their rags and hellish thinness, their anonymous deaths, minutely documented by those horrendous black-and-white photographs, were unsuitable for the sparkle of the silverware, the euphoric brio of the cocktails of those fantastic years. Or as if that madness of diabolic evil that had befallen the Drowned had authorized for the Saved a casual lack of scruples: was it for this reason—only this?—that there was not a single individual in Bepy and Ada's circle who did not feel authorized to violate bourgeois precepts, making sexual advances to the wife of his best friend or the underage daughter of his dearest colleague?

Evidently the inferno had abolished prohibitions. If this collective repression had not existed, how would Grandma Ada—whose two little cousins and a dozen other relatives the Nazis had annihilated (even though in the family, out of delicacy, they preferred the euphemistic expression "taken away")—have managed to participate with such emotion in the drying of her hydrangeas every summer?

Nothing strange, in the end: Bepy and Ada felt they were owed. That was all. Usually people who have risked their lives develop, after the trauma, a circumspection disguised as nocturnal nightmare or daytime presentiment. The Sonninos, instead, granted themselves a special full immunity, supported on the one hand by the conviction that those who have the courage to endure such an enormous disaster are equipped to overcome later, certainly lesser events and, on the other, by the awareness of their right to compensation, guaranteed by any monotheistic religion and by every liberal legal system (so manifestly in contrast with the laws of human destiny). History would have shown them that it's better to be hunted by the Nazis at twenty-five with the hope of making it than to be sixty years old and flat broke, at the mercy of public disapproval, in the heart of a cruelly indifferent Western democracy.

Frivolity, sarcasm, impudence; a penchant for sophistry, deceit, and false pretense; imprudence, incapacity to evaluate a single act, prodigality, sex mania, lack of interest in anyone else's point of view, reluctance to recognize one's own failings, feigned strength of character that is only weakness, and above all a peculiar variety of optimism spilling over into irresponsibility: that is only a tiny fraction of the mixture with which they habitually take you in, putting your back against the wall, the germ with which they poison your body, but also the cocaine with which they intoxicate it. And if only I had had the courage to hold them to their responsibilities, if only I had had the insolence (in which I was so deficient at the dawn of my puberty) to enjoin them: "I beg you, I implore you, isn't it time to admit your mistakes? And look reality in the face?" I'm sure they would have gazed at me with contempt, to burn me immediately afterward with a philosophical quip like: "The young master is requested to give a definition of *reality!*"

Wasn't it precisely through this all-embracing relativism that, almost thirty years earlier, Bepy had managed to persuade that freak of nature my father to consider his albinism a unique distinction and opportunity, the trademark of his future personality?

The unexpected educational success that Bepy had with my father—which no one later gave him credit for—originated in the deliberate overturning of every pedagogic paradigm: Bepy chose to magnify the differences and incongruities of his phosphorescent little firstborn. And by dint of saying over and over to him, "You are unique, un-re-peat-a-ble, you have hair like a Martian and skin like a polar bear's . . .," he had witnessed, not without pride, the miraculous strengthening of that so precociously deformed creature. One could say that Bepy's stroke of genius consisted in diverting little Luca's attention from the eccentricity of his absurd appearance to the constraints of formal impeccability: shame on you if your shoes are dusty, the crease in your trousers is crooked, you block a woman's path, succumb dialectically or make a bad showing athletically. Because the most important thing is to remember that nothing is important enough to deserve our emotional engagement or interfere with our material comfort. And so one must talk and talk, never stop talking, not be silent in order to listen, not listen in order not to be silent, acquire a talent for the last word, the unforgettable remark.

Maybe memory has played the trick on me of transforming Bepy into a decalogue on the proper behavior for living to the maximum with the minimum effort.

Let's take the time when my grandfather, during a stay at the Cristallo in Cortina, after a sumptuous breakfast in his room—with all the sparkling five-star extras that he can't do without—locks my brother Lorenzo and me, not yet adolescents, in the bathroom to make us defecate and, irritated by our protests ("What if it doesn't come out?"), repeats: "I don't care." "Please, Grandpa, open the door." "I forbid you to flush, I want to see! It's a matter of mental health!" Well, all he's doing is demonstrating to us how a certain bellicosity is the right medicine for the puerile wimpiness of our generation and our epoch.

Bepy is crazy, excessive, but he is a champion in the art of derision and duplicity. A creature forged by the Fascist twenties, sweetened by an overdose of causticity and republican humor—a living contradiction who could be accused of anything except not being drastically faithful to himself.

Even when, centuries ago, Teo, his second-born, at just over eighteen, decided to get a summer job to pay for a Jungian analyst who would help him understand his desire to emigrate to Israel not as a manifestation of Oedipal hatred, or as anti-patriotic, but as an "adult" aspiration (this attribute moved the Sonninos to tears) that would mark a turning point in his existence . . . Even on that occasion Bepy, to oppose his son, resorted to his matchless cynicism:

"What's the use of analysis? Haven't you had enough of such inanities? Unless you've hit on an institutional way of talking to a lady about getting laid. In that case you would have my approval."

"Come on, please, leave me alone."

"I'm serious. It's filthy hot in Israel. There's no water. Giordi Spizzichino told me that the desalinization plants break down on average every three days. You can't even take a shower every night. And of course those Yids are lousy cooks. Don't you know that Rachele Loewenthal has had chronic dysentery ever since she's lived in Haifa?"

That's Bepy: a tough character whose unconscious empiricism was always expressed in personal cases. He pulled out of his hat a throng of friends and relatives—all with improbable names—who had had, done, risked, tried what you, innocent little you, were about to attempt, on the one hand unprovided with that sublime emotional life vest that parents all over the world call "experience" and on the other overwhelmed by your sentimentality.

"I've de-de-de-ci-ci-ded," stammered Teo, as if he wanted to kill his father by machine-gunning him with syllables.

"No, you have not *de-de-de-cided*," mimicking him with impunity. "You don't decide like that. You reflect and then you decide. You know what you need, my dear boy?"

"Be-ep-y-yy . . . Pleeeease . . . don't teeeellll me . . ."

"A game of tennis, a massage with cologne, and, to finish off, a good fuck . . ."

"Pointless, Papa. I've told you that . . ." Teo whispered stubbornly, his voice trembling, because he wasn't used to contradicting his father and didn't know how to speak seriously to him, although for his entire life he had been trying to learn how to do both.

"The club has admitted a lot of delightful young women this year: just what we need. If you'll only calm down, have a good shower, dress up, and, above all, pay attention to your papa, I assure you that by tonight . . ."

"Come on, Bepy . . . Doesn't any *other* thing exist for you?"

"Not only does nothing *other* exist but I distrust all those frustrated *goys* who proclaim the marvels of the *other* . . ."

"It so happens that at this exact moment of my life what interests me is only and exclusively the *other* . . ."

"It so happens that I don't give a fuck about it. You are not leaving! Give me one good reason, for God's sake!" the old man snapped, noticing the ineffectiveness of his arguments and maybe for that reason getting sullen. "You know, Teo, that I am monstrously reasonable. And so I need a 'why.' If you give me this fucking 'why' you can go to Australia if you want. Or to the moon with Neil Armstrong."

Incongruous demand. Rhetorical question. The answer is there, in plain sight: in the blue shirt open to the curly forest of Bepy's chest, in the insolence of his biceps, in the watery splendor of his smile, in the skin that smells of roasted coffee and chlorine, in the indestructible self-assurance, in the ingenuous crushing pansexuality, in the body that never stops shouting, "I've made it. I know the recipe for the good life . . ." Yes, why look elsewhere? The answer is easy. He is the answer we're looking for. He, the Father, and then Luca, his emissary in disguise, his firstborn—his *bechor*. There it is, Grandpa, there's your fucking "why."

Without, however, forgetting that that overbearing display of insensitivity is above all strategic: the self-justifying mechanism that any father in flagrant bad faith mobilizes to protect himself from that nuisance which some illustrious charlatans call "sense of guilt": the easy way to avoid a hard truth: who else, if not he, the Father—with his machismo, with his extraordinary if temporary success in life—is responsible for the unhappiness, the inadequacy, of his second-born? Who, in the late fifties, transformed that smiling snot-nosed kid, always searching for impossible-to-find Eddie Cochran or Jerry Lee Lewis records, into an angry teenager, unable to find himself except in his own religious feeling, and the desire to flee to Israel?

(But isn't this another way of getting bogged down in the muddiest mire of the twentieth century? Haven't you had enough of the sins of the fathers? Or the rage of the sons, not to mention their belated repentance? Aren't you fed up with intergenerational clashes? He, Bepy, doesn't feel responsible for anything. He doesn't want any nonsense. Life, after all, is simple. *The Nazis wanted to kill me for reasons that I still don't know. I made it. And was young enough to start over again. Don't ask me how or why. I'm not a guy who has ready answers. I'll shout out my happiness. I'll sanctify my good faith. I'll reward my offspring materially. Then it's up to them.*)

But it can't be said that this cynicism is a shortcut by which Bepy clears his conscience. Anything but. It's a costly operation for a spirit so naturally inclined to an indulgent fluidity. It's simply a way of taking sides: long live simplification, long live sentimental sterility. (Find me someone who resists the enchantment of his own slogans, who isn't madly in love with his own idea of the world.) Bepy was born to simplify. Nor does he understand—and will not, even at the end—that levity can sometimes be the prelude to indifference. And indifference, in turn, the viaticum for disaster.

And on the other hand life, for the immoralist and voluptuous Sonnino couple—with all their levity and all their sodden rhetoric of levity—turned out, in the end, to be a bad business. But without their ever giving it the satisfaction of an honest acknowledgment.

Because the Sonninos—it's good to keep in mind—are allergic to inner life.

It was Dr. Limentani—surgeon at the Jewish Hospital and Bepy's second cousin, not to mention his tennis partner in the Sunday morning doubles matches at the Lazio Rowing Club—who first warned him, inaugurating the chorus of friends and family eager to persuade him that the essential thing is to save your skin. And, of course, tact is a rare commodity in the Sonnino household:

"The operation is indispensable—maybe we've caught it in time."

"Risks?"

"The risk is total!"

"No, come on . . . You know what I mean . . . Impotence?"

"God, Bepy, this is the most serious thing that's happened to you."

"I asked you if there's a risk."

"And I've told you yes. There are a thousand risks . . ."

"Then no!"

"Come on, Giuseppe, it's no joke this time."

"No."

"You understand that it's madness? Suicide? Things

change, you just have to . . . and then it's not at all a sure thing . . ."

"No!"

"You're being a dickhead, as usual!"

Bepy chooses to die: slowly his body melts away, the muscles liquefy like ice cream in the sun. Giorgia disappears in the magma of an unappeasable desire, while Ada returns yet again to look after him.

Bepy, by now, isn't even the double of the elderly macho man who asked me (his twelve-year-old grandson) to show him my genitals, so he could check on their aptitude for future erotic battles. His face, almost completely covered by a prickly beard, and his eyes, excited by morphine, give him an aura of asceticism obviously antithetical to his character and his history. Yes, Bepy's face, a few lengths from death, is a marvelous apocrypha of mysticism. It's as if, for Bepy, the outer world were tending toward a progressive uniformity. Perceiving us remote and interchangeable, it's as if he were digging a tomb within himself. He has never been so closed up in himself. The glassy gaze he turns to us seems uncorrupted by prejudices. For him by now my grandmother, my mother, my father, the Filipino woman who nurses him, even his apocalyptic visions—just like that pitch-black bubble by which he will soon be absorbed—are all the same, emissaries of the milky chaos into which the world has been transubstantiated.

He lies in the bedroom of the mortgaged house in the Parioli (where he moved after the bankruptcy and the brief American interlude), which preserves a semblance of refinement, barely spoiled by a worn sheet or a chipped cup, things that exasperate my grandmother as much as the inexorable demise of her husband. Sunk down in his bed, resistant to the idea of having no escape, even though his room looks like a pharmacy, overflowing with medicine bottles (from the innocuous aspirin to the more invasive painkillers), all he does is repeat phrases like "Tomorrow, if I feel better . . ." without bothering to finish them. Or he stares dreamily at the Michelangelesque buttocks of my Cape Verdean nanny and lets himself go in dreamy comments: "So this is paradise . . ." Or again, turning to his wife, heedless of our presence, or maybe excited by it: "Say it, that you never enjoyed it with anyone the way you did with your Bepy . . ." Even though Giorgia remains the only true protagonist of his delirium, with special reference to that "blow job of '79." The blow job given by a love-struck adolescent to a fifty-year-old who is about to know the shame of financial ruin and exile.

It's strange: obscenity has never been his forte. Sex, yes, but obscenity never. Now, though—maybe because his brain can't accommodate the idea of his imminent nonexistence, can't absorb a distasteful concept like lack-of-a-possible-future—he seems to have found an outlet in the obscene. How can our Bepy, the personal enemy of vulgarity, who taught us to avoid it, abandon himself to a horrifying verbal incontinence at the most serious moment of his life? The fact is that the sanest man in the world has never thought of death except as an abstract hypothesis that only concerns "other people." And his obscene ravings, which Professor Limentani with secular empiricism and Jewish piety ascribes to the effect of Tangesic, seem, rather, the sign of a brain's refusal to accept that it is dying: a sort of pathological degeneration of our Bepy's usual delirious optimism or, if you prefer, of his endemic cowardice—if you can't change something, obliterate it. Obliterate, Bepy, while you've got time. Hasn't this, perhaps, been the essence of your life? Your most inadmissible secret?

This is why, in spite of the pain and the very obvious impediments of his condition, he continues to shave and to sprinkle his cheeks and hair with cologne, in the same touching and thoughtless way that, in the days after his financial collapse, he persisted in lavish habits and irresponsible purchases. As if a part of his body and his intelligence had difficulty registering that unbearable circumstance, or required an illusion of normality.

By now Bepy is concerned only with his own body, his own physiological confusions, as if his body had become the entire planet, as if it were composed of valleys, plateaus, mountains, and oceans: every so often, resorting to an incongruous scientific term, he whispers, "I have to urinate," or "I have to defecate," as if he were announcing the arrival of a flood or an earthquake. It's as if now that his body's days are numbered—now that the burden of the flesh weighs more than the universe, now that the body has gone mad, now that the body responds only to itself, now that the great Bepy has replaced his unmistakable scent of limewater cologne and Tuscan cigars with that spiced miasma of diseased excrement—he had suddenly discovered that nothing else ever existed: only the body, the body alone.

Ada Sonnino's last words were uttered a few days before her death, during our Sunday walk in the city center: an essay in impropriety worthy of an eighteenth-century libertine, and even more eccentric considering its provenance—in the most chic of octogenarians, who seemed to have hidden the secret of a girl's beauty and a mature woman's charm in a solitary pearl that gleamed on her neck, hanging from an invisible wire of white gold. At the time, arteriosclerosis had ruined her brain. The only mental activity granted to that skinny old woman, once the loveliest girl in the Roman Jewish community, with her narrow Egyptian nose and black hair, was the ceaseless recitation of the names of the stores, as if the sex mania that had consumed her and her consort for their entire lives had been sublimated, forty years later, in an unpredictably verbal form. Was this how her brain, packed with brilliant and dramatic memories, tried to escape itself? Was this the senile version of her long-term strategy of dissimulation? A living monument to Oblivion? Who can say! Yet sometimes, in a kind of metaphysical epiphany, the circulatory illness that had led to her delirium abandoned the field to small drops of wisdom. And you never knew whether to take them as the fruit of the photographic memory of certain sick minds that randomly repeat phrases from many years earlier or, rather, as a temporary return to reason, prelude to a new plunge into darkness.

So who is this woman? This venerable old woman who in the chaos of Via Condotti grips my arm as if she had nothing else? Is it possible that this jumble of trembling bones is what remains of the beautiful girl who ruined her husband, as people say? She to whom Bepy could deny nothing? Is it true that Bepy bought her silence? Is it true that Bepy was at the mercy of this woman's megalomania? Is she the evil one responsible for the rise and fall of Our Man? The black widow? Is she the one we've been looking for since the start of this investigation? Is she the one we should be blaming? No one has forgotten that a few days after her husband's departure for the United States she, in the grip of hysteria, unable to accept that her princely life had gone up in smoke forever, and frightened by the possibility that the fatal news might reach her "bridge friends" of Via Paisiello—that they might smile about it the way she had thousands of times smiled at the misfortunes of others—refused to return the furs her husband had just bought and not yet paid for. My father tore them out of her hands, as if to make her understand that the good manners of the wealthy had given way to the violence of the newly indigent.

And yet: I was struck when Ada Sonnino, looking at me with those wild eyes, after reading aloud all the signs along Via del Babuino and preparing to start on those of Via Condotti, said to me, like an oracle:

"Daniel, if some day your girl should discover you in bed

with someone else, tell her that you were sleeping, that you don't know how that little whore could have ended up on your mattress, deny the evidence. Women want only to be lied to . . ."

I know it's not the most edifying discourse one might expect from a grandmother near the grave. I know perfectly well that some will consider that point of view antiquated, and degrading for a woman. It's certainly not something for International Women's Day or feminist collectives or the philogynist Sunday supplements. And yet it's a useful background for understanding how the mysteriously indissoluble bond between Bepy and Ada continued to be nourished—after the death of Him—by some vague sense of guilt in Her, the sole survivor: the regrets and remorse of a woman in her dotage, like, for example, her failure to persuade her husband that the operation on his bladder was absolutely necessary. How could she have allowed that wretched man to immolate himself on the altar of his unbearable machismo? Why had she let that virile body—whose skin, as rough and hard as a knapsack, had so excited her ever since the long-ago time when, at the height of the racial campaign, they had met and come together, blessed by the friendly bombs of the "allies"—dry up and wither?

Bepy not only had faced the final passage without letting himself be touched by gloom, or by the empty stupidity of Fundamental Questions, but had almost succeeded, for the last time, in persuading us that virility was a value worth sacrificing your life for.

Midget in dark suit, whispers a suave voice inside me, like the announcer at a fashion show: soft midnight-blue skullcap and sunglasses stolen from my mother (even though they're not graduated), because they look very "American funeral." I'm almost handsome, affectedly grief-stricken in my Brooks Brothers boys' department blazer and the temporary blond forelock that caresses my forehead.

The ageless Rabbi Perugia begins the ceremony without preamble. He seems irritated. His lips barely move. The idea is that the words come out of his mouth like a rote prayer. The idea is that, even though he knows Hebrew, he doesn't understand them or stopped listening to them ages ago.

But here comes a black Mercedes 500, fresh from the car wash, moving as slowly as if it were just another hearse, and stops right at the dark group, in the square in front of the gloomy chapel of the Jewish cemetery. Like a movie star, Giovanni Cittadini (Nanni to his friends) gets out of the car, Bepy's lifelong friend and swindled partner: he's in dark gray, a shadow of consternation obscuring his usually clear gaze. He is a marvelous sixty-five-year-old who smells of camphor and jasmine: an articulated giraffe whom, if you didn't know his proverbial restraint, you might take for a penitent fag (a kind of repressed homosexuality expressed as an irritable misogyny). He, too, wears a skullcap, uncalled-for homage to the Perfidious Jewish Brothers, with definite comic effect: a walking oxymoron. His figure has nothing Jewish about it: too lanky, too much confidence in his carriage. Escorted by two ephebes of indecipherable sex austerely garbed as *garçons d'honneur*, he passes in review the widow, the older son, the younger, the grandchildren and so on in a sequence of pleasantries. Only now as he is looking me in the eye with the intensity of someone who has many things to say do I understand that he has nothing to say to me. He swaggers, continually adjusting the jeweled cufflinks of his white shirt, as if he thought that he, and not the corpse, was the true star of this cemetery gathering.

It's surprising to see him at the obsequies of the unworthy man who—according to what people are murmuring—stole a lot of money from him. *So has he forgiven him?* is the question going around. Not only has Nanni, in his worldliness, been generous toward Bepy's relations, getting them out of a bind and restoring them to a decent life, but he has now found the generosity to attend the funeral of his disgraceful former friend who dared to come on to Sofia, his stupendous blue-blooded wife. How could Nanni the Magnanimous forgive Bepy the Irredeemable? Many are the motives for resentment, both legitimate and illegitimate, that the Magnanimous can claim against the Irredeemable: and this time business doesn't enter into it, or even the loyalty of lifelong friends. There are several matters outstanding that Nanni, with all his good nature, has not yet forgiven. One above all: Giorgia, the sublime seventeen-year-old seamstress. Not that Nanni was in love with her. An infatuation, an exuberant impulse, that's all. The sort of thing that happens to a man like Nanni—past forty, of sterling character—after a life of honorable conjugal service. An interest in an enchanting young thing. Nothing more. Let's say that Nanni liked to talk to her, flirt, come up with a different trick every day to make her laugh. Isn't it fantastic to see a girl laugh? Let's say that he had rediscovered a taste for taking a shower in the morning and spending a quarter of an hour choosing a tie.

Let's say that for a while he couldn't wait to get to the office to see if an encounter with that girl would cause the same slight alteration in his breathing as the day before . . . In short, given such premises, it's plausible to consider that the small family scandal involving Bepy and the young seamstress—the traumatic discovery on the part of Ada of her consort's dissolute relationship based on seaside weekends and urine parties— made Nanni ill disposed, and made him feel like a fool. Yes, it couldn't have been easy for a proud man like him—and so puritanical—to accept the idea that just at the time when he had begun to wonder about the advisability of inviting her out to lunch Bepy had been fucking her for more than a month. *A minor, can you believe that? A minor. My little baby* . . .

And yet this archangel—come on, folks, such a distinguished man!—came anyway: he is here among us at the funeral. He even seems moved. And in a further sign of the easing of diplomatic tensions he has brought with him his blond grandchildren, in twin gray coats whose mother-of-pearl buttons make you think of sparkling Arctic surfaces: two creatures so angelically abstract that I want to lower my gaze, as if, instead of at the funeral of my grandfather, I were caught up in the spectacle of my own human degradation. Only now do I realize that it's a boy and a girl.

It's as if the appearance of the Aryan disguised as a Jew with the two cherubim had confirmed in those present—whether close relatives or distant friends—the idea that that son of a bitch Bepy died at the right moment, at the summit of disgrace, young enough to rouse in others an assuaging pity but not so young that every past depravity can be forgiven. Bepy was one of those temperaments capable of finding full harmony in the effervescence of youth: during the brilliant sprint that was his existence, he had already passed through all the significant stages on the way to degradation. Why hang around any longer?

Bepy wasn't born to live by expedients, to run after servants and secretaries, cheat them for a little cash, as he did in his last years. He's a charismatic figure, who needs a stage to perform on. Let's close our eyes and see him in his white dinner jacket, inspired expression, golden mustache, and insolent smile revealing his wide incisors, like Clark Gable, while he sips a glass of champagne on the bridge of the Michelangelo, beside his wife and the whole daring bunch of pleasure-seekers, out to conquer New York! So let the bastard die. Yes, he died at the right moment. He wasn't the type for jackets deformed by the incipient hump of old age. Not the type to bear infirmities and physical handicaps stoically. You could say—as some maintain—that his life would have been even more perfect (in the mythopoetic sense) if only he had killed himself a few years earlier, at the time of the financial crash. That humiliating coda of the last five years, the ruin and disgrace, was just a vulgar surplus, the work of some decadent artist without talent. Try to imagine Bepy being able to tolerate old age, the ugly old age of deafness, of senile delusions, of memories, the weary gait and the widespread, trembling legs of prostatic incontinence. No, that wasn't for Bepy Sonnino. Never was a death more mercifully timed. Bearing witness to this is the emotion of those gathered, completely focused on what he was and not on what he might still have been.

For the family it's a liberation. No doubt about it. It seems that everyone is looking at the children and grandchildren and thinking of the troubles brought on them by the Iconoclast, who, after building up and consolidating, in the course of a life, an admirable prosperity, turned it to shit in a couple of months. The financial crash that was the talk of the textile industry in the early eighties. Who doesn't know the story that consecrated my father, Luca Sonnino, as the involuntary hero of an epic all our own, an end-of-the-millennium Jewish Buddenbrooks?

*

When, at the age of twenty-three, Luca abandons engineering, dazed by the promise of "easy money," he is already one of those scions of the good Jewish bourgeoisie who get into a rage if, arriving at the office in the morning, they don't find a fresh rose in a crystal vase. At that time Bepy is still solidly his hero: a showman, with the hands and tongue of an illusionist, one who needs only the contrast between the fitted suit of ice-colored linen and the perennially tanned face to bewitch you. A schoolboy's game for him—a man endowed with dangerous seductive capacities—to promise you a thrilling future. Until then, Bepy had been not only the ideal guide—who, after all, removed my father's hair shirt of differentness?—but also the guarantor of unrestraint. Natural to listen to him, to let that auspicious smile penetrate, persuade you.

But when Bepy, victim of unexpected idiosyncrasies masked as Napoleonic splendors—everything but the recession behind which he will soon take cover!—ruins everything, getting himself into inconceivable debt, defrauding friends and enemies, Luca is a spoiled thirty-year-old. For Bepy it's bankruptcy and the imminent risk of jail. The tinfoil castle of the Sonninos has crumpled. Among their friends are those who discreetly rejoice (*Christ, they were so full of themselves!*), those who disappear, those who interpret the facts as a warning from the Omnipotent: how much longer would He have allowed someone like Bepy Sonnino to challenge Him with such impudence?

But there's no time for self-pity. Bepy has pulled off a hundred swindles: he's being hunted by the *carabinieri*, the tax police, bankruptcy trustees, maybe even by evil-minded dwarfs in the pay of furious usurers, and God knows who else. All he can do is flee immediately to the United States. Yes, from one day to the next he acquires, with his last cash, extorted from my mother, a plane ticket to New York (the Concorde, naturally: even escape claims its comforts), and flies off to Angelo, his younger brother, who after the war opened a Roman Jewish restaurant in the heart of Manhattan. Da Angelino: a delightful place that family mythology (or mythomania?) insists is frequented by Frank Sinatra, Sammy Davis, Jr., Barbra Streisand, and many others; on the wall a photo going back to '59 (the year it opened) that captures Marilyn Monroe, with a shy smile, in one of her last embraces with the ineffable Arthur Miller. Specialties of the house: marinated zucchini, Jewish-style artichokes, meatballs with celery, mozzarella *all'imperiale*, strictly kosher Chianti, and a background of old Italian tunes crossed with violin melodies reminiscent of the works of I. B. Singer. Bepy's circus, his amusement park, changes only its domicile, moving to the banks of the Hudson: the mood and the menu are the same—a meat loaf of careless amorality in a sauce of Jewish megalomania.

But let's try to imagine, on the other hand, the storm that is overwhelming my father, on the other side of that ocean: just thirty-six years old (shit, three more than I am now). The echoes of an opulent life of luxuries and possibilities that seem a posthumous mockery of his current straits.

Our house, in the days following the catastrophe, seems to have been transformed into a Charity Agency. Bepy had the impudence to telephone us (collect): "Everything's O.K., guys, don't worry about me. It's magnificent here!"

Worry? About him? Are we nuts? Is he out of his mind? At this point Bepy even finds the nerve to ask us to send his summer dinner jacket (*Sorry, guys, but you can't live here without a dinner jacket! And in the wool one you die of the heat . . .*).

My father insults him. Yes, for the first time he insults his hero. An insult thousands of kilometers long crosses the Atlantic in the blink of an eye. My father shouts, taking refuge in the comforting shell of self-pity: don't you understand, you dirty bastard, what kind of life we're living here? Every day a different creditor . . . We're under siege: upholsterers, silver-smiths, furriers, tailors, car dealers, even the café next to the warehouse. All those retailers who had faith in you, all those big shots who gave you credit—they're all lined up holding out colossal bills.

It's exactly like that: every time the telephone rings and a frigid voice asks for Bepy, Luca shudders. He knows that he will have to equivocate, invent nonsense or avoid the truth, he will have to calm the fury of the caller, who for the sole fact of having a claim on an overdue bill feels authorized to be rude. How did we get ourselves into this mess? All mankind seems to have an account outstanding with Bepy. There are even some unlikely creditors who throw an operetta-like light on his depravity. One day Johanna shows up, a Cape Verdean maid who is a friend of my nanny, a Creole with the figure of a music-hall dancer. She lost her truck-driver husband in a car accident. Well, only now that Bepy has fled does she, in tears, find the courage to reveal to my parents that she had a rela-tionship with him, entrusted him with millions of lire, her hus-band's death benefits, everything she had, to be invested by Seór Giuseppe—money that Bepy, obviously, never bothered to give back. We don't dare tell her that it undoubtedly made its way into the immense financial mishmash, the bloodthirsty beast that Bepy tried to keep at bay as long as he could, and we pledge to return it a little at a time. At a certain point money must have lost any value for him . . . just like people.

Only now do we realize that the dazzling wealth of recent years was supported by a perverse latticework of bank loans and a dizzying whirl of postdated and bounced checks: the grand illusionist finale of that tightrope-walking Mandrake.

And this time it's certainly not admiration that crushes my father but, if anything, rage.

What do you feel upon receiving a phone call from the director of a bank, one who until yesterday treated you with respect, one you've never given the time of day to, whom you have habitually pitied because he wore trousers without cuffs and was convinced that a loud tie held the secret of vitality? And what does it mean that now you're sitting on the hot seat, in front of this individual, who has suddenly become grim? He, the dispenser of fortunes, the croupier of modern life, solemnly utters the edifying little speech that makes his job like a preacher's. He says to you—with restraint, as if it cost him something (only now do you suspect that he's never liked you: you, with your inch-and-a-half cuffs, and your solid-color knit ties)—that you are ruined: there must be at least twenty people in Rome who if they meet you (as he says this a little smile escapes him) . . . Your life style's going to have to change, you're going to have to consider the hypothesis that the grand future you imagined for your children has to be readjusted (What does this have to do with anything? Why are you telling me this? What do you know? How dare you?). "Sell everything, even the silver: I don't see any other practicable way to stem the mounting tide, Mr. Sonnino. I'm saying this in your interest and for your integrity." What you can't bear are the wholesale ethics lessons. It's typical of bank directors to impart them. That's why you blanch when he ventures to say that the disaster is the "inevitable consequence" of your family's bad habits, your father's unscrupulousness (as if capitalism observed the strict ethics of the virtuous!).

The pain of having to communicate it to your wife, who if she didn't marry you for money certainly did so for freedom (and money is tied to that). She is probably wondering whether, having married a rich man, it's necessary to assume the burden of his financial failure. (How many wives are there who, in analogous circumstances, seeing their social status plummet from one day to the next, wouldn't ask for a divorce?)

The terror of running into your father-in-law, that calculating millionaire, whom you will never ask for help (or maybe yes, you will?). What does this turmoil produce in the vulnerable constitution of a man over thirty?

Luca has character and talent, and above all the desperate optimism of one who has had an easy life. After a moment of discouragement, at the first creaking in the pleasant adventure of marriage he grits his teeth, just as the humiliations are multiplying in that vortex of sold cars and pawned furniture. The deputy sheriff asks you what has become of your father. What has become of his collection of paintings. "Where, Mr. Sonnino, are the Burris and the Sironis that you had insured?" You don't know, or pretend not to know. Maybe he's run away, sir. And before running he sold them. You would like to implore him, you would like to go down on your knees before him. But you were not brought up for that. You were brought up to arrogance. It's certainly not your fault. Everything happened so quickly, sir, so unexpectedly. A real tragedy.

Among the thousand things that you don't want to do, among the thousand outrages you wish you didn't have to submit to, there is one the mere thought of which makes you almost faint with anguish. It's been months since Bepy paid the Torlonia princes the rent on the hunting lodge, and you know that as soon as possible you'll have to go there and settle the debt, collect all Bepy's things and meet the contemptuous gaze of your aristocratic landlords. You find the courage one Saturday. You park your car under the shed, between the reddening chestnut woods and the lodge, eccentrically furnished by Bepy according to his turn-of-the-century dandy's taste. The slightly musty odor of the damp leaves pierces your chest like a dagger. Calm down! Calm down, Luca. Basically you never much liked this place. Maybe precisely because it seemed to you (and even more so today) the flower in the buttonhole of Bepy's style. The symbol of that rustic megalomania mixed with an absurd Hemingwayish vitality. This estate north of Rome, extending over three hundred acres of woods, has always been your father's Sunday oasis. Until a few months ago, that wretched man, in the grip of his death wish, organized hunting expeditions there or midnight parties with vulgar whores and Irish whiskey. Calm down, Luca! By now you've survived the trauma. You can allow yourself a little irony and a little self-containment. You spend two hours filling suitcases and boxes with Bepy's unmistakable belongings: half-full bottles of cologne, muddy boots, Sicilian tweed caps, unlined, well-worn loden coats, silver and leather flasks that still stink of grappa. Now it's time to devote yourself to the riding department: you empty an entire closetful of caps, whips, encrusted spurs, until the foamy bitter odor of horses that saturates the thin canvas gloves hits your nostrils. But it's only as you're picking up the guns and cartridge cases in a corner that a thought surfaces which shouldn't properly belong to you: *How much money thrown to the winds for the pure fun of throwing it!* And now the most difficult part: with a feeling of nausea you start to remove the hunting trophies from the walls. Bepy was the unchallenged king of boar hunting. Embalmed trophies at home and in the office with which you always identified your father's foolish ferocity. An exuberant and expert hunter: little composure, big charge, just as in business, just as in life. Flashes of the first hunt you went on come back to you with disgust: his irritation at your difficulties with the surroundings and your physical inadequacies, and then the tribal ritual that he imposes on you—to bite into the heart of your first (and last) slaughtered animal.

But is there something of him, of Bepy, that you want to hold on to?

If you think about it, there is one day. To be more precise a morning, waking up in a hotel. We're in the late fifties: Bepy is in London and he has brought you with him, for the first time: you, Luca, *Daddy's little albino*. You occupy a big room on the fourth floor of the Savoy Hotel. You have been wakened by a thin, kind little Negro in a red shirt with silver buttons who, with a spectacular gesture, has removed the covers from dishes to reveal a treasure of gilded muffins and bacon and eggs and sausage, spreading through the room a pungent smell of grease. Bepy has wet his lips with a sip of coffee, leaving the rest of the breakfast to you. At this point the memory gets more vivid, as if it were not a memory but one of those images tattooed in memory. It's little more than an instant. A few seconds. A series of snapshots: Bepy laying his ironed suit on the unmade bed. Bepy caressing the immaculate handkerchief after inserting it in the pocket. Bepy pulling the reddish maple shoe trees out of the dark-brown suède Trickers. Bepy at the window making sure there's no spot on his tie. Bepy unbuttoning the shirt he'll put on. Bepy with no modesty stripping completely, displaying his bronzed skin, in such contrast to your snowy complexion. And, finally, the dense steam that emerges from the open door of the bathroom, smelling of shower, of soap, of talcum powder, of cologne, of Tuscan cigar: it's the vaporous part (the choicest and most intoxicating) of Bepy's soul.

Why? Who is Bepy?

Your impression is that you are among the tools of a magician. This musty hunting lodge contains the secret of success of Bepy Sonnino, formidable collector of tin myths and platinum swindles.

That's who Bepy is.

And if someone, looking at the rosewood coffin that holds this improbable corpse, were to question, in an impulse of pedantry bordering on bad taste, the mystery of his failure and his end, he should know that Bepy was not a crook but simply one of the many individuals who hate to appear what they are. It's not at all easy to be a shopkeeper who is doing the utmost not to seem one. And Bepy had nothing of the shopkeeper about him. In thirty years of work during which his star had joyously shone, he had engaged his entire self in the attempt to make others forget his profession as a wholesaler of fabrics—although he was unanimously recognized as the cleverest "rag merchant" in central Italy. In reality he was an actor, an illusionist, a snake charmer, his own scriptwriter.

If in 1960 you were a sales rep in the world of textiles you knew that if Bepy Sonnino loved you he would make you rich with the narcissistic and capricious joy of a benefactor. But beware if you alienated him. You were finished. Because he continuously asked others to surprise him. So that he could display his unforgettable enchanted smile.

During the summer, he had appointments with the sales reps on Thursdays, at four in the afternoon. Each of these suppliants—makeshift dandies—who were kept waiting on Thursday afternoons knew that, in the luminous office cooled by a prehistoric air-conditioner, he would find Bepy just risen from a long nap and a reviving shower (Bepy adored showers), wearing a beige linen suit and a clear-blue shirt. Driven by an unwritten law or by a spirit of empathy, the salesmen were induced to enter the presence of that *arbiter elegantiarum* not only impeccably dressed but with a complexion that expressed complete spiritual well-being. The Sonnino mythology recounts that some went so far as to use makeup, but I have no confirmation of that. Naturally, if you displeased him that day, Bepy would not show any irritation; you would intuit his disappointment from the modesty of the order and the distraction of his gaze. The salesmen hung on that hospitable smile, charmed by the mellow voice, intoxicated by the odor of just drunk coffee that Bepy emanated. They felt welcomed and judged at the same time. Bepy had the habit of adjusting the knot of their tie as if they were high-school students. For a few minutes the money stopped being important. The salesmen knew that he would shower them with compliments, and yet they were not surprised that that flattery—rather than offending them by its ordinary, almost obsessive repetitiveness—continued, after many years, to inundate them with joie de vivre. And not until a quarter of an hour later, when their skin came into contact with the damp summer heat that in Bepy's office had been abolished by the efficiency of the air-conditioner, did they suddenly realize that they had been at the theater, that, suspended in that refrigerated oasis, they had temporarily interrupted the struggle for a living and long-term gain. Only then, emerging from the non-time of that Oriental spell, did they understand the uniqueness and the pointlessness of the performance. And they felt content and irritated at the same time.

Bepy was an ingenious and shameless flatterer, what in English is called a confidence man: that was how he snared you. His fawning wasn't sugary; it had something intrinsically masculine about it—he was like the enzyme produced by an overexcited body. He came to believe in the compliment he was about to make. How many times, in the presence of famously ugly women, did Grandpa dissolve in reckless eulogies: "My dear, I've rarely seen you looking so splendid." That bold, affectionate tribute lavished with such conviction by the Prince of flatterers was enough to transform the unfortunate woman—at least once in her poor, faded existence—into a Greta Garbo. There was no teasing in his praises: and no one could ever establish if the flattery was of more use to those who received it or to the one who dispensed it.

So in the hands of that Jewish Midas everything becomes "splendid," "marvelous," "inimitable." There is no vacation that he didn't enjoy, no restaurant where he didn't have an "unforgettable" dish. Life, to hear him describe it, speeds along in a gilded carriage. His adjectives are slaves of the superlative, just like his hyperbolic adverbs: "outstandingly," "miraculously," "stupendously." And, what's more, even later on, in his misfortune, Bepy will never lose the ability of the great pop artist to turn shit into gold.

(It's strange: I knew Grandpa during his ruin—the shadow of failure threatened the smile of that always good-humored individual—and yet even then his histrionic capacities were lively to the point of topping everything else: so that every dive he took me to eat or sleep in became the "best pizza in Rome," or "the most charming and panoramic hotel in Ravello." His acquaintances, even the most modest, were all "billionaires." It was a fairy-tale delight to listen to him. And perhaps that's why, in the twelve years I spent with my grandfather, although he displayed a clear preference for my brother Lorenzo, his *bechor*—maybe, who knows, because of their shared athletic brilliance and social charm—yes, in those twelve years I never stopped thinking of him as a force of nature.

It was as if the stories of his rise and fall had somehow become attached to him, to the point where—when Bepy struggled with himself and the world to persuade himself that nothing had changed—it was easy for me to superimpose his figure on that of certain middle-aged actresses who had tumbled into the abyss of non-success, and were spoiled by the bitter memory of their long-past limelight: that is, an *old glory!* Time and retrospection, after his death, modified the image of him I had inside me forever. If I think of him freely, without prejudices, I am hit by a summer gust of heat: yes, but a summer that no longer exists, a summer that heightens chromatic contrasts with a Fauve violence—yellow shorts, blue shirt open to the curly forest of his chest, age-spotted arms, face extremely tanned, in contrast to the sparse tufts of platinum hair, and eyes that preserve all the radiant astonishment of the Sonninos. The golden brightness of Bepy's pate makes you think of the cupolas of Jerusalem in the incandescent Israeli sunsets. We are at the beach in Positano; he has come to see us for a few days. It doesn't surprise me that everyone knows him, bartenders, concierges, shop clerks, fishermen—he calls everyone "my dear" or "my love," lavishing phantasmagoric tips. My childish heart is bursting with pride as he, leaning at the bar of the Buca di Bacco, drinks an iced tea with lemon granita and offers me a sip, just to taste. *What did Grandpa tell you? Isn't it delicious?* He is glowing. In an instant the man of long ago has returned to dazzle, protected by the impression that here nothing has changed: here no one knows about his failure and the successive humiliations. Time seems to have stopped. Everyone treats him as if life hadn't reserved so many reversals for him. Only then, seeing him strutting, hair wind-blown like a yachtsman's but without a yacht, aviator Ray-Bans and hairless calves, can I get an idea, and who can say how approximate, of what my grandfather might have been in the period before I was born. And then Bepy gives me a pat, smiles, and starts telling me: "You know, grandpa's darling, once there were so many of us, and we were so tight, that we could determine the economy of the entire coast. One time your grandmother got mad at a rude restaurant owner and in a day he lost a hundred customers. Yes, around here the fashionable places weren't fashionable enough unless they had the Sonninos' blessing. There must have been at least seventy of us. Once we rented the entire hotel Le Sirenuse for more than three weeks. They all came, the Castelnuovos from Florence, the Levis from Milan, Elio Segre from Turin, Giudy Almagià from Ancona, even your aunt Rachel, straight from Cannes. No one was absent. We were a tribe. Twist. Midnight swims. Gallons of alcohol. Playing hearts or poker until five in the morning . . . It was magnificent."

No, I can't say how much is true, invented, or hyperbolic in Grandpa's bursts of nostalgia: this Gatsby-style epic that infected us both on the beach at Positano! I know it's not essential to establish that. Or at least it doesn't interest me. If on the one hand Bepy's flights made me feel part of something greater than myself, a sort of last descendant of this family-tribe, of these dwarfs, stale Byzantines at the mercy of their final season, these gaga half-Jews who had escaped extermination and had admirably known how to enjoy themselves and squander, on the other hand today they make me sad, as if I were some disgruntled executor, one who has to pick up the shards of an inheritance undermined by terrible mortgages. I'm one of those alcoholic American Indians who camp out in the increasingly cramped reservations in the cult of yearning for times that cannot return.

I don't in the least know how the figure of Bepy drifted through my memory until it came to embody my original problem. I have no reason for personal rancor. If anything, it's legitimate to speak of a reflexive resentment, provoked, retroactive. That, yes! And even if starting at a certain point of my life he no longer existed and the space that separates me from him is wider than the one I occupied with him, Bepy continues to appear from time to time in certain hypertrophic expressions of my father, in the luminous gaze of my neo-Israeli uncle, or in various erotico-vitalist exuberances of my brother's, but above all in certain affectations of gallantry and snobbery that, unexpectedly, emerged from my own acid heart of a younger son and a survivor.)

Not until it comes time for the kaddish does the realization dawn that among the mourners there are only nine Jewish adult males—one less than a minyan, the minimum number needed to perform the rites. Not being Jewish, my brother and I are excluded. My father and my uncle are dismayed, while Rabbi Perugia—with his glutton's florid face—counts again, in the hope of finding someone who fits the requirements. But the scene is a composite and, to the eye of a *true Jew*, disheartening: a band of converts, forced converts, mixed bloods galore, atheists of Marxist extraction, Apostolic Roman Catholics, salesmen swindled or benefited, French cousins, American sisters-in-law, academics, old flames, insurance agents, even half-ruined and nostalgic bank directors . . . This is the human jumble that has flocked to the funeral of the unworthy Bepy Sonnino, a man carried away, from childhood, by his *desire for assimilation,* a man who shamelessly—but perhaps not deliberately—shifted the threshold of his morality a dozen steps beyond the mean of normal persons, and forty beyond that of his austere Jewish ancestors: a man whose *chic corpse* (the only written instruction Bepy left is that he wanted to face eternity in his chalk-striped Savile Row suit and his black Lobb boots) seems to be a demonstration of how optimism untempered by a sense of reality can annihilate a man in the space of a few years. They are all moved, and not because they have lost their reasons for personal resentment toward the dead man (who doesn't have a wife or daughter lusted after by that wretch? who can't claim at least a little monetary credit from him?), but because they are all aware that life without Bepy Sonnino will have a different savor.

Finally we see a small man walking toward us, flowers in hand, his expression mournful: Mario Debenedetti. It's the anniversary of his wife's death. The rabbi asks if he'll join us for the kaddish (orthodoxy imposes that such requests be granted: it's a mitzvah), but old Mario, skinny and wizened, without even looking up, stings us with the most unexpected response:

"I won't pray for that son of a bitch—he still owes me a pile of money."

We're stunned; even the rabbi is oddly short of words.

It's time to step up! an internal voice enjoins me imperiously. "There's me," I venture, and I say it with mounting pride. I want to show that I'm someone who knows how to assume his proper responsibilities, although I'm aware that my gesture will cause dismay. Between me and that rock in the ground there's no difference. "But, Daniel, you can't," whispers my father. "Why can't I, Papa?" "What do you mean, why? You're not Jewish." "O.K.," I say, annoyed. "Granted: I'm not Jewish. But you have to admit that I'm the closest thing to a Jew you've ever known."

It's here that he starts laughing: it's now that my father doubles over, guffawing like a madman, unable to stop, in front of all those grieving people, in front of the monumental tombs, at the conclave of Sonnino corpses whom our Bepy—without the hoped-for solemnity—is joining. It's just then, right after hearing me pronounce those words full of resentment, that my father bursts into uncontrollable, helpless laughter. Such inappropriate hilarity feeds—and in the succeeding weeks will continue to feed—on strange, vexing questions: how did Teo, a holy man by now, forget an adult Jew for Bepy? What would Teo's former analyst, the piece of shit, say about such a lack of attention? Is he using his field of expertise—religion—to revenge himself on Papa? And why did Mama let such an important detail get lost? Is Giorgia still in the middle of it? Bitterness toward Giorgia? Bitterness against all the Giorgias who preceded and succeeded her? Does Bepy have to pay for it? And why does my son Daniel, who isn't Jewish and isn't even thirteen, suddenly, with a priestly air, show off as if he were King Arthur of Camelot or the long-awaited Messiah? How could the rabbi ask Mario Debenedetti, the most indignant of Bepy's creditors, to honor his death?

Evidently my father's laugh is fated not to end, because even when he seems to have reached the saturation point, and is trying to regain the proper composure, my mother intervenes energetically to offer the rabbi, who is increasingly disconcerted, a tempting counterproposal: she asks if at least Lorenzo, her firstborn son, can do it: "After all, signor rabbi, no one will notice . . . And then Grandpa would have been pleased that one of his grandsons . . . You're not going to put off the service until next week? Surely you know that people have come from Lausanne and Budapest?" After all, even the troublesome Bepy Sonnino (toward whom my mother will never stop feeling every sort of rancor! Some gossips assert that the pervert even *came on* to her, imagine, his extremely chaste daughter-in-law) deserves a rapid flight to the Jewish empyrean. The rabbi is indignant. What are you thinking, dear people? In front of a dead man? In front of the bloodless remains of *Yoseph Sonnino* (as he called him, restoring him to his origins, removing him *in extremis* from the tyrannies of the flesh) you put on this performance? This is why the rabbi is against mixed marriages. You never know how it's going to end up. It's not right to waste Jewish seed in this manner. And shit, with what results?

I'm hurt. My father was clear. *You aren't Jewish!* he uttered, with the mordancy of a new Minos. And, if you think about it, it's not the first time he's come out with that. It's not the first time he's insulted me that way.

My mind runs to the day when, at the age of ten, I was taken to the cemetery for the first time, to mark the return of Grandfather Graziaddio's remains, which had been stolen by a group of neo-Nazi hoodlums. I was overwhelmed by the solemnity of the tomb of my forebears, all marble and Corinthian decorations. Spontaneously I asked my father if it was already decided where I would go, and heard him say that it wasn't a question of place, the place would be there, but I couldn't be with him and all the others. I asked him to explain, to be more precise. But he wouldn't answer. So I asked him if it was that he didn't want me with him. He said that he wasn't the one to decide about certain things. "Daniel, you're not Jewish! There are rules and prohibitions that are superior to us . . ." and blah, blah, blah . . . Thus Rabbi Sonnino to his son Isaac! I deduced from it that these rules and these prohibitions sanctioned my exclusion and my undesirability. That tomb, in spite of appearances, didn't belong to me. It wasn't so difficult to understand: a negligible, quibbling genealogical defect was depriving me of my property. Of a comfortable corner in the beyond. Well yes, an odious corruption in his DNA was evicting a poor child of ten from his slice of eternity!

And now the saying returns: *You're not Jewish!* But this time with the aggravating circumstance of all those people around. It's a public humiliation. A severe and unambiguous condemnation inflicted by one of the few individuals who should protect me. It seems natural to me to glance at the sad-looking blond girl who is holding Nanni's hand and be overcome by a paralyzing blast of shame. Suddenly I understand that the pain of my humiliation is in some sinister way connected to the presence of that girl with eyes the color of a sea breeze. I understand that if she weren't there I wouldn't be suffering so much. I even reach the point of realizing that what goaded me to come forward (which then determined the rest) derives from my sudden desire to be a hero, inspired by those eyes which I will never be able to look at again. It is to them— to those eyes—that I dedicate my humiliation. It is before their vigilant and teasing inflexibility that I must swallow this absurd pill: simple crude historical truth: *You aren't Jewish!*

You aren't Jewish! Why does it astonish you, really? This is simply your fate: to be a Jew for the Gentiles and a Gentile for the Jews! Nor should it be surprising that an adolescent should ardently wish to be Jewish. There is nothing astonishing about a child wanting to be like his father. A Jew like so many others.

Because today it's a trip to be Jewish. Lamented, looked after, exalted: that's the verbal troika that defines the condition of the contemporary Jew. There are people who, against all logic, do research to verify their descent, not from yet another wig-wearing count or marquis but from a pious sixteenth-century Israelite. A type like Montaigne, all home and family. Incredible. A Jew in the genealogical tree: the grand distinguishing dream of the twenty-first century. The heraldry of the New Millennium. The brand that can make you painfully urbane and politely provocative. It can't have escaped you that the era of penis envy has been replaced by this era consecrated to envy of the circumcised prepuce.

Is this why you've emphasized the part of yourself that in other historical circumstances you would have hidden? What's the difference if Daniel Sonnino, with this name and this Woody Allen-like profile, rather than coming into the world in a bright July of 1970, had been born in a grim January a century earlier in a Lithuanian village . . . Well, there would have been little to boast about.

Daniel, how real is your anti-Jewish resentment? How much of the comic curtain-raiser is there? Who can be sure that outside you, while you rail against pro-Semitic rhetoric, another self does not sit, seraphic and circumspect, intently contemplating your furious double? A clever self, without scruples, who, with the clinical eye of an old theatrical agent, looks at you with sympathy and says, Eh, not bad, that idea of the half-Jew pissed off at the Jews. A little old, maybe, but always in favor. Not bad, this pride of the half-breed. Half-breeds are hugely popular this year.

Otherwise, why write that book? What's the point of writing a book entitled *All the Anti-Semitic Jews: From Otto Weininger to Philip Roth*, and including yourself implicitly in that rich list, when everyone knows that you are neither Jewish nor anti-Semitic but would like to be both? What easy game is this? Why attribute to those magnificent writers what you thought of yourself in relation to the Jews, why not focus attention, with the honesty of a diligent professor, on what they themselves thought of their relations with the Jews?

For the oldest reason in the world: cunning, sustained by

the desire to live, to get the most out of the little life has to offer. Make it extreme. Render it attractive to others, at the cost of the deception inflicted on oneself. Those who loved your book have simply confused cunning with good faith, the spectacle of sorrow with sorrow, and exhibitionism with the truth. They believed that that sting was communicable. That there is nothing more authentic and fascinating than a half-Jew who drives out the Jews. A half-Jew against the Jews. A half-Jew who accuses the Jews of racism and a half-Catholic who accuses the Catholics of ecumenism. Those who liked your book didn't understand the ease or the dishonesty of such an operation. They didn't take account of History: hasn't it been centuries, millennia, since the Jews have been saying bad things about the Jews with the sole purpose of saying good things, and since the goyim have been saying good things about the Jews for the sole purpose of saying bad things? The heart trembled, under the impression of being in the presence of something whose truth was demonstrated by the uncomfortableness of the proposition, by its morally and politically reprehensible nature. In a world in which we are all in desperate search of something to hate, of someone to fight to the death, how perfect this little Jewish hater of Jews. That is, that essay of yours is merely a grand anti-Semitic manipulation, devised to the detriment of your guiltless relatives, and to your advantage: that sense of pride which infuses you with a masochistic violence mistaken by too many for intellectual honesty.

It was the chance encounter with Aunt Micaela's feet that hurled me into the vortex of depraved fetishism.

Micaela Salzman, the daughter of Russian Jews who had emigrated to Israel in '49, had married my father's younger brother on the wave of a kibbutz passion that arose a few days after the end of the Yom Kippur war and vanished in the first weeks of marriage. In 1983, during my sixth consecutive summer vacation in Tel Aviv, Micaela was an unsatisfied thirty-seven-year-old who (except for her surly attractiveness and a pathological fondness for the pleasures of chocolate) had none of the requirements for membership in our byzantine family clan. Not coincidentally branded by my ultra-snob grandparents a *shotè*, a nutcase, Micaela had found nothing better to do than to complete her own confused existence by marrying that misfit Teo, the second son whose departure from Italy in '73 to join the Israeli Army had literally worn out his apprehensive parents with worry. It doesn't much matter that the contribution of Teo Sonnino to the Israeli cause was very modest (apart from moral support, of course), because exactly two days after his enlistment he had come down with measles, which kept him far from the battlefield.

At that time, it was the bellicose version of Teo Sonnino that I knew best: that of the rare Roman visits, when, dismantling the apparatus of castrating religious rituals, he went back to playing the role of the wildman who, twenty years earlier, had appeared at the wedding of his super-bourgeois brother at the Excelsior, on Via Veneto, in shorts and T-shirt, yelling, like the Messiah in the Temple:

"Isn't it time to put an end to these nauseating spectacles out of Cecil B. DeMille?"

To then break down in tears, so as to move the eternal Rabbi Perugia, who in the following months devoted himself to Teo's social reinstatement through intense religious instruction: with the sole effect of transforming a detached and confused student into a fundamentalist Jew. But Christ, what a relief for Teo to get rid of twenty-year-old resentments, of the sentimental shiksa met at school, the BMW parked in the garage, the mystical Jungian analyst, that humiliating sensation of failure, and, especially, the blackmail of that family, at the time still respectable and well-to-do, in order to dedicate himself totally to the Jewish cause! Here, finally, a purpose in life, so laboriously sought, becomes concrete in the anachronistic form of emigration.

From then on all he needs is contact with Italy to remind him that his vocation consists of resisting the arrogance—masked by condescension—of his father and brother (what a strange way of defining the problem!). At that point you can imagine him as a sixteen-year-old, and understand the suffering that those two effervescent personalities caused him from the first moment of his life, but also the uneasiness that his insolence must have roused in them. In the Sonnino household there is not much indulgence for challengers, not because of a reactionary spirit but because of an endemic skepticism. Besides, I couldn't do anything but vacillate between sympathy for the fugitive, dictated by the affinity of my condition—being simultaneously the grandson of Bepy, the son of Luca, and the brother of Lorenzo Sonnino (three supermen in a single family really shows a lack of tact and moderation)—and solidarity with the recipients of so much reckless fury.

This year, in spite of the preceding summers, either we lost control or things stopped functioning. "Bad year," my father summed it up in his inane Sonnino-style optimism: we are gathered to mark the first-year-without-Bepy, and we're over come by an unknown emotion. It can't be said that his death left a veil of melancholy; it's as if an uncertainty tending to incredulity had been released into the air.

But above all my cousin Gabriele (known as Lele), the only son of Teo and Micaela, had had a tumor in his testicle and had undergone surgery to remove it. I'm afraid they sent me to Tel Aviv to help in his convalescence.

Lele isn't even a stand-in for the delicate dark-haired boy of a year ago. Where Donatello's David—with wavy black hair that, as his father proudly revealed to me, sent the girls in his class into embarrassing swoons—had gone to hide I wouldn't know. In his stead this mono-testicular larva who wears a hat to hide the symptomatic bald spots.

My psyche is already too undermined by hypochondria to withstand my cousin's tragedy, and my education too closely molded by paternal positivism for me to ignore the genetic precedent. And the soup is made when you add to the unlucky picture my terrible relationship with my testicles: thanks to the searing memory of the torture-baths with my brother Lorenzo, imposed by my mother, when that bastard, in a proto-pederastic raptus, crushes them with his foot. Not that he always succeeds, but the gesture is enough to make me jump: a painful practice that, however, stimulates deep fonts of pleasure. And because sometimes in those same circumstances Bepy breaks in (it must have happened twice, but something compels me to transform his incursions into a daily rite) and orders us, with an air of black camaraderie: "Let me see your cock." My brother doesn't show much embarrassment in the grotesque exhibition of his jewels. For me, though, it's mortifying. And in the end I have to stand up and expose my trophy, shrunk by water and embarrassment.

In the meantime I've reached the age where one witnesses with dismay the proliferation of friends and acquaintances who do nothing but brag about virtuosic masturbatory *happenings*. The contest for the longest spray gained a certain popularity in my decrepit, very exclusive school in Piazza di Spagna. And me? Why doesn't anything happen to me? Am I abnormal? Impotent? Will I never see the dawn? Is my sexual life consigned to an inexorable sunset? Will I never violate the deep mystery of reproduction? Will I never emerge from the fog of indecision that makes me desire the girls in my class to the point of tears but prevents post-orgasmic satiety? No, Dani, calm down: some don't develop till fifteen. And if at sixteen I'm still like that?

A prey to these anxieties, I left Rome to find my cousin in that unhappy state. And to observe, furthermore, in the bathroom in Tel Aviv, that one of my testicles, as if in the spirit of family emulation, is suspended at mid-height, as though it were stuck in my groin. Should I interpret this asymmetry as a sign of infirmity? I would like to ask Lele how it began. How he became aware of it. How the illness made its way in. But I promised my parents not to make allusions. To treat him naturally. As if nothing had happened. As they ordered me to do, looking me in the eye ("You're a man now," my father said, with a certain rabbinical imprecision, to that thirteen-year-old nuisance his younger son). O.K., got it. How do you *treat naturally* someone who isn't natural? How can a boy so altered not be offended by your effort at pretense? Or by your show of humanity? Is this why Lele avoids me? Or is it simply fear? Death? To feel it nearby, creeping in past the loving assurances of your parents. Past their faith in God and in medicine. Lele is only a child. Certain things don't happen to children, they shouldn't happen. Is this what he can't admit to me because he hasn't been able to admit it to himself? The reason that he avoids every attempt of mine to start a conversation?

And then homosexuality, the paradoxical stumbling block in the life of every normal little boy, yes, the incredible revelation, the sexual orientation that for many years to come Lele will keep reined in, explodes just at the moment when the illness first requires his attention. A sign: here's what he thinks, he—a boy molded by maniacal paternal extremisms—has had a sign from the Biblical Avenger, a divine punishment brought on by those illicit thoughts about his friends. The abnormality of those thoughts, the frenzy of those thoughts, has made his cells go mad. While his friends think and talk only about girls, Lele can think only about his friends (but without being able to talk about it). It's almost a liberation to notice it: Lord, how the young Hasidim excite him, with their skinny sidecurls, their indecently solemn expressions, their protruding lips. Not to mention soldiers in camouflage: beret, hair shaved high on their necks, bulging triceps, raucous impudence, vocation murder. He can't tell his father. He can't tell anyone. But that tumor has liberated the beast within him, the remarkable shrew that has been agitating inside him forever.

Homosexuality, that's the legacy of the disease. Its Gigantic Recompense. The illness is only the way of coming out of it safely. It's the path of redemption. So he thinks, childishly insistent. So he likes to tell himself in the wake of mystical paternal meditations, and while the body slowly responds to the treatments the soul secretly grows ill.

It's no joke, homosexuality. Or at least not in my very secular, very open, very liberal family. When my father encounters one of those delicate Anglo-Saxon homosexuals at work, all fruity wine and Renaissance art, he breaks into ecstatic expressions of jubilation: "I met a fascinating gay Australian designer!" Yes, in short, homosexuality is a great thing if it strikes the children of others. But ours? Well, let's say that around here we have a rather aestheticizing vision of homosexuality: it can be as beautiful as a dress by Valentino, provided it's not one of us who's wearing it. Let's take the day when, just twelve but already anguished by my failed development, I show up at the bedside of the dying Bepy and ask him, almost without thinking, "Grandpa, what if I'm gay?" and see his face temporarily regain the red of rage and of life: "Good God, Daniel, the Lord gave you a dick like that to fuck, not to take it in the ass!" Verbatim.

Not long ago Lele stopped to see me on his way through Rome: we hadn't met in years.

There he is at last, suitcases in hand and a fake smile on his lips: there he is, the most *different* different I've ever seen.

I've never understood if that capacity to change his skin, Lele's salamander-like mimicry, is yet another version of our family's histrionics or if, more simply, it should be ascribed to the aptitude of homosexuals for disguise or even to the lack of personality that afflicts many refined but talentless individuals. But I have to confess that after so many years it amused me to be with this unpredictable type. Lele was like a Mediterranean-charming version of the writer David Leavitt, with that Maoist chastity of dress, harmoniously combined with a shy manner that seemed to allude to a sort of mystical integrity. I found it equally surprising that a boy so slender had, over the years, immensely broadened the margins of his buttocks and that the gleaming black of his hair had been diluted by tiny white dots that gave him a Parisian look.

We had lunch at the Hungaria, because Lele insisted on it. It reminded him of the days of Bepy and Ada. We went there for the most marvelous and truculent hamburgers in central Italy: an epiphany of eggs, cheese, mustard, ketchup, and onions. And during that meal, drowning in a cocktail of beer, Xanax, and mayonnaise, drunk with self-satisfaction and embarrassing memories, Lele recounted how he told his parents about his homosexuality, almost fifteen years after he had discovered it, and for ten of which he had been practicing it feverishly.

Anyway, Lele's story was nearly identical to those which I had imagined or had read (for example in the novels of his illustrious double David Leavitt) about an ordinary bourgeois boy confessing his homosexuality to ordinary parents, incredulous and dismayed. The typical story that I could have found in a documentary about the human race made by a curious Martian. Yes, it's true, this case externally presents different characteristics, such as a mother who was not at all protective, a fundamentalist Jewish father, and the specter of a grandfather who in his time considered homosexuals on a level with Nazis. But here, too, the demon of banality reclaims his dark dominion: since the specter of the grandfather, being a specter, can no longer do much harm; the mother shows her more humane and understanding side; and, in spite of his ethical strictness, the fundamentalist Jew, faced with the ineluctability of his son's condition, can only surrender.

Now twenty-seven, Lele, having lived for five years in picturesque Provincetown, and having obtained a degree in creative writing at a university not far from Boston, with Norman Mailer, no less, returns to Tel Aviv, just before Yom Kippur, yes, for the commemoration of the Jewish Day of Atonement, right around the anniversary of his father's flight from Italy and his marriage to Micaela. All things considered, a nice handful of solemn anniversaries ready to be desecrated by the pederasty of that pervert! And for the occasion, who knows whether out of nonconformity or in open hostility to his father, Lele shows up with hair the color of straw, tight pants, three-inch platform shoes, and with the dramatic intention of bringing his parents up to date on his uncontrollable appetite.

Teo is perturbed by that eccentric attire. Yet, having struggled all his life against Bepy's hypocritical conventionality, he certainly can't reproach him. How not to feel upset, though?

Until now Teo has always believed that freedom is expressed by wearing jeans and a T-shirt. That freedom was a refuge from ostentation. It never occurred to him that one can be free by exaggerating the contrasts, emphasizing whims and affectations: the freedom to dress as a woman, for example, or to go around the world completely naked, or to take it in your mouth from a big black man from Illinois. Only now does he seem to discover that freedom is not only your own legitimate desire to emancipate yourself from your father but also the equally overwhelming desire of your son to emancipate himself from you.

Therefore let Lele be an exhibitionist and may God help us.

So when, two days after the Yom Kippur observances, at which Lele behaved impeccably, the son says he wants to talk to his parents, to tell them something serious and important, Teo is struck by the grave, threatening tone. But then he smiles to himself, preparing to get out his wallet. Lele must have got into some trouble: his spoiled son is in debt, or has seen a motorcycle he can't resist. Ever since he was sick he has tried to get his parents to compensate him for it. He began with motorcycles at fifteen and ended with that bizarre idea of studying literature in America (a genuine drain on the already diminished finances of Teo and Micaela). But Teo is so happy that Lele is here, that he has confided his intention to leave Provincetown and return to his own country; he is prepared for any economic sacrifice, as long as it makes him happy. Even better, he will astonish him, he won't even let him finish speaking, he will pull the checkbook out of his pocket and say, "How much do you need?," leaving his wife and son amazed.

But it's not money that Lele needs: if anything, it's understanding and especially—even if his new emancipated ideas won't let him admit it—absolution. That's why, without betraying embarrassment except in his whirling exposition, he starts on the speech that he's been preparing during the course of an entire youth. For years, in fact, he's been pondering the words he'll have to utter: he has always been aware that at a certain moment euphemisms would be of no use. *There will be a breaking point,* he has repeated to himself a thousand times. An instant after which the world will have changed. For this reason, in the long training period leading to the Great Speech he has persuaded himself that the only path is concision: the immediate attack, without preamble, diving into the heart of the matter, as old man Mailer taught you. But, in spite of his praiseworthy intentions, as often happens with speeches one has imagined too many times, Lele's confession turns out to be elliptical and confused, and, worst of all, he makes the mistake of beginning with a litotes and continuing with a dizzying series of negatives:

"I'm not a heterosexual. I don't like women. I've never liked them. I've never had the least doubt that I would like them . . ."

Until finally, in the face of his parents' bewilderment, Lele regains lucidity:

"I've been through some difficult years, but now I'm fine. I'm lucky to have gone away early, to a city where it's the heteros who are considered abnormal. I know that for you—especially for you, Papa—it must be a shock. And yet I can't be sorry. Not for the fact of making you suffer. I'm a believer in sexual freedom. There's not much else to say. Except that I don't want you to poison your life by trying to understand where you went wrong or how you failed, and all that other stuff, both because there's nothing wrong with my way of life and because I've always been like this, since I was twelve. The tumor has nothing to do with it. Nor the operation on my testicles. I was like this even earlier, even without knowing it. I've been living with a man older than me for almost three years. The only thing I'm sorry about is that—at least for now—you'll have to give up the idea of a grandchild. I'm not in a position to please you in that. Although I can assure you that the organization I belong to—I've been a member for almost ten years, and I'm the vice-president now—is fighting for that, too, to liberate us from yet another outrage, this shameful discrimination against our basic freedoms, this institutionalized homophobia. Look, Papa, you should understand. You who do so much for the Jews. You see, you should understand that for homosexuals it's the same thing. People judge us according to the same criterion."

Why is my Lele so generous with details?

This is Teo's first question, rising instinctively, even before the news has been absorbed, followed by a second: why is Lele talking in the impersonal tone of a revolutionary newsletter? Why is his son speaking ideological propaganda at such a traumatic moment? Is he wrong or is his son using a cruel truth to torture them? A cruelty that maybe reminds him of something: his own cruelty toward his brother and father—a cruelty that at the time seemed to be in the service of a just cause but today no longer makes sense. For example, what does the allusion to the impossibility of children have to do with it, or that terrible, unthinkable living together? Is it really necessary to blurt out everything? Wouldn't this be better: "Papa, forgive me, I've sinned against nature. But I will do everything to redeem myself. I swear on the holiness of this country!"? Why did he send him to the United States? Can he still be saved? How could he not have understood what was happening to his son? Is it possible to turn back? Can he introduce him to a beautiful, eager girl? Maybe with a sexually liberated woman captain in the Special Forces he would feel as comfortable as with a man?

Come on, let's not ask too much of Teo Sonnino. Christ, his mentality isn't sophisticated enough (although it's a lot more so than Bepy's) to imagine his son possessed by a mustache-wearing macho man from New England. And you have to consider that gays are like Jews and like blacks: it's fine to love the idea that they represent, it's fine to know that they exist, but it is absolutely annoying to hang out with them.

"Well, do you want to ask me anything?" says Lele, with an air of challenge, irritated by his parents' astonishment. Who knows why, he had imagined that they would slap him, and who knows why he's sorry that they haven't even made a move. Who knows why, in ten years of fantasizing about this scene, he had imagined a lot more agitation, both in himself and in his parents. How could he have believed that his words would have a musical counterpoint, like a soap opera? But now the critical point has been brilliantly passed. Now it's up to you, Daddy, and to you, Mama dear. After years of painful indecisiveness, he passes the ball into the trembling hands of his parents.

Micaela tries to cry. But the tears won't come. Teo's mouth is furry with the micro-organisms of anguish. One thing he wants explained, immediately. One thing that in the first instance seems to him intelligent, that he can't and won't keep inside, even though right afterward he will regret having even conceived it.

"Lele, can we at least ask you, if not to hide your devia—that is, your sexual preference . . . yes, that is, you understand . . . can we ask you not to flaunt it with those eccentric clothes? . . . After all, what's the point? I don't show off my virility, or what remains of it . . . Narcissism is a failing, if not exactly a sin. What's the point of hair that color, son? And those women's shoes? Don't you, too, find that they add nothing? Didn't we teach you respect . . ."

Yes, it's Teo speaking. It's he who for the first time in his life is putting within quotation marks the odious word "respect."

On the other hand it takes him only an instant to realize that he has fallen into the most banal trap set by his son's treacherous hysterics. What? He who fought against the family formality is now asserting superficial, self-serving trivialities?

Even he has reached the point of speaking of respect? Is it possible that the man expressing himself in this conservative manner is the same hippie type who challenged the dandyism of his father and brother with his slovenly clothes? He, the sixties rebel who mocked bourgeois custom with his T-shirt and shorts amid the morning suits of that sensational wedding reception? How can he dare to be indignant at his son's extravagance? How long has he been such a hypocrite? So Pharisaic? Is it the air of Israel that has changed his head?

Lele's thrust is inescapable. And Teo can't complain, he's the one who provoked it.

"No, Papa, you can't ask that. There isn't one honest way or one dishonest way of dressing. And if you have decided to tell me how to dress only because I'm in your house, then tomorrow I'll go and find somewhere else. Besides, it would be difficult for me to live with a person who has such a conventional idea of 'respectability.' Someone who gives clothes such decisive importance . . . Or are you just ashamed of me?"

"No, of course not, don't be that way, I didn't mean that and you know it. I just wanted to say that a picturesque manifestation of diversity ends by being inauthentic, parodistic. A pose. A fashion. And therefore harmful to your cause. That's what I meant to say. Isn't that what I've always taught you?"

So he feels slightly reassured. He feels he has given the conversation a promising turn, while the consciousness of his son's homosexuality enters into him, twisting his guts.

"And in any case, Papa, you should know that, although in my own way I am a believer, and although I respect your feelings (you saw how good I was yesterday at that charade of Yom Kippur), I can no longer accept a religion like Judaism that's based on racism and homophobia. And I should warn you that in the next elections I will vote against those fanatics of the Likud!"

What strikes Teo most sharply is that his son—his only

son—not only has a lot of ideas about everything but can't wait to get them out, to share them with his parents. At the same time Teo has the unpleasant impression that all the ideas expressed by his son are more or less explicitly hostile.

And this is really the death blow. This is the revenge prophesied (or hoped for?) by Bepy. "You'll be sorry," Bepy had said to him many years earlier, when he was still a man with self-confidence, when he was still rich and respected, when he was light-years away from the contemptible swindler life would make of him. When he was still an invincible and venerated man. "Don't go," he had repeated with the incongruously prophetic cadence that his voice sometimes had. "What does Israel have to do with anything?" he had asked him. "You have everything here. You're not one of them. You have nothing in common with that desperate people. You're not a fighter. You will not expose my grandchildren to hatred, to assassinations, to wars. I know war . . ." And then came the prophecy: "You'll be sorry, I don't know how, but I'm sure you will." So he had spoken many years before, when Teo decided to leave. And those words were heavy, yes, Teo had nourished them in himself like a small tumor. Earlier, during Lele's illness, then during the exhausting quarrels with Micaela and the endless financial hardships, and now in the face of this revelation, he had heard them surfacing, until they jolted his consciousness. "You'll be sorry," he had said to him. And Teo—Teo the Superstitious—had had the impression that they were evidence of wishful thinking rather than an unhappy prediction. A vendetta, in other words. "I hope your son makes you endure what you are making me and your mother endure, you damn foolish kid." That's the sense of that "You'll be sorry." So at least Teo, in his emotional instability and his literariness, had interpreted it. Not as the protest of a fearful parent but as a reprisal. And now that he feels secure, now that his father has socially committed suicide, now that his influence has ceased to harass him, now that he has been dead long enough so that not even his ashes could vibrate with joy, now "You'll be sorry" returns to Teo's mind. Now that he has found a reason for living—counter to his family's dissipation—in the principles of Israel, in the morality and the force of this government in trouble, in the spirit of conservatism that nests in his Israelite heart, he discovers he has brought into the world a son who—after longing throughout his adolescence to flee the country so laboriously won by his father, in order not to do military service, in order not to jeopardize his own corrupt existence, out of pure cowardice—has chosen this abnormal *thing* that our ancestors, with a sense of disgust, called "sodomy," and numbered among the mortal sins. Here is the punishment: he who has sought the authentic far beyond human possibility is rewarded by having given his name to this dissolute freak of nature. He who embraced with such warmth the most orthodox Jewish tradition ends up with this Labourite queer for a son.

Teo Sonnino in 1983 was the badly paid editor of a newspaper close to the Likud and in just a few years of valiant service had won his stripes as a fierce enemy of the Arab people.

A man of integrity or a hothead?

Reading his editorials you were amazed that they had been written by the cordial and smiling man who, on summer nights when the moon was full, sat, solemnly absorbed, on the deserted beach of Tel Aviv, embracing an acoustic guitar marked by the bad weather and excesses of the sixties, and humming "Across the Universe"; and that many years earlier that same man, at the start of his Israeli infatuation, had been a militant revolutionary. It would be simpler to associate that display of muscle and journalistic intransigence with the bony face and visionary eyes of a Zionist of Russian origin: some hateful son of a bitch who, having suffered all that an average man would consider far beyond the threshold of tolerance, had developed a fierce disdain for life, for his own and everyone else's. No, those sharp words did not fit the pacific silhouette of Teo Sonnino, or his eyes, which exhibited the sky-blue glaze of wonder. But his charm, apart from an extraordinary eclecticism and an ironic sort of human sympathy, seems to consist in contradiction. From birth he has nurtured in himself a stack of inconsistencies. That's his appeal for some. And what irritates everyone else.

Subversive in his youth, he hates the secular liberals of his family with Dostoyevskyan ardor. Until the seventies: when, during the Yom Kippur War, he breaks with his friends of the extreme left, accusing them of having bought into the Arab cause and sold out Israel. He calls them anti-Semites, Nazis, stupid Third Worlders, but finds equally nauseating the open-minded, unprejudiced way that Bepy evaluates the Middle East question—that moderate champion of equidistance, that dandy too worried about keeping the champagne cold to think about the History-that-is-overwhelming-us.

(God, Teo, how unfair you are!)

Even many years after his son's departure, Bepy couldn't forget the day he had seen Teo cut from an issue of *L'Europeo* the photographs of the eight Israeli athletes killed during the Munich Olympics in '72. Bepy had in his eyes his nose his ears his hands the excitement of those days. He remembered the boy with the scissors, he remembered scattered on the kitchen table the photos of the young boys who were dead for the sole fact of representing Israel in the world. He had found all this so touching. He had admired his son's involvement in that drama as a sign of his sensitivity. He had even deplored his other son's cynicism in minimizing a tragedy so symbolically relevant (Luca was like that: he hated symbols). But how could he believe that the next step, what followed that macabre album of photographs, would be the decision to go and live, fight, procreate in Israel? He wouldn't have thought it possible. And yet if only he had known how to interpret that sorrowful sequence of gestures. If only he had known how deeply touched Teo felt by the death of those boys who were his own age. If only he had known how to listen to his son's sighs. If only he had understood how hard that murder had shaken him. How it had entered into him. How difficult it was for him to clear it out of his system. If only he had been able to intuit that Teo was unable to free himself from the facial expressions of the young athletes. The expressions printed on the pages of a weekly. The expressions of living boys who are now dead: the slightly arrogant one who feels he's on top of the world, the thoughtful one who has transformed the profession of champion into something paranoid, not to mention the clever one who seems to expect infinite amusement. If only Bepy had been sensitive enough to understand all this. If only he had been able to imagine in his heart the most predictable but also the most unthinkable scenario. If only he had not dismissed with a smile the poster of Jerusalem in his second son's bedroom. If only he hadn't reacted with the usual shrug of the shoulders to Teo's increasingly annoying habit of talking about the importance of Israeli politics and the disgracefulness of anti-Israel propaganda. If only he had been able to offer his son a less dogmatic language, if only, during the long evening meals, he had harshly prevented him from talking about the Arabs with such acrimony. ("They're worse than the Nazis!" he had heard him say once. And yet Bepy's back had yet again avoided breaking into a sweat.) If only he had countered his unrecognizable son's fundamentalist nonsense with gentle and persuasive reasoning rather than the usual bucket of cold sarcasms . . . Well, maybe, then . . .

There are at least a dozen more "if"s that Bepy could have used to torture himself in the years following Teo's departure, to try to understand retrospectively all that he hadn't understood at the time, and to delude himself, perhaps, that if he had only picked up on one of the flashing signals sent out by his son he could have prevented him from fulfilling his own destiny, which was ultimately not tragic in the least.

In those years there must have been at least a hundred Roman Jewish families worried about their loved ones who had decided to move to the other end of the Mediterranean, to Israel. These families were united not only by terror of the arrival of some traumatic news concerning the fate of their heroic relatives but also by a seething sentiment of pride for that (almost ascetic) choice. It was as if these families had paid a tribute of flesh, blood, and chromosomes to that Great Mother, in superstitious protection of their own petty lives, senseless well-being, and, especially, safety. Hearing them speak—these Jewish relatives of Israeli Jews—one might have said that a mysterious force kept them in thrall to Italy, preventing them from joining the family members dispersed throughout the streets of Haifa and Jerusalem or the elegant residential neighborhoods of Tel Aviv. Because if on the one hand they spent their lives comparing Italian-European instability to the superhuman competence of the Israelis (and loved to praise the civic-mindedness of the Israelis, the bureaucratic efficiency, the military and scientific successes, the agro-genetic experiments—gigantic grapefruit and seedless watermelons sweet as ambrosia—the ecumenical-communitarian experience of the kibbutz, the new writers, the ancient yet brand-new language, the overpopulated universities full of geniuses . . .), on the other hand they had no intention of leaving Rome. Every Passover they formally promised (as their forebears had done for millennia) that before the next one they would move to Jerusalem, but then, evidently, suitcases in hand, they had second thoughts.

And yet among these hundred families that had a relative in Israel there was one that didn't give a damn about Israel, that had never dreamed of moving there, that, if anything, was more inclined to show its gratitude to Rome, to Italy, to all Europe for having responded marvelously to the demands for work, profligacy, and freedom of each of its members. This nucleus was formed around the patriarch Bepy Sonnino, so far from being venerable that he couldn't stop asking himself how his younger son, so handsome, so congenial, so athletic, so loved by women, so protected by the family, could have fled to that hostile and crazy place called Israel.

But Teo would never be free of the smiles of the murdered athletes. It was his closeness, his juxtaposition to those boys that upset him. Judaism had nothing to do with it. He wasn't a partisan. Those dead boys moved him, they took his breath away (more than the many other dead people in the world and in History, more than the dead of the Holocaust) because when they were alive they had been exactly like him. They had his long hair. They listened to his music. They loved blond girls with green eyes. They smoked his unfiltered cigarettes. His joints. They must have experienced the sixties with the same feverish excitement. That's what his father and brother couldn't understand. He could not take no interest in all this. He had to be a party in the case, he was in it up to his neck. Otherwise his life would have been monstrously without meaning. And those faces would continue to torment him. That's why he had diligently, patiently cut them out. That's why he had put them in a folder. He had written and rewritten the names of the athletes a hundred times, under the illusion that the grim effect produced in him by those Middle Eastern cadences could be exorcised by habit.

And Bepy, dismayed, had seen his son—in whom he had tried to inculcate the totally Sonnino idea that in life one must set aside the past in order to project oneself gently and unconsciously into the future—grow morbidly attached to those bygone faces. But he hadn't been able to understand how that iconographic fetishism was only the prologue to emigration: an emigration that Bepy considered a thoughtless, imprudent flight toward a deeply remote past, and hence something both stupid and sad.

Only now, ten years later, and an Israeli citizen, has Teo Sonnino espoused the "hard line," proclaiming himself the enemy of "peace at all costs," and of the dismantling of the Jewish settlements in the Occupied Territories, an advocate of the indivisibility of Jerusalem and its spiritual inviolability, one of the most unyielding supporters of Prime Minister Shamir and a supporter of the extremist methods of Ariel Sharon in Lebanon. Only now has his position become irremediably fundamentalist. Restore the Gaza Strip to those . . .? You're joking! If anything it's them, those thieves, who should have to move. Those lands belong to us. Yahweh gave them to us. They've been ours for millennia. The tombs of the Patriarchs are there for us. The U.N. resolutions? We believe in Yahweh, not the United Nations.

Teo hasn't learned to bear the fact that his Italian relatives—Bepy but also Luca and all the others—are moved by the Palestinian crisis. It's something he can't think of calmly: that pathetic display of sentimentality. Those contemptible melodramas. The children sent to die just for the satisfaction of displaying their lifeless little bodies, for the sole cynical purpose of upsetting the world, so that when we are bombed everyone can happily exclaim: "Well, boys, it can't be said that you didn't ask for it . . ." The Palestinians are a wholesale factory of emotion and rhetoric, Teo thinks angrily. And he doesn't confine himself to thinking. He writes it every day. Tireless. That's how he ended up occupying a prestigious place in the list drawn up by the P.L.O., under the heading "fundamentalist Jews to be eliminated."

Isn't it really irresponsible, almost scandalous, on the part of apprehensive parents like mine, to send me for my summer vacation to the house of a man hated by the increasingly aggressive Palestinian terrorists? The palpable sign of a strong sense of fatalism on the part of my parents, which the prudent Catholic Philistines of my mother's family considered (with reason?) an outrageous presumption of invulnerability: so excessive as to involve even small children.

It made a certain impression, however, to see Teo leave for work in the morning in his creased linen suit—its cream color intensified by the tan of his hands and the blue of his eyes— and, before getting in the car, parked imprudently in front of the house, take off his jacket, crouch down, crawl underneath to make sure no one had planted an explosive device or tampered with the brakes, as if it were a routine, like taking off the club or the wheel lock, and then slide out, distractedly wipe himself off, put the gun back in the holster, smile at me, and depart with a squeal of tires for the newspaper.

As if fear had stopped celebrating its obscure office secretly and, bursting from the shadows of clandestinity, had become an organic and luminous substance, burning lava that melts into the atmosphere, mixing with the perfume of orange blossoms. Fear that everything will disappear. That suddenly a chubby teenage girl, out shopping for something or other, will be caught in an explosion: pieces of her scattered in the midday heat. Fear that that bus will go mad. That a vile shadow will set off a tremendous detonation. That the sky will become lead. That the sidewalks will buckle. *That someone will shatter the equilibrium of the day* in this strange country wrenched from the desert, populated by a dense, heterodox population of fair-skinned types who protect themselves from the sun with an overproduction of melanin and dark-haired Sabras accustomed to challenging it: this dirty and unadorned country, which tries only to be inessential, where the young people are drugged on Coca-Cola and the old strive to detoxify themselves of a rage that has been accumulating since the persecu-

tions of the Pharaohs: yes, this strange desert strip, vehement-
ly made green, which the Jews of the world call "nation": this
country that seems composed of atoms of terror. Everything
here is silencing. Even the incredible sunsets have the color of
blood. If someone were looking for a macabre diversion, popping a balloon in a public square would be enough to sow
panic, to see well-dressed young executives returning from an
aperitif in the gracious neighborhood of Jaffa throw themselves in the dust to escape destruction. Hidden under the civilized clothes, under the ostentatious elegance, under the aspiration to normality, under the hedonistic vitality are battle uni-
forms and gun belts and, under those, in the thoracic cavity,
angry hearts that find it hard to demilitarize themselves.

Well, those fears seem to combine with my own in this
exhausting summer of '83. Fear of not being a man. Fear that
my nose will never stop growing. Fear of going blind. Fear that
others think I'm as ugly as I do. Fear that the interminable adolescence that awaits me won't live up to my expectations. Fear
of not being able to satisfy my desire. Fear of having cancer in
my testicles just like my cousin. Fear of never seeing a single
drop of semen spurt from my timid Circumcised One. Fear of
remaining stuck in this swamp of erotic doubt.

How could I have imagined that I would be drawn out of
the nightmare of sterility thanks to Aunt Micaela's feet, and
that this would represent a definitive turning point? Of all possible candidates: Micaela Salzman, the slender Ukrainian girl
whose rough beauty had literally overwhelmed Teo, at their
first encounter in the kibbutz in the Golan Heights, was the
involuntary cause of my emancipation.

One afternoon I found myself in the dusty living room of
the house in Tel Aviv in that half-light artificially created to
combat the scorching heat. My aunt was wandering through
the house, with her faded adolescent's delicacy that roused me

like nothing else. In her hand the ever-present chocolate bar. All she did was eat chocolate, perhaps to alleviate her growing disappointment. She always had specks of chestnut around the edges of her mouth, clouds of hazelnut cream, commas of cocoa that gave her a movingly childish look. The miracle was that that diet based on saturated fats didn't have the slightest effect on her gentle, slender profile except for a slight prominence just above the pubic area that, besides, was so alluring that I would have gone to sleep and died there. Micaela continued to be harsher every day with me and her son, as if she were taking out the resentment she felt for her mad penniless husband on the innocent offspring of his family. The outrage is that she reproached Teo for not being the man he had tried all his life not to be: a fulfilled and reassuring type like my father. A real man, in short, who, after freeing himself from Bepy's disasters, had resumed sailing over the calm waters of prosperity, with a beautiful house, a sports car, and two promising sons (you see how this innocent Russian girl had transfigured my family). I already felt how my mysterious and illicit attraction for that woman was linked, in a way that I wouldn't have been able to define, to her bad humor (was I preparing myself for the Calvary of my adolescence, which would consist of falling in love in record time with girls who openly despised me?).

That afternoon we were alone. Some change fell out of Micaela's hands. Immediately, in keeping with the gallantry that her presence inspired in me, I bent over to pick it up. At that point, on the floor—in a subordinate position that would seem to me, over the years, preliminary to the search for pleasure—crawling on all fours like a truffle dog toward my aunt, I was aware of an odor that came from her feet. At that precise instant, with my head pressed against the floor and my nostrils flaring, I received the gift of the minor deity who sanctions the triumphal entrance into adulthood (this time the attribute "triumphal" truly seems adequate). My underpants filled with the warm liquid that I had been waiting years for. And after that day my life was no longer the same.

I went through adolescence stealing panty hose from the houses of my classmates, from my friends' girlfriends, from my aunts, from my grandmother, exposing myself many times to the risk of discovery. Kleptomania for a fetishistic purpose became a mission, besides being a painful need bordering on dependency.

The inclination was so uncontrollable that at school I began staring at the extremities of my classmates, for five consecutive hours in a row. Sometimes my ladies wore see-through stockings and ballet shoes. But look, there, suddenly, Monica Lambicchi, at a nearby desk, sublimely ugly, with glasses and braces, decided—unconsciously distracted—that the moment had arrived to take her heel out of her shoe. That little game was enough to inundate my groin with pain. Well, that space between shoe and heel was for me a metaphysical place, deserving of absolute veneration, of a new mystique: a place outside of time where every aspiration converged. I caught myself dreaming that the Benign God of Israel would burst into the classroom, eager to grant a new wish: stopping time and space for the private use of this sexually excited son. I saw myself gliding among the sleeping wax statues of my school-mates. Landing beside Monica Lambicchi, who is turned to stone. Sticking my penis in the dark crack between foot and shoe and instantly reaching orgasm. Emerging from that delightful fantasy I felt my manhood pushing painfully against the fly of my jeans. A few minutes later, losing all self-control, I stuck my right hand in my pants pocket, which had a hole in it for just this purpose, and began to work. Suddenly I felt that heat and excitement were painted on my face and the moment was approaching. Until I broke out in the usual bracing shower, aware that ninety per cent of the class had watched my performance with electrified disgust.

These were the only rebellious gestures, the only reprisals I allowed myself. It's as if Daniel Sonnino, the Greatest Thief of Female Panty Hose in the Northern Hemisphere, ordinarily a cowardly student, was able to find courage only in degradation. Look, I think that this should be the subject of considered reflection. Why in the world was my small store of courage indissolubly bound up in my humiliation? If I had seen my father drowning I would never have found the strength to jump into the water and save him. And yet if in order to possess Monica Lambicchi's stockings I had been forced to undergo a terrible trial, like walking across a deep canyon on a string, probably, driven by adrenalin and that pain in my groin, I would have accepted the challenge, and maybe I would even have made it! And the articulate form of courage that surfaced, sometimes—the most self-damaging recklessness—could not be vanquished even by censure and general scorn.

Not even the enigmatic legend that appeared one day on the gray door of the girls' bathroom—"Dear girls, don't shake hands with Daniel Sonnino. You could get infected"—not even those words, written in black block letters that every girl could see, managed to persuade me, after a few days of mourning, that the time had come, once and for all, to abandon that almost daily practice.

I would go as far as blackmail to obtain new relics. I dreamed of threatening Monica Lambicchi (*I'll kill your father!*) if she didn't give me her sneakers in a sealed envelope and with a photograph of her grind's face. I dreamed of those Japanese megastores where, to supplement their stipends or make ends meet, young women students sell their used intimate garments to slobbering old men (or young men) like me. I was elated by the marvels of Japanese culture. By that Oriental insight into human nature.

So suddenly my life is transformed into a permanent fashion show: on the stage of my consciousness is an ongoing parade of sandals, ballet shoes, espadrilles, loafers, flats, with which I have only to associate a face (even the most improbable) to trigger the miracle.

My sixteen-year-old's room is a museum of horrors. Baskets, drawers, closets overflowing with stockings, socks, slippers, shoes. No one can understand better than me the uncontrollable taste serial killers have for collecting. (But perhaps I'm wrong to use the word "taste," which seems to imply a considered and aesthetically conscious choice. It's really a compulsion to steal that you can't do anything but indulge.) From the start I catalogued that mountain of dirty stuff with a Cartesian-encyclopedic order: age of the victim, year of the theft, number of wanks devoted to it. Here is my photograph album, my drawer of emotional memories, the inventory of things lost, the object of my untamed idolatry. It's stronger than I am. With each of those relics I have enjoyed, fantasized, exulted, and wept. Here is the counter-story of my brief life as a diligent child, with his high marks for behavior, his extreme naïveté, whose failing is that he too closely resembles an academic in embryo, and is crushed by the warmth of a perfect family.

But there's one question that continues to bug me: why, after so many years, the rhythm of my onanistic performances hasn't diminished at all with respect to the one ostentatiously inaugurated twenty years ago in the land of Israel?

It's insulting to dispose of that irreducibility with stale psychological formulations like: *Daniel, you anestheticize yourself by masturbating because you're ill bred and frustrated.* Nor is a well-known historian-anthropologist convincing: *You're the last repository of that decadent mentality which has given much to, but has also taken much from, the intellectual generation that grew up between 1850 and 1945.* Nor does the pathological hypothesis seem to fit: *Give in to the evidence, you're a chronic pervert!,* which I would have believed several years ago, before nocturnal surfing on the Web revealed to me the secrets of solitary humanity.

No, that's not it: this time I want to astonish myself; it would be easy and monotonous to get away with yet another self-denigrating outburst. I would like, instead, to inaugurate an intense, if brief, moment of self-justification.

Masturbation is the highest expression of freedom—second to which one can place only literature (which unfortunately has rules too rigid and obstructive to support the comparison)—that my body has been able to give itself in the past thirty-three years. A freedom that surpasses even the unrestrained sex mania of certain rock stars, over whom I have the advantage of being able to fuck simultaneously, or in the span of those elective ten minutes outside of History, women who've been dead for years, like Marilyn Monroe, without the risk of being taken for a necrophiliac; old classmates without hearing talk of traditionalism; TV starlets without having to become, in turn, a celebrity; the wives of my friends without having to betray them; the sister I've never had without committing incest; university students without perpetrating any abuse; blessed virgins without indulging in blasphemy; eleven-year-old Lolitas without violating the penal code; good-looking young men without changing sides . . . All this from my comfortable domestic gallery, protected by the intoxicating anonymity of the Just.

You'll have to be content with the Viking grandeur of that stranger who stands out amid the end-of-July airport chaos, instead of enjoying your slim anxious mother, as you might have naturally expected: the sight of that pale fair-haired giant has stifled your enthusiasm, making you slow down, in the hope that the figure of Her will suddenly emerge from behind the impatient stranger.

You'll have to manage without Her, this time.

"Hi, Dani . . ." the man smiles, coming toward me.

I couldn't bring myself to ask him why my mother, after sending me on a study vacation to Cornwall for an entire month, after repeating to me on the phone, more times than necessary, how empty the house and her life are without her little chipmunk, couldn't find the time to come and meet me. Was I to interpret her words as a cynical expedient to comfort my complaints of homesickness from across the Channel? And why send that man? What meaning did it have? Why this unease within unease?

And while a high pressure zone had literally immobilized the air, so that it had become a damp condensation that pasted your clothes to your skin and tortured menopausal women returning from Polynesian vacations, I was practically paralyzed by an emotion I inevitably suffered from in those years at the end of every boldly adventurous vacation. As if the world were about to cave in. As if the sadness were fated never to end. It was an experience of death in miniature. I still wasn't fully aware of how unhappy I was, all right. If anything, I had an embryonic conception of it. That vision was enough to tighten my stomach. I was certain that I would never be able to eat again. At least not through that mouth, that esophagus, that stomach, which felt almost atrophied, as if they belonged to someone else, who was not me.

The August process of desertification seemed to have dried up the fields and the trees and the rails and the asphalt and the spirits (mine certainly). Everything had a pale cream color. That vapor-saturated air was a friendly replica of my innocent desperation: the echo of a distress that was acting below the surface. Everything was infinitely smaller and more sordid: the airport, the parked cars, the taxis, the guards, the Tyrrhenian wind, the city where I was born and lived, even the names of things . . . Like a wanted man in a foreign land, I felt nostalgia for the cliffs and hated the cement! Maybe even my apartment—if I ever got there—would be dusty, hot, neglected, dark, and suffocating. Everything was strange and unknown around here, and above all threatening. You had the impression that soon even your muscles would surrender to the midday heat, liquefying on the asphalt like strawberry ice cream.

Would I ever get used to that life again? To that city? To those people? To that language?

And meanwhile I didn't know whether to embrace that man, or let him embrace me. I chose an irresolute abstention. Grabbing the suitcases, I felt myself pushed.

"Leave them, you must be tired . . ."

"You know what time we had to get up this morning?"

" . . . "

"Four. And the plane was at five-thirty."

Now you are infinitely unhappy, in the grip of pure adolescent overreaction (a personality disorder that will continue to afflict me, even to the ancient age of thirty-three): life is behind you. Everything you've left will never return: friends, England, host family, delicious buttered toast, liters of tea with milk that every morning flays your guts, the small hotel in London turned upside down the night before departure by the energy of that phalanx of pimply boys to which you proudly belong. To contain that destructive euphoria a dozen bobbys with nightsticks and mustaches were called in. Right after passing through customs you realized you hadn't said goodbye to any of the boys. That you had run away to take refuge in your mother's arms. In the toasted odor of the skin of a woman over forty. But instead you found this strange man, this uprooted giant.

"Don't you want a cup of coffee?" the man returned to press me.

Only after this sentence did I understand that my unease was not even comparable to his. It was he, my father, who had to be accepted. Say the right thing. Relax and relax me. Lead the game, in short. He knew very well that this was *his* institutional job but he knew that no word could worse define his role (and our relationship) than "institutional." I would have liked to say: "Papa, I don't drink coffee, I'm only fourteen. I drink milk, sometimes tea, never coffee." But I couldn't bring myself to call him Papa and so I avoided the rest.

"O.K., let's have a coffee," I said abruptly, to get out of the impasse.

This seemed to placate him. We had something to do. And together, too. I looked at him as he attacked the steaming cup. He was clumsy, quivering, as if unable to dominate his giant hands. He moved jerkily, maybe because of his strong astigmatism. There was nothing harmonious about him. But unlike his younger son, who was extremely skillful at disguising that stock of awkwardness and terror as a circumspect slowness, he seemed to voluptuously abandon himself to it.

"So? What do you think?" he asked me once we'd reached the airport parking lot, his eyes lighting up.

It's exasperating and typical not to pick up the allusions of a man you want to impress.

"What?" I equivocated.

"What do you think of the surprise?"

"What . . . surprise?"

"Come on, Dani, don't you see what I'm leaning against?"

"It's new?"

"Very new."

"It's yours?"

"Ours!"

Out of the darkness of the garage I saw emerge the pleasing aerodynamic lines of a sports car, presumably luxury. You could almost see yourself in its metallic blue, lose yourself in the perfect wavelike curves of its sides.

"Shit, Dani, it's a Porsche. A Carrera. I thought you liked cars."

Turning up the air-conditioning to a glacial temperature without paying attention to my annoyance and my sweat, and setting off like a race-car driver, he perfectly embodied the image of exaggerated sparkle and absent-minded insensitivity with which I identified my father. His physical self was as immoderate as his behavior: some obliging psychologist would have said that the man attacked the world before being attacked by it. This ill-contained impetuousness must have been the antidote, produced naturally by his body, against the poison of his own anomaly: the surplus of energy and competitiveness deployed since his school days—the first time that, emerging from the soft family womb, and coming into contact with the hostility of the planet, he had understood the unease he caused in others. Yes, he was different. Totally. He was an elegy of difference. Is there anything more original than a six-foot-four-inch Jew, half-albino, nearly blind, dressed with a refinement (rarely affected) that makes you think of those

British businessmen who aren't embarrassed to break the austerity of a gray chalk-striped suit with an ostentatious Art Nouveau tie? Is there anything stranger than this amusing cross between Edward Windsor and Bruno Schultz?

Was a supreme taste for masquerade and performance all part of it? Merely the distinctive trait of those eccentrics who, incapable of accepting themselves as such, hide behind a comfortable stereotype? Beware of depriving him of his carnival revelry. The reason he rode horses (although he was afraid of being thrown and although he hated sports in general, and although his height in the saddle, even on the tallest horses, made him a Don Quixote-like parody) was to show off jodhpurs of the type worn by the British cavalry. Just as the reason he traveled hundreds of kilometers to Cortina every February was to show off cashmere polo necks (unsuitable, in his incontestable judgment, for the city) that made him look like an existentialist *chanteur* long after time has run out. The whole reason he loved the changes of season (and often anticipated them) was the desire to renew, after long months of monotony, his own wardrobe. Like a true artist, Luca Sonnino started with a detail, and on that detail he constructed the world. If, for example, he acquired a pair of socks of a color that had hints of rust, once he got home he enjoyed—with the euphoria of certain informal virtuoso painters—orchestrating around that pair of socks a whirlwind of ties, shoes, handkerchiefs, until he finally made a decision, sadly saying goodbye to all the abandoned roads, the paths not taken, of his sartorial fantasy.

So beware of dressing him in a track suit or a pair of comfortable Sunday jeans! He would feel lost, he would fall back into the inferno of his primordial condition—what he had tried all his life to escape. He would have felt his hard-won harmony with the world break up into a new disharmony. He would not have survived the squalor of an average life of jogging and Sunday soccer, of elementary tastes and suffocating banalities. From the early years of childhood he had felt that his gigantic body had to be smoothed, softened, even hidden, possibly by English fabrics but also by a refined dialectic and a combative spirit, or, otherwise, had to be supported, intensified by a good dose of vulgarity and arrogance. He had crushed the world, he had crushed that younger brother of his, so much more handsome and delicate, he had crushed his wife, he had crushed his employees and his colleagues, just to affirm his own personality.

He turned on the stereo. Pushed a tape into the machine.

"Listen to this!" he said, more to himself than to me. Naturally he played it at an insane volume. Looking at him you would have said he was inhaling the music with his nostrils, as if he were breathing it deeply, or even swallowing it, in order to inject it into his veins: as if his already imposing body were asking only to explode with impatience and happiness. So the music lost its transcendence, until it was almost solid, concrete, like one of those summer-at-the-beach mint popsicles he had no fear of biting into. He was enthusiastic about his new stereo system. "You have no idea," he said, "what it means for someone of my generation to listen to music on a car stereo with this definition. I still remember Bepy's first radio, it was torture. Scratchy. You couldn't hear anything. And yet it was like a miracle."

Progress with a capital "P."

My father experienced any technological improvement as a personal success, or at least as yet another triumph of the very intelligent species that he had the honor of belonging to.

"So, do you like it?"

It was a song by Supertramp, "Goodbye Stranger," a comically prophetic title. He liked the song. It was big that summer. And this was his way of saying to me: "Hey, kid, I'm not nostalgic." And in effect he wasn't nostalgic. Not so much because he had nothing to feel nostalgia for (on the contrary) but because an intelligent man—according to the special significance he attributed to intelligence—couldn't, and shouldn't, indulge in nostalgia. For my father the Future was the dwelling place of the intelligent. He hated both apocalyptics and traditionalists. It was essential to be stubbornly interested in the present. That was the right recipe. Not at all like the fathers of my friends, not the *popular songs in my day* type. His approach to music was the inevitable emanation and dazzling epitome of his bond with the universe: curious, sometimes even courageous, if not really experimental, certainly omnivorous and hence totally immune from any prejudicial snobbery. He casually mixed novelties with evergreens: from Thelonius Monk to Supertramp, in an aesthetic acrobatics that was part of his insatiable love for the world. Rapacious love for his time. Voracious love for the West and the twentieth century, purified of all their frightening filth and transfigured by the magnificent dream of progress that in those very years—the years of his maturity—had taken off again.

Only then does it occur to you that maybe he came to get you without your mother to show you his new Carrera. Only then do you realize that you haven't gone overboard with compliments, or covered with enthusiastic interjections those wraparound seats smelling of leather, the poetic roar of the engine that any of your friends would be carried away by. Do you think he's upset? It's hateful to hurt his feelings. It's strange, sometimes you have a sinister pleasure in torturing your mother. But with him it's different. Making him suffer gives you a lump in your throat. He wasn't born to suffer. He really wasn't. You're mortified at not having expressed all your amazement at that car. Almost desperate at having been unable to let yourself go. (What's worse than the meeting of two shy souls?) You would pay to have a greater intimacy with him. But it's not your fault. You hardly know him. He's been away for so long. Far away for so many years. For almost ten years you must have seen him at most a couple of days a month. It's only natural that he has the effect on you of a stranger. Or rather, of a special and subtly unwelcome guest.

The guest of honor. The one for whom my mother always mobilized her superb hygienic-organizational machine. So that her husband, once at home, didn't have to worry about anything. Could feel like a pasha. Remember, Dani, don't annoy Papa . . . Remember, boys, Papa's coming home tonight . . . Remember, Johanna, tonight my husband will be home for dinner . . . So the directives seemed to unfold in our heads, and then creep into our consciousness as if they had been programmed to welcome the idea—deviously instilled by my mother—that Luca Sonnino deserved both the respect due to a sovereign and the pity inspired by a martyr.

I can't forget that when he came home I perceived, even though I was so small, the erotic vibrations of his young wife, yes, of this woman who for reasons independent of her will had ended up with a globetrotter husband, a young woman—neurotically obsessed with emotional sobriety—forced to spend the best years of her marriage separated from her husband. Just as I can't forget the ineffable sadness—and the desperation with which she tried to hide it—that fell over her face when he left again. A sadness strictly hidden by modesty and irony (these were the sentimental coordinates from the beginning of their relationship as classmates). Our evenings at the airport, with him so elegant in his double-breasted Daks overcoat (*the same one Churchill wore at Yalta!* he boasted), stank of pathos. At least as I experienced them. This is the important point: as I experienced them.

In my memories, in the sordid whimpering of my psyche, certain black-and-white snapshots return. Desperate emigrants with their bundles departing for America. Eastern Jews tired of pogroms and onion sauces. Lean Calabrian laborers seeking their fortune, leaving behind wives and children, to be hurled into a mysterious future of humiliation and hunger. To embark on a rusting ship in third class is the most attractive destiny you can imagine. Not to have any idea what the future reserves for you is your perpetual condition. But here things are different. My father leaves on airplanes, stays in big sophisticated hotels, leads a comfortable life; he's a fan of French cooking and wines, never misses the shows at the Royal Academy in London or the retrospectives at the Museum of Modern Art in New York, of which he is also a member. Probably there is some attractive assistant who accompanies him, to take care of him where a man wants to be taken care of.

Though seeing him there in his mustard-colored coat, ready to board yet another plane, does not rouse in me any special emotions, I find absolutely unbearable the anguished vortex in which my mother struggles just after his departure. We go home and she pretends to be calm; in reality she is gripped in a vise of terror at the unlikely hypothesis that the plane will crash or the taxi taking my father to the hotel in Frankfurt will skid on the ice and ram into the guardrail. The imagination of that gentle creature is packed with hair-raising images of blood and steel. Her diaphragm swells with the heavy breath emanated by the Unthinkable. Her heart is brimming with the last moments of her dying husband. And until the all-clear phone call arrives, until he informs her, with his characteristic aseptic detachment, that he is in the hotel, has had a shower, and is under the covers, she can't sit still. Time slows down, the minutes weigh on her. And it all seems to melt in the miraculous ringing that cuts through the nocturnal rarefactions of an elegant Roman apartment. She waits before answering in order not to give the impression, either to us, or to him, or to herself, of being apprehensive, and then, once she's answered, utters those words that in my mind function as the conclusion of a liturgy: "You're there? Already in bed? Which? That old Frank

Capra film? Splendid! Go to sleep, we'll talk tomorrow . . . Do you want me to give you a wake-up call in the morning? No, you know I like doing it . . . Then sleep well, love . . ." At that point the world changes, transformed from a squalid hostel to a luxury hotel in the mountains. The lady is euphoric, even chatty. The lady is not so neurotic as to think that her adored and distant spouse could meet with the most grotesque accident, such as tripping as he gets out of the tub and falling fatally on his head, or dying in his sleep from a blocked artery. The lady is young. The lady is content. The lady is very happy to sleep in an empty bed drunk on the thought that thousands of kilometers away the quivering fulcrum of her anguish is safe and sound, sinking into a foreign mattress. It pains her a little, now. But it's hardly more than a fleeting thought that, in any case, is part of the indecipherable range of emotions that keep her clinging to the mysterious idea of that strange man. An idea now miraculously cleansed of the sinister breath of the Unthinkable.

An idea, it has to be said, incapable of reviving when he makes his occasional Roman appearances, with his bundle of vices, indifferences, urbane vacuities, cruel conjugal egoisms, and ever more uselessly sophisticated purchases. At that point their relationship shifts from the starry heights of a dreamed-of, longed-for Empyrean to the frustrating Tolstoyan customs of marriage.

And then it starts all over again, like an infinite merry-go-round: because it isn't easy, it's not at all easy to go to bed at night knowing that your husband or your father is on yet another flight taking him from Indonesia to Mexico. It's a scene that you—about to go to bed—can barely imagine: not without that cosmic anxiety that tends to cover the astral distances between you and your relative. Because it's true, you're in bed, under the quilt, and outside it's cold, it's raining or whatever: and it's not easy for someone who's been in bed for hours, for someone who feels protected, enveloped in a kind of languid blanket of darkness and silence, to imagine husband or father—this intergalactic traveling salesman—suspended at nine thousand meters over a magnificent and terrible expanse like the Indian Ocean, at a thousand kilometers an hour, trapped by an external temperature of sixty degrees below zero and by air so rarefied you can't breathe. It's a thought that freezes the blood. A thought that encourages insomnia. A thought that can't be calmed even by the soporifics of Statistics (how many airplanes *don't* crash every day in the world? How many taxis *don't* have accidents every day in the world? How many people *never* return home again every day in the world?). All you can do is imagine your husband or father as a traveler, with his habits, his strict rules, partly inspired, partly mad, partly silly, like the one that forbids him peremptorily to wear shoes without laces because one's feet swell on an airplane. That's it, that's how your husband or your father breaks away from the threatening sky where you've confined him. That's how he comes back to earth among the living. Tomorrow you'll see him again. Tomorrow you'll be able to go and pick him up at the airport. Sleep, boy. Sleep, gentle lady. Sleep, both of you. There's no reason to stay awake. Airplanes almost always land.

And maybe it would have been different if she had realized that for him things were fine like that.

Basically what you have to understand is that he is one of those men of our time who not only have no home, in the sense of a fixed dwelling place, but don't seem to need one. Put like that, it may appear exaggerated, but his home is the world: if not all of it, a considerable piece. More at ease in the antiseptic labyrinths of the duty-free shops, in the meticulous cubicles of Japanese restaurants, in the impersonal luxury of the Hiltons, even in the hazy sarabands of waiting rooms than in his own house. Maybe because a man of that extra-large size doesn't know what to do with domestic coziness: he needs big spaces, crowded lobbies. My God, that prince of surfaces inhabited his years with overflowing enthusiasm. Here it is: the upscale version of the *wandering Jew*, the chic transposition of Miller's salesman. No one could understand better than he the sublime poetry of a McDonald's in a desolate service area in West Germany at a given midnight in December. No one could be moved more than he at the sight of a fourteen-year-old Ukrainian girl, protected by a pair of faded jeans and a lice-infested windbreaker, waiting for the bus, blowing on her hands in the cold. He loved certain modern scenes. Saw the intrinsic elegy.

And the singular thing is that he had a self-ironic awareness of his tendencies. For example, when someone asked if he was tired, or if he was still out of synch because of the time change, he answered that after many years of traveling he had gotten the better of jet lag. He said that for him jet lag didn't exist. That it was a ridiculous suggestion. He who has the world in his pocket knows that in essence it never stops being illuminated. And finally he would add, with a pinch of amused vainglory, "Let's say I feel like Charles V: the sun never sets on my empire." That self-definition seems to me to describe perfectly the persona that my father had constructed for himself, almost in opposition to the intemperances of nature: yes, that's my father there; on the one hand the arrogance of claiming improbable victories, on the other the continual declaration of rationality.

More and more every day he was a slave of his habits, spoiled by solitude, totally in thrall to crazy rituals that if you didn't know him you would have called superstitious. One with his suitcase and toilet kit. I've never met a man who could be identified with his own accessories like my father: the smell of his skin—that mixture of virility, unfiltered Players, and astringent bergamot aftershave—spoke of his personality and his vocation better than any exhaustive discourse. Luca Sonnino experienced his clothes viscerally: the checked Brooks Brothers shirts—like Moravia!—under a blue blazer, the regimental ties with a Windsor knot, the white handkerchiefs, the natural-leather English shoes, the tight-waisted overcoats with velvet lapels, the broad-brimmed hats were only the concrete offshoots of his soul, guardians of a moral choice, or, more accurately, of a vision of the world.

There are those who say that a human being's first great love story is not the adolescent agitation provoked by a classmate, or, even less, that elective connection between twenty-year-olds that usually at the most dramatic moment develops into bourgeois matrimony, but the first unforgettable extramarital adventure. It's there, in the betrayal of the young husband or wife, that one feels the adrenaline flow and the heart explode. It's there that, like Dr. Zhivago, you feel so lost, so painfully exhilarated, so mired in something supernatural and tragically unjust that you want to confess it to your spouse, not to hurt but to share your illicit happiness and your inevitable guilt with the person you think of as your closest friend. I don't know if this marvelous moment arrived in the life of my father and what effect it produced on his overexcited organism. I imagine it did, if only considering the logistical anomaly of his marriage and the experience I've had in the meantime—if indirectly—of the typical marriage. It's natural: it happens to every man who isn't paralyzed by religious-moralistic aversions, just imagine an individual like him, well-to-do tenant of the comfortable part of this world. And yet, despite all the other men in his family, despite Bepy especially, despite the whole race represented by Bepy, Luca was absolutely discreet. In the difficulty I feel even today in accepting that my father was a man and my mother a woman and that I am the product of their humanity, I can't help noticing that my father's reserve had something elegantly refined about it. His intimate life was a mystery as impenetrable as his inner life. The job of sentimental desertification that his parents had done on him, so that he would forget (or at least not dramatize) his very singular appearance, had had the collateral effect of making him proudly enigmatic. Yes, he was an enigma purged of the viscosity of enigmas. As I've said: for Bepy the pleasure of adultery was in the possibility of showing off. For my father—assuming he practiced it with the assiduousness of his dissolute progenitor—it was probably something much more profound (burning and unconfessable passions) or much more superficial: hormonal jolts, erotic appetites satisfied by the occasional traveling companion. Maybe because he, who at first sight might seem impervious, he, who loved to display a cynicism that he was totally exempt from, and that, when it was turned against him, made him suffer tremendously, hadn't forgiven his father and mother for flaunting their respective conquests. Or maybe because his peculiar idea of style—only sometimes overflowing into a venial coarseness absolutely in accord with his Orson Welles-like physique—couldn't conceive the possibility of being so shameless in erotic matters. Or maybe, much more simply, like all physically eccentric people, he had developed a timidity that obliged him to hide any sentimental rapture, from the most conventional to the most illicit. The usual Sonnino problem: neurotic modesty confused with euphoric levity. The fact is that a soul so tender deserved another body. A small body, like Kafka's, bony and difficult. And instead nature had made him that way, and he had had to invent another self, a self that was in accord with his physique, a robust self. Was this his secret? This the incomprehensible secret that was manifested in the continuous alternation between timidity and competitiveness, arrogance and vulnerability? This the unconfessable mystery of Luca Sonnino? And maybe then his body had grown so large in order to better guard that secret, as in the Middle Ages enormous fortresses were built to protect a reliquary?

Anyway, and I know I'm not wrong, the secret of my parents' marriage—from the outside so anomalous and irrational—lay entirely in the wife's capacity for being present and the husband's for being absent. For her it was enough to see him emerge from the baggage area of the airport at Fiumicino, with his gangster's overcoat and broad-brimmed hat, to feel an irrepressible sensation of irritation. Just as for him it was enough to come across her suddenly gloomy expression to understand that now, after that long, exhausting journey, he had to climb the Russian mountains of that moody wife.

"We're not going home?" I asked him, as he turned in the wrong direction.

"No, to Positano."

"Positano?"

"To Nanni's house."

"Why?"

"What do you mean 'why'? Let's put it like this: because I am your father, because I am six-four, because I earn a lot more than you, because your survival is tightly bound to my wallet. I think I have all the necessary requirements to decide both for me and for you. Satisfied?"

"You didn't say anything to me . . ."

"Next time we'll do a press release."

"I didn't mean that, but . . ."

"Dani, I'm on vacation, I'd like to relax and enjoy myself. Nanni invited us. It seemed proper to accept."

"And Mama?" I finally found the courage to ask. *Maybe she's dead and he doesn't know how to tell me.*

"She's joining us tomorrow morning."

"But," I whined, "I don't have anything with me . . . bathing suit. Bermudas. Beach towels. I'm tired. I have a suitcase full of dirty clothes . . ."

"Nonsense! Mama packed you a suitcase with clean clothes

and everything you need for the beach. Anything you don't have we'll buy this afternoon. After all," he resumed a moment later with a facetious smile, "a man like you doesn't travel with suitcases. A man like you redoes his wardrobe every place he goes."

Extended pause.

"So? You're not going to tell me anything?"

"What?"

"Everything."

Usually it was Lorenzo who took charge of these detailed travel reports. The job of exaggerating, twisting, inventing was entrusted to him. My role was secondary. I was a silent witness. An actor, not the protagonist. My job was to assent, to deny, sometimes sigh, in extreme cases even emit monosyllables. But this time it was up to me. Lorenzo had stayed in London, to do an intensive course, for three more weeks. The truth was he'd decided to stay because of a girl. I couldn't say if it was more unusual or more distressing to see my brother infatuated. Isn't it always terrible to discover a self-confident person caught in some sappy amorous web? Don't you find unbearable the sight of a proud man made sentimental and tame? Well, that adorable dispenser of skepticism—the natural counterweight to the languors of his little brother—at the sight of that boyish girl with glasses, a sort of elegy to a fresh and springlike Rome, had fallen head over heels.

Lorenzo was much more like my father than I. And it's not just a matter of physique. Or charisma. It doesn't matter that when people listened to him they felt influenced, almost subjugated. I don't mean the marriage of agnosticism and corrosive sensuality. His anomaly—what made him so profoundly close to his father and so blatantly different from every other individual—was sentiment, the purity of sentiment, the scandal of sentiments: the painful accord between generosity and the desperate attempt to hide it through that verbose display of cynicism. In our small nuclear family two good persons who seemed bad coexisted with two bad persons who seemed good. It was the clarity that could be sensed in Lorenzo that disturbed many people but exercised a morbid fascination on them. That severe, honest way, only apparently ruthless, of judging others.

Well, he was only seventeen, and he already seemed to have mastered the art of being listened to. He who one day would put his intellectual fervor in the service of the liberal cause, as an independent journalist, with that shocking book on Raymond Aron (who knows why the Sonninos only write shocking books?), was then a Marxist. The only Marxist in our high school. And everyone was afraid of him because of it. He didn't have my weakness. He didn't want to be like everyone else. He loved being what he was. He wasn't a conformist like his younger brother. He wasn't the slobbering lady-in-waiting to the reigning prince and princess. He had constructed an independent personality. He seemed to challenge the little bastards of our school, the ones who called him a "Communist cockroach," because once in religion class he had defended the sacred-inviolability-of-democracy. My father recognized himself. "At his age," he would say, "I was exactly like Lorenzo, with the only difference that I would never have worn those terrible double-breasted jackets, like a hero of the Risorgimento."

"Do you want to know why Lorenzo stayed in London?" I asked him.

"It's a start."

"He has a girlfriend," I said triumphantly, sure of the impact this phrase would have on my father.

"Really?"

"Yes . . ."

"So?"

"What?"

"The details!"

So I tell Luca Sonnino exactly what Luca Sonnino expects to be told, giving the murderous ogre a meal of his favorite food, soothing his eardrums with the sweetest gossip they can receive. I tell him that his firstborn was the best English-speaker in our group, so a course was set up just for him. I tell him that in the mini-tournament of countries organized by the school, the final soccer challenge between Italy and France was decided on an overhead kick by Lorenzo that was emphatically compared to Pele's in *Escape to Victory* (why do his successes excite me more than mine?). I tell him that Syria, Lorenzo's girlfriend, is the prettiest and most popular girl. I tell him that Lorenzo had a fierce argument, from which he naturally emerged the winner, with a boy—a notoriously brazen blond kid, not to mention glaringly envious of Lorenzo, though not of me—who claimed that all Jews are stingy and always defend each other. I tell him that when Lorenzo speaks everyone listens, as if they couldn't help it.

What am I doing?

Simple: I'm compensating my father. I'm following the gooey maternal instructions. I transfigure the British successes of my brother in order to be forgiven for my failed enthusiasm at the sight of the Carrera, for not having managed to embrace him, for almost not having recognized him. I give him what he needs. I serve him his preferred cocktail: security, success, the sensation that everything has a meaning and that that meaning is vaguely kind to him. That his sons will make it—like him, better than him. That's why, as I speak, I hear his deep breathing (the manly, heavy breath of Winston Churchill). That's why he presses his foot down even harder on the accelerator. Somehow he has to let out the excess elation that is sometimes more unbearable and piercing than grief.

Am I lying, then?

Of course I'm lying. Anyone who has the least experience

of life knows that to make our neighbor happy there is no better recipe than the lie. And anyone who had seen my father in
that precise instant breathe in so vigorously, as if he were seeking to grasp even in the air something ungraspable—if only
someone could have heard the tone in which he continued to
repeat "Really? Is that really what happened?"—would have
said that I was right.

Luca Sonnino was the creature most like a polar bear I've
ever seen: regal, fierce, incredibly tender. Besides the tangible
elements like his broad shoulders, his clumsiness, and his
albinism, the resemblance was also in his Gargantuan appetite,
his sky-blue gaze that was a mixture of gentleness, anger, and
impatience, the ungainliness of every movement on land offset
by the agility he showed in the water. That's it, it was as if that
snow-white body had an amphibian predisposition. As if it had
come into the world to dominate the terraqueous elements.
When he walked he had the bumbling arrogance of Gérard
Depardieu, but in the summer at the sea or in a pool he dove
like a whale and swam rapidly, raising masses of water like the
propeller of a motorboat. The thick lenses of his glasses made
his eyes seem like billiard balls. His white-blond beard almost
touched his swelling chest, while his nose had the Jewish
effrontery that made you think of the Ashkenazi exterminated
forty years earlier by the Nazis or of certain Jewish dandies
who overran the Viennese salons in the time of Felix Austria.
He had come into the world almost completely blind, and
thanks to an operation after the war had gained those two or
three diopters needed to read, with immense difficulty, a dic-
tionary, get a driver's license, and earn a lot of money in the
textile business. Although nature had amused herself in being
so unfavorable to him in certain things (sight, clumsiness,
phosphorescent hair), she had sneakily compensated him, giving him that imperial air which mysteriously commanded

respect. His complexion was so distinctive and his physique so imposing that as his son you knew that in the most crowded square in the world you would recognize your father among thousands of other anonymous individuals. You could say anything about his looks, except that they could pass unnoticed. Bepy had done his utmost to transform his son's eccentricity, which might have seemed made to order for generating inferiority complexes, into a sort of pride. What Bepy, because of his cultural bias, could never have tolerated was that his son should develop a self-pitying or even loser's spirit. He had taught him to swim at Capri in the fifties by pushing him out of the boat into the sea *where he couldn't touch*. He had taught him to take cold showers. To eat the guts and head of a fish. Not to have scruples about women. To hunt deer. Not to be embarrassed to be the most fashionable. The result Bepy obtained was certainly not a giant clone of himself. The son had mediated the vitalist histrionics of his father into a sort of aggressive competitiveness, in a way that closely resembled, as if in a mirror, the utter rejection of that educational method by the other son, Teo. Luca, his *bechor*, the favorite, was someone who would always have a clear idea about the world, and who would want to express that idea, who would want to perform, one whom professors would say had a gift for lucidity, and whom women would detest for his combative eagerness to speak.

After all, in view of the premises, one could consider the commitment of Bepy and Ada Sonnino to their adored Luca, that freak of nature, that Viking who came from who knows where, an absolute masterpiece of pedagogy. They had succeeded in transforming him into a man who was at once normal and extraordinary, civilized and uncultured, shy and barbaric—removing him definitively from the handicap of his difference to make him the tender arrogant man he was.

In spite of the effort spent to be like everyone else, in spite of the struggle to be accepted, so the color of his hair would lose its meaning for others, in spite of the normality won at a high price in the course of an entire adolescence, my father, on the threshold of marriage, hadn't managed to free himself from the unanimous perplexity of the world. And his choice, a small girl, of another religion and another world, had made things more complex.

It was an *affaire*, my parents' marriage. That needs to be clear. Otherwise all the rest can't be understood. The path that led them to the altar was arduous and filled with perils. No one wanted that marriage, no one had sought it or endorsed it. Because since the world began no Jew has enjoyed having his son marry a Catholic and no Catholic aspires to have a Jewish son-in-law. In the end, however, they all resigned themselves. The two opposing parties—although without equanimity; on the contrary, with bitter acceptance of the inevitable—gave in. You are making a mistake, they all said. This business promises nothing good, they insisted on emphasizing. But finally they gave in. The Sonninos capitulated quickly. More because of an intrinsic inability to tolerate a domestic struggle than because of a sincere moderation of their views.

While on the other side, the side of the Bonanno family, the storm raged. The whining chorus of mothers, fathers, grandparents, distant friends and relations rallied to condemn the choice of the reprobate. That is to say that for them it was more difficult. It's always more difficult for the majority to accept the minority. Who are the Jews? They have never known any. It's the first time they've had any contact. Unfortunate people, who have suffered. Rich and malicious people. Avaricious and clever. People who have noses of a certain shape. People who mostly go bald. Sly people who cheat you. That's who they are: usurers and textile merchants, bankers and jewelers. It's their own fault. What's the point of remaining Jewish in a world of Catholics? What's the point of not eating certain choice foods? What's the point of acting so snobbish and victimized? And then where did they get him? With that strange-color hair. An albino afflicted with gigantism. And are we a hundred per cent sure that he can bring healthy children into the world? How can our dear girl have made such a bizarre choice?

But come on, it couldn't have been otherwise. It's precisely his abnormality that attracted her. She was always like that, always on the side of the losers, the disinherited, and yet deeply ambitious and secretly smitten by Hollywood. As a girl she wanted to become a nun. But she couldn't tear herself away from her giant Cary Grant posters. An uncle had brought her a memento from the United States that she religiously preserved: an original poster for *The Philadelphia Story*, going back to 1940, a few years before she was born, featuring the young faces of a dazzling Grant and a swooning Hepburn. Asceticism and luxury found unhoped-for harmony in the heart of that dreamy high-school girl. During Lent when she was a child, she always brought her most precious possessions to the poor on Mission Day. She would have stripped herself of everything to make the needy happy. Who knows why? The malicious say out of pride. The kindly point resolutely to a precocious sense of altruism. The cynics claim that the two go together marvelously. What impulse if not charity mixed with grandiosity can have induced her to fall in love with that ungainly sugary Gulliver? What does she want from him if not the privilege of protecting him, if not the pride of displaying him? He can't charm us. What abyss lies hidden behind those tailored clothes? What artificial world produced this fashion plate? Why does he continually defy moderation and ridicule, wearing an immaculate panama in summer, in winter a felt borsalino? Why does he always speak so ostentatiously? Why is he obsessed with show? Why does he have an unrenounceable need to be provocative and hyperbolic? Have you seen how he tastes wine, how he sniffs it, how he rolls it around in the glass? Good God, is he vain! The answer is simple. How could we miss it? This poor boy is simply broken and desperate. That's why he is attached to her. Because she, our girl, in spite of appearances, is a strong little thing. She's the dominant figure. She will be the moving force in this disastrous and splendid marriage. She will be the one to keep it afloat if it's worth the trouble, just as she will be the one to sink it if circumstances require.

So at the first invitation to the Sonnino house, the Largo Argentina penthouse that overlooks a formidable slice of Rome, the future in-laws, different in history and ideas, find themselves facing one another, ready to do battle. Let's enjoy this confrontation. Let's study it, like a game of chess. Let's drain it, down to the last drop. Starting from one fundamental assumption: no one will come out a winner. They'll all lose. Because they'll all have a strong sensation of defeat.

The coarseness of Alfio Bonanno, my mother's father, has something solemn and disturbing about it. He's thickset, and his opaque blue gaze expresses the obtuse pride of the self-made man who hates frills. His massive protruding chin recalls Benito Mussolini but the oblong shape of his eyes is unmistakably Mao. A man who speaks little and slowly. His goals and his vision of the world are of a piece with the self-made man's colorless aspect. Practical, frank, distrustful, unmystical but devout Catholic, puritanical, sexophobic, Pharisaic, and profoundly afraid of the world. It's impressive to see Bepy and Alfio, both so out of their element, shake hands, fake a smile, and try to come to an understanding in the fluorescent frame of this fragrant habitation. Life has brought them together without their having lifted a finger. They have both done what they can to dissuade Romeo and Juliet. But, faced with their obstinacy, they could do nothing but consent. That small, enervating battle was joined while their offspring were in high school and then university. Now that they're grown up, you can't stop them. All that's left is to limit the damage.

The Sonninos' terrace is a perfect square whose sides are decorated with red and white tufts of geraniums and daisies; it's a jumble of walls of a desert-yellow color. The surrounding frame is Rome by night: the charm of the flaking ochre of the rooftops. That background odor of cats and early summer. It can't be said that all this doesn't have an effect on the Bonannos. They look around, frightened and distrustful, wondering how "true" it all is. "True" in their particular language means "solid," resting on a "secure financial base." For the Bonannos, solvency is an ethical value. For the Bonannos, to live beyond one's means, "to bite off more than you can chew," to pay interest on a bank loan, to flaunt wealth you don't possess is not only affectation and weakness of character but moral perversion, and, if not exactly a crime, certainly an infallible criterion for judging one's neighbor. Years later, when the inexorable financial disaster strikes the Sonninos, the Bonannos will greet it with hearts that waver between sorrow for their older daughter, and her involvement in such a drama, and the sinister pride of having observed yet again how lack of prudence and an inflated passion for ostentation lead to ruin. In their eyes, the Sonninos (and the fate that was about to be cruel to them) would become the living proof of how right they—the Bonannos, with their frugality and with all the rhetoric of frugality—had been from the beginning: yet further proof of how that first devious challenge had been only the worldly version of the eternal conflict between Good and Evil, embodied once again in an innocuous bourgeois custom.

Many say that the problem between these two opposing families is religion. That between them there must be, if not a doctrinal dispute, an anthropological incompatibility. Let me say that this is outrageous nonsense. A generic, conscience-soothing pack of lies. The differences and disagreements

between these two couples are so deeply rooted and unyielding that one might paradoxically say that the only point of contact between them, beyond their common membership in the
human race, is their Judeo-Christian origin: they share the spirit of the Commandments. Yes, indeed, the fact of being Jews
and Catholics unites them much more than all the rest: much
more than having lived for many years in the same city or having shared the same historical experiences, for example.

It's the summer of 1967. The summer when the world
began spinning. A few weeks have passed since the end of the
Six-Day War. The atmosphere in the Sonnino household,
although they are all too snobbish to completely enter into the
mood of the Jewish community, is nevertheless electric. The
dailies with banner headlines piled on the tables. Come on, it's
thrilling for those who lived through certain times, who saw
their own ten-year-old cousins deported, who had to hide, who
endured the violation of their own homes and the flaying of
their souls, for those who trembled at the thud of German
boots and the steely din of their death orders on that fatal
Sixteenth of October, to see such a formidably equipped
Jewish army under the leadership of that Jewish messiah of a
general Yitzhak Rabin annihilate the far more numerous Arab
enemy. We've already said it, basically: the Sonninos are not
the type to get excited about Israel, not the type to send
money, not the kind of Jews for whom *Israel above all*. Israel is
no more than one of the tangible offshoots of Jewish Memory
regarded by them with diffidence. No, the Sonninos are of
another type: proudly attached to their duty as sober expo-
nents of a critical spirit and objectivity. We ask a lot from
Israel. Justice and democracy. Tolerance and secularism. From
the Israelis, permanently at war, we claim exemplary behavior,
like pilgrim fathers, like the last frontier: inflexibly hard but
severely just. But this time no, it was impossible to contain our

excitement: we were moved, we suffered, lost sleep, cheered, truly feared that Israel might cease to exist, disappear from the face of the earth, a new Jewish genocide and another dream transmuted into tragedy. We immediately had the impression that things would be different this time. We understood that the stoicism with which the parents waited to be massacred taught their children the absolute necessity of fighting. You can't understand the pride that fills Bepy's heart. Incredible that in the space of a few hours the small Israeli air force (shit, the Jews have an air force, too!) destroyed Russian jets made available to the Egyptians and the Jordanians, insuring absolute supremacy in the air. And that those armies, made up largely of illiterate and unmotivated masses, surrendered in the face of a small, compact army, overflowing with motivation.

All this left in the souls of Bepy and his family a grim elation. It's strange to continue to be occupied with insignificant things like keeping the business going, receiving salesmen, organizing masked balls, fucking underage seamstresses, while in a part of the world not that far away the Israeli Army achieves a crushing victory. For several days everyone in the family continued to buy five dailies, disappointed by the Italian papers' progressive loss of interest in the extraordinary event, grieved by the Arab-loving bias of the majority of the commentators. As if flawless journalism would be bound to extol the unaccustomed power of the Israeli Army every day. For several nights Bepy has barely slept. He gets up, listens to the radio, watches television. He is annoying and irritable. He suffers from that syndrome of the periphery—that sense of decentralization with respect to the events of History—that will soon lead his son Teo to emigrate to a place where History still exists and local news has only a decorative importance.

That's why when Alfio Bonanno asks him, "So, everything all right, Mr. Sonnino?" and Bepy assumes an expression that betrays concern to the point where the other asks, "Is something wrong?," Bepy, wondering if Alfio's making fun of him, winks, "Well, yes, you know, with what's happened!"

"What has happened?"

"Well, in Israel . . ."

"Ah, yes, I think I read something . . ."

That's exactly what Alfio says, leaving Bepy speechless. *Ah, yes, I think I read something* . . . With this statement, apparently harmless, Alfio confesses not only his utter alienation from the Jewish cause, not only his rudeness, not only his metaphysical egoism, but a total lack of attention to international affairs, to current events, to History. He confesses his modest vision. His distressing mental perimeter. And this indifference, this detachment, can't help but annoy the Sonninos.

Come on, Bepy, no need to torment yourself. This is Alfio, you'll get to know him. He is the human being with the narrowest horizons you—who were born and lived in your Jewish theater—will meet in the course of your existence. Alfio is a provincial who made a fortune through stubborn determination, through the constantly celebrated myth of saving and secure investment. No books. No movies. No analysis. No wanks. No elegance. No sophisticated cooking. No ideological confrontation. No excitement. No sport. No team to root for. No unrealizable dream. No adultery. No leap that goes beyond the ordinary religious rites learned in childhood and never forgotten. No nonsense in his head. A man who is on the side of suffering because he has suffered. A businessman who has no talent for business but adores martyrdom. One who owes everything to himself and to the sacrifice inflicted on his family members. One who loves to make apocalyptic predictions. One who has built his own fortune on others' consumption but is not disposed to consume in turn. An unexpected dissident from Keynesian capitalism. A prophet of the civilization of the practical. A man who doesn't want to circulate his money, preferring to leave it where it is. One who has learned diligently, and even with a good dose of humility, that you have to buy your shirts at Caleffi, your ties at Battistoni, sweaters and shoes at Cenci, and that suits should be ordered from an old, trusted, not too exorbitant tailor—but who endemically detests any kind of blustering pecuniary show. One who does not like to travel. Because the best thing he ever saw, his center of gravity, from which he basically can't and won't distance himself, is the village near Macerata where he was born. The village where today he's treated like a king. A son who made it and who to demonstrate it bought the entire wing of a building, of the town hall. And now everyone respects him. Everyone bows to him. The rest for him doesn't exist. Come on, Bepy, don't be angry with him. Alfio has nothing against your Six-Day War. If anything he's got a problem with the Jews. Not in a special way, however. His prejudice has something democratically ecumenical about it. His discrimination (rather, distrust) involves all those who don't share his origin, his generation, his view of the world—and that's about five billion or so people. Isn't it perhaps his right as a man from the Marches to distrust the Abruzzese, the Sicilians, the Tuscans, the Jews, the French, the blacks, the Alpine troops? Not hatred. Hatred is a waste of time and time is . . . No, don't say it! . . . Alfio is mad for clichés: he admires the stubborn precision of the Germans, just as he deplores the sloppy negligence of Neapolitans. What the hell can your Middle East dispute matter to him, then, if he lived through the Second World War, the one that should have concerned him, in terror mixed with a deep unconsciousness? How the hell can you expect him to care about your little war if even today his boast is that he didn't take sides, at a moment when the choice was, if not exactly a strict necessity, a demonstration of character? The important thing for him is not to attract attention. The important thing is to respect one's superiors. Flatter them. Never be

disrespectful. Be monstrously efficient. Think about work
even in moments of relaxation. Talk about work even at the
funeral of one's best friend. Not only out of opportunism but
because life for him seems to be completely taken up with the
conscientious fulfillment of a pre-established order. A social
order that isn't to be violated. Pointless to discuss it. For him
there is nothing more odious than chatterers. Any aspiring
artist is a chatterer. Any dolt with imagination is a chatterer.
All those who are confused, or who simply want to express
themselves, are in his eyes chatterers. People should be judged
by what they have been able to construct, not by what they say.
And for him their constructions have to be solid and tangible.
Land made suitable for building. Apartments to sell and rent.
Here is a Fundamentalist Believer in the God of Bricks, my
dear Bepy. The first thing Alfio asked himself when he entered
your house is if it belongs to you or if you are a mere tenant
(he is loaded with tenants and considers them pure scum,
bloodsuckers), then he asked himself how much it might be
worth, and finally if fixtures so refined and subject to wear and
furnishings so sumptuous were indispensable. He understood
from the affected manner of your greeting that you host the
germ of the chatterer. And he is happy to have identified you.
He considers himself someone who flushes out chatterers. You
mustn't expect anything from him, except what he is capable
of giving: some sensible advice that explains his exemplary
life, his exemplary fate, his exemplary rise. He hates men with
beards, because they savor of the subversive. He can't look at
red sweaters because they savor of Communism. His sexual
phobia has nothing to with decadent disgust for sticky female
intimacy: it's a matter of decorum and opportunity. In spite of
appearances, he's not an extremist, if anything he's a moderate
puritan. Anything can be done provided the world doesn't
find out about it. Adultery in a completely theoretical way
doesn't have to be rejected. Provided no one discovers you

(which is very difficult to guarantee in advance). Provided you don't deviate from your immutable mission of saving and accumulation (which, in his indisputable opinion, is impossible). In time the form has so hardened and crystallized as to become substance. That's why he's ended up believing that he is what he isn't, like you, dear Bepy, who want to let others think that you are what you are not. Beware of calling him when he's in the bathroom. Try it, he won't respond. That doesn't mean he doesn't have physiological needs. More simply, no one must know. That's all. No one must know that Alfio Bonanno in the middle of the day feels the urge to defecate.

So, Bepy, don't be annoyed. You've got a tough nut here. You'd be unlikely to meet in your circle a man so hard and unassailable, so pathologically insensitive to the charm of your worldliness and prestige. It is absolutely pointless to display your smile, to flatter his wife ("Signora Bonanno, has anyone ever told you that you have lovely hands?"), pointless (indeed damaging) to show off such an impeccable chalk-stripe. It's pointless to show him, as you're doing now, your collection of modern paintings, your Burri, your Mafai, your precious Modigliani, because the only question you will hear addressed to you—as in fact happens—is whether you're not afraid to keep such valuable pieces in the house, if you're not afraid of theft. And thus, although to you it may seem petty, Alfio is showing you the truest, most human part of himself. His most sensitive point. I'm talking about fear. He's a man who is afraid. So tall, imposing, in appearance indestructible, he's a man who shits himself. He's a fortress with cracked walls who by instilling fear in others tries to exorcize his own.

What's he afraid of?

Everything: not only death, illness, infirmity, doing the wrong thing, but simply turning a corner, coming up against the anger of somebody powerful, seeing everything he has built

shattered. He loves to sow fear. He is a preacher of the imminent apocalypse.

And so have no illusions: nothing of what you are, nothing
of what you have tried to be in your whole life, works with him.
He is fiercely immovable in the face of your charms, your
seductive powers. And no one understands you better than
me. Because you are failing precisely where I will fail millions
of times: in the difficult operation of seducing him. He isn't
seducible. Not by people like us. What you are experiencing
on this infernal evening I will experience my whole life, every
time I see him.

Because Alfio regarded me, maybe because of my resemblance to my father, maybe because of the Jewish features
sculpted in my face, as the child of sin. The very incarnation of
my mother's mistake. He would sit there in his big flowered
armchair, placed in the center of the immense living room of
his immense house on the Aventine, from which he seemed to
dominate the whole world: and suddenly he would look at me
and say to my mother: "Daniel is sly, be careful, he's sly, you've
already been taken in once . . . You see that nose? He's got a
big nose! The same nose as his father and grandfather . . ."
And he couldn't stop laughing at this physiognomic observation of his that seemed so perfectly revealing. Biology was all
for Alfio Bonanno, even if he didn't know it! And my mother's
indignation was to no avail. To no avail my own indignation, or
the media clamor of political correctness. He continued unper-
turbed to make fun of my nose, fluctuating, as was his way,
between the serious and the facetious. You see, Bepy, I think
I'm the first Jew in the history of humanity to have suffered
discrimination from his own grandfather. The first Jew in
History with an anti-Semitic grandfather. For all Jews there has
always been the family, at least that, the ultimate resource, the
last refuge, and yet in my house anti-Semitism laid traps with
the same strong determination that ran through the Jewish

spirit. What a scabrous schizophrenia, dear Bepy, are you preparing for me on this unfortunate evening in 1967? If only you knew how it will end up, you would behave in a very different way tonight with your future in-law, a lot tougher, to keep the evil deed from being committed. You would, perhaps, do your utmost so that what cannot, what must not, be joined will not be joined.

"At least you've insured them?" asks Alfio, alluding again to the paintings.

"Of course I've insured them," Bepy answers, annoyed.

Finally they are interrupted by the maid: Dinner is served, sir.

The main dish is a classic of the Sonnino household. To tell the truth it's an archeological relic dug up for the occasion. Both because of the difficulty and the time required for its execution and because of the excess of calories that defies Bepy's dietary prohibitions, it was at least ten years ago that Grandma Rachele's Pasticcio Dolce was banished from the convivial habits of the Sonninos. But this time Bepy has insisted that the cook stick to a strict philological program. Nothing added, no adjustments. And so there is the browned timbale of sweet dough—which inside holds a savory treasure of ziti, meatballs, and mushroom *ragù*—displaying its classic cylindrical profile to the proud masters of the house and their two diffident guests. Bepy gazes at his grandmother's unforgettable *pasticcio* with an almost comical pride. But for Alfio it's enough for his palate—spoiled by the customary pleasures of simple carbonaras and sirloins—to be caressed by a burning mouthful of timbale for him to dismiss the operation as a pretentious abomination, a sweet-and-sour concoction. "Just like those people!" he will burst out hours later to his wife. "Pretentious people, concocted, sweet-and-sour." Yet Alfio, faithful to his pauperist proclamations, cleans his plate, irritated by the foolish chitchat of the wives. Evidently no one dares to confront the subjects that are the reason they've decided to meet. Bepy is strangely intimidated. Besides, only that morning he was drilled by his son: "Remember, Papa, be tolerant, give in as far as possible, and don't talk about religion."

"But what kind of people are they?" Bepy asked, curious.

"Different from us. They're closed, opaque. But they adore Fiamma."

"Why aren't you and Fiamma coming?"

"I don't know. She asked me. She said it was her parents who wanted it that way. Insisted. I think he has something to talk to you about."

"But what type is he?"

"Impeccable character. Something of a windbag. But it's essential that he agree."

"Do you at least know what they want to discuss?"

"No. The important thing is for you to be tolerant."

It's the memory of these words of his son that has led Bepy to put off the moment of truth until after dessert. But at this point, while Ada serves coffee in the living room, Bepy comes to a decision.

The beginning is unforgettable, a cross between *Guess Who's Coming to Dinner* and *The Betrothed*. Bepy starts off with a declaration that could offend anyone but, instead, galvanizes those present:

"Now, at the cost of seeming discourteous, I can't conceal my bewilderment . . ."

Thus Bepy: decisive and theatrical, even if he's not really all that opposed to his son's choice. He and Ada have already metabolized the shock of marriage with that girl (although my great-grandfather has bizarrely nicknamed her the Canaanite. "Are you going to impose the company of the Canaanite on us again today?" he keeps asking that strange grandson, so much whiter than he is). But Bepy can't resist the temptation to flatter his listeners: he wants to subscribe to the anxieties of his future fellow in-law. He wants to be *completely* on his side. And how can that gentleman Alfio disappoint the expectations of such an unpredictably diligent flatterer?

"I'm glad you think that way, too," he responds dryly. "I didn't dare to say so, but since you've brought up the subject . . ."

"Now, look, it's not a matter of racism or other foolishness . . . or even of compatibility," Bepy hurries to explain, "in fact I should add that I've met Fiamma and she seems an enchanting girl, so tiny, so shy, in short a true love: my Luca is crazy about her . . . Still, I think there are many obstacles to this union, some, I would say, almost insurmountable . . . My wife and I both think—and we've said so to Luca—that a mixed marriage can be disastrous, for example, for the children, assuming they want to have them . . . A problem of identity . . ."

Any spectator of this scene other than the ineffable Bepy would observe Alfio's face assume an expression of severe irritation upon hearing the words "my Luca is crazy about her." This phrase, which unexpectedly slipped out, would be enough to understand what really makes these two families incompatible and the union between them pernicious.

"My Luca is crazy about her" is an expression that reveals the personality of the one who has uttered it: you have to be theatrically immodest, you have to have a flat and codified idea of love, even if you don't exclude the primacy of feelings, you have to be familiar with at least a handful of serial romances and have seen an equal number of American movies, you have to have betrayed your wife at least a dozen times, you have to have frequented the exquisitely immoral milieu of Roman rowing clubs, you have to have little regard for the value of words, you have to have gone beyond any Jesuitical embarrassment, you have to not give a damn about the susceptibility of others and be deprived of empathy, you have to be pretty strange to say to the sober Bonannos, in reference to their tender virginal daughter and her wretched love for that Jew: "My Luca is crazy about her."

"I'm glad we think the same way," Alfio repeats, assenting. "Look, I'm telling you I have nothing against *you*, in fact I'm sincerely sorry for what happened to *you* . . . but we would have preferred our Fiamma to marry an Italian boy."

"Italian? In what way?"

"Italian Italian, what other way is there?"

"Why, isn't Luca Italian?"

"Well, you know, you understand what I mean. Besides, my daughter told me that Luca didn't do his military service . . . nor did you, if I may . . . and you know, for me the draft is an essential stage. A decisive experience in the life of a man. Profoundly formative."

"It's true, neither I nor my son did military service. But for reasons very different from those which you evidently imagine. And not certainly because we're not Italian . . . Though it may surprise you, we're just as Italian as you are!"

"And so?"

"In my case the racial laws prevented it. But I think I served my country. I was a partisan . . . As for Luca, well, he was unfit for service because of his eyesight. Nothing to do with his nationality."

Bepy has uttered these words with increasing irritation. He is bluffing, of course. He likes to claim that he took part in the resistance, although, strictly speaking, his subversive activity was limited to hiding fearfully in the mountains.

"Look, I didn't mean to offend you . . . In fact I'm pleased that you alluded to your son's, so to speak, *physical* problems . . . Let's say it's something we're concerned about. That is, what I wanted to say to you is that we would like to have assurances . . ."

"In what sense?"

"Well, that is, we would like Luca, for precautionary purposes, to undergo some tests. We were thinking of an andrologist or a geneticist or something like that. We'd like to be sure that he can have children, and that he can do it with the minimum risk . . . I mean, for us a marriage without children is absolutely inconceivable!"

"Excuse me, it seems to me you're exaggerating. Luca is absolutely normal. From every point of view."

"But why are you getting excited? I think I have the right to know who I'm giving my daughter to . . . To protect her . . ."

"Yes, in the same identical manner in which we have the right to know who we are giving our Luca to, but I haven't asked you to show me your daughter's police record. And in any case I find it grotesque and old-fashioned that you speak to me as if certain things depended on me. My son is of age and responsible, and so is your daughter. So I don't see how our opinions can influence them in any decisive way . . . It's disconcerting to have you asking, lightheartedly, tactlessly, that my son undergo clinical tests, as if Luca were a freak of nature . . ."

"But no, look, the discussion has taken an unpleasant turn. I know perfectly well that at this point the game is over. That our children are going to get married. I've resigned myself and I think you have, too. But I am an apprehensive father. I have the right to be an apprehensive father. That's the only reason I've asked for assurances."

"May we know what you want, besides asking my son to submit to such a humiliation?"

"Well, if I have to be direct, I would like the wedding to be held in a church. Besides, Fiamma has told me that Luca isn't religious. Whereas she is very devout. I've looked into it. Our priest would be willing to marry them, although Luca, of course, has to agree to baptize his children . . ."

"This really seems too much. I'm sorry, at least give them the right to choose."

"Who?"

"The grandchildren."

"Why? My parents chose for me. And yours chose for you, obviously. Why should we behave differently? And to be married in church it's essential for him to promise to baptize the children."

"I understand, but it isn't essential to get married in church. You speak of a church wedding as if it were a favor you are bestowing."

"Well, in a certain sense it is a favor the priest is doing for us . . ."

"A favor he's doing for you, certainly not for me, my wife, or Luca . . ."

"But, really, I thought . . ."

"What did you think? That we would thank you because your very generous priest has granted us the honor of marrying our son? Do you think it's a favor to Luca's grandparents?"

"Well, I thought you would be happy about the possibility."

"What possibility?"

"The church wedding."

"Look, Alfio, although it may seem to you extraordinary and upsetting, if we didn't like being Jews we wouldn't be Jews. It's not an *inexorability* that ties us to Judaism. If it were of interest to us to become Christians we would have chosen to believe in Jesus Christ two thousand years ago."

End of Round 1!

With this declaration of Jewish pride the first conversation concludes. And all the rest, all that follows, seems, at this point, irrevocable.

"You really were tired!" my father said. "You must have slept for two hours." We were at the Naples toll plaza. The horizon of metal and reinforced concrete was about to unfold before our gaze, the broad Vesuvian plain disfigured by centuries of abuse, the inevitable purgatory before the paradise of the Amalfi coast. Which soon, very soon, perhaps around the next bend, would appear, with its astonishing views. I was tense. I knew that my mother wouldn't be there, that my brother—the delightful refuge for my timidity—was far away. But I became truly agitated when Papa said to me:

"Tomorrow, or maybe the day after, Nanni's granddaughter should be arriving from Capri. It seems to me she'll be in your class next year . . . Nanni told me that she's fed up with girls' schools."

"So it's only Nanni?" I observed, in a whisper.

"I think Giacomo's there, Gaia's brother . . . Have you ever met him?"

"I don't think so," I lied. The memory of Bepy's funeral was still vivid, thanks to the presence of those angels. I had forgotten almost everything else about that disastrous funeral but the two children—them I couldn't forget.

"A strange, difficult boy, quite neurotic, I'm afraid . . . He reacted badly to the death of his father. Shit! For Nanni it was a tremendous blow. Really, to lose a forty-two-year-old son, and in that way."

Then let's make this trip continue on to the end of the world, to the extreme tip of South Africa, so as not to deal with a situation that seems insidious from every point of view. I feel no sympathy for Nanni. He's one of those dandies in their sixties of Bepy's entourage, who speak with affectation: a man who wears beige vests and honey-colored suede shoes, ordered strictly from Vogel. Who has white hair with silver highlights and fine wrinkles on his cheeks. In other words, the type of man who inspires in me an annoying sense of unease, who speaks to me as if I were an adult, claiming an intimacy he shouldn't allow himself. To have to be a guest—worse: an intruder—in that magnificent house that I've seen only from a distance, to have to entertain those two children who, I don't know why, I imagine as much more expert, much more self-

confident that I will ever be in the course of an entire existence, sharpens my resentment toward my parents. Couldn't
we go to a hotel? Haven't we always gone to a hotel? After my
father's comments, I imagine Giacomo as a conceited kid who
will despise me at first sight: a romantic aesthete of the death
wish, like so many I've known. But in particular it's the eyes of
the little girl that torment me. How will I find the courage to
meet them? How will I be able to sustain the gaze of that lovely girl who witnessed the compound assortment of gaffes
accumulated by us at Bepy's funeral? Who knows everything
about my grandfather and my family? Who's had a chance to
observe our painful inferiority? How can a being as unre-
spectable as I am gain the trust of a girl it's impossible to lie to?
Up to this point lying has protected me. But now? How will I
manage now, without my beloved lies? I'm going to see drop-
ping into my class this girl who, in an instant, will destroy
everything I've laboriously worked for: the shaky tower of my
infinite mystifications will collapse right before my own poor
eyes.

The fact that she, Gaia, is coming from Capri strikes me as
mysterious. What does she do in Capri? Who does she stay
with? Also, I find it alarming, to put it mildly, that she wants so
much to leave a girls' school for one that's co-ed. Enterprising?
Desire to have fun or know the world? To rise up frothily from
the beribboned riverbed of a haute-bourgeois female institution and pour herself into the world of boys overflowing with
testosterone? All this seems to me terribly opposed to the
mournful image I preserve of her. My father called it being
"fed up." And although I have a modest, secondhand experience of the infinite feminine universe, so fascinatingly inconceivable, how can I not notice—if only taking into account my
latest misadventures—that being "fed up" is the principal
defect of girls? What makes their human adventure troubling
and inscrutable?

But, above all, what was the meaning of this trip? After all, I had just gotten home. I had so many things to think about. So many things to hold inside I could feel myself exploding. I was a boy brimming with new emotions. That's the destiny of that long summer of 1984: to brim with new emotions. Mama, Papa, what is the point of all this new adrenaline in circulation? It's time, rather, to settle: to be on my own, to settle. To shut myself in the house for at least two weeks *so that everything that has happened can settle.* I was still filled with the experience of the previous night, that short sleepless night in the London hotel . . . That night when each of us tried to express what he had inside: to expand beyond the normal limits, to play, as they used to say, our last cards, before the long winter of the superego's proscriptions extended its threatening hands over our lives.

Weighing on me still was the moment when, during the carousing that had wrecked a small hotel in the Arab neighborhood of London, my brother came back to the room, anxious to pack his suitcase. It was two-thirty in the morning, he was completely sweaty, his hair a mess, a vague dazed smile on his face that he made an effort to hide but that every so often melted over his face as if he had lost control of his muscles and facial nerves, a smell of cheap beer that seemed to come from his mouth and clothes and so much agitation. I knew, because it had been going on for weeks, that he was flirting with Syria, that shiksa with the hazel eyes.

"Did you fuck her?" I had asked, pretending that it was normal and didn't send a wave of amazement coursing through me.

"No, or at least I don't think so."

"What do you mean, 'I don't think so'?"

"That if it wasn't fucking it was pretty close."

"Did you *neck*, then?" (Who knows why adolescents, enemies of vagueness, are so obsessed by the desire to catalogue everything that concerns them, and above all what concerns sex.)

"More!"

"What?"

"I don't know, Dani. I'm overwhelmed, and I didn't even like it that much. At first I did, but then . . ."

And at that point he stuck out his hand and urged me to smell his index and middle fingers. Only then did I realize that the fingers were tensed, and probably had been since he came in, as if ossified or paralyzed. Intuiting something, I circumspectly sniffed those fingers, to recoil instantly in disgust.

"Is that what I think it is?" I had asked him.

"Yes."

"You fingered her??"

Again a display of terminological propriety: is that why "fingered" had come out of me, a word that in the rest of life I would be reluctant to use, even in analogous circumstances? Besides, I was disconcerted, if not really upset, by a stench that recalled ammonia or the docks at the little port of Ponza. It seemed to me the start of a new epoch. A door had been broken down. The insurmountable wall had been scaled. And all at once, with a unique, intense inspiration, my body had been invaded by that miasma that would never abandon it.

This a first memory to reflect on, to give in to: something that made you gasp for breath.

But that wasn't all: many small emotional splinters had given my boy's life a broader perspective. Only a few evenings earlier, in a discotheque for kids in that village in Cornwall with its frozen sunsets, I had danced—even I had danced: do you see me dancing?—with an older girl, a German who vaguely resembled Eva Braun, so tall that my head sank into her cool, Teutonic cleavage. And then I had seen my brother setting out to conquer that difficult prey, that Syria, who had an elfin look that made you think of the angelic nurses of the Hitler Youth. Yes, in a single evening the two Sonnino brothers, barely pubescent, branded with a genealogy of shrewd

Jewish fabric sellers, and subjected since birth to intense anti-Nazi propaganda (to the point that their very correct mother had refused many times to buy German toy soldiers, forcing them into historical perversions like arraying American armies against the English), had amused themselves with, respectively, a double of Eva Braun and a fugitive from the Hitler Youth. So all this had made me dream of an alternative, had made me grasp the meaning of many things. I needed time to recover. I needed to lose myself in remembering. This was the recipe for returning to normal life. I didn't need Positano, Nanni Cittadini, and his whole family. I didn't need the emotional stakes to be raised, pernicious neurotic codas.

I already had all I could wish for.

I'm talking about the confused and explosive mixture of erotic instinct, love of novelty, desire for social and emotional recognition, and action without a precise goal, which by some strange mechanism is transformed into languor, a throb as long as a lifetime: the World's Biggest Mystification, the one that all fourteen-year-olds come up against, the impression that there exists nothing more urgent and more essential than that languor: the aching stomach, the lack of appetite, the tormenting desire to dissimulate (no one must know!), the seraphic devotion to the Incorporeal . . . That's what I'm talking about. Nothing but that: that loss of self. That confusion about the world that sometimes leads the gentlest and most introverted of adolescents to a crime of passion because he hasn't been taught to accept the unjust, terrible rejection of a girl his age. No, I'm not talking about love. Not true love. I'm talking about the atmosphere that encourages it: the amniotic fluid from which it will sooner or later arise.

Disoriented and nostalgic. Aware of being in the wrong place. The only thing you need is to shut yourself in a room. Lock yourself in. Turn the music up high. Even better if you put on the Big Hits of your era, the ones that marked your hours of freedom and emancipation. That British cocktail of Rod Stewart, the Police, Phil Collins, Dire Straits, Eric Clapton: the islands that compose the variegated archipelago of your imagination, your generation's pantheon . . . And fly far away. To Cornwall, and then to London. And vice versa. Pause for a while on some individuals or even simply on facial expressions. Dig out the memory of that resounding kick that won your brother the applause of a gallery of international girls and filled your heart with pride. Or the breasts of your Eva Braun. Make those emotions live again. Rock them inside you. Let them expand to the point where they take you over. That's what you should do. What you feel you have to do. Are you ready? Are you ready to take in everything? Are you open and amorphous? Ready for the storm? Ready for the loud earthquake? . . . And while on the horizon the hairpin turns of the coast are looming, along with luxuriant mantles of solaria and bougainvillea covering rocky walls, while the gaudy crèche that is Positano appears suddenly on your left, and on the right, gray amid all that blue, the elongated outline of Nureyev's island promises worldliness or solitude, you repeat to yourself that something is changing: irreparably.

I s it so difficult to make money? Is there a recipe for accumulating so much that it makes you sick? What is the path that leads a shrewd, well-off fabric seller to wealth so great as to be at the service of many generations?

These are not the ravings of a novice Wall Street broker played by a young Michael J. Fox in the faded revival of some movie from the eighties. They are, if anything, the obsessive lucubrations of a thirteen-year-old bewitched by comic books, by literature, and by the hypercompetitive era he has happened into, which tends to place his future as a man in the intoxicating context of the America of the movies, and who, instead of devoting his imaginative resources to standard dreams of glory, becomes fixated on money, on everything it means and everything it can buy.

The story of Nanni Cittadini's money seemed to me the biggest, most disturbing adventure that had ever happened to someone I knew. I'm afraid I have to add that it interested me morbidly, in fact in a sinister way, because it seemed to me the counter-story of my own family: the other half of the sky. It represented the alternative dialectic to the inglorious fate of Bcpy and the rest of us. And the value of that story was in its comic-strip implausibility: those boys who suddenly find themselves depositories of unhoped-for fortunes. No, for Nanni no millionaire aunt died, nor did he strike gold in the Klondike. His story was fascinating, but it had the value of not turning a corner into the fantastic, of always coming back to the realm of the

inexhaustible narrative machine that is twentieth-century capitalism. One of those stories that transform a computer-junkie
kid into the richest man on the planet, or a young Russian Jew
escaped from Stalinism into the most important movie producer in Hollywood. A story basically not too heroic, even in its
unbelievability, which filled my dreams to a point of painful
delirium. I told and retold myself the story of Nanni Cittadini's
social rise with visionary enthusiasm: the enthusiasm with
which someone my age would naturally identify with a comic-
book superhero rushing to the rescue of his golden-haired
beloved. Here's my secret teenage pastime. But also my Calvary.

For Nanni it all began in yet another contest with Bepy.
Both were convinced that they were extraordinary connois-
seurs of artistic things, and, through a dilettantish and omnivorous habit of collecting, had from their youth cultivated an
aggressive competitiveness. Furniture, paintings, sculptures
filled both Nanni's big villa (bestowing on it the cold air of an
unlucky provincial museum) and Bepy's luminous apartment,
much more culturally organic in its choices.

One day, thanks to an acquaintance of his wife, Sofia, a
Neapolitan princess, Nanni gets his hands on two obscure
paintings that have up to now been attributed to a student of
Luca Giordano. He offers them to his former partner (he and
Bepy have long since gone their separate ways), who almost
laughs in his face. It's been years since they've done business
together, years since they've bought art at auctions public and
private. But Bepy doesn't share Nanni's "junkman's spirit,"
that taste for accumulation without quality. He aims at valuable pieces. And besides by now he's specializing in modern
paintings. In short, in the end Nanni buys those old daubs
himself because Bepy didn't want to contribute a cent.

No mistake, among the countless that Bepy will make, from
now until his ruin, will have the importance and the mocking
flavor of this failed acquisition.

And he knows it when Nanni, his suspicions aroused by a date on the back of the canvas that doesn't correspond to the period when the two paintings are supposed to have been made, has them appraised, submitting them to a detailed X-ray examination that yields surprising results: behind that monotone patina of paint, stupendous chromatic contrasts attributable only to one, unmistakable hand have been sleeping for centuries. It's exciting to have them restored: and really astonishing to see two Baroque marvels slowly emerge from the shadows of oblivion. If for Nanni the incomparable light disinterred by the restorers is enough so that he feels the need to call on the venerable Sir Denis Mahon, for Sir Denis it's enough to see that explosion of violent energy to give an enthusiastic response: Michelangelo Merisi, better known as Caravaggio, there's no doubt! Sir Denis's expertise furnishes more precise information: the paintings are datable approximately from 1608 to 1610, Mr. Cittadini, probably done by Merisi during his final flight, back from the island of Malta, and before he set sail for Civitavecchia, a few days before his premature death. The greater and more compelling is a version of "The Beheading of Holofernes," in which a self-portrait of the artist appears: a malevolent bearded figure in the background, whose harsh sneer seems cut in two by a dazzling ray of light. The other is an "Annunciation" full of second thoughts, with a grim-faced Madonna alla Anna Magnani and an archangel like a Pasolinian thug.

So Nanni locks up those two winning lottery tickets in the form of seventeenth-century canvases in a bank vault, and on them—on their value and their prestige—constructs (like that Mark Twain character who possesses a million-pound banknote) his fortune. Yes, thanks to the two sleeping Caravaggios—original copies of which ornament his new house—Nanni can finally practice the profession he's always dreamed of. So he throws himself into art, becoming in a few years the heavenly father of the offshore art market. He manages his affairs by means of accounts scattered throughout exotic fiscal paradises, like Isola Margherita, or the Cayman Islands, contemplating the sweet, miraculous growth of his patrimony with a childlike stupor. All the rest—from the purchase of the estate on the slopes of Via Aldrovandi to his collection of custom-built cars—is only the logical result of that sudden and unstoppable wealth. Wealth that—although it doesn't induce him to get rid of the business that has guaranteed him, up to that point, prosperity and comfort, in addition to the possibility of buying those two lucky pictures—makes him radically change his opinion of himself and, in part, his way of life. Let's say that he holds on to the business with the good-luck spirit of a Scrooge McDuck who keeps the first dollar he's earned.

And the comparison isn't at all incongruous, or sacrilegious: if you don't believe it, ask my father, who recalled the saga of Nanni Cittadini with the verve and bright eyes of one telling a comic-book story with a resounding happy ending. He loved to show the newspaper clippings of the time that magnified the fortune of that impromptu collector. His enthusiasm seemed to me all the more insane considering that Nanni's sudden good fortune coincided with Bepy's no less unexpected failure, and that if only the latter had agreed to join in his friend's deal his entire existence (and ours!) would have been completely different. But it seemed even more incredible to me that the fate of so many people could have been decided by a little paint spread with a brush on a canvas by a murderous beggar who had died in mysterious circumstances four hundred years earlier.

Every Christmas my father bought two bottles of very peaty malt whiskey—the Lagavulin 16, nothing special, really—to give to Nanni.

It was like the annual visit to a shrine of the Madonna: a habit halfway between superstition and payment for grace received. Already at that time Nanni Cittadini was, for my father, a living legend. I don't know how the mechanism of idolatry had been grafted onto a man who proudly loved to profess his Enlightenment secularism. It was enough to hear him talk about Nanni to understand that that compendium of anecdotes—most often evoked with euphoric intonations—was equivalent to a boundless love. As if Luca Sonnino had reacted not so much to Bepy's death as to the last infamous years of his life by establishing a new, immutable idol, rather than with a legitimate skepticism based on experience and disappointment. Yes, precisely because Bepy had been for him what few fathers can be for their sons—an incomparable model—he now felt the desire to find himself another.

When my parents met, my father was still completely under the spell of his filial devotion. To the point where after the marriage the enchantment had spilled over into their conjugal routines. Nothing the young bride did could correspond to the sacred model of life that Bepy had until then tacitly embodied in the eyes of his son. That's why even the first signs of Bepy's financial disaster were greeted by his firstborn with indulgence and optimism. A false step. Only one false step in an exemplary life. It would take a lot more to deconstruct that sanctuary of freedom and open-mindedness . . . It took all the rest, all that followed the disaster—Bepy's weeping, his lies, his plaintive blackmailing demand for help, his inability to accept his sudden poverty, the small pathetic deceptions, the petty tricks, the shameful flight and return—to disillusion his son in a drastic, definitive way. Only then had my father, just thirty-seven, with that great story of love and disappointment behind him, felt the irresistible need to invent another hero for himself: less brilliant, perhaps, but certainly more stable and promising. Only then did the longing to replace one

utopia with another take shape in the thin, loose-limbed figure of Nanni Cittadini.

Every year, having bought those two bottles, we went to the
usual rendezvous with old Cittadini like two very refined beg-
gars.

Nanni's establishment was a succession of tables piled high
with rolls of fabric; every gust of air coming from the door
raised clouds of dust. It was a squalid place, out of a Russian
novel. (I've known several millionaires in my life, and one
thing I've learned: they have an inclination to modesty and
sobriety, not as a matter of style, as they let you think, but out
of supreme arrogance. As if to say: *I'm too rich to worry about
showing off my money!*) Walls threatened by gray islands of
dampness, broken armchairs, straight chairs with torn seat
covers, a faded grayish Christmas tree. The employees wore
long brown coats and had the disheveled look of people who
are unhappy with their pay and with the backbreaking work.

But here's Nanni, emerging from a fog of cobalt and temporarily bestowing himself on us. Even his hair, with its bluish
highlights, and his eyes, even the skin, if you look hard, make
you think of the sky: the whole accented by a cardigan of a
blend of blues that pulls a little over his protruding stomach.
A mystic vision. The archangel Gabriel in a living body:

"I'm sorry to have made you wait . . . But here you are, my
globetrotter and his little squire!"

Nanni liked to allude to my father's nomadism. It was something that amused him. Or maybe it was a way of reminding us
that that line of work, extended and expanded by the years and
by my father's undoubted talent to the point of guaranteeing
for us a new, unhoped-for prosperity, had been his idea, that
without his logistical and economic support it could never
have developed as it did. He liked to emphasize that it had
been he, Nanni Cittadini, valuing my father's abilities and his

culture, his aptitude for cosmopolitanism, who had promoted him with those clients in Manchester and that lady in Peking. It was he who had transformed the spoiled son of a former wholesaler in a tight spot into one of the most respected executives in the field.

Furthermore, Nanni liked to use theatrical and falsely sympathetic expressions. He must have found irresistible the contrast between the melancholy of those surroundings and a parodistically polished manner of speaking.

Nanni also liked to shower us with compliments that we didn't deserve, just as he would not have liked to pay them if we had deserved them.

Nanni showed an affection for my father so evident that people were moved.

In spite of that, the old man Cittadini, with his cashmere turtleneck sweaters, his affectation of austerity, his collection of custom-made cars celebrated in a big photograph on the wall, annoyed me. And the curious fact is that the reasons for my precocious hostility coincide with the reasons for my father's opposite feelings. Luca Sonnino is happy that a man should be superior to us: richer, happier, more refined. In fact he is charmed that such an individual should greet us with moving affection. He isn't horrified to enter the establishment that once belonged to him. The thought that if only Bepy had made a small contribution to the purchase of those two paintings everything would have been different didn't drive him crazy. The idea—so obsessive for me—that there is nothing more terrible than to lick the edges of fortune, to touch it giddily with your fingers, only to see it evaporate before your very eyes, makes no impression on him. I know I'm wrong: I should be grateful to Nanni. Isn't he the Eminence Gris of our redemption? But at eight—just as at nine and ten and so on— one should have the right to ingratitude. I can't keep from despising him with the cordiality forced on me by my status as the son of a beneficiary and by my good upbringing. Just as I can't free myself from the impression—certainly incongruous—that Nanni has only to push a red button, like Goldfinger in the famous Sean Connery movie, to destroy my family. Not only do I hate Nanni's paternalistic air but I can't bear my father's inability to share my bitterness. A voice inside me whispers that Nanni helped us—but did he really?—only in order to grant us this offensive indulgence. No one gives something for nothing. Exactly what my father doesn't understand. Why, Papa, do you let yourself be treated this way by such an unbearable arrogant man? Is it possible that you don't see what to me seems so plain?

The truth, madly avoided by my father, is that Nanni has never stopped hating Bepy. And that hatred has survived even his rival's indecorous death.

The story is well known: Bepy is still an enthusiastic, sturdy member of the Fascist youth when he first meets the delicate fair-haired Giovanni. There is no great sympathy between them. Not, at least, what one might expect, considering the continuation of their friendship. The contrasts in character, the same that will so cruelly determine their fate, appear in Nanni's irritation at his future partner's boasting. And Bepy, on the other hand, is too involved in his own affairs to pay much attention to that quiet, aloof boy. And yet it is as if each glimpsed in his friend the other half of the sky.

So after the war they open their first wholesale fabric business, Solemex, the biggest, the most famous. Known in the trade as Ugo and Raimondo, for their resemblance to Tognazzi and Vianello. Same explosive mixture. On the one hand, Nanni, tall and thin, sweet, all starched collars and British humor (of the sort that hasn't made the Brits laugh for a couple of centuries); on the other, Bepy, short, tanned, virile, courtly, erotomaniac, with his Pantagruelian appetites.

They make money, in those years. Diabolical couple. Well-oiled commercial machine. Bepy is a talented buyer and an irresistible seller, he's like the handsome actor in some movie from the sixties boom. Nanni, with his degree in engineering, is an accountant of exemplary diligence and rigor. By now Solemex is rightfully considered the most important establishment in central Italy.

In the late sixties, Nanni realizes that something isn't working anymore. He has the sense that the heroic-pioneering period of the two young partners is over. He scents the odor of recession. And then he fears his partner's delirium of omnipotence: Bepy has lost any sense of reality, as if he had forgotten that the purpose of a commercial enterprise is to make money, not give lessons in bravura or style. Besides, Bepy, in order to finance the excessive luxuries of his family (parties, cars, servants, vacations, clothes, jewels), draws on the account unrestrainedly. He buys, buys, never checking his solvency, careless of his own financial situation, as if he had an unlimited trust fund. Nanni is worried and irritated. He, unlike Bepy, worships accumulation. Over the years, he has capitalized well, investing and diversifying his activities: construction, treasury bonds, art collecting, money lending—real money, not papier-mâché. Prudence and speculation: those are the Patron Saints who assist that shrewd dandy. So he begins to work out the idea of a separation, with a persuasive secret thought: Bepy is no use to him anymore. In fact, he is harmful, people increasingly gossip about him. Nanni is clever: he doesn't have the brilliant talent of his partner, the infallible nose for buying and selling, but by now he has learned, absorbed; he knows the moves. Bepy unexpectedly shows himself anything but reluctant, the divorce is a good idea. He has suffered in recent years from his partner's cowardice, is exasperated by his apocalyptic preaching. A dead weight, that's what Bepy thinks of Nanni. Ballast to his attempt to take flight, for the ultimate miracle: a solid, inexhaustible wealth, like that of some of the northern industrialists who now treat him as an equal, inviting him every summer to their luxuriant wooded slopes in Stresa and Bellagio, where Ada Sonnino is introduced as a black-haired statue sculpted by Capucci.

Then, one day, things fall apart, thanks to an incident that has no relation to fabric. That day Bepy asks Nanni for help: he should telephone Ada, tell her that tonight her husband will be at the office late, with him, they have work to do. Often the partners are supportive in these things, each calling the other's wife. This time, however, Bepy was evasive. To his partner's questions he answered that he had found a wonderful woman, a tough nut, but no details. Usually he is more generous with particulars, because for him the fun of adultery is never separate from a bold theatricality in talking about it, transforming it into public boasting.

Nanni almost forgets about it until, coming home, he is surprised by the unusual absence of his wife. The surprise becomes anxiety, anxiety a terrible suspicion: that that wonderful woman, the tough nut Bepy mentioned, might be his wife, Sofia. Why should he be surprised? It would be typical of Bepy. He loves such acts of bravado. Yes, typical. How many times has he committed similar abuses, to laugh about them later in company? What does his pleasure consist of? Simple: Bepy has his partner telephone his wife, in order to be free of any trouble, and in the meantime prepares his little black-and-white pied-à-terre-with-lights-dimmed to welcome Sofia, and fuck her in a triumph of diverse flavors. "Where is the signora?" Nanni asks the maid in a pained voice. "The princess telephoned, she is having dinner with a friend . . . She told me to prepare the vegetable soup for you, sir . . ." Nanni is beside himself. What to do? What to think? It's an unprecedented and maddening situation. Usually not only does he know what to think, and have full control of things, but he is rarely beset by nerve-racking worry. He would like to find his wife. But where? "She didn't say who she was dining with?" he asks with fake absent-mindedness from behind the newspaper. "No, sir. She said only not to expect her for dinner." Go there, in the middle of the night? Lurk outside his partner's bedroom? Never has Bepy seemed so disgusting to him. At this precise instant Bepy is, in his eyes, a monument of duplicity. Wait for them at the sheepfold, like any self-respecting cuckold? No, Nanni is cool, he likes to show lucidity and restraint. He will do nothing. He will suffer in silence. He will wait for Sofia to get home. And he will try to find out, without extorting any-thing.

Come on, Nanni, calm down: Sofia isn't that type of woman, plus she has always despised Bepy. Have you forgot-ten? Your adored little flower is a firmly convinced anti-Semite, and is so by culture and family tradition. Her purple-robed great-great-grandparents would have had the power of life and death over Bepy's skullcap-wearing great-great-grand-parents. And so? You've got nothing to worry about. But, at the same time, you have learned that what Sofia officially says she thinks is one thing, while her fascination with the exotic is another, and too often, in sudden and unsuspected bursts, it seems to surface from the inner fibres of your languid little kit-ten, like the spontaneous manifestation of a secret perversion that leaves you frightened. Who can assure you that in Sofia's inaccessible, womanly imagination, in the closed space of her feminine consciousness, Bepy doesn't represent the quintes-sential male? Sofia in bed is a champion, a fury: hot and unin-hibited. You've never satisfied her fully. Don't bullshit your-self, Nanni. It's true. It's your unconfessable punishment. In sexual intimacy, her body, normally stiffened by aristocratic self-possession, seems to soften voluptuously. Her temperature rises and she melts as if she were clay. This you can't forget, or underestimate. The thing you envy about Bepy is his unstop-

pable, notorious sexual appetite. His convulsive and compulsive eroticism. He's one of the few men who don't experience
post-orgasmic relief. And, besides, since high school Bepy has
felt an illicit pleasure in stealing your girls: he must be a recur-
rence of Jewish revanchism. ("I fucked another snotty shiksa!
Plus I stole her from that jerk!" That's how Bepy expresses
himself, with that vulgarity, that explicit racism.) At least so
you've always thought. As a boy you were the handsome one,
the young conqueror, but how much game, fresh or seasoned,
has passed through Bepy's bed since then, for long periods or
short, subverting that trend! Bepy, by now, can go anywhere.
He fears nothing. He has no dignity to defend. Only a little
while ago he stole Giorgia, the young seamstress at the shop.
You'd just about fallen in love with her, and he fucked her.

Nanni doesn't want to precipitate things. Or make scenes.
He loves his wife too much. How could that bastard? With his
wife? "A tough nut," that's what he called her. Sofia a tough
nut, as if she were a high-class whore.

When Sofia gets home suspiciously late, suavely enveloped
in her mink, Nanni is waiting for her in bed. He hears her moving about with circumspection, sees the light come on in the
dressing room, and then the incandescent reflection of her
pearls, or maybe her teeth. *A glance will be enough for me to
know.* When Sofia comes in, she kisses him too ardently. Nanni
has the impression that his wife's gestures betray a soft languor,
that she's hiding a smile. Suddenly he feels a fierce pain in his
chest. Sofia is beautiful and flushed the way some women get
when they've made love. You will never have the evidence. You
will never find the courage to subject her to the banality of a
detailed interrogation. In a moment she falls asleep, while her
husband stews in his caldron overflowing with insolubly torturing questions.

In the late seventies the separation is inevitable. Nanni is
annoyed, he can't bear even the sight of his partner. He hasn't

forgiven him. Every gesture of Bepy's irritates him. The Byzantine affectation of his dress and his speech is repugnant to him. Sometimes he gets lost in the small black abyss that opens between two of Bepy's incisors. He feels the hatred mounting as the thought that his Sofia might, trembling, have met the mouth of that third-rate pseudo Clark Gable (Bepy is flattered by the chance resemblance). Nanni realizes that he's always detested him, ever since high school. He understands that he has gone on with him up to that point precisely because of that hatred. Yes, he has always hated (or envied?) his boldness, his insolence, his amorality, and a lot of other things besides. So he decides to break up the thirty-year partnership, ending, too, one of the most successful and prosperous fabric businesses of the Roman postwar period. The adventure of Ugo and Raimondo has reached the end of the line. Each will choose his own destiny, with full autonomy.

They make an agreement like true gentlemen. Nanni is willing to settle generously. In exchange he keeps the old place on Via Caetani and above all the name of the firm. Solemex is his, now. Grandpa opens another wholesale business. He has always hated the old things, traditions: he's a modern type. He has money to invest. In the beginning, business seems to swell with an impressive facility, and then it suddenly deflates, exposing him to the inconstancy of a thousand unscrupulous speculators, from whom his shrewd partner has protected him his whole life.

When Bepy fails, Nanni, who by now shares with him only a few small unimportant shops, is barely touched by the breath of the disaster. He'll lose only a little something, which time and gossip will take care of transforming into a hyperbolic figure, enveloping his figure with an incongruous aura of generosity. Nanni is as ready for sanctity as Bepy is unprepared for hell. Nanni is solid, he fears nothing and no one, now the business is secure, Caravaggio has changed his life and Sofia is at his side.

*

"Wow, nice loden, fellows!" exclaims Nanni, during one of those Christmas visits, fingering with a professional gesture the sleeve of my father's overcoat, and then, turning to me, a skinny little bird with glasses, asks with a condescending smile, "How does it feel to have the most fashionable dad in Rome?"

That's what I mean!

Stamped on this phrase is the unmistakable Sonnino brand—one of the best bits of Bepy's polymorphous repertory—mediated by Nanni's gussied-up rigidity. I'm old enough not to let myself be taken in: it's so obvious that Nanni has filtered certain of his former partner's affectations! Just as it's glaringly obvious that he doesn't have the delicate touch, he's not as credible. He pays for the inauthenticity of the apocryphal. Although confident of himself, Nanni remains the man put in plaster by Bepy, screwed with gracious contempt. Now, dear Nanni, play the great man, thousands of miles away from your ex-partner, who, in the meantime, is serving his transatlantic sentence. But we all know that you're only a replicant, a warmup act. Houdini is far away, and you are enjoying yourself behind his back, clumsily distorting his tricks.

But that complimentary question addressed to me by Nanni—"How does it feel to have the most fashionable dad in Rome?"—literally delights my father. I see that big pale man melt like a little virgin. How can he not understand that those words hide the ironic disapproval of a millionaire toward the son of a failure, who in spite of everything, as soon as he got back on his feet, rather than save keeps on buying designer clothes? Or is this only my childish paranoia?

Why does my father—aware that old Cittadini knows our situation in detail: Bepy's inheritance of bank overdrafts, the orgy of hungry creditors, my mother racing to cash checks right and left—show up here wearing that marvelous loden coat and the broad-brimmed green hat that wouldn't make a poor impression at St. Moritz? Isn't he afraid of boasting? Doesn't he want his appearance to correspond to his bank account? Or maybe this is an idea that only the son of that neurotic poor mouth my mother could conceive? Maybe I would be less uncomfortable showing up at Nanni's dressed like a son of the people: faded velvet pants and worn purple pullover. Then maybe I wouldn't feel this anxious displacement. Then maybe I wouldn't have trouble seeing myself in a pre-established role and behaving accordingly. But this way the air is tainted. Everything is clothed in hypocrisy and the obscure emptiness of the unsaid. Also because there's one thing I can't remember without distress, because of all the successive, unthinkable implications. It's like putting tinfoil on a bad tooth. Like pain that makes you jump up and down in your chair. Every year old Cittadini rattles off the same old nonsense:

"Eh, Daniel, is it true you like to ski? Your father says you're a champion skier! What do you say to coming with us to Cortina? My grandchildren are there."

"Why not, Daniel? Thank Nanni, like a good boy . . ." smiles the most unconscious, pure, blind father who ever trod the boards of paternity.

There is nothing to do but smile in turn. Both Nanni and I know that it's a convention, there's nothing behind it. In other words, he invites me in the certainty of my refusal, just as—on my side I pretend to hesitate, artificially pondering, knowing I can't accept. The only one who seems ignorant of this exquisite worldliness, in his candor, is my father. He doesn't seem to understand the reasons I can't accept Nanni's invitation. Pointless to explain. He wouldn't understand. If I tried, he would shrug his shoulders, get angry, calling me a dreamer or an obsessive. And I wouldn't know what to say because in effect Nanni's way of keeping us at a distance isn't obvious: if anything it's a subterranean rejection, ungraspable, that mixes a little anti-Semitic contempt, reproach for the vulgar display of shaky luxuries, and superior class consciousness.

Maybe Nanni appreciates my father just because Judaism seems to have taken a different form in him: a refined neurasthenia, genetic deviation like the Warburgs or the Rothschilds? Or maybe the help given to my needy father is the offering made for the sins committed by his conscience against the Jewish people? He is one of those *goys* who, confronted with the evidence of their own prejudice, shelter themselves behind the usual formula: "Come on, I have more Jewish friends than Gentile . . ." which is certainly true, but denotes a form of Jew-loving exhibitionism, the prelude to racial hatred. It's those anti-Semites who have chosen to live among the Jews, with the spirit of a zoologist who studies the wild beasts of black Africa, without ever forgetting his gun. In him affection and caution are mixed into a gray paste. Was Himmler right when he reproached his compatriots for having no sense of History, for sinister egoism? "We all have a Jewish friend we'd like to save . . . But we have to think on the grand scale!" that fierce, insatiable strategist said to his men. For Nanni, perhaps, my father, so elegant and respectable, so loyal and straightforward, was the Jew who made the exception, just as the clever conman Bepy was the one who had confirmed, at least in his eyes, the rule. And, besides, my father's indulgence for anti-Semites had something anachronistically Oriental about it.

This is why my father doesn't understand my position. Yes, it's splendid to go to Cortina. Splendid to ski on New Year's Day. And what a delightful fantasy if Nanni's "little grandchildren" are those two ethereal angels framed in the photograph over their grandfather's desk. But what a burden to go with those people who know the poverty I come from: they'll always treat me with indifference. If in certain circles rich Jews are barely welcomed, poor ones couldn't even number among the servants. You know what I'm saying? And Nanni, furthermore, corresponds exactly to the physiognomy of the repressed anti-Semite. Maybe he married an Altavilla, yes, a princess, as androgynous and blue-tinted as he is, this Neapolitan topaz who sparkles in her sumptuous dwelling, just to protect himself against the attack launched by the curly-haired crowd he has frequented—for motives of lucre—since the early years of his life. Does Nanni use his consort the princess as an antidote to the Jews? Is this what he's doing? Is she his life preserver in that shark-infested sea? His pass to the high society that has always obsessed him? Come on, let's spend the day with the rude, clever Shylocks of Piazza Giudia, or the Byzantines of the London art market, or the ruthless Jews of Genevan high finance, but how nice to return home—warm, sugar-coated Art Nouveau in the green-and-ochre heart of Rome—and find waiting for you the marble smile of your Fifi (as her friends call her, as you like to call her, with the lower lip that grazes your incisors in a sensually syncopated manner), celebrated a thousand times by the covers of the glossy magazines: yes, because the princess, ever since she became shamelessly rich again, likes to be photographed beside her husband, her grandchildren, and a very annoying mastodon of a Great Dane . . . It's an innocuous vanity. Sofia is a true stalwart of the glossies, the first lady of sophisticated gossip. She's always interviewed at Christmastime in her Empire-style living room, where some valuable pieces that survived the dissipation of the Altavilla fortunes live alongside Nanni's new acquisitions. Any idle woman who goes to the hairdresser to see for herself can enjoy the wise advice of Fifi Altavilla (she didn't want to get rid of her unmarried name, if anything it's her husband who sometimes likes to gratify himself by using it) on how to set the table for New Year's Day or how to greet an important guest. The princess displays a refined good sense and illustrates, as if it were an antique, the family harmony that she and her rich husband have so naturally established. She is one of those awk-

ward noblewomen who have canceled out the debts of ten generations of wastrel princes with a marriage that in the end turns
out to be extremely convenient. She had the perspicacity to bet
on the right horse. It was a miraculous encounter: one day
Nanni—from a traditionally monarchist middle-class environment (in '46, in spite of the terrible example offered by the
Savoys in the Fascist *ventennio*, he voted against the repub-
lic)—during a boar hunt in the Anglo-Saxon countryside north
of Rome organized by some dying landowner, met the young
Sofia, heiress to a fortune of land and estates threatened by a
conspicuous number of mortgages. They really fell in love. It
happens when each possesses what the other ardently desires.
Extravagant wedding but austere life, according to Nanni's
ironclad convictions. So that, after the unexpected access of
wealth, life changes its flavor and its rhythm. From then on she
spends her time in bemusing charity work, anachronistic
patronage of poor portraitists or promising designers, or
imparting, for a fee, lessons in *bon ton:* she has opened a school
with the idea of teaching the maids of the bourgeoisie how to
set a table and how to serve. Nanni adores his wife, doesn't let
her lack for anything, crawls at her feet. It's his only weakness—otherwise he is a viper with a calculator.

But how does the death of Riccardo, their only son, fit into
this edifying portrait? How is it possible, if you know so well
how to organize your life, if you have full control over it to the
point of placing the three forks always on the left, the spoon
always near the knife, and for goodness' sake, never the napkin
on the plate . . . How is it possible, if you have impressed a
Cartesian order onto your existence, furnishing it with all the
loving customs that in the end transform it into such a pleasant business, that your son, as his only response, kills himself?
And we're not talking about an unbalanced son, a reckless type
with a passion for producing problems wholesale. We're not

alluding to a hypercritical or depressed ex-adolescent, the usual angry young man of the sixties. But of the ideal son, the one you created in your image and likeness, purifying him of your petit-bourgeois coarseness, the scion who bestows further luster on your life. A Nanni Cittadini with his rough edges of diffidence and philistinism smoothed. We're talking about the son who didn't cause trouble, the son with a brilliant degree in architecture, the fearless skier, the graceful tennis player, the impeccable rider, twice champion in the "Cortina winter polo" tournament, upon whom you imposed a titled and indigent wife, who brought into the world two irresistible little angels, and who, above all, never failed to respect you. If there's something that doesn't fit—but it's a retrospective thought, the thought of someone who knows how things ended up, the reflection, after time has run out, worthy of a talk-show psychologist, which comes to your aid only now, an ideological perversity of this perverse era—it was your Ricky's *excessive* respect. There are plenty of people who kill themselves, for the most various reasons. Plenty of people who kill themselves because nothing good has happened to them or because they'll never attain what they consider an acceptable lifestyle. I'm afraid that Riccardo Cittadini belongs to the clan of those who shoot themselves because they have done things too respectably. One of those concave personalities who are skillfully manipulated, programmed to always say yes. Yes to an absurd marriage to an aristocratic fortune hunter. Yes to two children, who trapped him for good. Yes even to the proposal to work under the authoritarian control of his father, frustrating his desire to be an architect. ("You want to be a laborer? You want to work for others? You want to be an employee? Is this what you want? If that's your highest aspiration help yourself," Nanni told him contemptuously.)

So wasn't it perhaps natural that Ricky, without warning, without giving any obvious signs, without losing his good humor, on the wave of a frenzy for freedom, should write in capital letters a definitive NO, shooting himself in the mouth on an ordinary weekday?

And yet there is an element of this experience that Nanni can't forget. Ricky, shortly before shooting himself, had had an extramarital affair. In his sentimentalism, he had taken it too seriously. To the point of questioning his marriage. And to think that it was Nanni who had hired Chiara, that whore! And he had immediately realized that between her and his son there had arisen that complicity which is sometimes established between sales girls and the son of the owner. He had left it alone. He knew how certain things went. Finally one day Ricky had found the courage and showed up, trembling, to announce his intentions to his father: divorce, and marry Chiara. "Don't even mention it!" Nanni had answered, coldly, but nonetheless worried. Ricky had been astonished, he couldn't reply, hadn't found the courage to contradict his father, to defend his own position, his own love: he had, as they say, imploded.

Nanni also recalled that, before firing the girl, he had felt the need to consult with Bepy. Although Nanni had never been able to stand the influence Bepy had on Riccardo, he had thought that this time he could use that influence for another purpose.

And what did he hear from Bepy?

"Come on, don't exaggerate. If your son doesn't want to stay with his wife why should you make him? Don't force it with that boy! He's a lot more fragile than you think. You don't imagine how susceptible normal kids can be. They're the ones who really are unpredictable. I'm telling you out of personal experience. It may seem like nonsense to you, but I can assure you that children who hide their vulnerability behind a façade of happiness are the most determined: they're the ones who, in the end, do unimaginable, spectacular things. Look at Teo! If

someone had told me that Teo . . . Yes, all right, you know what
I'm saying . . . I would never have thought . . . But at the same
time I urge you not to be melodramatic. Basically it never
seemed to me that there was a great love between your son and
daughter-in-law. It wouldn't be a tragedy for anyone, my
friend. And all right, yes, there are children in the middle, but
it doesn't seem to me that the lady is the ideal mother. These
are things that happen. You'll see that once it's over you'll all
be better off and you won't feel any particular resentment.
That's a healthy, secular way of looking at things, my friend.
And then why do you always have to be so pessimistic? It may
be that the girl really loves him, that this time money doesn't
have anything to do with it . . ." Bepy had said with the care-
lessness, the frankness, and the cynicism that he used only in
conversations with those close to him, reserving his notorious
hypocrisies for the rest of the world.

*By God, it's easy to play the liberal with other people's chil-
dren. But I'd like to see him in my place,* Nanni had thought,
with hatred, regretting that he had yet again given that swelled
head an occasion to show off his superiority. What a hypocrite!
*He made all that fuss just because Teo went to live in Tel Aviv,
and now he dares to preach to me.*

Only now did it occur to him that the immediate rapport
(by an almost epidermal selection) between Bepy and Riccardo
might depend on a similarity of character: they were two spineless men, who didn't know what it meant to honor a commitment, two unscrupulous egoists ready to ruin everything in
order not to give up their own comfort. And now a question
burned in him: was it the inner comparison he had made
between Bepy and Ricky that drove him to that consummate
severity? So it was as if he had wanted to punish Bepy through
Ricky, or vice versa: so it had gone. Only at that point, in fact,
and without hesitation, had he offered money to Chiara, exult-
ing in the observation that she was just waiting to put the

check in her pocket and disappear. Everything seemed to be forgotten when that sudden shot changed—forever—his life. And although feeling the injustice of such a position, Nanni couldn't separate the death of his son from the psychological influence of which he had been the object on the part of that Mephistophelian corrupter Bepy. Was it possible that only now—after everything was over—Bepy's words should return to his mind? "Children who hide their vulnerability behind a façade of happiness are the most determined: they're the ones who, in the end, do unimaginable, spectacular things." Possible that he had failed to appreciate them then? Nanni thought again about those words the way the father of a condemned man obsessively recalls the bureaucratic formulas with which a judge has declared the end of his son. Just like that: the words—which Bepy had uttered in his usual carefree tone—resounded in Nanni's mind like a death sentence. So Nanni felt the irresistible need to persuade himself that his former partner was responsible for Ricky's death, even though this time poor Bepy had done nothing wrong. For Nanni it was evident that Bepy had had the inconsiderate audacity to predict that unpredictable gesture, just as it was evident that Bepy had offered Ricky his example of unpunished adulterer and world champion of irresponsibility and self-indulgence. And, on the subject of unlucky divinations, Nanni himself—although he couldn't possibly imagine how tragically well-founded his prophecy was—felt that one day Bepy, too, would in some way kill himself.

Unlike many fathers condemned to survive their own children, Nanni had at least found someone to accuse for that absurd, outrageous death.

On the other hand, if this death had done nothing but add further luster to the Cittadini family, conferring on it that slightly sorrowful aura that distinguishes all great dynasties, if this misfortune had rendered the Princess Altavilla a modern figure of the most noble Dignity, it's also true that Ricky's death, in its obscene unpredictability, in its obvious unfairness, had destroyed Nanni's life, corroding his spirit and nullifying all that tumultuous success.

But there is something much more serious to consider.

Because, as for me, I'm certain that when we get home my father will rush to tell my mother: "You know, love, what Nanni said to me? That I'm the most fashionable man in Rome!" And then I'll see surface in the lady's gaze a veil of irritation. Go on, you try to explain to the daughter of the builder from the Marches, who lives in penitence for her sins against the Family and against its Patrimony, the poetry of her vain husband . . .

Over the years my mother has changed, but her husband insists on not understanding it. She is no longer the shiksa dressed with the tight-waisted girlishness of Audrey Hepburn, so in love with a wealthy son of Israel that she marries him, challenging the veto of two families and an entire hostile society. The girl who on June afternoons appeared on the balcony, biting into the red pulp of a watermelon slice, her mouth dripping, with her heart entirely open to the future, has disappeared. Of that dreamy creature some deeply rooted features endure: the emotion when she hears the first notes of "Moon River," the soundtrack of *Breakfast at Tiffany's*, or the moving melody of "A Summer Place" (predilections that, if I just had the whim to interpret, would overwhelm me, if only for the intrinsic sensuality of which they are evidence). A few small, unimportant vanities persist, which she gives in to with masterly discretion. But officially she has renounced the sighing idealism of Juliet. She has returned to earth. She has wised up, as happens to responsible adults. No one would believe that this prudent forty-year-old, literally tossed from one commitment to the next, might have had a different life, made up of

unrealizable dreams and fairy-tale hopes, or that she could
have felt so much emotion watching certain Billy Wilder films.
Or that her breast conceals the heart of a megalomaniac. How
is it credible that this woman, continually at the mercy of the
sacrifices imposed by her own maternity, could have at one
time—however remote—thought of herself with the vibrant
dreaminess of a debutante? And yet you have only to approach
her with a little more attention, puncturing the membrane of
your cynicism, to discover the surprising similarity between the
egotistical little princess of the past and this busy woman. She
has merely shifted the fields of her possible achievement: she
has mediated, softened, transformed, hidden them. But they
still exist. They are whole. She is for the programmatic *defer-
ment* of happiness. She nourishes herself on expectations and
plans continually put off . . . If she buys a pair of shoes or a new
coat she is inclined to wait as long as a year before putting
them on, in order not to squander the intoxicating sensation of
newness! Her night table is piled with cuttings from newspa-
pers or of whole inserts that promote fashionable spots. If you
unfold them you'll see a lot of circles, lightly drawn by her pencil, to greet the arrival in our marvelous city of a new Mexican
restaurant or the reopening of a forgotten museum. Naturally
she is wary of transforming these paper (bookish?) desires into
reality. Even if it should be said that the very few times (usually because of a strong push from her husband) she finally
resolves to visit one of these dreamed-of places, her disappointment is intensified by a kind of prior skepticism.

But in spite of such convulsive incompatibilities, today she
defends her rickety marriage tooth and nail. Out of stubborn-
ness? Love? Love, certainly, but with what hidden muddy
depths . . . In the deep part of herself persists the idea of a family like the ones in films or advertisements, like the ones she
dreamed of on her adolescent balcony: a candy box filled with
"family harmony" and "personal success," by which she is

almost obsessed. Every obstacle that postpones that velvety dream is experienced as an epochal drama, with a depression that can degenerate into desperation. By now she is insensitive to certain games of prestige. She is vaccinated. She no longer commissions photographs at Luxardo, or dresses at Capucci, because she knows that the fatuous pleasure of enjoying them will be followed by the punishment of having to pay for them. The marriage's first, rosy decade of folly and dissipation is up in the attic. History. Fiamma has confronted the financial crisis with a spirit contrary to her husband's: all on the side of austerity and bourgeois karma.

Is that how real ladies and gentlemen behave? This question floats in her mind. She responds with a propriety of substance (and not of form). She exasperates my father with her careless dress, she seems to do it just to irritate him. When they were young he treated her with an air of superiority, he was the worldly Jewish haute-bourgeois, and she the little beggar of *My Fair Lady*, the one who had to learn everything. At that time she was ashamed of her family's vulgarity, of her half-illiterate grandmother, of having to share her apartment—although it was large—with uncle and cousins. How could she forget the day when, invited to a meal at the Sonninos', she had crossed the threshold of that inaccessible Temple for the first time? Her knees trembled and she couldn't get out a complete sentence. The anxiety roused in her by the refinement of that dining room, the elegance of the china and the silver, the formality of the servants, the somewhat stiff decorum of the diners, the frivolity of the talk . . . Was this the sense of inadequacy experienced countless times by Sabrina, her favorite movie character, played, of course, by Audrey Hepburn? The saga of the passionate Cinderella, daughter of a chauffeur, who, after various adventures, falls in love with and marries a scion of the Larrabees, millionaire Long Island dynasty, thus achieving an incredible social ascent. Certainly my father is not the heir to the vast financial and mining fortunes of the Larrabees, nor does he possess the carefree charm of William Holden or the gruff fascination of Humphrey Bogart, but my mother, after all, is content. Is it from that film that she drew the inspiration for the way she dressed and spoke? Is it from that point that she understood what she was authorized to dream? And who knows what became of the real Sabrina . . . Maybe the Larrabees went bankrupt, like the Sonninos . . . Or who knows if Sabrina, like Mme. Bovary, got tired of her cold, impeccable husband right away . . . Who knows, maybe she betrayed him with her brother-in-law? Maybe they divorced . . . who knows, maybe she asked for millions in alimony . . . Who knows, maybe the great Bogart was already too old to satisfy his wife sexually . . . Who knows, maybe their love ends . . . And who knows how many other who knows . . . All I know is that if it were possible to stop the course of life at certain memorable peaks of love, as happens in Hollywood comedies, my mother would be the happiest woman who ever appeared on the stage of this world! Because her vocation for happiness had something unreal about it. Besides, come to think of it, they're all dead: Bogart, Holden, even Hepburn; and yet my mother, every time she sits in front of the television and puts on the cassette of *Sabrina*, upon reaching the epilogue—where the big ocean liner heads for Europe, with the melancholy dreamer ignorant that her dark, handsome heir will unexpectedly appear and she will soon be flooded with happiness—feels again exactly that sensation of fulfillment that Proust's "moments outside of time" give us: a feeling of euphoric hope, as if she were still sixteen and had her whole life before her!

But when it came to striving, to becoming adult, getting into hand-to-hand combat with life, she, the shy daughter of that rich, rude builder, didn't back down. While all around her the Sonninos are running off, seeking comfort in unreasonably optimistic predictions, while they (who once so intimidated her) can't stop asking themselves how the disaster could have happened, she rolls up her sleeves, showing a courage, a devotion to the cause, an astonishing nobility in defying adversity. At that precise instant Audrey Hepburn dies, and from the ashes of that feline American actress my mother is born, just as I know her. Her new nuclear family, which started out so well, and about which she has so often fantasized, can't go to pieces now, not like this, not for this setback which she and her husband have nothing to do with, or almost nothing. She will do what ninety-nine per cent of young wives on this planet in analogous circumstances would refuse to do: she will save her marriage. That's the new impulse, more combative than the one that impelled her to marry a Jew: stay with her husband, be involved with him and his affairs full time, disregarding if necessary the censure of her own family and a lot of other sensible people. That's how she shows her character. This is courage. The rest is nothing.

But now, after the crash, the moment of vindication has arrived. All this assumes in her the shape of an ideological protest, moderated by a congenital piety, the incapacity to raise her voice and embarrass others. She's anarchic, but, like all people who enjoy appearing disillusioned, deep inside she hasn't given up a dream of happiness and pleasure: she has only buried it socially. The back seat of her car seems like a gypsy's, overflowing with stuff (shoes to take to the shoemaker, pocket diaries full of loose pages, the shopping for my grandparents, old tape recorders to be repaired). That chaos, however, which my father can't stomach, represents my mother's total availability to others, her inextinguishable granting of credit and, at the same time, her efficiency, but it is also the image of an impertinent iconoclasm. When we park near school, she, who has done her utmost to get into the city center, avoiding the surveillance of the traffic police, entrusts her car to a homeless man who pretends to watch it, but in reality settles himself comfortably inside to protect himself from the cold, leaving in the driver's seat a stench of alcohol and armpits. This is my mother. A delicate creature who could scale a mountain. An anarchic populist who feels herself a lady or vice-versa. For too many years a victim of the Sonninos' style, suddenly she has moved to the counterattack. She has sold out to the enemy, but always like a boat on the ocean, steering a course between gentleness and sudden bursts of bitter rebellion.

If my father managed to forgive Bepy, helping him return from the United States, doing all he could to set him up again, forgetting everything, even the failure to buy those life-saving Caravaggios, my mother, instead, wouldn't pardon her father-in-law for anything. Isn't it strange that the devout Catholic Fiamma Bonanno is so little inclined to the remission of the sins of others, while her Biblical consort seems to have unlimited resources for forgiveness and not bearing grudges? In any case Fiamma wouldn't forgive Bepy. Not because of the money: that for her always played a marginal, or, at most, symbolic role. Money is not an instrument of advancement or happiness, it isn't meant to acquire things, comforts, or services; it is only, God willing, a guarantee of social respectability. It should have been conserved for that, rather than used.

And it was for *formal reasons* and symbolic ones—so dominant in her—that she always considered her father-in-law if not a wicked man certainly an irresponsible son of a bitch. To the point of sometimes being irritated with her husband for his indulgence toward his trouble-making father. "But he's my father!" he would timidly defend himself. "And I'm your wife!" she would reply, coldly, emphasizing that her claims were always neglected. "And those are your children," she would add, giving to the scene a melodramatic flavor, like a soap opera, which was not typical of her. So my parents taunted each other, but always with a mixture of mutterings and admonitions. My mother didn't want us to hear, nor did she want to

humiliate my father in front of his children, obtaining, however, the opposite effect, because, by conducting these whispered
quarrels in secret, all she did was endow them with mystery and
fear, and for me they became a source of constant anxiety. She,
who in the eyes of the world seemed the lady of Magnanimity
and Mercy, was in reality lacerated by rancor-filled rage. And,
strange as it may seem, the accusation she didn't have the
courage to direct against her husband—and which emerged
only occasionally in uncontrolled nervous outbursts—was my
father's inexplicable lack of bitterness, his generosity, his infidelity to every hostile sentiment . . . The fact that he had forgiven his father went along with that passion for wagging his
tail with so much affected dismay to Nanni Cittadini, that rat
who had sunk my grandfather, and the rest of us with him.
"He's the only one who helped us! I can't bear your cynicism!"
His voice rose. "If you think lending money at twenty per cent
interest is a philanthropic act . . ." she nailed him, impassive.

It's true that my mother had never had much sympathy for
my grandfather, or for his whole circle. I think that for her,
brought up to behave as if she were poor (for Grandpa Alfio,
a man who vaunted a wealth he didn't possess was worse than
a confessed mass murderer), her father-in-law represented a
negative model. But she waited for the crash to color her intolerance with the crude tones of hostility. Since that fateful
morning in '82 when Bepy, in a tight spot, had asked her for a
million lire and she had signed a blank check, to discover the
following month that he had filled in a much larger amount, to
pay for the Concorde to the United States, showing further dis-
regard for our situation—since that day my mother had sworn
revenge. But, I repeat, not because of the money. No, that was
only a symbol for my mother. For the betrayal of trust, if anything. Certain things were important to my mother. One's
word given. Honoring a pledge made. A promise is a promise.
The sacredness of the social contract. Given the circumstances,

her contempt for the Sonninos was inevitable. Not because they had ruined her youth, forcing her into a precarious situation and a sense of guilt toward her own extremely respectable family. No, not for this. The question is more complex. And runs into ethics, above all (like everything regarding that Jansenist in skirts, my mother). Her inner life was a mixture of adjustments and ironies that only sometimes deteriorated into the vortex of a bad mood, but her moral universe tended to the absolute. She was a neurotic creature, suited to generating neurotics. The thing she couldn't forgive my father for was not the Sacrifice he imposed on her but that It wasn't recognized. She wanted to identify with the victim. This would have been enough for her. My father, resistant to certain Dostoyevskyan morbidities, couldn't ever content her, even if he should have.

What did the Sacrifice consist of?

Placing before her own interests—always—those of others. An oblatory delirium, because this was the life she had chosen: to occupy herself full time with her unreasonable parents, her hypochondriac mother-in-law, her maladjusted children, her homesick Filipino maid, her whining dependents, the tenants in her and her father's apartments, and a lot of other people besides . . . All in her court. That plethora of the "insulted and humiliated" who saw in her an inalienable reference point— precious, irreplaceable Teresa of Calcutta—and who always telephoned a minute before we sat down for dinner, maybe because she was incapable of putting up barriers. She was always reaching out and available, like a punching bag or a mouth harp.

Once at a catechism lesson I was subjected to, in the attempt to convert me to the religion of my mother, or, at worst, purify me of the dross of my father's, I came upon the myth of Lucifer: the fall into Hell of the beloved angel of the Omnipotent. Immediately I had a feeling of familiarity. I had seen that myth come to life in my mother, but reversed. She was the opposite of Lucifer: a creature of the shadows, of dark sentiments and a striking neurotic willfulness, who had chosen to expiate her inclination to evil in a paradise of caring. But deep inside her persisted what with a certain pomposity we might call a "nostalgia for the darkness."

At the same time, in a peculiar imbalance, in the recesses of my mother's psyche lurked a boundless pride, overflowing into hostility and resentment for anyone who was "undeservedly" happier than she, her husband, and her sons. Her investment in these three talented individuals was absolute. They couldn't disappoint her in any way. She couldn't have stood it. And the reason that she sometimes lashed out at us was that she had to express the bitterness of an unhappy investor. Naturally she would never let such vainglorious thoughts escape, in front of her sons, or anyone else, perhaps because of a modesty that many took for indifference, and because—considering herself an emancipated girl of the sixties, who had picked up a little psychoanalysis and experimental pedagogy—she knew that placing insurmountable obstacles before children of a good bourgeois family was equivalent to an indirect invitation to avoid them, if not reject them. That didn't keep her from deviously manifesting reproach for our failures.

Yes, Mama dear, it was enough to hear you breathe or look at the wrinkles puckering on your forehead to understand how many and what expectations you nourished for the life of your sons. The usual story, the formative error par excellence: the sweet little princess, mad for Audrey Hepburn, becomes an unhappy adult and pours her cup of frustrations into the bitter receptacle of her children.

Sometimes it seemed I'd caught her with her gaze lost in emptiness: maybe she saw me already in my tuxedo, in an auditorium at the Nobel foundation in Stockholm, ready to receive the prize that I deserved for my unforgettable literary work. Did she think we didn't understand that inside she was certain that Lorenzo—her dear Lorenzo—would one day be president or chief executive of some great organization, or else it *all* would have been meaningless?

But when the successes my mother strove so hard for did arrive, her behavior changed immediately. She didn't like to display her exultation. One of her sons had had a small personal triumph (an exam passed brilliantly, a book published, a raise, a dazzling lecture)? All she could do was hide, vanish into the wings like a busy stage manager. As if to let it be understood that the merit was ours alone, or at most the unquestionable didactic talent of her husband. When it was communicated to her that her son Daniel had gotten the highest grade possible on a high-school exam, for a theme on the intrinsic stupidity of political engagement—a record that, while modest, should have repaid any mother obsessed as she was by the scholastic performance of her sons—she remained unmoved. She refused to tell friends and acquaintances, although she thoughtlessly told her husband, who, for his part, began to brag publicly, as if that meaningless grade for a high-school essay on disengagement were the prelude to a glorious literary career. My mother at that point no longer existed. She must have felt a masochistic joy in removing herself, like the melancholy hero of a Western who at the moment of triumph—when the town, freed from the bad guys' violence, acclaims him—goes off solitary into the night, alone with his horse and the starry sky. It was a game she played all out. An Oriental discipline of *annihilation of the I*, in favor of a cosmic happiness. What my father, with a certain psychological imprecision, called the *movie-extra syndrome*. So, while she might be eating her heart out, she was wary of asking us questions. She left to my father the job of subjecting us to an exhausting third degree. *But then what did they say*—he pressed us, ingenuously smiling—*Come on, tell me. Were they jealous of you?* He wanted to decant that pleasure, re-create it, in the hope that it wouldn't vanish, renewed by the brilliance of our accounts. That's why he was eager for details and clearly radiant, while she hid, perhaps because she knew that happiness—true happiness—isn't social but extremely private, to be enjoyed in secret solitude; or perhaps because of the inhibitions dictated by her excessive discretion.

Yes, my mother was disposed to sacrifice. But she wanted to be repaid with interest. Seriousness for her was a value, just as for the Sonninos it was an irrelevant option. And, although it might seem an easy paradox, the odd thing is that while she did her duty with the incredible lightness of a smile, the frivolity of the Sonninos was heavy and suffocating—and, as the story of my uncle Teo's flight and rancor demonstrates, terrifically obstructive.

That's why my mother felt a stifling annoyance for everything that *being a Sonnino* implied. A tone-deaf band of braggarts, dishonest, happy-go-lucky egotists, who lived beyond their own possibilities. And when one of these defects took shape in the heart and behavior of one of her children, she blanched, as if he had been transformed into an uncontrollable little monster, a new Sonnino to destroy.

I still remember when my brother, having won a place for a doctorate in journalism at the Bocconi, found himself in that gynaeceum of career bunnies and lost control, leaving his longtime girlfriend in order to embark on a rabid libertinism (the cause of annoying rashes on his groin—perhaps a subliminal fury against his own instrument of pleasure?—hair loss, and a scratching sense of guilt), the prelude to marriage with the restored ex-girlfriend. My mother's reaction in those days of crisis was symptomatic. Panther in a cage. Wounded beast. As if she had perceived the spirit of Bepy Sonnino becoming incarnate in the flesh of her son. She went deviously to work, telephoning my future sister-in-law every day, boycotting the new girls, subtly reproaching her son, and working in the shadows like a grim Richelieu. The crazy thing is that, at the time, it seemed to me natural to take my mother's side (who knows if I would today?), as if she had brainwashed me. For her the mortal sin was to make others suffer, to forget who had helped us. What she detested was her husband's anti-memory, that propensity of his to transfigure an individual and then let him fall into the record book of oblivion and disillusion. Never in a dispute between us and the world would she choose her sons. My brother had made a pledge to that girl? Had he deluded her with the typical Sonnino methods (a blend of magniloquence, brilliance, and gallantry)? Well, then, he couldn't pull out now, he must respect his promise, even if he would later regret it . . . And happiness? There's no place for that, Mama? Yes, but not at all costs! Or else what meaning does life have, boys? And when my brother, having destroyed in just three months his conjugal happiness and a good piece of his life, showed up at home to accuse her publicly of having forced him into a reparatory marriage (when there was nothing to repair), my mother defended herself with that air of an outraged little saint: "But I didn't make you do anything . . . You did it yourself . . ." Unexceptionable response. My mother had a dominion so absolute over our consciences that she had no need to impose choices and actions. We acted according to her will, without her having to worry about demonstrating it. And submitting to the silent, conspiratorial plans of my mother was equivalent to selling your soul to the devil. You could be certain that she would make your life pleasant, filling it with every possible comfort (exotic travel, cars, affection, understanding, money, organization, timely interventions . . .), but the price was always too high. And she, habitually so shy and evasive, at the moment of victory was implacable. But how, dear, with all that I've done for you now, can you go back on your word? One doesn't do that. Commitments are commitments and have to be respected. And if you, in an access of adolescent enthu siasm, told her that you hadn't taken on any damn commitment, that, if anything, it had been she who, unasked, had put you in the world for the sole purpose of overloading you with commitments, you would have to endure the ironic curl of her contemptuous lips.

Yet again she didn't take the trouble to utter words or engage in discussions. (Ugh, discussions were stuff for chattering Jews!) Implying them served her cause more effectively. And Lorenzo and I must have seemed, in the eyes of the world, two big demijohns overflowing with a sense of guilt toward that mother too good to be true.

But one December day, a few hours before an eighteenth-birthday party I had been invited to, it happened that my mother, just returning home, came into my room, attracted by the sound of a tape that Uncle Teo had sent me from Israel. The song was "A Summer Place," in a hazy, embellished version by Henry Mancini. So we stood facing each other, I in my rented dinner jacket and she in her wet Army raincoat. Then she grabbed me, and, overcoming my serious childish shyness, urged me to dance. We began like that, without saying a word: her face was alight, completely uninterested in her clumsy inessential cavalier, totally immersed in a memory, or in an atmosphere, or something like that, and just at that moment I had the unpleasant impression of having in my arms a human being who was not at all familiar. A living, breathing, idealistic, imaginative, sensual, thoughtless, adventurous creature . . . I had the would-be Sabrina in my arms, looking out the window, her hands and chin red with watermelon, the girl I had so often heard mentioned but had not yet had the honor of meeting. I was so confused and bewildered that, if I hadn't suddenly come to my senses, I would have introduced myself, "I'm Daniel Sonnino," and then asked her, "And who are you?" What a foolish question! I had in my arms only a young girl who was thinking about herself, happily not giving a damn about the children whom destiny would one day presumably inflict on her.

PART II
WHEN CLASS ENVY DEGENERATES INTO DESPERATE LOVE

1. Course in Applied Mythomania

In January of 2000 I received a telephone call from Professor J. R. Leiterman, glory of comparative literature in the United States, not to mention enthusiastic opponent of the unforgivably autobiographical theories expressed violently and cleverly in my first book, *All the Anti-Semitic Jews*.

The ineffable Dean Leiterman was pleased to invite me to a seminar organized by the University of Pittsburgh with the prophetic title:

THE FATE OF JEWISH LITERATURE IN A TIME OF FULL ASSIMILATION AND ISLAMIC THREAT.

He said he was certain that a provocation from me would have the power to stiffen the flaccid bow ties of the supercilious professors on the other side of the ocean.

I accepted happily. Free trip and new people. Just the thing for a depressed academic.

Could I perhaps have foreseen that, while I was fantasizing about the tone of my talk, someone, on the other side of the world, would be pondering how to destroy the World Trade Center? Fate decided that the conference be postponed from the spring of 2001 to the fall of that year, in the midst of the planetary cataclysm; that I had promised Giorgio Sevi, a high-school classmate who for years had been making money in America, to meet him in Manhattan; and that during the night drive from Pittsburgh to New York (in a rented car) I received a telephone call from my father informing me, in a voice pasty with emotion, of the death of Nanni Cittadini.

Who knows why people are so eager to announce the death of a fellow-human, as if the only truly *inexorable thing* were perceived as the most unpredictable. To the point that a moment after registering the news of the death I was racking my brains to think of whom I could in turn communicate it to. Until I was devastated by the realization that the people whom that death would interest hadn't been in touch with me for fifteen years. And that that span of time—interspersed with an unsatisfying ration of academic satisfactions—had been inserted between me and them without my ever stopping to miss them.

Thus, in the middle of the night, like Hamlet before the ghost of his father, but with so much more amusement and so much less anguish, the phantom of that man who had just died appeared to me. I see him rising on the dashboard and smiling at me, in the image steamed open by memory, immersed in his Eden of cashmere and peaty malt whiskey, in his improbable millionaire's dwelling at No. 7 Via Aldrovandi, yellow and Art Nouveau, like the embassy of some second-rate country. I see Nanni Cittadini—Nanni himself: the Patron Saint of my class hatreds, the grandfather of the girl Gaia, who simply ruined my adolescence—embodied before my incredulous eyes, while my father, that fine man, continues to philosophize on the phone, "He's the last of Bepy's generation to go," and inside I tell him off: *For goodness' sake, Papa, when will you stop idolizing that clown?* And it's a masterpiece of filial devotion to contain my hilarity. Generally I don't find the death of an octogenarian moving. But, given the circumstances, my usual indifference to the death of an ordinary octogenarian is transformed into a kind of euphoria, inspired by the death of that particular octogenarian.

I promise myself to get through the Giorgio Sevi experience as quickly as possible in order to return to base immediately: I want to attend Nanni's funeral. At any cost!

What a pleasure to let myself be thrilled by the news, my heart strangled by memories of Gaia, Gaia, Gaia, in the grip of that disembodied melodrama that belongs to us Sonninos! As if she had never existed, as if she had been a fantastic myth of my summers on the Amalfi Coast and my winters in the Dolomites, smelling of ski wax and vin brulé, as if she hadn't inflicted any suffering on me, as if in fifteen long years I hadn't mythologized and demythologized her at least a dozen times, as if I hadn't endured the persistence of that thought so darkly determined to survive.

Well yes, Nanni is dead! And you are the most enthusiastic undertaker in history. Run to the city of the triumph of death, triumphant in turn at the death of a particular biological organism that, from the age of eight, you detested and envied to the point of nausea. You hated Nanni Cittadini with your whole self. That's the only thing you've never been ashamed of. And although a posthumous hatred might seem as pointless and foolish as an unrequited love, maybe because of a faint superstitious perversity you don't want (or don't know how?) to get rid of the one or the other.

And who knows if it wasn't the euphoria generated by the news or by that jumble of questions getting tangled up inside me—*Who is Gaia? Where does she live? Is she married? Does she think of me every so often? Why should she think of me? Has she reached the age when ninety per cent of girls begin to dangerously resemble their own mothers and even their grand-mothers? Does she belong to that category of thirty-year-olds afflicted by boring idiosyncrasies and obsessed by the specter of failure? How will she take my presence at the funeral? Do I have the right tie?*—that prepared me for immersion in the most anguished Manhattan since the time of its epic founding.

Finally, balanced heavily between the Hudson and the East River, and enveloped in the pink bubble of dawn and a blue morning fantasy, the island offers me its profile: devoid of the ungainly steel twins.

Observing the mutilated horizon, and trying to purify it of symbolic emotional implications, is difficult: as when, several months ago in a restaurant in Parioli, I ran into Silvia Toffan, a classmate once at the top of the hit parade of our upscale high-school world, who had lost her beautiful lower limbs in a tragic car accident. That's why this absurd spectacle of absence, the urbanist masterpiece of the third millennium, chokes me with horror, but also with a kind of sinister Samson-like enjoyment: two distant myths of my adolescence (Silvia Toffan and New York) monstrously lacerated.

The day is phenomenal. The contours hover between red, purple, orange, and a radiant blue. My rectangular honey-colored car is reflected in the bluish-glass mosaic of a skyscraper. I slowly skirt an autumnal postcard-like Central Park, passing in review luxurious apartment buildings guarded by regal African-Americans in uniform, and then the Guggenheim, the Metropolitan, the Frick.

But it's only when I enter the jangling din of midtown— amid the army of Pakistani taxi drivers who, to exorcise the distrust roused by their turbans, have hung small American flags on their rearview mirrors—that I realize with relief, and in spite of my first impression, that Manhattan has found nothing better to do than go back to being Manhattan.

"This, too, will soon be consumed," opines a guy on the radio in an apocalyptic tone. As for me I *consume* his voice along with blueberry pancakes saturated with butter and maple syrup, sitting at the counter of a not too crowded coffee shop in the Fifties. It's as if the sound of his voice, with the help of that weighty candy-like mush, were dragging me by the lapels back to the summer of '86, and my third consecutive— not to mention last—study vacation in Boston. Gaia existed. And a lot of others, if you think about it, existed. At the time they all had the underestimated merit of existing! Say it, who-ever you are: *this, too, will soon be consumed . . .*

The idea of making a reservation at Morgans came from my father, of course. With certain things, I lost control a long time ago. "It's a postmodern delirium in a Philippe Starck style, all forties furniture and dizzying lines," he said to me the other night on the phone, having recourse to one of his typically fatu-ous expressions, after torturing me for a quarter of an hour in an attempt to extort the truth about the reception of his son and his son's ludicrous anti-Semitic ideas in that Jewish redoubt of the University of Pittsburgh. And I, after having, in turn, tormented him by telling him about my loss of control, and the censure of the most intransigent audience I've ever faced, gave in and took his advice, violating my reactionary nature, which asks from hotels a decadent luxury, Art Nouveau style, on the edge of pure grandiosity . . . Christ, two hundred and sixty dollars for this minuscule lobby? Not to mention the concierge, who, affected by a very American smile-paralysis, barely lifts his eyebrows on finding before him a guy like me with nothing of the usual clientele about him.

After having a shower in a cubicle, in that room for Lilliputians, and sleeping till late afternoon, I get up and go down, with my thirty-year bundle of inadequacies, to the bar of the hotel, for the rendezvous with the past that even as I slept was torturing my guts. I would pay in diamonds to avoid this meeting.

And yet only when the door of the very speedy elevator opens slowly on a room that is all high decibel sounds and soft purple light caressing the perfect teeth of Apollos in Calvin Klein and the curves of international Barbies who inspire a pantheistic intoxication—only then do I feel really doomed.

How to believe that the preppy with the starry smile, like a Brooks Brothers salesman, who rushes toward me in this noisy bar on the east side of midtown is Giorgio, our successful émigré? An individual so irrelevant that when, a few months ago, he phoned me in my tiny office at the university—"Hey, Daniel, it's Giorgio . . ."—I felt the need to stall for time: "Giorgio?" In return I got an encouraging confirmation from that voice: "Giorgio Sevi! I found your number on the university Web site. I hope I'm not disturbing you." "Good God! . . . Giorgio. Where the hell are you? Where are you calling from? . . . Imagine, Giorgio . . ." racking my brains in a last effort to associate with that name the thin figure of a boy whose only special qualities in our school days were an agreeable charm and a barely sufficient intellect. In those days everyone knew that Giorgio and I were the opposite ends of an affective segment at the center of which shone, in all his glory and good nature, our high school hero: DAVID RUBEN, known as DAV.

But that equidistance from the object of so much admiration, rather than solidifying a friendship, made Giorgio and me—out of a mixture of incompatibility and competitiveness—fervent enemies. To understand it you have only to look at us fifteen years later as we shake hands distrustfully, not only with the mutual impression that seeing each other is pointless but with the sharp consciousness that someone or something essential is missing: it's millennia since we felt so acutely the absence of Dav.

Who, although he hated to hear it over and over, was the dazzling double of Tom Cruise. The fourteen-year-old who had kindled the fantasies of hundreds of girls in our school, contesting the primacy of the Hollywood star in his *Top Gun* jacket, whose glossy image decorated the diaries of my fanatic classmates.

Although Dav was the only other Jew in the school, he was

my glowing antithesis, as if Judaism, which in me had worked in extreme caricature, had spared him: and the outrage consisted precisely in that kind of attractiveness, so politely reassuring, that is usually the prerogative of high-ranking Gentiles but in his case was marked by a name and last name that were not only exotic but so unequivocally Jewish: David Ruben. *Of the jewelry Rubens,* my mother would explain with a little pride and a little envy, and in the same tone in which she would have said *the real-estate Pipernos* or *the steel Savellis.*

On the other hand it was evident that our blond Tom Cruise, nearly eight inches taller than the original, had paid a tribute to Semite iconography with a nose whose tip pointed slightly downward: but it was equally clear that he owed his irresistible democratic ascendancy to just that somatic imperfection.

How arduous it was for Dav to gain his standing in a school near the Spanish Steps where the majority of the students used the word "rabbi" as a synonym for "miser" I couldn't say: but I suppose behind it was the same logic that had led Silvia Toffan—indescribable sapphire with the splendid if temporary legs of a pinup girl—to insist during a memorable geography quiz that Kashmir was a lice-ridden region of India that had got its name from Burberry twin sets.

Our physical and temperamental differences had not kept Dav from shadowing me like a bloodsucker, just as they had not diminished my impression that he was what, if I could have started over, I would have chosen to be. Yet my devotion, mixed with envy, was never clearly manifested. I would never have given up the appearance of disdainful insensitivity to the world's Davidian enthusiasms, sensing that, beyond being co-religionists, this was the core of our union: the reason that the Dean Martins choose to hang around the Jerry Lewises is the capacity of the latter to mock them where everyone else exalts them. On the other hand, you wouldn't be the idol's favorite if he, in turn, didn't know he was your secret aspiration. And what's the point of waving your hands or raising your voice to get attention if all he has to do is smile to enrapture a gaze only temporarily attracted by you? People (especially those around sixteen) show a natural indulgence for beauty and a chronic irritation with intellectual effort. The only thing left was to profess a monotheistic religion, staring at the fetish of our screaming blond girls with the admiration of one who would never learn to compete.

When Dav, because of a slight myopia, was compelled to put on his first pair of glasses—not too different, basically, from the ones that had poisoned the life of so many boys like me, absorbing them into that subgroup of adolescents commonly known as "four eyes"—they seemed an element of consecration. His handsomeness assumed in the eyes of the world a moral legitimacy, becoming both serious and dreamy. And how can I forget that, as I walked through the halls of our seventeenth-century school beside the newly spectacled David Ruben, the atmosphere filled with the unmistakable chatter of nymphets? How can I forget that at the same time the leadership of the David Ruben fan club, founded a year earlier by a group of girls from the foreign language school, called a special meeting to discuss whether the Idol, with that earth-shattering idea of wearing glasses, should be called—in public and without fear of denial—"the handsomest guy of all time"?

The creature to whom "the handsomest guy of all time" owed the bronze glow and the eager restlessness of those who are content but won't make up their minds to be happy was Karen, his mother.

I considered meeting that woman to be a genuine "inebriation at first sight." Then again I would never be totally detoxified of that aphrodisiac cocktail whose ingredients I couldn't stop enumerating to myself: forty-two-year-old blonde, polyglot frivolous aloof designer-clothes-wearing snob, sapped by intermittent moodiness, and absolutely beautiful.

I'm afraid the lady repaid my veneration with indifference: those years stand out in memory for my talent for hanging around people who could intensify my sense of futility, but no one managed to give me such a vivid impression of my human irrelevance as Karen Ruben. It would be euphemistic to say that she didn't consider me someone worth talking to: I simply didn't exist. I didn't belong to this planet. She said she had met Bepy, many years before, at a party on a terrace in Positano. She said she had put up with his flattery. And had been unable to forget him. And she said it as if she were awarding me a prize, or rather an important testimonial. That's why, whenever she saw me (it might happen ten times in the course of the same day), she would say, reflexively: "You know, your grandfather was really a fine man, so chic and respectable . . ." That judgment—which many of Bepy's angry creditors would have considered somewhat incongruous—was spoken with a sigh, and the amazement of someone noting a paranormal phenomenon: the genetic corruption that could cause the descendant of a *très charmant* man to be a chronic jerk.

Karen was allergic to the past. It might have been said that there was something unhealthy about the way she was anchored to the present.

And who—looking at her—could have guessed that she had emerged from an inferno?

It was as if the tragic story of her family had left no traces. At the same time, however, counterbalancing the impression of a nonexistent past, the stain that time had left on her could be perceived in the anachronism of her style of life. Perhaps because I was a new reader of nineteenth-century novels, I found it easy to identify in Karen the living incarnation of many rarefied turn-of-the-century heroines. This, if nothing else, made the masturbations that I devoted to her, during

afternoons at the Ruben house, a tribute to my love for decadent literature: to have in my hands and under my nose a pair
of Karen's pantyhose was equivalent, in my fantasy, to possess-
ing X-rays of the diseased lungs of Claudia Chauchat. How
could I not be aware, besides, that, during my lightning
marathons in the Rubens' bathroom, Karen's voluptuous lisp-
ing "r"—Franco-Prussian glamour that was also engraved in
David's tongue and palate—brilliantly served the cause of my
excitement? "Hey, kid, there's a lot of saliva for you here!"
whispered the Lady of my fantasy to her Fanatical Onanist—
she whose flesh and blood version I would find a few minutes
later in the living room, at the pool, in the greenhouse, or
wherever she had chosen to be.

Karen's inferno had the name of a place, so trite as to be
unpronounceable.

Buchenwald.

In that site adjacent to Olympic Weimar, her parents—distinguished Alsatians—had been annihilated when she was still
too young to suffer from it or to preserve any memory of them.
Karen had grown up in Paris with a great-aunt who had
escaped the Hitlerian slaughters (as the wife of a Catholic
diplomat), and whom Karen had pompously taken to calling
maman. And then there had been the years at Le Rosey, the
Genevan boarding school, as is proper for a girl of the good
French bourgeoisie. Le Rosey so that she would come into
contact with that fruit salad of industrial aristocracies and
blue-blooded nobility that would forge her tastes and aspirations. Karen had found herself mingling with the jet set that in
the late fifties celebrated its rites at St. Moritz and the Côte
d'Azur. Although she was beautiful in her own, original way,
endowed with impeccable manners and basically rich enough
to sustain that fabled life style, she had never managed to free
herself from a kind of syndrome of the excluded: what she

envied her friends, both boys and girls, was their families. Large families, falsely or authentically united: she envied the gatherings, the noisy festivities (especially Christmas), the white-haired, whiskered patriarchs, and the big group photos. On the other hand the shame inspired by the void behind her led her to lie, to invent relatives she didn't have, to make up travels during summer vacations to aunts and uncles she had lost even before coming into the world. Thus—in the long-lasting and insistent invention of her own family—Karen had developed an insane mythomania. It wasn't at all clear why she was so ashamed of being an orphan. Especially since, at that time, there were many unfortunates (a cousin of Bepy's, for example) who, hit by the same catastrophe as Karen, by the hand of the same murderers, had felt the need to construct around those exterminated relatives a kind of mausoleum of Memory. The opposite of Karen, who, to get rid of her dead, had built an invisible temple dedicated to Forgetting and Averting. Why feel so much embarrassment for something she had no responsibility for? Was it possible that she had reached the point of considering unrefined the way in which her parents and grandparents and all the others had been murdered?

Mystery! One of the few things I've learned in life is that people find the most various and idiotic reasons for being ashamed: presumed, invented faults, madly transfigured by those who feel them as a fatal disease. Basically, if it's a mistake to say that Karen's misfortune was in itself respectable, it's just as big a mistake to dismiss such a tragedy as if it were something to be ashamed of and eliminated.

Especially since this cancer ruined her life.

Many times, in fact, she was close to marrying the man of her dreams. But then? Then she desisted. And for the usual foolish reason: she couldn't bear the family of her betrothed. She came to hate what in reality she was in love with: those structured families that made her feel inferior, filling her with the poisonous bile of envy. And, besides, after a while the fiancé of the moment claimed the right to meet Karen's parents, of whom she spoke continuously. At that point she preferred to throw to the winds her own happiness in order not to confess that she had lied, that no parent existed. That's why it shouldn't in fact have been surprising that in the end she married Amos Ruben. Here was a man upon whom to exercise her undoubted superiority. He has nothing she can envy and at the same time has everything she needs to orchestrate her revenge. Amos is simply the first man for whom Karen doesn't feel the need to prepare a polluting sequence of colossal lies, and so the man with whom to create a family without the risk of going mad. Yes, because Amos appears to her as the classic uprooted, embarrassingly rich Jew who will lead her to a brand-new city, where she can invent a new life for herself and practice with impunity her schizoid mythomania.

Tripoli, the city Amos comes from, seems to have tinted his complexion yellow: his skin shines like the jewels that the Ruben family has been selling for centuries, or like dawn in the African desert. When he meets Karen he is just another refugee from Qaddafi's purges, who has transferred his business to Geneva, the classic high-powered merchant marked by the spiritual simplicity that characterizes men who have a nose for business. From precious stones to luxury watches, nothing escapes the finely calibrated olfactory sense of that Libyan Croesus. His life is sober, not at all luxurious, divided between the atelier he has set up in an apartment on the Rue de Rhône (Ali Baba's sparkling cave translated into the heart of Europe, where the future spouses meet) and the synagogue of Geneva.

David—when by pure chance we found ourselves sitting next to each other in the first year of middle school—is perfectly aware of his mother's lies: and not only feels no pain about them but is self-confident enough not to make a mystery of them with his friends. His strategy, in all ways similar to his father's, consists in trying, within the limits of the possible, to indulge her. So, when Karen asks, *"As-tu téléphoné a tes grand-parents à Genève?,"* it's easy for the great Dav to swear to her that he's done it. And you have to admit that it's not just any-one who could assure his own mother that he has telephoned two distinguished old people who died some thirty years ago and who—for the record—never lived in Geneva.

Karen had imposed on herself two not unrelated missions: on the one hand to de-Judaize Amos, on the other to create out of nothing a respectable pedigree for Dav. And if the realiza-tion of the second proposal turned out to be not at all difficult, the first created some problems. Because, although Amos is at the mercy of his wife, he nonetheless shows a certain Oriental resistance to upsetting his own habits. Karen is going too far: let her make her son a *goy*, let her send him to a school run by priests, let him observe Christmas, Easter, Ash Wednesday, let him hang around with all those insipid blondes, fill the house with all those snobbish *goys*, but why should her domineering extend to the point of keeping him, Amos Ruben, from living in his own way, as he was taught? No, he doesn't see why he, too, should play along with his wife's foolish screenplays. He is a Jew. He has fled from a country and from an era in which that condition was considered a problem. And for that very reason he will not allow anyone (not even that sublime woman opposite him, to whose erotic power he is far more than vul-nerable) to keep him from living as one. He feels the need to honor the obligatory holidays and to give economic support to his relatives scattered throughout Europe. Besides, Amos is too clever not to know that those relatives are, at the same time, the sorrow and the shame of his wife. So in order to live quietly he has decided that the more his wife bugs him with stories of her invented relatives the more he has to spare her the troubles of his own, flesh-and-blood family members. For her part, Karen, like all unstable and unsatisfied persons, isn't aware of her husband's indulgence. And she often baptizes members of his family with insulting epithets like "Bedouins" or "Berbers." So that when Amos, after finishing his spaghetti, in his notorious way wipes his plate clean, Karen rebukes him, "My dear, control yourself, you're not in the midst of your Bedouins!" She has forbidden her husband to invite them to their house—those Bedouins!—and to have them meet Dav. If Amos respects the first of these bans, it often happens that he deliberately violates the second, especially since his son—free of his mother's snobbishness—has manifested a surprising curiosity about the part of himself that has roots in such distant and exotic places. Yes, the boy, to Amos's great amazement, displays an attraction for his real relatives: who knows, maybe because his mother has forced him to live for so long among those ridiculous phantoms.

The Rubens' villa was on the western slope of Section 1 of Olgiata—the oldest and most exclusive part of the neighborhood, which was built around the Golf Club in the mid-sixties, after the original subdivision of the land.

During our high-school years that pretentious castle wrapped in ivy and set in the fabled isolation of pines and oaks in the most British section of northern Rome provided the background for countless parties, all flowing together in memory into the December mega-party enveloped by red hedges and purple vines, the one that Karen pompously called, and, following her, everyone else, "the turkey party," but which custom had helped contract into the expression "the turkey."

A cult event in our crowd, and for reasons that had little to do with sophistication, nothing with Catholic mysticism, and a lot to do with a worn-out form of Jewish-Hollywood tradition. And O.K., these eccentric Rubens insist on dinner jacket and long dress (Christ, we're only teenagers and barely fifteen years from 2000), and submerge you in this atmosphere too strongly scented with mistletoe, and yet the sensation is splendidly retro: the brief journey from your own house to the Ruben villa is made in a car of the time, like an exciting journey from the euphoric Italy of Craxi to the glossy America of Eisenhower.

Being invited to the turkey doesn't constitute a privilege but only a very pleasant diversion. Both because of the guests who are thrown into that unaccustomed space, and because of the organizers, so anxious to respect the iconography of Christmas that they don't skimp on the pretentious decorations, to the point where the house resembles the background of an ad for panettone.

The mania for piling on refinements may express more clearly than any other sign the neurosis of the organizer. There may not be on the rosewood strips of the dining-room parquet all the warmth that was hoped for but only the rhetoric of warmth, deftly orchestrated by Madame Ruben. Nor can it escape the guests that that performance—although its pagan-consumerist implication tends to be exaggerated—is staged by a Jewish family. Nor that Signora Ruben, hostile by age-old tradition to the idea that Jesus was the long-awaited messiah, loves to celebrate the birthday of that crucified successful Jew in a way that no Catholic could equal. (Come on, Karen, what would your grandfather or your father think of the genuine emotion that assails you as you listen to *From Starry Skies Descending* . . .?) Nor can one underestimate the fact that the only adults present at the dazzling December kermesse (besides the waiters) are Amos and Karen (Lord, what improbable names!). Just as the event's American flavor should not be neglected. What does that thirty-five-pound turkey stuffed with apples and chestnuts have to do with anything? Or the illumination of the garden with orange and purple spotlights hidden in the wisteria? Or the swing music of Sinatra or Bobby Darin? Or the truck and the station wagon parked under the shed? Come on, folks, we're in Rome, not Connecticut!

But who would suspect that this joyful worldly custom hides, in the wings, such a throbbingly painful nucleus? The pain of a woman who is emotionally invested in an event that should at most amuse her. Who could imagine that this inscrutable woman could abandon herself to a merry-go-round of irrational apprehensions? How can we accept the idea that we represent for her much more than she represents for us? That Karen would pay any amount to penetrate our brains and understand what we really think of her, of Amos, of Dav, of the Villa Ruben and above all of her incomparable *dindon* stuffed with chestnuts?

This Calvary began at the end of every November, when the guest list was compiled. The Rubens ended up inviting an exorbitant number of people, in order to absorb any possible defection and to exorcise the horror of the void that frightened Karen during the whole month of December: what if no one showed up? Such things happen. Things that leave an indelible mark. Is it possible that our happiness is completely entrusted to the kindness of others?

As soon as she sent out the invitations Karen began to wonder if they would reach their destination, and if the recipients would have the sense to respond in a timely manner. After a couple of days she went on the counterattack, subjecting Dav to constant interrogations: "Your friends are really very badly brought up." "Why?" "Well, they haven't responded yet!" "But come on, Mama, it's still three weeks away!" "Do you think it's so easy? Do you think feeding that troop is a joke? I need to know—pre-cise-ly—how many you'll be!" "O.K., tomorrow I'll ask around." "Nooo, it's not nice to ask, it seems almost as if . . . We're not tax collectors." "So what should I do?" "Manage it in a way that they'll tell you, *mon petit.*"

"O.K., I'll try, but calm down." "Uff, I'm totally calm! I'm just doing it for you. What does it matter to me, your little party . . . but my parents taught me to do things right. That's all." Naturally Karen always concluded with a phrase that alluded to her upbringing by that nonexistent family. And David was silent.

Over the years Karen had come to realize that the best day for the turkey was the second or third Friday in December. Through a series of circumstances that it would be difficult to rationalize, Friday evening guaranteed a significant number of prestigious attendees, whereas Saturday seemed to rule them out.

But there was the Amos obstacle to take into account. That his wife should organize a Christmas party in their house already seemed to him an ironic eccentricity of fate, but that she should impose it on him, for such foolish reasons, on the evening of the Sabbath, well, this was really intolerable! Naturally she wouldn't listen to reason and in the end he yielded, not without resentment. And let's say that Amos's hostility contributed to making the air even more stifling. On the other hand this was not the only case of religious superposition. It wasn't unusual, for example, that, on entering the living room of the Ruben house, on an ordinary December day, you would be confronted by the unexpected sight of a large, heavily decorated Christmas tree sparkling with lights beside which burned a menorah lighted by Amos. That sight—which would have delighted any promoter of intercultural exchanges between the great monotheistic religions—literally drove Karen into a rage.

So, in the days leading up to the party, when she activated her by now well-tested organizational machine, you could see her going around the house with the list of guests in her hand. Never stopping her obsessive counting, she associated every phone call received by Dav with a possible defection. It was as if every ring of the telephone were equivalent to a lashing of her eardrum. That was why the hatred she felt for people who cancelled at the last minute had biblical proportions. She swore to God that she would go to every party she was invited to. Yes, in those days filled with suspense, Karen, in a sudden onset of religious feeling, would pray: she prayed that no one would die. Or at least would have the good taste not to expire until the party was over. That no calamity should strike our city. That no planetary war render the mere idea of that party a grave offense to decorum.

The day Karen's faith hits an obstacle that causes it to waver dangerously has gone down in history: it all happens when, a few hours before the turkey, a sharp stone, hibernating for months in Amos's kidneys, has the disastrous idea of rousing itself, to begin its arduous course toward the abyss, and gets bogged down at the bottleneck of the urethra. It takes Amos, historically subject to kidney stones, only an instant to recognize that blaze of paralyzing pain that radiates over his whole back.

Is the turkey in danger?

David, summoned home urgently, finds an incredible sight awaiting him. Karen—whose features have been redrawn by anxiety and rage—is crouching beside her husband, who lies, like Marat, in the big bathtub, surrounded by a dozen bottles of Fiuggi water: the watery steam has beaded his forehead and the characteristic yellow of his complexion seems to tend toward a dark forest green. It's as if pain, and the fear that the pain will return in the form of those frightening spasms, had put him in a state of permanent alert that stretches the muscles of his face and his arms, which have something Michelangelesque about them. If, on the one hand, Karen is caring for him, on the other she can't keep from torturing him with bitter recriminations: "How many times have

I told you that you shouldn't drink all that ice-cold Coca-Cola after dinner? You know what I say? I'm not going to buy it anymore!" "Come on, Mama, leave him alone, can't you see he's suffering?" "I'm saying it for his sake!" "Mama, if you want we can postpone the turkey!" "What does the turkey have to do with it? We're talking about something much more serious: the health of your father! And who says we need to postpone it? Your father is fine, he just needs a little rest. Let's not make a fuss. Some ailments just have to be played down. I'm not saying it for myself. You know it doesn't matter to me. But it's not nice to upset everything right now. It's not right. Think of your friends from Florence! They'll have bought their train tickets already. Think of all that stuff I've ordered. Think of that poor thirty-five-pound turkey. It would be wasted . . ."

In short, the show must go on. The mortal sacrifice of the turkey must not be in vain.

So with a Mosaic gesture Amos raises one hand to give his assent. He is fine, they mustn't worry about him: "Your mother is right, nothing's happened, it's impossible to cancel everything now." With what gravity does he utter these words! He is almost moved by his own courage until a tremendous spasm shakes his kidneys again and his cheeks are bathed in small, uncontrollable tears.

Besides, although Karen would never have admitted it, she didn't at all mind if her husband remained in the tub during the turkey. Ah yes, because the only thing over which she hadn't managed to exercise adequate control through the years was Amos's behavior during the turkey. How many times had she seen him help himself to indecorous quantities of food at the buffet, and sit in a corner with his head sunk in his plate, like a prisoner. Or raise his voice too high, or suddenly turn on the TV, or eat his soup noisily (after that Karen had removed all liquid food from the menu). Not to mention the times when the good Amos started conversations with the children of his clients, toward whom he assumed the slightly servile attitude that some shopkeepers display toward the most prestigious of their habitual customers, the counterpart of the brusque tone reserved for occasional ones. "Greetings to your mother," Amos would say in a mellifluous tone that made a Shylock-type impression, performing an imperceptible bow the sight of which made his wife almost faint with shame.

"Why don't you go sit in the other room for a while, *mon cher*? You won't bore yourself with these kids. I'll bring you a nice plate . . . you seem so tired," she said, affecting a warmth she didn't feel. But he, always moved by the attention of his wife, reassured her: he was fine. He liked the company of the young people: "My dear, calm down, don't be nervous, it's all delightful."

No, this time, thanks to that blessed kidney stone, she would be spared the torture of seeing her troublesome boor of a husband in action!

Dav's behavior, during the turkey, is no less surprising that that of his parents. Maybe under the influence of his anxiety-inducing mother and the iconoclastic Amos, he betrays signs, if not exactly of nervousness, of obvious irritability, as if he wished to be elsewhere. He usually drove his mother crazy, coming back from a golf game late in the afternoon. Barely in time to have a shower and don his dinner jacket, reducing his room to a battlefield. Not that he is uneasy in the role of master of the house in full dress uniform. Rather, he seems to fail in the most elementary duties of hospitality: for example, he's the first to serve himself. He eats like a desperado, especially meat, as if to recover the protein consumed during his athletic feats.

It's almost as if, like any self-respecting child, he is taking care not to participate in his mother's stupid raptures.

Or perhaps he's still thinking of a game that didn't go well.

We all know that his neurosis is sports, that is, athletic competition. We all know that he can't stand losing. We all know there is nothing that influences his mood more negatively than a defeat. We all know that even in the most friendly and insignificant game Dav is aggressive to the point where he feels offended by a teammate incapable of understanding that winning that game is a matter of capital importance.

Maybe this is why when it comes to the other things in life he has an Olympian meekness, which borders on indifference. Is it that in him the desire to humiliate others—that vice which cheers and poisons the lives of us all—is used up in a true desire to defeat his adversaries on the playing field? What is the origin of such magnanimity? Can one say that Dav belongs to that category of boys so satisfied with their present that they feel no need to stick their faces into the future, through imagination, to be happy? Dav has the good fortune to desire what he possesses and to possess what he desires. He doesn't know hope but only the ordinary practice of his own pleasure. He loves himself, without suffering, without idolatry, but with warmth and indulgence. He loves to sleep naked at night and see himself disheveled in front of the mirror in the morning. Just as he likes to swim, to take a shower, to eat enormous steaks and equine quantities of vegetables, spend the summers in America trout fishing or surfing. He does nothing in a professional way. He is quickly bored. In the long run he likes to show off his own infidelity to himself. Dilettantism for him is a moral category. Every passion is exalted by that body which conceals its mystery in an unexpected profundity.

If it's true that Time is the true enemy of the Rubens and that that's why Karen has repudiated the past, then maybe one could hypothesize that Dav has simply abolished the future.

In short, what use is the future if you've had—at the right age and without any sacrifices—the best that life can offer? What do you make of hope if your mother, beyond dreams of glory, has had the good taste not to project onto you any scholastic or professional ambition, and if your father is too displaced to claim from you the dynastic pride that one would expect of the offspring of a family with a solid patrimony?

David is free, freer than all of us, and he has clear ideas about how to spend his freedom. He doesn't disdain luxury but he doesn't idolize it. For him it's completely functional. They have precociously provided an unlimited credit card with which to satisfy his every whim, but he seldom indulges in the sort of compulsive consumerism that poisons the lives of most of our girls.

In other words, David's secret can be summed up in a rather crude formula: don't have a past to respect or a future to desire.

Once he said to me in a serious, anguished tone: "Without sports I would be a social misfit." These flashes of critical self-awareness were perhaps the only germs that attacked the health of that triumphant boy. That's why sometimes his heart seemed inclined to a kind of catatonic suspension that bordered on depression. That's perhaps why during the turkey, although surrounded by so many guests he should have been attending to, Dav remained apart, in a daze, inhaling delicacies, while his friend-valet Giorgio Sevi, much decorated veteran of that party, welcomed and entertained the guests in a state of exaltation, as if he were the master of the house.

Boredom was the thermometer of David Ruben's life: as soon as that spiritual disease appeared in him, an army of antibodies intervened to push him toward new, alluring diversions. If he was bored it was evidently time to change something. To put aside old passions and choose new ones: change was the way to not let yourself be lured by death.

Riding has had its day? It's time to fish.

And then, like those children who enjoy getting ready for imaginary battles more than fighting them, David prepared his future as a fisherman, buying the equipment, circling with a pen on topographic maps the lakes and streams that he would violate with his green rubber boots, foretasting the pleasure of early-morning risings and departures in the middle of the night. The miracle is that these private passions in a flash became collective, infecting us all. So our lives were marked by Dav's latest folly, which in a few weeks became ours, too, at least until that capricious *maître à penser* decided that we were ripe for another change of route, for a new, impulsive trip.

And yet Dav couldn't care less about others: as if they vanished before his eyes. He was too superior to take them into consideration.

Why waste time, like his mother, trying to figure out what others thought of him? Rather than trying to keep up, wasn't it healthier and more fun to let them follow you?

Not that Dav was without vanity: the resemblance to Tom Cruise, for example, flattered him more than he was disposed to admit. Proof of this is the fact that he often defended himself, even without apparent motivation, with phrases like "Hey, enough with Tom Cruise!," which served only to publicly reaffirm how remarkable the resemblance was. And ultimately the similarity he claimed with that star of the big screen wasn't physiognomic but ideological. Dav liked the handsome sons of the American middle class, those who had won roles as protagonists in the films of the time: he was captivated by their sneakers, by their checked shirts, by their sunglasses, by their sleeveless down vests, and above all by the extraordinary normality of their way of life. Often he reproached his parents— who knows how seriously—for not having emigrated to America. God, if only they had! He saw himself strutting like a cock, running down the football fields to be greeted by the sharp cries of cheerleaders. That was his destiny. Not the small dull country in which they had confined him. He would have traded any invitation to a fashionable rendezvous proffered by yet another little countess (courted on his behalf by Karen) for a Big Mac or a pepperoni pizza, at the time, at least in our world, genuinely rare. The strange thing—and it denoted again the appealing eccentricity of his point of view—is that Dav preferred the hinterland to the America of the coasts: the worst, the meanest, the part no one loves. He liked to play at being the typical teenager growing up in the Midwest, in an isolated house surrounded by flat acres of corn: baseball, billiards, ice-cold Buds, hearty breakfasts, barbecue, country music, and sex in motels with washed-out blondes wearing braces. Indignant that in Italy you couldn't get a license at sixteen, he had made his mother buy a pickup with which he, barely fifteen, amused himself, illegally bouncing over the road bumps of Olgiata right before the eyes of those indulgent members of the bourgeoisie (so happy, basically, to see in action the one they consider the son they missed, yes, the son that every young lady hopes to have one day and that every lady regrets not having had).

Although Dav was, in spite of himself, one of that select list of names whom the discotheques of the time fought over—to the point of offering money (as is done today with the starlet of the season) to get exclusive rights and be sure of their presence on Saturday night—he preferred (though not particularly snobbish he did have periodic bursts of annoyance) to gather his little court at home and set up, in the movie room, yet another weary viewing of *Once Upon a Time in America*. It was his film. The quintessence of what cinema and life should hold for a man like him: heroism, anarchy, violence, loyalty, sentimentalism, blood, romantic love, carnal love . . . And, oddly, at the time it escaped me that that suggestive and stylized epic dramatized an event of violent Jewish assimilation: *Once Upon a Time in America* is the story of two street criminals, sons of Jewish émigrés, who want, at any cost, to conquer the New World. It's strange that I didn't even put the question to myself and didn't understand that the emotion Dav tried stubbornly to master and to hide, at the end of the arduous screenings of *Once Upon a Time in America*, derived from a kind of profound, almost unconscious empathy with the two heroes, brilliantly portrayed by Robert De Niro and James Woods. It's obvious that that film worked so well for Dav because it was full of Jews; it's obvious that if it had been full of Italian-Americans it wouldn't have had such a shattering impact on him.

This was David Ruben, our Dav: a concentrate of adrenaline, crazy initiatives, and remote feelings, a bourgeois version of Sordi's *americano a Roma*, so enthralling as to infect an entire community of boys to the point of inducing them, without any coercion, to watch the same film every Saturday night for a whole year. It was really great to let yourself be led by that son of a bitch who, unlike the rest of us, was able to elaborate a completely autonomous world view, and who acted on our inner selves in a way that we wouldn't have been able to explain to anyone who hadn't had the privilege of being a friend of David Ruben, alias Dav.

Well, the consciousness that Dav's world seemed to have engraved most enduringly—and with a violence that made one think of the crime of plagiarism—was that of Giorgio Sevi.

At that time Giorgio was afflicted by boring good looks, certainly exaggerated by the maniacal regimens he inflicted on his body. The surgery he had (secretly) undergone to fix his ears, which he considered too protruding, had had the effect of rendering his charm even more insipid. The nature of that physical attractiveness seemed such as to impress you at a first meeting, when your brain, almost distractedly, placed Giorgio in the category of "good-looking guys." But it was unfortunate that that judgment couldn't stand up to a steady friendship or even an occasional one. Already by the second or third time you saw him, you spontaneously felt critical of the chiseled nose, the artificial ears, eyes that seemed to be drowning in their own fixity. This poor boy seemed to be the innocent victim of the spell cast by a mocking witch, who had amused herself by transforming his handsomeness into something mysteriously irritating. Giorgio's face recalled those annoying background noises that you become aware of when suddenly they stop bothering you. Just so: only when Giorgio's eyes disappeared from your horizon could you understand how much their inexpressiveness had annoyed you. That had made Giorgio one of those sturdy mannequins who in high schools all over the world are popular among younger girls, leaving indifferent (if not actually disgusted) those their own age.

I would like this aesthetic dysfunction to be entered into the record as "Drama No. 1."

Giorgio couldn't have done more: impossible to have a body more sculpted. Yes, perhaps to the pair of weekly visits to the tanning salon he could have added a third, or given his skin another dose of moisturizing cream and his hair another of the magic elixir that prevents baldness. But what's the use if, as every chef well knows, the accumulation of good ingredients—far from guaranteeing a real advantage—serves only the foolish god of overrichness? Giorgio had a gleaming steel Rolex worn strictly on the right, Ray-Bans twenty-four hours a day, a down jacket, an Enduro motorcycle, gelled hair, and a pretentious proclivity for joking and personal contact. In his world, among old friends and relatives, in the nucleus of his institutional supporters, this was enough to make him someone with a great future. But among us, as he realized with dismay, things worked differently. What he had a lot of us had—and this inflation was enough to disqualify even his best gifts. The Ineffable was required, that *je ne sais quoi* which Giorgio couldn't grasp, being limited to painful attempts to guess at it. Everything he had worked for since birth, everything he had laboriously constructed, seemed irrelevant here. What else could he come up with, then? And how to react to the irrational success of young men full of verve but totally without his muscles and resistant to his daily, almost homosexual toilette? Giorgio was like those cameras whose lens never gets the scene in focus. His readings of reality were always pathetically out of focus. Is this why he laughed at remarks that were not amusing and remained unmoved at scenes that were utterly comical? Maybe his misfortune consisted in being intelligent enough to understand the irritation he roused but not enough to remedy it.

And this is definitely "Drama No. 2."

Once at a surprise birthday party of his—organized by his brother, much to his annoyance—I happened to encounter the Sevi parents, who, anything but retiring, were ready to explain to me several things about their son. I noticed the father above all: he wore a wine-colored Armani jacket that barely contained his massive body, blessed by a face that bore unequivocal signs of his peasant origins: narrow eyes, leathery skin, hair painted by Mantegna, and a wrist sparkling with bracelets. What truly gave him away him was the way he talked: Signor Sevi did all he could to push into the depths of his diaphragm the intonations that revealed his humble birth. He was one of those individuals who learned their dialect before Italian and who, in order to become free of the dominating influence of the first and throw themselves completely into the arms of the second, make frightful, self-punishing efforts. It was as if this man, when he spoke—above all with his son's friends or with his wealthy clients—felt himself constantly on the edge of a precipice. One more move of the tongue, a consonant forgotten or unexpectedly doubled, would be enough to hurl him into the abyss of his social origins. But in spite of this small impasse, Signor Sevi had a confidently self-satisfied air, a sign that life, given the premises, had repaid him for every sacrifice. From son of a very humble family to respected businessman who had crowned his miraculous ascent with marriage to the belle of the neighborhood. That triumph, embodied, in his eyes, at least, by two sons of promising attractiveness, was further celebrated by a villa at Casalpalocco whose garden full of palms, cica trees, and lantana mimicked a Caribbean island. At the center of the brightly lit living room shone the immaculate square of a baby grand piano, on which Manuel, Giorgio's younger brother, entertained guests with an embarrassingly mistake-filled version of *Für Elise*, swelling his parents' hearts with a tonic pride.

During that unfortunate party at the Sevis' house, at which I saw Giorgio flare up several times, stricken by his father's blunders and his mother's habit of addressing everyone with the crude Roman colloquial "Hey you," I understood how, in a short time, he had been transformed into one of those boys who, although their parents have given them every material and emotional advantage, can't help being monstrously ashamed of them. It was as if, having worshipped those kind benefactors, throughout his enchanted childhood, with the gratitude of innocent eyes, he now couldn't help seeing them and judging them through the scrim of snobbery that we had been happy to give him for his sixteenth birthday ("Drama No. 3").

But for "Drama No. 4" (the most outrageous and detailed) we have to move on to a "classic" in the pool at Dav's house, the next to last year of high school. We usually go there on Saturdays in the summer, in the early afternoon. Karen is marvelous: on the table under the gazebo we always find trays of sliced watermelon and cantaloupe sitting in a bluish sea of ice. And while we play water polo and the girls sunbathe in dazzling bright-colored bikinis, reluctant to get wet because chlorine is the enemy of melanin, Giorgio, extremely tanned, sitting on the edge of the pool, displays a well-toned physique and an allusive striped bathing suit: he has struggled all winter so the gentle promontory outlined by his dorsals will stand out. He is flexing his arm and making a fist to show us the shape of his triceps. The garden is invaded by euphoric, syncopated music. A mix of hits by Kool & the Gang, simply adored by Dav and by all of us. Suddenly Giorgio, seeing Diamante Arcieri standing by herself and watching, openmouthed, some sixteen-year-olds dancing together like lesbians, calls her over.

Diamante is a dark-haired girl with emerald eyes that seem to have no seductive cunning. One of the rare starlets who aren't stuck up in a school that is an industrial producer of unbelievable vamps, and where financial and physical discrimination is considered not a social distortion but a sign of profound culture. Not that she's easygoing, but her elusiveness seems to depend more on timidity than on arrogance. She's a girl who often stumbles in class, never answers questions, whose hands constantly drop things, whose face turns red for no reason, whose fascination seems to consist in the mystery expressed by that apparent air-headedness. The story is that her father, the majority shareholder in a pharmaceutical company, has a jet. It is said maliciously that she is the only girl of our crowd who has resolutely refused Dav. That rumor has given her an aura of metaphysical inaccessibility, and, in a predictable osmosis, made her, so tiny and insecure, the incarnation of the Impossible Girl.

Is this why, Giorgio, you play the fool with her? Is this why you court her continuously? Because you know that, if you feed ambiguity about a nonexistent relationship, one day you'll be able to say that there was something between you, certain of not being contradicted? That you, Giorgio Sevi, succeeded where David Ruben failed? Is this why your voice is so loud when you call her? Is it possible that every act of yours is subordinated to a self-promotional calculation? And possible that that calculation is always dramatically mistaken?

Now Giorgio is calling her:

"Hey, Diamante, climb on me with both feet. Check out these abs."

"Are you crazy?"

"Come on, don't be scared, it's like walking on a slab of marble," insists our showoff.

She gives in, and, first with one foot, then the other, climbs onto his stomach, getting the attention of the bystanders. Just then the most unpredictably embarrassing thing that could ever happen happens. (We're at the climax of "Drama No. 4.") Giorgio, because of the exertion, emits a long, noisy fart, and she, out of consternation, falls in the water. And while everyone laughs convulsively, Giorgio dives in the pool, pretending to be rushing to the aid of that girl he will never again, for the rest of his life, have the courage to look in the face.

So it seems logical to think that the reason I've been summoned to this flashy bar in Manhattan fifteen years after the events described above is that our Giorgio wants to avenge that long-ago flatulence. So that our new impeccable Giorgio can amuse himself at the expense of the old farting Giorgio. Because there are certain humiliations you can't get free of easily. Because certain shitty adolescent images aren't invalidated by any statute of limitations. They remain attached to you forever. Giorgio wants to cancel out the effect of that laughter, that uncontrollable, irresistible laughter that infected us all, that submerged him until he was liquefied in the blue of the Rubens' pool.

On the telephone, when he got to the point of inviting me, offering the hospitality of his apartment on the Upper West Side ("even a week if you want, Daniel, I've got a ton of space!"), I realized from his breathless insistence that the extraordinary things I had gathered about his professional success must be true: but so threatening and so insecure as to drive him to track down an old high-school acquaintance—so much the better if it was the vile, irritable Daniel Sonnino, even at the cost of burying our unofficial high-school hostility—so that he could at least thrust them in my face. In the end I convinced myself that he wanted to use me as an ambassador to our old friends, toward whom he preserved an unresolved resentment.

It almost seems that for Giorgio the moment has arrived to call in the chits. To collect long overdue credits. Besides, if you've made so much money, how can you enjoy it completely unless your old friends are informed of the details? Unless your Diamante—then indifferent and today distractedly married—knows that you, you yourself, the farter, have made it? And how can it escape me that Giorgio's real companion—the phantom companion—is Dav, that platinum shadow who moves in the blurry backgrounds of our existences? It's for him, in his name and against him, that Giorgio has constructed his life. It's no coincidence that he came to America to seek his fortune, to the country that Dav taught him to idolize. It's no coincidence that he has turned to me, Dav's best friend.

Does Giorgio want me, upon returning to Rome, to convene the high school crowd to celebrate his triumph? To become the promoter of this zillionth *Big Chill,* translated to the putrid banks of the Tiber, where, instead of the dead, the most alive among us is glorified?

Amen. I'm here to serve him.

Go for it, dimwit. We're in the right place, in the guts of the city of colossal fortunes and epic disasters. Let it out, kid, now that you've made it. Now that you're a knockout in that blue chalk-stripe, with the regimental tie that goes so well with the colored-thread cufflinks and the silver curls à la George Clooney. Now that you've gotten what none of us will ever get. Now that you've become what you ardently desired to be. Now that the notorious fart has stopped vibrating. Now that, in a single magisterial blow, you've cancelled out the four dramas of your almost perfect adolescence.

*

But while a waitress with a welcoming smile and a nonexistent skirt comes to serve us, I read in Giorgio's eyes the expression of desolate surprise that even I would try to hide if, after fifteen years of extraordinary success, I was meeting a classmate—an irritable pain in the ass who went down in history as the author of the craziest threatening letter ever written and delivered to an eighteen-year-old of the upper classes—transformed, by time, into an inoffensive ball of fat. That's how I presented myself to him: a good sixty pounds heavier and a hundred thousand hairs lighter with respect to the last time we met. I'm here: with the moist eyes of one who eats, smokes, and drinks continuously, to fill his existential voids, erotic impotence, and a certain creeping rage. I'm afraid that the effect I've produced in his soul isn't too far removed from the one produced in me by Silvia Toffan and by mutilated Manhattan.

How could it have happened?

How can somebody let himself go like this?

Where did this aging cripple come from?

Where's his hair?

How many tons of food has he consumed to put on that belly, that neck, those massive cheeks?

That's the stew of enigmas expressed by the intelligible gaze of Giorgio Sevi, to which my brain seems to respond with a kind of self-inflicted interrogation:

Why are you here?

What's the sense of being here?

Why did you agree to see him?

Why are you so submissive?

Why can't you control yourself?

Until the interrogatory fury becomes general, extending to the entire world, like a Greek chorus:

Can someone explain to us why an individual who has over-

come a thousand traumas, who could speak about the latest, splendid book by Saul Bellow in front of a hundred thousand people packed into a stadium, a guy who—though not a womanizer, or a philanthropist, or particularly pleasing or sympathetic—has had his exciting encounters and his formative experiences, a solid individual, after all . . . at mere contact with one of his old high-school friends turns pale, is once again the frightened child, the stammerer who in the presence of an angel-like Aryan girl didn't know where to put his hands? O.K., so someone solve this mystery for us. Why is he so terrorized, as if he were facing a jury or a firing squad? Why does he keep spilling his drink on the floor? What is different about this Giorgio from all the thousands of people our Daniel meets every day who put him perfectly at ease? What is it that he still has to resolve? What further proof of his value does he have to provide to the community in order not to feel overwhelmed by this indecent specter of asininity?

"So, tell me about yourself," Giorgio says at a certain point, to get rid of that mounting impression of discomfort. "Is it true that you're married?"

"Not true, no."

"I'm confused, then."

"I'm afraid so."

"Then were you about to get married?"

"Never even thought about it. But tell me about you!"

"I can't complain . . ."

Pause. He starts again:

"What would you say to a steak at Smith & Wollensky?"

I make a slight gesture of assent. One of my father's places. Very bourgeois, a little out of fashion, but not bad.

"Though we might need a reservation," he says then, disappointed by my willingness. "If you don't get a table at the back, where it's more sheltered and quieter, it's a torture."

"Look, Giò, for me it's all the same." (*All the same? Do you hear yourself? Are you mad? Why are you talking like this? Why do you want to give the impression that you're not an exacting type? You are an exacting type! Why hide it? What the hell is happening to you?*) "And Cipriani?" I say then to let him see that I'm an expert. "You know, the owner, the son of the old Arrigo, is a friend of my parents'."

Nothing has changed since then: pretensions, imperturbable pretensions tempered by false nonchalance.

"The most fantastic lasagne in Manhattan," I add triumphantly, to go along with his tone. The absolute superlative is a legacy of those years; grammatical euphoria was the currency of our continuous one-upmanship.

"Well, if you want to meet the crème de la crème of Italian yuppies abroad, showing off their shit Palm pilots and Daytonas . . . help yourself," he stings me, affecting scorn.

"Anyway, how are things going?" he asks again, after yet another swallow of his bloody Mary and yet another pause. "Don't tell me that Daniel Sonnino has lost his voice? Tell me about your wife, at least!"

I'm afraid that this obstinate curiosity about some presumed consort of mine is merely a diversionary tactic in preparation for the information about himself that he is going to lavish on me. In fact he ardently wants me to be married because he can't wait to counter the sinister and melancholy monogamy of an unsatisfied bourgeois with the polygamous excesses of a successful man.

Isn't that what we're here for?

So let's get hit by a torrential seminar on happiness.

He's a manager in an American-based multinational food company. He's the director of the frozen-food division. He has, as they say, shot ahead and routed the competition from older colleagues, thanks to some surprising marketing intuitions. Having thirsted throughout his adolescence for approbation, he couldn't do otherwise than make his profession the study of the mysterious gears of consensus. He is paid to seduce, and from what I can see he's really good at it.

Evidently it's important to let me know that he lives in Milan and New York, in two sumptuous apartments paid for by the company. He has the nerve to complain about the inadequacy of his salary: seven hundred thousand dollars a year, not counting production bonuses and stock options and skipping over many other benefits. Plus he's installed in an office up in the stars, on the sixtieth floor of the ITT building, has a caravan of secretaries, a personal trainer who follows him to the ends of the earth, a finely calibrated hypocaloric diet, a Mexican housekeeping couple and an entire litter of Labradors, a BMWx5, a collection of Harleys, a house in Southampton whose cellar has a pool full of live lobsters, and many other unimaginable things that would delight any boy who had grown up in the anguished and fictitious glory of our pretentious high school in the nineteen-eighties.

And how can such a depressing show of prosperity not unleash a metamorphosis in me? Inevitable. It was waiting in ambush. I can't repress it. It grabs my calf like a shark. I am at the mercy of the metamorphosis, like certain characters in the comics, like the Incredible Hulk. The atavistic adolescent in me has seized the upper hand over the so-called adult in a Manhattan bar. It's no joke to embody—even if at a fixed time, even if it's only an evening—the very idea of Failure! It's a nagging sensation that, after five drinks, intensifies. It's as if another self, much more powerful and at the same time much more fragile, had emerged, exhumed by the fear that meeting an acquaintance at the apex of ascent has inspired in me: a fear I thought I couldn't feel anymore, a fear overcome, attached to a past time of my life, a relic consigned to History. But—obviously—it was there. The fear of not making it. Of not being up to it. A fear of inadequacy. It's He—God the Avenger—who is speaking for me. Giorgio has resuscitated him. And now the zombie is here, among us again.

So I find myself talking nonsense, just as I did then, with the same painful intensity, with the same lowered eyes, with the voice that tries not to tremble, in a tone that is elated and desperate. Maybe what I've lost is the shamelessness of the professional bullshitter, the power of foolishly believing the lie I'm telling: what's missing is a little healthy practice! Maybe that's why the lies seem so different from the ones I prepared as a boy. Today I'm transfiguring reality, then I invented out of whole cloth. Back then my torrential speeches overflowed with girls I'd fucked on the beach, journeys to the ends of the earth, circumnavigations of Africa on fabulous yachts. Back then my lying had something about it of the heroically titanic.

"Did I tell you I won the competition for a professorship? But yes, you know, isn't that how you found me?"

"I thought you were an adjunct. At least that's what it said on the university Web site, if I'm not mistaken."

"Oh yes, probably since I just got it they haven't updated it yet, I mean the site . . ."

"Ah, I see . . ."

"In the meantime I've written a book. Well received. It must have sold almost . . . almost . . . ten thousand copies. Of course, not much in absolute terms, but for an essay in literary sociology it's like a best-seller. Especially since it roused some interest here in the States. Just think, only three months ago I gave a lecture at Harvard. You should have seen how many people, and what level. A hundred academics. An élite group. There, listening to me. Pretty gratifying . . . all with my book in their hand."

"So it's been translated?"

"Not exactly . . . That is, yes . . . I mean just a few copies, for the university . . ."

"By the way, where was the lecture?"

"What do you mean?"

"Well, what hall? What building? I know Harvard, I lived in Cambridge for three years. I did an MBA there: the best years of my life . . ."

"Actually I don't remember? You know, I was out of it . . . They led me around . . . It was raining . . . And after all it was a little while ago . . ."

And meanwhile I drink, I down my sixth bloody Mary.

And now the death blow.

"Are you writing something else?" He shoots me point-blank.

If I were honest I would answer: "No, I'm not writing anything." Ever since I wrote that fucking essay (whether for or against the Jews no one has ever figured out) I haven't been able to write anything. It's sad that one little diatribe has dried up all my creative reserves. It's pathetic that the greatest effort of literary muscle lavished by Dr. Daniel Sonnino—adjunct professor at one of the many universities of Rome—in the first thirty years of his useless existence should be consumed so rapidly on the pyre that he so vulgarly erected in order to destroy the image of his favorite Jewish writers. It's disconcerting that the *sole* occasion granted him should have been tainted by envy for the great, prolific writers who have saved and destroyed his life. It's discouraging that, setting out to write an essay, he built a mausoleum dedicated to Envy.

And instead I answer: "Yes, a novel. Almost finished. It's with an agent . . ." (As I utter these words I feel my head invaded by a sudden vertigo. It's been seventeen years—seventeen years!—since I was a raw youth tortured by burning dreams of glory, since I've done nothing but repeat to everyone, but especially to myself, that *I've almost finished a novel.* I think that the majority of my acquaintances have realized for at least a decade that I will never finish that novel, that it existed only in the fantasy of a megalomaniac kid. However, now *I* understand, while yet again I answer the question by saying that *the novel is almost finished* . . . It's one of the mechanisms of bad faith that help us to live. As when gravely and sadly I say to my students, "You know, kids, the novel is dead!" or "It's so difficult to write a masterpiece before the age of fifty. Look at Proust." Standard declarations that, if any one had wanted to decode them, would mean this: "It's not the novel that's dead, if anything I'm dead as a novelist even before birth. In any case, not to worry, because I've still got fifteen years to write *À la Recherche*." "But professor," a malicious girl once nailed me—may God get rid of her as soon as possible—"didn't Proust start writing *À la Recherche* at thirty-three?" "Well, we're not sure about that . . ." I corrected her pedantically.)

"Why are you going back to Rome so soon?" he asks after a long pause, and his tone has become (at least it seems to me) dry, almost inquisitorial. "Didn't you say you were staying at least a week?"

"You won't believe it!"

"What?"

"I'm going to a funeral."

"I'm sorry. Did someone close to you die?"

"Not exactly."

"So?"

"The funeral of Nanni Cittadini."

"Gaia's grandfather?"

"Precisely."

"Good Lord, are you crazy?"

"It's true."

"Shit, don't you ever have enough?"

"Well, it seemed like a nice thing . . . A conciliatory gesture . . ."

From this point on I'm not responsible for what I say. I don't know if what I'm about to recount is an event or a hallucination. I don't know if it really happened or if it's simply a consequence of drunkenness. A banal alcoholic rant. Or even the paroxysmic echo of my Catholic-Jewish Sense of Guilt.

Suddenly Giorgio turns serious and says:

"You're the most despicable person I've ever met."

"What?"

"You heard me perfectly well, spare me the role of the drunk."

"No, it's just that . . ."

"You always have been, anyway. I thought you would turn out better. And instead look at you, you're disgusting."

"Don't you think you're exaggerating?"

"I know guys like you. This city is full of guys like you. They even resemble you physically. They all have your anteater profile and the lenses of their glasses are scratched. Always ready to show off your books, your sensibilities, and the Jews and the Holocaust and all that other crap . . ."

"What does the Holocaust have to do with it?"

". . . And you claim that others respect you. Why? Do you have more rights than we do? Because if Diamante stands me up it's normal, she has her reasons and the right to choose . . . while if Gaia rejects you, Mr. Sensitivity, Mr. I Know Everything, Mr. Holocaust 1989, she does it for deep, obscure reasons, because she's a whore, an anti-Semitic head-giver. Can you explain that? What in the world were you thinking when you threatened to kill her?"

"Come on, it was just a manner of speaking. I didn't have any serious intentions . . . I was bluffing. It was a dialectic provocation. A surrealist gambit."

". . . And the most incredible, the funniest thing is that after causing all that mess, rather than disappear and never be seen again, you showed up at her party, you got drunk, insulting everything and everyone. He arrives, the inconsolable one, and ruins everything. All I'm saying is you could have vanished. Gotten out of the way. It would have been more dignified. And instead you started an election campaign."

"Election campaign?"

"Yes, the most unbelievable campaign of self-promotion I've ever seen. You tried to extort our solidarity. You wanted to convince us that She was wicked, that She had deceived you, frustrated you, that She was absolute evil . . . You remember when you dared to compare her to Adolf Hitler? Yes, that was the tone of your propaganda. And you know what the irony is?"

"I'm sure you're about to tell me."

"That a lot of us ended up believing you. Not me, of course, but a lot of people did. You corrupted them. That's what I think. And now after all these years you show up and you tell me this crap! And you tell me you're going to the funeral of Gaia's grandfather. As if nothing had happened. As if so many years hadn't gone by. As if in that grotesque letter you hadn't threatened her with death. Come on, Daniel, don't you know words like 'shame,' 'dignity,' 'decorum'?"

"I told you, I had no intention of killing her . . . It was a joke . . . Bullshit . . . But why try to explain it to you? Basically you've never had a sense of humor . . . Take that fart, for example. You made yourself sick over it . . ."

"What are you talking about?"

"Come on, don't be melodramatic, you know perfectly well what fart I'm referring to . . . Don't be modest! There's only one big fart that's gone down in History. And you have the honor of being its author."

"You're a shit, Daniel."

"Imagine, I ran into Diamante recently and she asked me about you: 'Have you seen the petomaniac?' and I started laughing, because I have a sense of humor . . ."

"What a shit . . ."

"O.K., you're right, there was no need to drag up that story. But you started it, after all. You're the one who summoned the ghosts. *You're the one who opened the drawers.* You know, after a certain age, it's better to keep them closed, those fucking drawers! And if you want to know what I think, I'll tell you that Gaia didn't have the right . . ."

"Didn't have what right? Can you tell me that? Didn't have the right to fuck, to give blow jobs . . .?"

"Well, it would have been nicer if she'd done it to one guy at a time. After all she was only fourteen."

"You wanted to murder a girl who gave blow jobs when she was fourteen? Is that what you're trying to tell me? You mean to say that if she had waited another couple of years, then you would have understood? You mean that if she hadn't been a minor you would have approved?"

"No, come on, putting it that way makes no sense . . . And cut out this bullshit: I didn't want to kill anyone!"

"The truth is that certain precocious girls should be glorified. Come on, Daniel, it's not a crime to give someone a blow job. It's a pleasure to do, and, if you really want to know, it's even better to get one. We're not in Iran. Our constitution allows anyone who wants to give or get a blow job . . . And instead you turned it into a huge mess, bringing up things that had nothing to do with it, diverting our attention from the facts . . . You were always taking our eyes off the facts. You weren't so smart as you thought, you were just a vulgar con artist, that's what you were, if you really want to know . . . I never understood why someone like Dav gave you so much credit. It's really a mystery! He should see you today. You're a perfect picture of failure. You and your future best-sellers! You and your totally invented Harvard lectures . . . You know what? I know Patagonia better than you know Harvard . . ."

"Have you been to Patagonia?"

While Giorgio gets all steamed up in what I still don't know precisely whether to place in the category of alcoholic hallucinations or that of historically verifiable facts, I unexpectedly find myself in a good mood. And then—I think to myself, lighting my faithful cigar, defying the prohibition of the bar and the indignation of the onlookers—if it's true that in those years I made so much noise, if it's true that I was the hypocritical Moralizer, a cross between Cromwell, Savonarola, and Tartuffe, if I bugged everyone in that disgraceful way . . . yes, if all that is true and not the invention of a furious ex-friend or of my alcoholic haze, then, in spite of the sensation of colorless vacuity that has afflicted me for thirty years, I really did exist.

2. Some Peace Amid the Clouds

Only now, after I've left Giorgio, pretending to be offended by his cutting words (the final lie in a painful encounter devoted to deception), now that, having arrived by taxi at Newark, stubbornly reflecting the whole way, saturated with crippled Manhattan fading behind and inside me in the rose-gilded mirrors of sunset, now that I'm about to get on the plane for the trip back to Rome for the funeral of old Nanni and many other things . . . Only at this point, after being literally hurled into my past, do I see appearing, in its revolting density, the story of Gaia, Nanni, Dav, and all the others. And as I give my ticket to the hostess and look around to make sure that none of my fellow-passengers has the hard look of an Islamic terrorist, I feel a throbbing desire to make my way again through that story: appropriate it for myself one last time. Start from zero, even if I have to work all night, suspended in my moving empyrean at thirty thousand feet above the Atlantic Ocean, traveling toward that magnificent sun-baked city where everything began.

I would love to be able to say that I didn't like Gaia instantly, that the sight of that pale girl with the diaphanous veins in her neck and wrists, that dear creature in the blue-and-white striped T-shirt, that teenager with a watery-green silk foulard on her head that made her look like Jackie Kennedy or a Pontormo Madonna as she climbed out of the wooden motorboat Riva at the wharf at Positano on a summer afternoon in 1984, left me indifferent. I would prefer to chalk it up to psychology, hide behind some suggestive definition: to maintain that the days of that unfamiliar life in the Cittadini villa, the continuing, unjustified absence of my mother, and the unbearable presence of Giacomo, who had instituted a "strike of silence" against Nanni and his guests, had weakened my nervous system to the point of placing me in the debilitated state of mind that precedes every amorous mirage. I would like to be able to say that that spell, a first taste of my youthful disaster, originated in a weakness, an inexorable hormonal need. Or even adopt a pathetic register, asserting that being in the presence of a delicate girl whose father had killed himself overwhelmed me to the point of mobilizing Jewish idealism and Catholic solidarity simultaneously. I would like to be able to say that I became infatuated with an idea, an idea that loomed over us all, a contagious collective utopia that imposed on the girls of that epoch the pursuit of a fleeting, almost abstract beauty. I would like to be able to say that the impression gained from the consciousness that she was perfectly aware of who I was, where

I came from, of the proportions of my inferiority with respect to her, excited my body in an ominous way. I would like to be able to say that the historical circumstances, the sort of *pax romana* established by President Ronald Reagan (that siliconed soldier of fortune destined to win the Cold War), had made me sentimental, lowered my immune defenses.

But I can do nothing other than give in to the crude truth.

Gaia, with her eyes the color of a sea breeze, was a knockout, and for reasons diametrically opposed to the ones I would cite over the years to myself and to my enchanted listeners. It's not true that I was attracted by the banality of privilege (a type of snobbishness elaborated later). Or that I was dramatically influenced by experiencing for the first time the masochistic paradigm that placed me in a position of clear subjugation toward someone my own age (she was exactly a year younger than me, but so much more aware . . .). I would be continuing the falsehood by declaring that she was like all the others, a product of her refined environment, with something arid and obsequious, one of the thousand clones of those years, a marble image of haute-bourgeois insubstantiality (in fact I'm afraid that such definitions are more suited to myself at that age). By that I don't mean that that passion, fated over the years to exhaust itself well beyond the threshold of obsession, did not rest on a subjective evaluation, on my very personal taste for diaphanous flesh. (It's almost obvious to say it: otherwise everyone would have fallen in love with her and everyone would have ended up writing her that odious letter . . .) I would like to scale back that subjectivity, however. I would like to make it clear that I was not in love with a porcupine or a mathematical formula or, still less, a patriotic symbol. Rather, a girl at the peak of her flourishing splendor, who had the requirements necessary to make half the adult population of Positano fall in love with her in that burning-hot 1984. That's what I'm trying to say.

Without intending, with this, to deny that I was in the right state of mind for complete abandonment. The apple was ripe for picking. The sequence seems treacherously perfect, like a Hitchcockian plot: first the vacation in England, which serves to show me the licentious face of the other sex, and the scabrous side of female sexuality itself (impressed in my nostrils was the stench given off by my brother's fingers: that miasma right out of a Sicilian fish market). Then there is the long (so it appeared to me) journey-ordeal in my father's Porsche on a dry midsummer afternoon through a Dantesque alternation of environmental abuses and paradisiacal visions. Nanni's luxurious house, with its rules of good citizenship and harmony. The exposure to the sun that colored my arms and forehead and bleached my hair. The view every morning at breakfast. The aromatic rumbling of the coffeepot on the kitchen stove. The veil of nutella that I spread furtively on my tongue to give myself courage. The crumbling yellow of the walls bordering the paths that every morning we walk along, my father and I, to go and buy the five daily papers, the car magazines, and the crossword puzzle weekly. The scent of suntan lotion. The brown skin of the local kids who show up on the slender strip of sand that constitutes the beach of Positano. The drawling English of Americans on holiday. The bright-colored cosmopolitan river of men with white caps and the rainbow pareos of their elderly ladies. The contours of imposing yachts docked in the harbor for days right before my eyes, but so unattainable they seem as fantastic as pirate ships! The memory of Bepy, who has been dead for just a year, evoked by iced tea with granita (an "on the rocks" version of Proustian reminiscence). The glowing lobsters of the Covo dei Saraceni. The pergola of vines under which we dine in the evening. The sour greenish taste of the single sip of Falanghina I'm allowed every night. The methodical echo of the waves from the private inlet under my window just before I fall asleep. Given such premises, I defy anyone not to fall in love.

Is it possible that the synesthetic tangle of these impressions altered the normal equilibrium of my system? And then look how everything tends to an indescribable fullness. With a single worry: how long will I hold off my pernicious tendency for accidents, an untamable and violent force that since childhood has caused me to spill a glass of water on the master of the house at least a couple of times a meal, or bump into a valuable object, shattering it? For how many days will I rein in my nature as a professional klutz, if everything in this house seems to allude to a metaphysical fragility, and if the excess of attention has reduced my movements to the brief, syncopated jerks of a pathetic Pinocchio?

Let's suppose that Gerhard Fischer, a vigorous middle-aged German, his forehead protected by a broad-brimmed vanilla-colored panama hat—the photographer for the now defunct magazine *Fashion Press*, specializing in articles on great vacation spots for pretentious Anglo-American couples—found himself in the summer of '84 doing a photographic essay on Positano. Let's suppose that our Gerhard had gone out in a small rented boat at six-thirty in the evening intending to be about half a mile from the coast a little before seven so that he could photograph Positano and its surroundings in a delicate twilight. Let's suppose that for days he had been waiting for that light: that seductive light absolutely forbidden to art, a light authorized only by postcards: that sunset light that Americans are fond of (as were the Venetians of the sixteenth century). Let's suppose that he were to find himself just opposite Nanni's villa at the precise instant my father and I parked the car and the usual platoon of minute domestic servants met us to help unload the suitcases, and I felt unable to breathe, as if confronted with something that offended me personally: well, I'm sure that Gerhard, in a completely different emotional condition from mine, would have begun to photograph rapaciously. I'm sure that he wouldn't have let that house escape him (although, given the dimensions of the complex, I ought to use the ridiculous term "fortress"), that he would not have given up the privilege of immortalizing that labyrinth of stairs, terraces, and overhanging white-orange structures cleverly perched on the side of the cliff, from the shady beach up almost to the starry heights of Monte Pertuso, bathed in the coppery light of early evening. Because, although it might appear incredible to you—almost humiliating—Nanni possessed a piece of the coast in one of the most evocative places on the planet, exactly equidistant between Zeffirelli's villa and the Hotel San Pietro. That's why the German photographer would have been astounded, wondering who in the world could have deserved to live in a vertical paradise like that.

The most interesting part of the place was the middle section: balconies and pergolas and a panoramic saltwater swimming pool, whose left wall had been left deliberately rough. Every morning a pump sucked the water from the sea and, after purifying it, poured it into the pool through a hole in the rock, like an artificial waterfall. Inside, the villa was a succession of arches and stone hearths that highlighted a restored floor from the early twentieth century: sparkling mosaic of turquoise majolica with designs that vaguely recalled Renaissance grotesques. The furniture, for the most part colonial, not valuable—as Nanni explained to us—had been collected by the former owner during a life of travel. That's why that hodgepodge of low Indonesian tables, aboriginal ornaments, Berber carpets, striped tapestries, and various chinoiseries made you feel you were in the anachronistic dwelling of an English civil servant on the banks of the Ganges at the end of the nineteenth century. Chesterfield armchairs of cream-colored leather, placed like sentinels at the windows, flirted with the white walls, saturated with light, and broke up the darkness of the decor. It was one of those houses-in-progress that the owners never finish furnishing. There was no lack of valuable pieces from Nanni's own collection, as he hastened to show us. He had recently discovered Art Deco, and, in the space of a short time, and at fabulous expense, had acquired a vase by Rene Buthaud, lacquered boxes by Sinobu Tsuda, a silver tea service by Puiforcat—*objets* that adorned the large living room and sent my father into ecstasies. The house's most precious possession, however, was the panoramic view that one had from the large floor-to-ceiling window, as if from the highest and most dizzying deck of a transatlantic liner. And it was magnificent to sit in one of those sofas covered in a pale material and let oneself be hypnotized by the boundlessness of the sea.

And yet the secret attraction of that dream house, which, with its glamorous contents, unpredictable openings, and unexpected, breathtaking views, seemed made purposely to torture a boy born in the early seventies and fed on the conviction that the entire world was being consumed in a wild competition for wealth, had no relation to that succession of precious objects and spectacular vistas . . . The secret, magnetic masterpiece of that house, which our Gerhard would never have been able to imagine, was a door.

That door, in essence no different from the others though kept strictly locked, seemed to protect an unimaginable secret. My mind—perhaps still under the influence of visits to English castles—imagined that it guarded an enormous, splendid, thick-walled room, not unlike the one inhabited by Henry VIII: Gaia's room.

Yes, that door guarded an expectation, and not a generic expectation, not a metaphysical wait, not the usual Godot or the trite *Desert of the Tartars*. I mean a circumscribed and circumstantial wait that seemed to have infected everyone: the expectation that Gaia, whose beauty seemed consecrated by this villa like that of Aphrodite by certain ancient temples, would deign to return from her little Capri vacation. Now, that there existed a girl, who was my age, and capable, solely by her absence and by the promise of an imminent return, of setting in motion the mechanism of that dwelling, seemed to me the strangest phenomenon I had ever witnessed.

And how could my surprise not be intensified by the incredible behavior of the old man?

He was simply beside himself. He seemed like the priest officiating at a pagan rite. As if he were waiting for the visit of a head of state, he did nothing but admonish the servants with tedious commands: "Consuelo, remember that for the fusilli with zucchini you are to use a lot of basil and no *parmigiana*, the way Gaia likes it . . . Why hasn't the plumber come yet? The water massage needs to be adjusted, otherwise my girl . . ."

Yes, this absent goddess, this blood-sucking vampire, to whom Nanni seemed to allude with every gesture of his hands and every syllable uttered by his mouth, was the spectral monarch who had been looming over the domestic arrangements for almost six days. For Nanni, evidently, it was more important to make an impression on his granddaughter than on my father. This to me was absurd, sacrilegious, painful, but above all exciting. One had the impression that the entire nucleus of that seaside town had been alerted. And that all this should happen for a girl whose face—very pretty, it has to be said, but let's not exaggerate!—seemed to multiply as in a vaporous obsession, in all the photographs scattered through the house, made my wait even grimmer. And the fact that Nanni's frenzy might be a small tile in a broader psychological mosaic (at the time totally incomprehensible to me) that, if someone had been interested in reconstructing it, would have—who knows—shown the ominous, but, in spite of everything, not tragic, figure of the suicide Ricky Cittadini, is a later thought that neither adds to nor subtracts from my pathos of the moment and my anxious astonishment.

*

Furthermore, the mystery of that closed door highlighted—by contrast—the immodesty of the adjacent door, which was almost always open. Not to close the door of his room was one of the many strategies adopted by Giacomo to differentiate himself from his sister and to exasperate his grandfather. The message was explicit: I'm not a mysterious type, I have nothing to hide, I do not follow this family's grotesque program of self-celebration. Look how that boy exposed himself to the startled gaze of the world. Not infrequently, passing near the bathroom, I saw him peeing into the sink with an affectedly ecstatic expression. And often he would strip naked and lie on his bed in view of the open door.

And then there was that damn "strike of silence," which brought with it other intolerable eccentricities. Not only had Giacomo determined not to speak a word to Nanni or my father or even to me but he had decided to abandon the sun. He lived as a recluse, his blinds lowered, as if he wished to differentiate himself in every way from the tanned tribe around Nanni's pool. Giacomo spoke only to the servants. This obsolete form of reverse snobbery wouldn't have particularly bothered me if one night I hadn't witnessed a singular scene. I had gone to the kitchen to get a glass for my father and stopped in the doorway dumbstruck. There before me were the four servants, for once dressed in normal clothes, sitting around the big rectangular table, which had been set, if possible, even more elaborately than Nanni insisted on every evening at his table under the pergola of orange blossoms. They were eating silently and in some embarrassment. Until I saw, standing there stiffly, and holding a tray in his hand the way you're taught in hotel school, an improvised waiter in a striped suit with gold frogs and immaculate gloves. It was Giacomo. Yes, Giacomo, serving dinner to his grandfather's servants. I had the wit to slip away before anyone saw me. But I couldn't get rid of a

strange discomfort. It was natural to wonder if that performance was repeated every evening, or only every so often. Or if
I'd had the honor of being present at a première. And then so
many other questions: Did he make them do it? Or was it they
who had coerced him? Did Nanni know? And if he knew why
didn't he intervene? Why did Nanni, whose severity seemed to
have something emblematic, show such careless indulgence for
Giacomo's eccentricities and the arrogance of his servants?
Was it a pedagogical strategy or a sign of surrender? Maybe
Nanni not only knew but was himself the one who'd had the
idea, who was the screenwriter and the director of that farce?
Maybe it was part of his notorious educational methods? What
did Nanni feel toward that boy? Affection? Shame? Pity?
Rage?

What will Gaia Cittadini think of me? (And who knows
why her last name was indispensable?)
This question was so fixed in my mind that sometimes I
woke in the middle of the night to look at myself in the mirror,
in an attempt to guess what might be the precise effect that my
person—that disreputable advertisement for the Jewish people—would produce on her.
And then I would go back to imagining the locked door,
would suddenly feel like getting up to make a furtive pilgrimage to that wailing wall, and, finally, went back to asking the
stars:
What will Gaia Cittadini think of me?
This question had the same desperate intonation as the one
that I addressed to myself many years later with regard to the
effect that my writings might produce on some cruel and indifferent mass-market publisher.
If I had only had a little more lucidity and cold-bloodedness
I probably would have managed to formulate questions that
were more exacting and appropriate, for example: *What might*

all these regal attentions do to the mind of a child? What indelible mark might they leave on her face or her behavior? But in my state of semi-prostration, made more acute by all that dazzle, I had been able to take refuge only in a single, tormenting question:

What will Gaia Cittadini think of me?

That's the mother of all questions: so that my subsequent five-year alliance with Gaia, marked by a series of indelible humiliations, is summed up in this question (*What will Gaia Cittadini think of me?*), far more than in all the temporary and varying answers I would try to give. Not only that: if an ounce of that now extirpated pain persists in any region of my body, I'm sure that it has to do with this tormenting query: *What will Gaia Cittadini think of me?* On the other hand I have the obscure feeling that if only I had changed the terms of the question, even so far as to turn it upside down—What do I think of Gaia Cittadini?—well, I think everything would have been different. And yet, strange as it may seem, not once did I find the strength or dignity to ask myself a natural question, indicating a certain critical spirit, such as: *What do I think of her?* Further: I'm afraid that if I had had the strength to extend this question to the whole crowd I spent my time with, if I had asked myself, trying to read my inner self, *Come on, Daniel, what do you think of them?,* rather than taking refuge in the trite and obsessive *What will they think of me?,* then, maybe, who knows . . . Besides, what distinguishes my brother Lorenzo's exemplary experience from my own so disastrous one may be the fact that he had the strength and the sense of irony not only to ask himself from the beginning *What do I think of them?* but also to answer in his own proudly graphic manner: *I think they're a bunch of paranoid shits!* There is no other significant difference between me and Lorenzo except that he managed to establish with that cruel world a boldly convex relationship, while I locked myself in an obtuse concavity. And this was enough, evidently: because our condition was otherwise nearly identical: we had the same father and the same mother, the same culture, the same money at our disposal, the same uncertain religious identity, the same introspective capacity, the same egotistical bent, the same dark eyes, the same incipient baldness, the same defective "s"s . . . And so you'd have to conclude that it was only a different mental attitude that determined his serenity and my loud crash.

(A few weeks ago I was lounging in my living room, embracing a big bottle of Coca-Cola, and reaching into a bowl of peanuts. I was watching TV, as I often am these days. Just reviving after the offensive tedium of my morning's work. Ever since I've had this precarious position at the university, ever since I became aware that my relationship with Sharon, my girlfriend, is in shreds, ever since I began stuffing myself every day with enough food to last a week, my life has lost any value or appeal, becoming a den for thousands of obsessions and other vices. I have no desire to study, to see other people, to go away, to go to a game, to teach, to visit museums, to write even a line on dead writers, to betray Sharon or, still less, imagine an alternative to her . . . I watch life run by on the dead tracks of grim fantasies about my classmates. I like seeing them die in weird accidents: I see Dav drown in a swimming pool full of Dom Pérignon. I see Diamante Arcieri hit in the forehead by a meteorite made of truffles from Alba. I see Silvia Toffan lose her arms, too, mutilated by an enormous Gucci paper-cutter.

The only enduring passions, right behind masturbation—which has lost the pioneering appeal of puberty to become a beloved companion for life!—are PlayStation 2 and satellite TV. Yes, my real existence, now, is the very brief interlude between a wank and an exhausting television session. I sit down in front of the screen, alone: and while everyone else is working—or at least has the decorum to pretend to do so—I set out on journeys through documentaries on vampires of the earth, sophisticated recipes, aerobics classes, detailed explorations of the savanna or the virgin forest, long digressions on Nasdaq, on hi-tech, on Japanese design.

Well, that day I was tuned in to one of my favorite satellite stations, Wishline Channel: yes, the planet of unrealizable desires, a channel that broadcasts auctions of stuff for millionaires at inaccessible prices—sultanesque yachts, panoramic Tuscan estates and Provençal castles, supersonic jets, custommade cars . . . Suddenly I literally jumped up out of my chair, as I saw appearing on the screen, incredible and unthinkable, Nanni's villa at Positano. Suddenly I was catapulted from the impersonal view of a TV camera into the confused bog of my past: suddenly I entered Gaia's room—of such a nature was my violation!—and Nanni's, and even the one assigned to me, while the voice of the seller tried to lure impossible buyers with conventional expressions:

"The astounding view from the small balcony looking out on the gulf is a fine companion for those who want to dine in the company of friends amid the most evocative scenery on the Amalfi coast . . ." said the voice, and I was stunned.

If Nanni adored that house, why did he want to get rid of it? What did Gaia think of all this? And how was I supposed to take it . . . ?

You don't need a degree in psychology to understand that these were the old questions, but they were no longer getting me worked up. I was inside those images, slightly irritated by the coldness of the descriptions, slightly disappointed by the fact that the rooms couldn't stand up to the brilliance of memory. The Positano villa seemed a dead place, a place where it was impossible to live or to have lived, a place that must have been inhabited a hundred years ago by men in wigs, by zombies, a place that emitted an odor of dust and dampness. Well, no, it resembled the set of a soap opera: an improbable house inhabited by improbable creatures—a disappointing myth. Certainly not the concrete space as I seemed to remember it and as it then appeared to me.

But a slightly diffuse shadow made it live again, canceling out the first impression.

Because, right after putting a cassette in the VCR and pushing the REC button to record the show for my father, I saw on the screen, reflected in one of the grand living-room windows, an image: the figure of a woman. I let the segment end while in me a strange anguish mounted that had nothing to do with the choking vises of long ago: it was a vertigo, as if the world had unexpectedly stopped turning. As if my life had been rolled up into the narrow space of an instant. And then, slowly, with hands that barely responded to the confused impulses of the brain, I rewound the tape to the offending point in the hope of stopping that shadow with the pause button.

Gaia!

There was no doubt. At least it seemed to me. A thirty-year-old Gaia. So a Gaia that made no sense. I was furious that I hadn't managed to see and record the whole program. Maybe in the first part of the show she had appeared just as the years had changed her. But why did I care so much? Curiosity, certainly. But also a subtle form of fetishism. With the hint of a death wish that accompanies every fetishism.

Was I suffering?

I asked with the same detachment with which I had asked myself the previous questions. No, I wasn't suffering. There was nothing overwhelming, nothing in that stolen image that fed nostalgia. I felt sick to my stomach, if anything. A bitter taste in my mouth, so that all I could do was cling to the Coke bottle and plunge my hands in the bowl of peanuts, as if to scrape the bottom.

But if I wasn't suffering, if I wasn't frightened, if I wasn't on the brink of emotional collapse, if I really couldn't care less, if that calm displayed to myself wasn't yet another demonstration of my thirty years' bad faith—as I never tired of repeating to myself—why were my eyes glued to the television? Why, with the intensity of a stray dog digging in the garbage, was I trying to seize, in the pale reflection in the window that the pause button made even fainter, incontrovertible proof of Gaia's presumed physical decline?

Maybe I needed my proper ration of expectation. The right dose. Nothing exaggerated. Maybe what distinguished the house of that time from the one of today was simply the expectation: take away from something the expectation and you lose its only treasure. Nothing has value without expectation. Expectation is God. There exists no other God beyond expectation. Expectation explains everything: why we go forward. Why we don't drown. Why we let ourselves be seduced by what is not in itself seductive. Expectation is the only passion of my life.

I don't know anything else. There is nothing else to know. And now, with the lesson over, I'll take up where I left off. Can you see Gaia climbing onto the wharf with the grace and solemnity of Jacqueline Kennedy and a Pontormo Madonna? Well, from her—and from her imprudent worshiper—expect anything.)

Only in the presence of Dav had I felt a physical unease vaguely comparable to that sense of oppressive weight that hit me on seeing that little sailor girl disembark from her motorboat. An instant was enough for me to feel afflicted by a so-called "ostrich syndrome": that defective mechanism which gives the Subject the delusion that to take away his gaze from the Object is equivalent to disappearing. And although I had chosen not to look, to avoid that astonishing vision, I was about to explode, saturated by an image that was already flowing through my veins. Like a blue brushstroke on the gray walls of my life. Like a shrill bucket of cold water after a sleep lasting for years. But at the same time it was as if the vague sense of inadequacy I had felt during six days in Nanni's house had found its ineluctable outlet in that cobalt stain. As if I had inhaled a balm of knowledge: only now did I see that my life up to now had been deprived of something fundamental: from tomorrow things would be different, everything that had interested me would interest me no longer, just as I would have to reconsider everything that concerned me.

What's the sense of looking down on yourself thin?, I would ask myself many years later. From a distance? And at the same time very close up? Why did I see every pimple, every blackhead, every small imperfection of my nose? Why did my nose suddenly occupy every present or potential thought? Why did my nose fill the horizon like a gigantic cliff? Why did my teeth press against my lips as if to show themselves in all their ugly imperfection? Why did a single molar seem as big and heavy as a boulder?

"Let me introduce *Daniel*, Luca's son, Bepy's grandson," Nanni said to Gaia, peremptorily biblical, as if he were reading a death sentence. And never had my name (Daniel) seemed to indicate such a stupidly concrete referent.

"CIAO, DANIEL," she said as if to rehabilitate it . . .

. . . It was then that I felt that the deal was done; it was then that I perceived my future in a strange backward glance at the end of which there was nothing but Gaia; it was then that I understood (with a clarity that today perhaps I tend to exaggerate) not only that I would never be liberated but that that outdated form of liberty would no longer interest me. That there existed a strict semantic correlation between liberty and death. It was then that I had the disquieting presentiment that the existence of that girl humiliated me and that the only way of escaping my condition of annihilating inferiority was to kill her with my own hands.

That's why an account of the next two weeks of our stay in Positano seems pleonastic and irrelevant. I don't even feel like recounting it. These words of Gaia's were enough, uttered (who knows why) with a vague southern accent (learned, perhaps, from her exclusive Capri visits and filtered by the membrane of my nervousness), to understand the extent of that inner earthquake. Do you understand where the novelty is, and the talent? She didn't say "ciao" rudely or indifferently. She didn't greet me the way you'd greet someone unimportant. She called me by name. She avoided the stereotype that had led most of the pretty girls I had met up till then not only to insolently devalue the importance of my name but to confront the question of my historical existence in a dismissive tone, underestimating my senstivity. She said: "Ciao, Daniel," as if to deconstruct the judgment I had made of her during that brief week of passion. She said "Ciao, Daniel." Literally. She didn't say "Ciao, Alessandro," "Ciao, Fabrizio." No, she said "Ciao, Daniel," and for that I can't stop thanking her, even after all this time, even admitting that the promising beginning was only a false start. Without, however, failing to note that that "Ciao, Daniel," uttered so naturally, which in a single instant shattered all my memories of childhood—right up until the recent, electrifying ones of my English vacation, the German girl who looked like Eva Braun, the ammonia-like stench on my brother's fingers—was the cause of everything else.

Allow me a last tiny footnote, before moving on.

Being conscious of one's own privilege. That's the indelible lesson of that memorable sojourn. Until the age of fourteen, until that strange vacation that hurled me, with a considerable temporal leap, from the agile laxity of the twentieth century to the rigid etiquette of the nineteenth, it had seemed to me that I was fully aware of my privilege . . . Until the age of fourteen, before Nanni's Positano villa in all its rosy eclectic brightness

opened its doors to me, I had always considered myself a privileged kid. I hadn't been subjected to the superhuman law of
relativity that renders all our convictions about the world inex-
haustive and precarious. Until then I had been only with families and persons of my level or a lower class. I had always
believed that my father's custom of exchanging a Mercedes for
a Porsche almost every six months or our long vacations
abroad or the pair of live-in servants or our apartment full of
rugs and paintings and the serene habit of indulging every
technological whim bore witness to a prosperity that if it could
not be called wealth came perilously close to it.

There's nothing to be surprised at. Such considerations are
made by children of that age much more often than one thinks,
much more than by adults, especially in certain circles. If you
then add to this family snobbishness a congenital tendency to
magnify everything, exaggerated by my young age and by a
precocious talent for comparison, it's easy to understand my
pain, a pain more burning and invasive than the love that was
rising inside me. The truth is this: social comparison occupied
my imagination—and that of my friends—much more then,
when it didn't make any sense, than today, when perhaps I
should be afflicted by it. And so all we could do—I and all the
others—was to lie, shamelessly risking the ridiculous and the
absurd. It was a matter of survival: to lie about the family
inheritance and your parents' bank account, about athletic
feats, about the fleet of cars, about expensive trips all over the
world, about girls had and virginities compromised, about the
length of your penis and your erotic performances . . . Good
Lord, bluffing about these things was the only way to breathe.
Who of us did not number among his family members an
eccentric uncle who collected Rolls-Royces? Who of us resis-
ted the temptation to reveal that his grandfather was the head
of a section of the Rotary Club, if not actually the president?
Why deprive your friends of the sight of your passport so that

they could delight in the stamps that attested to multiple exotic journeys? Who of us did not desire to conform our modest bourgeois life to the sacred dictates of influential ads for liquor and designer watches? What other resource was available to defend yourself from the pressure of that hyper peer group if not inventing places, situations, persons who never existed?

The crazy thing, comprehensible only today, is that almost everyone lied. No one—unless you were lucky, or were a Buddhist unaware of the collision of aspirations and reality—avoided the spell. It was the only shield that could protect you from the aggressions of others' successes. There was so much speculation on lies that at a certain point it was like finding yourself in a sort of Stock Exchange of social prestige where each person's stock had been clumsily overvalued by a pack of pathetic brokers. And now, for me, it was as if that stock market of lies were under the looming threat of an epochal crash. Much later I asked myself—with a retrospective dose of moralism and wisdom, but without obtaining an adequate response—whether, if that counterfeiting operation had been dismantled, life would have had a different savor. But perhaps it's a stupid and pointless question. It would be like asking how our lives would change if we were freed from the daily requirement of eating and drinking.

It was meeting the Cittadinis shortly after meeting the Rubens that introduced me to this different way of conceiving my existence, making me feel for the first time what presumably many of my less wealthy friends had felt toward me: a sense of inadequacy, a kind of shortness of breath. The drama of a runner who goes all out and is passed with apparent ease by another contestant with wings on his feet. My encounter with the Cittadinis and the Rubens showed me a wealth that, in an unpredictable way, undermined my self-esteem, that had nothing to do with the prosperity that my family assured me: a wealth that significantly marked—for good and for ill—the persons who had it. Just think of the neuroses of Karen Ruben or the fatal ones of Ricky Cittadini and his son Giacomo. Even the suicide of the first and the idiosyncrasies of the second had something so chic about them. This was enough, in my eyes, to cancel out the privileges I had always enjoyed. From now on, the house where I had always lived, where I was born and had not stopped for a single instant considering splendid would seem to me a pathetic hovel. And yet I was mistaken in thinking that what to me looked like the finish line for the Rubens or the Cittadinis was a source of joy and satisfaction. There was no limit to desirable wealth. There would always be someone at whom to point the red-hot stinger of human envy. Nanni Cittadini wasn't the richest man in the world. Nor was Amos Ruben. And so why wouldn't you think that both men drew from that painful observation a legitimate motive for humiliation?

4. Five Years in Miniature

Although I loved Gaia with solipsistic determination for five whole years, enjoying the luxury of unexpected pleasures (basically no less egocentric than the pain), I can't say that time taught me to know her. In fact, it almost seems as if time made the ambiguity of her personality and the enigma of her life more complicated. The only courtship I felt up to was my sly courting of her brother, Giacomo, which could be numbered among those diversional maneuvers that are the prelude to a pitched battle.

Besides that, I read some books (fewer than I would claim in the years to come), listened to a substantial number of bad but moving records, abused myself without restraint, visited the United States several times, went back to Israel with Dav; I even went to Australia and New Zealand with my parents and my brother. For the rest, I had leisure to intensify my hypochondria, stubbornly keep my virginity intact, and prepare, with genuine pedantry, my own ostracism.

T hings went more or less like this.

Starting in the winter of '86 I didn't miss a single eighteenth-birthday party of my friends and more important acquaintances. Thirty parties in all, so incredibly alike in every detail (a little the way it would be later on for wedding receptions full of penguins and geese) that I had the impression of having gone to a single, interminable birthday party, donning a dinner jacket at the rate of a lesser Gatsby, drinking more sangria than Hemingway, and popping aspirin with the ease of certain sixties neurotics. Let's say that I belonged to the first generation of adolescents who were able to experience freedom—won by our hotheaded predecessors—without too many traumas or vitalist outbursts, prey, if anything, to a feeble lack of commitment.

One thing is certain: Azzurra Paciotti, Silvestro Pallavicini, Giando Raspelli, David Ruben, and many others still hadn't had the courage, or perhaps the interest, to impress any mark of originality on their eighteenth-birthday party. As if they had slavishly followed a dull basic format: invitations printed by Pineider, a fashionable club rented for the evening (Jackie O', Open Gate, Cabala, Gilda . . .) or exploiting one's own cold country house (Cortona, Montepulciano) or seaside villa (Fregene, Capalbio, Porto Rotondo), long dress for the girls, black tie for the boys, catering by Ruschena, Strauss waltz at midnight, with the birthday boy or girl compelled to dance with the parent of the opposite sex, and then deafening music until five in the morning, the ban on hard liquor almost always violated, virginities delicately or desperately compromised. In these indispensable festivities branded by the stigmata of Roman provincialism, tens of millions of lire were lightheartedly invested. And the best that the birthday boy or girl could expect from the party was to end up being thrown, fully dressed, into a pool in the middle of the night, completely drunk, not to mention overwhelmed by an ardent desire to kill himself. Only thanks to my highly publicized neuroticism and my late-romantic aura did I manage to keep my mother from organizing such an extravagant obscenity for me. And it's still one of the few events-not-experienced that I have no regrets about, only an enduring relief.

This is the story of Gaia's party, which went down in history—with my decisive contribution—as the most disastrous and unforgettable. This is the story of my end. Of my failed revolution. Of my resignation as a spoiled rich kid. This is the story of the second Jew crucified by a Roman oligarchy. This is the story of my crucifixion, after which I would not rise. This is the story of my expulsion from Eden: the story that from the beginning I intended to tell, before losing myself in a labyrinth of stupid conspiracy theories.

The strange and comfortable life led within that snobbish institution where you were promoted by force of inertia and where I had gone along more or less quietly for thirteen years came to an end. That last year was dominated, mainly, by a range of unpleasant impressions that converged in the panic generated by an anguished, if provisional, realization.

Gaia eighteen? My girl grown up?

A joke in the worst taste. Decidedly inadmissible absurdity. Eighteen-year-olds are free, emancipated, adult. Plus, the eighteen-year-olds of 1989, to spite those of barely a century earlier, come home when they want. They drink and smoke to excess. Eighteen-year-olds have cars. Not to mention an uncontrollable aptitude for promiscuity and fornication.

It's fatal: love is one of those intense emotional experiences that make us puritans and reactionaries!

That's why Gaia's coming of age seemed to me an intolerable accomplishment. Above all, when school ended I would suffer a drastic decrease in the number of our encounters, slowly losing my capacity to keep an eye on her, to delay her illegitimate emancipation. At the same time, however, I couldn't help being infected by her enthusiasm. How could I not please her when she asked me to go with her to order the invitations or the cake? When she needed my help with the decorations, the orchestra, the lights . . .? How not back her up when, trying on her dress, whose straps were obviously too wide, she became indignant? Or when she told me, with the same concentrated anger with which a missionary nun might have told me about a genocide of African children, that a mistake had been made in the monograms on the white linen napkins? Well, yes, I was her counselor. Or rather a bifurcated lady-in-waiting. A pederast in love with a girl. A freak halfway between horrid Iago and pathetic Polonius.

How does a person get that way? Even today it's an inexplicable mystery.

How do you become an old maid before your time? How can a brilliant youth turn into an asexual amoeba? Cancel out by his own will all the force, all the impact of his young man's vigor? Disengage his own manly ambition? Destroy the erotic charge? How did he succeed in abolishing it? Is it possible that you didn't realize it at the time? That, like an incurable neurotic, you were so deep in your obsession, in the self-assigned role of superintendent of Gaia's Chastity Not to Mention Guardian of Her Holy Orifices, to gamble away all the chances and all the cards available for your happiness? That you were so blind as to believe that alternatives to that life of sighs and sleaziness didn't exist? So stupid you didn't understand that a masturbator of your quality wasn't born to be a hermit? Is it possible that you didn't see the obvious imbalance between your aspiration to abstinence (yours, like the one you arbitrarily attributed to Gaia) and the mad, tireless search for female garments on which to masturbate? So eager to surrender that you were content with a situation in which Gaia offered you only the crumbs of her many attractions?

You were her best friend, there you had succeeded, everyone knew it, you had secretly used the assistance offered free by her raging madman of a brother to gain her trust. But how could you ignore the fact that trust was the least alluring thing she could give? That you might have had greater hope with her if she had frankly hated you? How could you not know that social worker was not the most popular profession in that shit school, that training camp for the physically well endowed and the mentally disabled?

No, all this was beyond my understanding then, just as today it's glaringly obvious. There's nothing else to say: at fourteen, during that strange vacation in Positano, I decided to bury my virility, renouncing the grit, the verve demanded by my age to devote myself totally to a crazy cause. Yes, crazy, if only because it offered no hope, promised no reward. It was as crazy and futile as its promoter. I had made the most serious mistake a boy can make: not so much not believing in himself (that happens to the majority of adolescents) as bestowing on that lack of faith the blessing of metaphysical inalterability. I hadn't wanted to believe in myself. I had committed the sin of cynicism, absorbing the implicit message of that world: the devious, reactionary invitation to immutability.

And yet I would like to salvage a single day from the sea of those five years. To be more precise, I would like to salvage an afternoon in December of 1986 (a couple of years before that party of Gaia's), when the cozy comfort of my apartment is broken by the telephone ringing:

"Dani, is that you?"

"Gaia!"

"Who else?"

"What's up?"

"Are you doing anything this afternoon?"

"Well . . ."

"What do you say to a shopping trip?"

"But . . ."

"If you don't feel like it, no big deal . . ."

"Of course, sure . . ."

"Splendid, I'll pick you up in ten minutes."

And so here I am—it's really me, although I still have trouble believing it!—cold, with my legs spread, on Gaia's scooter: I'm sitting behind her, and she's wearing a red down jacket and a blue cashmere cardigan and wool gloves with bear cubs on them: her Neutro Roberts alcohol scent is sharpened by a slight hint of sweat. She glides through the traffic heedless of me. Maybe she doesn't hear my protests because of the fur earmuffs. Or maybe, as usual, she doesn't give a damn. We slide sinuously along the Muro Torto, handing out insults to drivers exasperated by life and by the approach of Christmas, and crown our scofflaw journey with a U-turn at Piazza del Popolo and a slalom through human gates over a deceptively uneven but incontrovertibly pedestrian terrain. And now we're on Via del Babuino, seriously intent on reaching Via Condotti before it fills with foreigners. It's just four o'clock, there's a dry cold that it's easy and nice to protect yourself from. A postprandial languor paralyzes the brain in that adamantine light. Everything is blessed by the porcelain shadow of evening spreading over the stuccoed walls.

Gaia and I are talking intimately.

What are we talking about?

About nothing. About how nothing is indispensable. About how nothing is instructive. How nothing makes you happier than nothing. She spends money with a frightening ease. She is the joy of incredulous merchants and neurotic salespeople. The unit of measure of her purchases is the dozen. *What do you think about this? You know who for? For Aunt Edna . . . This is for Dada, she'll die . . . This is for my nanny . . .* The bags multiply in time with the dizzying abundance of syllables. This verbal-consumer incontinence doesn't seem to have any relation to Nanni's endemic frugality, and even less to Grandma Sofia's careless extravagance. Her excess is violent, sometimes even arrogant, and yet so irresistible to me—me, Gaia's personal groupie: her glasses-wearing admirer who will never fuck her.

But what surprises me most—and I don't know if she bestows it consciously or with the pure instinct of giving pleasure—is the way she's treating me today. I have the impression that she's pretending to be my girlfriend. That she's granting me the unimaginable. Today is my lucky day, the memory of which will drive me mad in the long sequence of unlucky days. She smiles at me, she becomes flirtatious for me, she asks my advice, she tugs at me, she makes up funny nicknames for me, she treats me as if only Daniel Sonnino existed in the entire world, she has inserted me into the list of gifts to give and to receive, and for once she has the delicate good taste not to ask me anything about Dav . . . I would like to speak, to reply, to have my say, but she doesn't listen to me. I perceive, rather, the ringing of her spirit as it spreads over the steps of Piazza di Spagna, punctuated by the red and white of the cyclamens.

Gaia is, above all, my era.

Via Condotti at six-thirty on a December day in 1986 can't be compared to any other street I've seen. Probably for an equivalent you'd have to think of the Nevsky Prospect in the time of Gogol, or Washington Square placidly trod by the feet of Henry James, or Madison Avenue, where Edith Wharton's characters lived and suffered. A flaming of scarlet lights, a glow of red carpets and rubies in windows the color of amaranth, a fragrance of roasted chestnuts, an icy-smooth song by Bing Crosby is spread discreetly over a slice of the city on holiday.

Suddenly I'm startled by an unmistakable rumbling of her stomach that's like the muffled sound of a storm in a gothic film.

"Oops, what an embarrassing tummy!" and she smiles. "What do you say to a snack at Babington's? I'm exhausted!"

Now, can you see this docile and romantic Shylock, beside that lovely morsel of girl, enter a tea room on Piazza di Spagna, full of mahogany and wicker, and sit politely on a tiny chair, crossing his legs, taking the menu with the feigned assurance of a fifty-year-old, concealing his horror at the astronomical prices, and restraining his emotion as he watches the girl of his life unknot her scarf, take off her jacket, and place her gloves in a corner with the fluidity of a single gesture, then raise a finger to call a pseudo-British crone and order bergamot tea and two muffins with butter and orange marmalade?

It's good that you can see it. Because that's exactly what happens.

Since the start of this chronicle I've been looking for the right moment to allow myself a pleasure that I ought to deny myself: describing Gaia. Maybe the moment has come, now that she's not looking at me, now that her face is buried in the menu, now that she seems a little tired, inserted in that crèche of bags and packages, now that I'm not afraid of anything, now that I could do what, in analogous circumstances, ninety per cent of my friends would do: kiss her, whispering in her ear a secret that seems enormous but basically isn't much . . . Just now I allow myself the most intoxicating and outmoded among literary privileges: the ekphrasis of the beloved woman.

Gaia is a Britney Spears before Britney Spears, an inch or so shorter than the future model. Gaia is exasperated by a couple of extra pounds (which she considers useless and harmful) that she would like to get rid of, losing herself in Svevian promises of dietetic redemption and submitting to unimaginable doses of massage. Gaia eats with an unparalleled pleasure but at the slow pace of an aesthete. The slight hint of a double chin is the reason I love Gaia. Gaia is small and well proportioned. The Hungarian blond of Gaia's hair is inherited and her nose belongs to Brigitte Bardot. Gaia almost never wears a skirt. Everyone thinks Gaia is beautiful in spite of her slightly buck teeth. No one understands that Gaia owes her beauty to her uneven teeth and, in particular, to that small imperfection of the incisor, that imperceptible stain that, if only I had the chance, I would lick without stopping, for days, weeks. Gaia's breath has the scent of apricot and her skin the fragrance of cashmere. Gaia's voice makes you think of the saliva of an eleven-year-old. Gaia loves men's accessories: big watches, Clarks, cardigans, oversize shirts of Canadian woodsmen's plaid worn strictly outside her pants. Gaia, when she puts on an evening gown and a lot of makeup for one of the many parties she goes to, no longer resembles Gaia. Gaia looks great in riding gear. On those occasions, she displays the androgynous attractiveness of a Hussar.

Now, worn out with fatigue, I take off my glasses and with a habitual gesture rub my eyelids with my fingertips, as if I wanted to caress my eyes for the wonderful work they've done for me in the past couple of hours.

"You know, Dani, you have beautiful eyes? It's funny, with the glasses you don't notice . . . even though the lenses magnify them . . ."

I'm in silent ecstasy.

"I'm telling you the truth . . . Have you ever thought about contact lenses? You know, *like that you're not bad at all.*"

A very modest experience of Gaia is enough to know that these words don't count: they contain not a trace of desire (unless by desire one understands the wish to be universally loved). By that I don't mean to say that if I tried to kiss her she would certainly draw back. She might even yield on the wave of an emotional complicity, because of this soft and enveloping warmth. Or because outside—beyond the frosted glass—it's cold now. Of course she might yield. To explain to me immediately afterward that maybe there's been a misunderstanding, that she's attached, but that if she weren't who knows . . . That in any case she's flattered. That she would never have believed that I . . . That of course the right girl for me is already born and blah, blah, blah . . . Besides, compliments are the opposite of advice: usually (and especially in a relationship marked by an astronomical inequality) they count a lot for the one receiving them and almost nothing for the one lavishing them. I'm Bepy's grandson, I know about certain dynamics. Although I've always deplored the rhetoric of "experience" as a vaccine against pain, I have to admit that if at the time I'd had a little more experience—even though it wouldn't have been able to erase the effect of words that seemed a worthy conclusion to a fairy-tale afternoon—certainly I would have tried to put them in proportion, bringing them back to the level of the empty words with which beautiful women address the world and deceive their admirers. Not that I hoped for anything. I wasn't in a condition to hope for anything. I was frankly a desperate adolescent. But I wanted to believe those words. Yes, even my wanting was desperate. I wanted desperately to believe in the sincerity of her words. I needed to delude myself that if she hadn't been attached I would have been a possible alternative. That her emotional horizon could contemplate even a male like me. Yes, a male who needed some retouching: get rid of the glasses, add contact lenses, enlarge the biceps, round some sharp edges, et cetera, but, still, a male to take into serious consideration. One can't say, besides, that that illusion radically dismantled the idea that I'd had of Gaia from the beginning, and that is that she divided the world into two types of people, those who were *desirable* and all the *others:* and that if you didn't belong to the first group you might as well not exist, since you wouldn't have any psychological or physical tool with which to change that condition. Gaia was like the Calvinist God who bestows Grace or takes it away according to His uncontestable Will. Well, although it might seem a logical contradiction, at that moment I was able to bring the idea that Gaia took me into consideration as a male of her species into harmony with the idea that she would never take me into consideration as a male of her species. I was there beside her, perhaps as never before: breathless and tormented as an abstruse chemical formula, I felt that—although Gaia contained the reward for every possible desire, to the point where my name had no value without hers next to it—sex (notorious sex, the sex of the sexual revolution but also the sex prohibited in the centuries preceding it) didn't have a damn thing to do with it. That it wasn't sex that interested me. That sex, if anything, would have destroyed everything (as in fact would happen shortly). That sex was a foolish fixation of certain insatiable erotomaniacs (that whole large segment of horny Jews that joins Sigmund Freud and Philip Roth, and to whom I would be teaching a lesson in my anti-Semite book). That the idea of sinking my dick into the cavernous dampness of Gaia-esque intimacy was an absolute abstraction right out of metempsychosis or telepathy. That what I asked of her—or rather what I didn't have the courage to ask but couldn't help desiring passionately—was that she take me into consideration as a male of her species. That she elevate me socially. That she provide me with her blue passkey for Paradise. That she guarantee me the upgrade I thought I deserved.

But it's already time to pay and go. On the brown-speckled silver tray brought to me by the pseudo-British crone I place the American Express card recently restored to me by my father after three months of punishment, because, in the grip of some madness during a study vacation in Boston, I had bought, in a shop on Acorn Street, a small ship model from the early nineteen-hundreds, paying a hyperbolic sum close to two months' pay for an autoworker: a galleon that now sits on the top of my boy's desk like a mausoleum of my fin-de-siècle fetishism and my eighties consumer incontinence.

Until, on the scooter that's carrying me home, weighed down by a dozen or more packages and bags and perhaps because of all that tea I drank, or because of the motion or the now penetrating cold, I have a sudden attack of indigestion. I'm terrified. I run the risk of ruining one of the most beautiful days of my life by defecating on the seat of my beloved's scooter. I pray to God she's not aware of the little farts that I can't control. I pray to God that the cloud of sulfur is dissipating in the December cold. Then, jumping off the scooter, going up in the elevator, entering the house, squatting on the toilet to allow the volcano to erupt, I address to the Omnipotent my last prayer: God, make Gaia not interpret my urgent need to leave her—my refusal to crown a day for lovers with the standard flirtations of leave-taking—as a result of my intestinal upset but, if anything, as yet another demonstration of my dignity, as the seal of my emotional detachment, as a tangible testimony of my eccentric character!

Good God, what else have I got?

But in spite of this salvaged day I don't want to hide the fact that, in the five years of our friendship, it seldom happened that I wished for her presence. No, I didn't like to be with her. To see her was a cruelty comparable to the torture that condemns a man to a slow death by thirst, forcing him to contemplate, night and day, marvelous cascades of cold water. The only feeling that Gaia's vicinity inspired in me was the desire to disappear, to go far away, to die and be utterly forgotten. Her comments on other boys frightened me. It was tremendous when she pointed out that Signor X had fantastic eyes while Signor Y's neck was too prominent, not to mention that Signor Z had a head like a goat's. She seemed to have an inimitable talent for picking out physiognomic oddities and finding in any face an objective correlative in the animal world. The male universe, through her gaze, was reduced to the catalogue of a plastic surgeon: a sample book of noses, ears, jaws, and hairlines . . . The naturalist's ruthlessness that she put into remarking on even a small imperfection in the face of one of her friends was almost balanced by her genuine enthusiasm when she was in the presence of something she judged unexceptionable. So my panic when confronted by that proliferation of Gaia-esque comments on my friends' features was based not only on a banal form of jealousy but on a more perverse logic: her comment indicated an attention to men that—although superficially it might be laid to a simple scientific, or at most artistic, interest—my puritan romanticism kept me from attributing to her. On the other hand, because I was a boy myself, although without the qualities necessary to please her, it was very probable that, through a transitive property, she had subjected me as well to a careful physical examination when we met on the wharf at Positano or even at the time of Bepy's funeral. There you have it: that my nose, my ears, my cheeks, my complexion, my neck had been the object of attention and judgment on Gaia's part was for me absolutely unbearable. At those moments my image—which existed in spite of me, which rebelled against me, which mocked me in spite of myself, which could never be other than itself, over which I had not been allowed to exercise any control—crumbled inside me like a skyscraper hit by a wrecking ball. Only then did I realize, with utter panic, that my loathing of my image was based essentially on its incapacity to exercise any fascination on Gaia. I felt the terrible weight of immutability and of death. I could have done anything—earned a ton of money, devised a beautiful way of speaking, dressed with incomparable elegance, become a TV star, a great writer, or a champion in some popular sport, but my aspect would remain unchanged, in fact, would get worse. That's one of the things that Gaia forced me to discover too precociously.

Who can say how all this became transformed, on my part as well, into the idiosyncrasy of zoomorphizing reality (I am more and more convinced that the world view of girls like Gaia, in essence so unconsciously Darwinian, educated an entire generation). I imagined that the life of us high-school students was ruled by hierarchies not dissimilar from those which govern the oligarchic societies of ants and bees. And so I envisioned, for example, humanity divided into two big categories: on the one hand there were the *contemplatives*, who were entrusted with civil organization, and who had no particular aptitude for encounters with the opposite sex and so hadn't developed the exterior apparatus of charms and graces indispensable for amorous seduction; and on the other the *reproductives,* those who were assigned the duty of perpetuating the species, and so had been endowed by Mother Nature with all the superficial attractions that the contemplatives ineluctably lacked. Well, I had the impression of being an unfortunate hybrid: that nature had amused herself by giving me the body of a *contemplative* and an overwhelming aspiration to reproduce.

You had to stay far away from that girl: but only God knew how difficult it was. The problem was that distance from her didn't help me when I was distant from her, just as closeness didn't help me when I was close. I was terrified by the thought that she didn't think about me but I was even more terrified at the idea that she might take me into consideration.

Maybe I should have treated the whole thing more calmly. But for me it was a matter that had to do with Justice. Thus, when in a fake-joking mode I reproached my father for not having made me as handsome as an actor and he lost patience—"Good Lord, Daniel, what does that have to do with anything? You're better-looking than Sartre, Simenon, and Kissinger, and those lechers spent almost their entire lives fucking"—I would have liked to explain to him that the pleasure of being better-looking than Sartre, Simenon, and Kissinger did not in any way make up for the discomfort of feeling myself so much less good-looking than Marlon Brando.

Besides, through one of those processes of compensation typical of any elementary psychology, I shifted the pain of Gaia's indifference, which by its very nature could never have been turned against her, onto the people who loved me: they were the ones who paid. Wasn't it my parents who had made me that way? Wasn't it my parents who had first put me in contact with Gaia? Wasn't it they who hadn't made it to the same level as Gaia's forebears? Wasn't the failed acquisition of those Caravaggio canvases Bepy's fault? Wasn't it my family who had placed me in a society where to love a type-like-Gaia was a necessity, even more than an obligation?

Well, they would pay for it. It would be my concern, in the course of the only adolescence granted me, to poison their life through my capriciousness, my bad moods, my depressions, my sleeping too much or too little, my sullen responses, my terrible, stupid melodramas, my inelegant outbursts, and that suicidal inclination which—if they had been able to look into the heart of that utter coward their son—they could have calmly joked about.

For a long time Gaia's horizons were completely filled by her birthday party. The spirit of that future event seemed to have captured her heart.

It's a common belief that the good-looking aren't able to enjoy life completely. As if privilege promoted a kind of imaginative laziness. Or as if an overestimation of their outward appearance, to the detriment of every other particular quality, kept them from seeing the secret beauties of the real. I'm afraid that's a cliché invented by the ugly to console themselves. My experience, although very modest, provided me with examples of individuals like Gaia, Dav, Giorgio, Karen, Bepy who, although extremely satisfied with their appearance, had an eagerness for intellectual pleasures that was expressed in the inexhaustible search for objects to idolize. In short, they, who could have been passively content with the enthusiasm their bodies inspired in others, seemed to be stirred by a luminous energy that drove them to worship objects, situations, sometimes even people.

So that, long before the specter of her eighteenth birthday celebration took possession of her, I had witnessed the succession—within Gaia's inconstant pantheon—of countless consuming fixations.

Her fourteenth year rushed by in interminable lectures on riding, or more precisely on Costant (pronounced, naturally, in the French style), the Arabian stallion that Nanni gave her for her birthday, astride which the little Amazon raced over the fields of the Farnesina, facing ever more frightening jumps. Then it was synchronized swimming, which led her frequently to take off her pants and shoes in a gym, so that in her white shorts she could demonstrate for her friends the new figures she'd learned, while the hordes of wankers swooned (and one of them grew indignant); not to mention the PR job for a discotheque, where the compensation consisted of a couple of pairs of distinctive sunglasses worn uninterruptedly for an entire year and then unexpectedly sent to the garbage compactor of her memory. Then it was Boris Becker, just seventeen, playing at the Rome International a few months before he won Wimbledon, soon supplanted by Alberto Tomba, with whom Gaia said she had skied for an entire Christmas at Cortina, and who—she claimed cheekily—had made explicit advances. Then came Christopher Reeve, the actor who played Superman. Then a song and its singer: "Every Time You Go Away," by Paul Young of the sublime hair, many years before he detoured into rock and roll. Until she reached a climax of falling in love with a mythological character: Hector, the son of Priam and husband of Andromache, whose story of tragic dignity she had learned in a translation from Greek, and whose romanticizing influence penetrated deep into her teenage heart.

But is it possible that it didn't cross my mind, as I watched that reckless postmodern Eve leaping like an acrobat into the fiery circle of a new temporary passion, that if a flesh-and-blood boy arrived in her life, and she devoted herself to him with the same ardor she had reserved for her papier-mâché idols, my worst nightmares would be realized? That soon nature would transform her abstract passions into concrete loves? Is it possible that my brain had abdicated its institutional function of gathering the facts? Possible that the idea hadn't occurred to me that in our group the most likely incarnation of that ideal boy—the one who, more than any other, seemed to comprise the athletic, physical, intellectual gifts of Costant, Boris Becker, Alberto Tomba, Christopher Reeve, Superman, Paul Young, Hector of Troy, and all the others— was simply Dav, our Dav?!

And how did old Nanni react to the extemporaneous exaltations of his granddaughter?

It might seem natural that he would undermine them. Isn't discouraging others perhaps his greatest talent? That refined executioner's list is extremely long, and doesn't seem to spare even those dearest to him: his son, whose death the world charges him with, his rebellious grandson whose folly exasperates him. Not counting his spendthrift partner and his employees. And if he's spared his wife it's solely because she's the only person who intimidates him: she opened doors for him that would otherwise have remained eternally locked. And then there's nothing to be done about it: in the face of that woman's enduring sexual charisma, Nanni continues to demonstrate his frailty.

With Gaia things should be different. No reverential fear. No master key to the world. No erotic pressure (except perhaps in a sublimated way). Nanni could dispose of his granddaughter as he pleases, if only he wanted to, just as he's done with everyone else: yes, dispose of her like a new, unpunished Humbert Humbert.

Who's stopping him?

It's obvious that he doesn't want to stop: Gaia is his life. Gaia is for him what Dav is for Karen, what Giorgio is for his father, what my brother is for my mother: a glorious manifestation of how life can have meaning: perfect marriage between power and action. Nanni adores that girl. He is at her mercy. It's she who commands. She has to be indulged, blandished, because now the game is entirely hers.

When Gaia was nine, Nanni had only to see her, in the evenings, sitting at her desk drawing stick figures to melt into infinite tenderness. And later the same emotion, veined with pride, would be embodied in the photograph, placed obliquely on the desk in his office, of Gaia dressed for riding: the velvet cap, with her honey-colored, silken hair peeking out, the deerskin gloves, the polished black leather boots, the tight-waisted gray blazer, the close-fitting white pants with patches at the knees. But above all Nanni has impressed in his memory his first encounter with that young lady, only a couple of hours old. Born six weeks premature, she weighed barely three and a half pounds. There she was, right before her grandfather's eyes, in all her purple fragility. Wrapped in a pink blanket, she let him glimpse a little red face, sulky and astonished behind the glass of the incubator. It was love at first sight.

And then you can understand how, after Ricky's death, Nanni found it natural to compensate her for the affection he feels he deprived her of. Nanni himself: the same inflexible father who harshly kept his only son from divorcing, now, with his granddaughter, discovers the pleasure of understanding and the euphoria of compromise. His refusal to let Ricky divorce—which in fact killed his son (his weak, spineless, tender son)—was fed by the same requirements and the same good faith that today impel him to be generous. Precisely because Ricky's self-destructive act erased everything else, disposing of every strict educational principle. And now Nanni has to be aware that if it weren't for that girl, if it weren't for her historical existence and her volcanic vitality, everything would be ruined.

She is the second chance God is granting him. She is the salvation of his family and of his soul. That's why Nanni is prey to the fear and the slightly crazed eagerness of mothers who, after losing a child, bring into the world another and another and yet another . . . Just as he is pervaded by the convulsively protective desire of those fathers who, having seen their first daughter die in a car accident, swear that they will exercise a suffocating control over the second.

He will make her happy precisely where he made his son unhappy. Yes, he will make her happy for two, even for three. This is the new cause that Nanni will live for. His new battle. His new strategy. Make that girl happy. Because happy people don't kill themselves. Because happy people don't think. Because happy people don't judge. Because happy people are submissive. Because happy people do things properly. Would you like your children to do what you want? Well, then, pay attention to Nanni: don't force them: make them happy! Their happiness is the most valuable weapon for blackmail that you will ever have at your disposal: your genuine ace in the hole. Nanni spent the first part of his life making money, the second gaining a social position, now, in the third, the last, inaugurated by an inexplicable gunshot, his goal is the joy of his sweetheart. He has an unpaid account with her and with happiness. He feels he is a debtor and a creditor at the same time. Yes, he has to compensate his little girl and through that compensation he wishes to be compensated. Because Nanni, too, has something to be compensated for: even the ice man has his accounts to settle.

Maybe Nanni's affection for that girl is too compromised by admiration and idolatry not to be harmful. In effect, despite appearances, Nanni hasn't modified his perverse way of thinking: just as, through an abstract love of justice, he established theoretically what Riccardo's conjugal responsibilities were, now, through an equally abstract idea of compensation, he has established that the happiness of his granddaughter is bound to her freedom.

But it's time to speak of the most famous waiter at the Bar del Parnaso (if for no other reason than that he's the only real protagonist of this story): seraphic institution, silent conscience of the neighborhood, and perhaps even more, with the vigorous-arrogant aspect of an Arab. In the depths of his gaze glowed sparks of a Middle Eastern pride. So that we kids called him the Arab, even though he was from Cisterna, and this gave him an exotic quality that he was proud of. Often at cocktail parties and dinners (especially in summer) held on the flowery terraces in that part of Rome one might come across a sort of nocturnal reincarnation of the Arab, in a white shirt with gold buttons and frogs, and with a bald head as shiny as a samovar. And only in those circumstances, amid all those nouveau-riche eccentrics in coral necklaces and chiffon, did you clearly get the idea of the Arab's mystical majesty!

The Arab. The heroic repository of Roman exclusivity, much more than a lot of pallid exhibitionists from those years.

The rest of us could basically be indulgent and tolerant toward those who came from nearby neighborhoods or even farther: but the Arab was intransigent, fierce. Like a good snob, he was easily offended. He examined the customers sitting at the tables, ready to order, and he understood immediately if they were Pariolini D.O.C. or frauds, incautious adventurers in a foreign land. If it had been up to him, he would have erected unbreachable walls to defend against the barbarian hordes. For him that elegant little slice of northern Rome was a bulwark of Western civilization, besieged by the vulgarity of the world. Once upon a time it wasn't like this, he would say sadly. And to show us that he had flushed out another *gate-crasher* (so he called them, as if it were a private party, or as if an entire neighborhood of Rome had been transformed into an immense estate whose control had been entrusted to him), he uttered in a loud voice cryptic expressions that the intruder would never have been able to decipher, and that for us were an unmistakable jargon. And if in order to gain his good graces some stranger called him "Arab," he stiffened, emitting a slight sigh of irritation. Evidently not everyone was authorized to treat him with such familiarity.

When Dav made his entrance, wearing that green American college jacket whose twin I had in turquoise, the Arab sprang forward, immediately got rid of the customer who had made the mistake of occupying Dav's place, and invited his favorite to sit down. "How is your mother?" he asked solicitously, to then gaze dramatically, dreamily upward: "Ahhh, that lady is stupendous, a princess. I remember when she brought you here. Everyone looked at you, you were both so beautiful." The Arab was a poet with the mellifluous and plaintive voice of a shrewish pederast: hair in a crewcut and, on his eyelids, black eye shadow. The nostalgic bard of twenty-seven-year-old couples who on Saturday mornings strolled among the dried-out flowerbeds of Piazza delle Muse, with baby carriages, buckskin jackets, dove-colored suede shoes, and Dalmatian puppies on a leash, the Arab often launched into tedious digressions on good taste.

David, used to the Arab's flattery, evaded it without embarrassment and waited for his cappuccino to be served. While the Arab caressed him with an indulgent gaze, maybe because he saw in Dav—who knows if rightly—the unquestioned god of that race of immortals, one of the few who could defend the integrity of that place which, to listen to him, had become a seaport. The Arab was sorry that the Rubens so many years earlier had decided to change neighborhoods, ending up in that distant villa which he, in his snobbishness, situated more or less in the tundra. At the same time, in his superstitious way of interpreting every event symbolically, he had seen in the Ruben family's move one of the clear signs of the decline of civilization.

But above all the Arab got sappy about what he called "the couple of the century": David and Gaia.

It's destiny! One day these children will find each other, this sentimental necromancer had once opined, causing me pain that, even if I had described it to him, he wouldn't have understood. The Arab's nose for "affairs of the heart" was infallible, but his empathy for suffering was not. And assuming that his judgments, although so temperamental, were marked not by racial factors but for the most part by more profound aesthetic intuitions, he had immediately understood, from the time they were children, even before they knew each other, that a Gaia Cittadini was made to end up in the arms of a David Ruben and vice-versa.

But the Arab's real passion—in whose infinite vortex all the others seemed to converge—was a book. To be precise, "the most beautiful book ever written" (the Arab, too, like the boys and girls he served, was a slave of the superlative): *War and Peace*, by Leo Tolstoy, whose prophetically bearded image the

Arab kept a tiny copy of in his wallet, like a sacred picture. I had learned from my father (who claimed to have known the Arab many centuries before my birth) that his passion for that book went back to his youth. Yes, the Arab had been reading *War and Peace* for more than thirty years. He had gone so far as to study French on his own at night, in order to "appreciate it completely" (something he was proud of: especially since the few times a "customer from the other side of the Alps" happened into the Parnaso it was truly entertaining to see the Arab show off, in a loud voice, his ridiculously nineteenth-century French). Some episodes of *War and Peace* he had reread fifty, a hundred times, more than the most scrupulous specialist: Prince Andrei arriving in his carriage at Lysye Gory, with his quick step and that shadowy, proud face. The heroic encounter of Andrei and Napoleon Bonaparte. Pierre's intimate diary. The story of his Petersburg drunks. The Arab could confidently recite long extracts from these scenes, without omitting a comma, each time reviving the emotion that, over the years, he had learned to excite in himself more and more fully until it became something unnaturally genuine.

Among all these scenes, the one that was most deeply engraved in his life as a snobbish dreamer was the great reception in honor of the Emperor Alexander: Natasha's debut in society, her first dance with Prince Andrei, and, in particular, the birth of the love between the two future fiancés: "Prince Andrei was one of the best dancers of his time. Natasha danced magnificently. Her little feet, in satin dancing shoes, did their work rapidly, lightly, and without her being aware of it, but her face shone with joy and enthusiasm," the Arab declaimed in a stentorian voice whenever he saw Dav and Gaia coming. He used those few phrases as a sort of pagan benediction.

I had long ago stopped suggesting other books to the Arab, having given up hope of transforming that idolatry of his for one book into an authentic love for literature. And that is to say that I had tried with Stendhal, with Flaubert, with Mann, even with Proust. The best. But every time, as he returned those old family volumes, the Arab's face displayed a slightly fastidious expression, as if to say: "Thank you for the suggestion, my friend, but, you see, once you've read *War and Peace* you are condemned to read nothing else all your life!" And who's to say that he wasn't right?

In any event, the identification with Andrei and Natasha that the Arab had awarded to Dav and Gaia was simply incongruous. They were nothing like the Tolstoyan couple. To get an idea you'd only have to consider the tremendous difference in size between the giant Dav and the small Andrei, or compare Natasha's black eyes with Gaia's sea-blue ones. And how could you not take account of the difference in age between Andrei and Natasha, which finds no correspondence in this pair of contemporary adolescents? Plus, if you thought about it, the Arab's comparison had nothing hopeful about it. The love between Andrei and Natasha is the story of a passion aborted, not lived. How could the Arab not remember, having read *War and Peace* hundreds of times, that at the end, after the death of Andrei, Natasha marries that "horrible elephant Pierre" (Arab's words)? Once, driven by my jealousy of Gaia, I dared to make that objection to the Arab. But his reply seemed to me of such a rigorous intelligence that I was silenced. "Don't talk to me about that," he said in the tone of one who is recalling a too unpleasantly painful fact. "You know something? I find the two epilogues of *War and Peace* truly outrageous. I wonder how the Count"—so he called him, as if even that great writer, dead for almost a century, were one of the many titled idlers who every day had the honor of being served by the Arab— "could have . . ." Yet the fact remained that the association of the David-Gaia couple with the Andrei-Natasha one was a real interpretative distortion. Thank Heaven, the Arab didn't give a damn about the congruities. He had a need to read what he insisted on considering his own "world"—the universe of which he was only an occasional witness and a faithful servant—through the rose-colored lenses offered him by the titanic Count Tolstoy.

Here's what the Arab's madness consisted of: seeking a trace of the epic in a decade that had violently abolished all mythology.

My father had once smilingly asked me: "Has the Arab chosen the Andrei and Natasha of the season yet?" Not without pain I had answered that the couple of the year was the one formed by David and Gaia.

"Well, you know, it's hardly the first time the Arab has chosen a Jewish Andrei. You know who Andrei was in my time?"

"Who?"

"Teo. Your uncle. Think of it. Before he went nuts and moved to Tel Aviv . . ."

Suddenly I understood why my father always started his intercontinental phone calls to his brother with the same enigmatic formula: "So, how's our Israeli Andrei?"

"Well, Nanni must be happy for his granddaughter," he added immediately afterward. "Ultimately the Arab's opinion is worth more than a title offered by the government of this country."

I'm afraid my father was right.

A book can determine the life of a man in an unpredictable way. The Arab, in essence, was merely a new Don Quixote who had chosen to believe more in an epic written many years before his birth than in everyday life. What distinguished him from the pathetic Spanish model is that the Arab didn't feel qualified to be the protagonist, and so had chosen for himself the no less demanding role of witness. Now, it may seem absurd that he saw a correspondence between tsarist society at the beginning of the nineteenth century, based on the honor of war and a sophisticated code of behavior, and a small group made up of the children of the nouveau riche obsessed with wealth and physical appearance, and yet the Arab's intuition had a freshness about it: what joined those two so distant worlds was the oligarchic and violently hierarchical structure by which both were ruled.

And perhaps the Arab's genius consisted in the fact that, instead of being angered by that inane ruthlessness, he had become, over the years, its Homeric bard. ´

June 8, 1989: fifty-two hours to X hour: the event is approaching, with the roaring impatience of a summer storm. Everything is ready: the Cittadinis' garden is prepared to welcome five hundred guests; the bottles are on ice; the invitations have reached their destinations; the Rome section of the *Messaggero* is already talking about the event as something not to be missed; the rights for the photographs have been sold to a gossip magazine, and Nanni has guaranteed that the proceeds will go to a Catholic organization that provides for malnourished Peruvian babies. And then there are my mother's friends—those women in their forties who play canasta on Wednesday afternoons—who have subjected me, over a warm pizza and a sip of Twinings, to a serious interrogation: "Do you know who made the dress? . . . Is it true that they spent a fortune on white truffles alone? . . . That they rented a plane to bring people from England? . . . That she'll descend a staircase garlanded with flowers? . . ."

It's the third time in a row that Gaia has stood me up. And to say that, as usual, she was the one who called: she wanted to see me. She wanted to hang out a little with her "best friend" to give her head a break from all these "frightful" obligations. She just wanted a little peace and quiet to catch her breath. Although we could take advantage of it to go over the preparations (in fact she had a desperate need for confirmation). And then not only does she not show up at the appointment but she is careful not to let me know, sending, in her place, that unhinged older brother whose inescapable illness I've been dealing with, like an extremely lazy missionary, for way too long.

That's why, as I'm sitting at the Parnaso, it's so painful, humiliating, but not at all surprising, to see Giacomo coming toward me from Via Eleonora Duse swaying like a ship that is about to sink.

"What do you say I sit down?" he asks me in a loud, slow voice. "Gaia couldn't come."

Is there even the slightest relationship between the delicate *putto* I saw walking beside his grandfather at Bepy's funeral and this large, amorphous creature who has sat down beside me without waiting for my consent? Although I've been able to follow the span of his existence day by day, I still have trouble believing it's the same person. Good Lord, Giacomo has been disfigured by time. I have witnessed, in astonishment, the unfolding of the opposite fates of these two siblings. He increasingly locked inside the armor of his dementia, increasingly the slave of a neurotic overeating, and she, on the other hand, every day more self-assured, every day a step higher on the hierarchical ladder. He increasingly shadowy and elusive and she so fascinatingly cartoonlike. I've seen his artificiality transmuted into real suffering and her miraculous spontaneity become a seductive drawl. By now Giacomo's inherited beauty can hardly be grasped behind that mountain of fat. He seems to have employed the years of his adolescence in getting rid of the magnificent image sculpted into his DNA. His blue eyes, so similar in energy to those of his sister and his grandfather, endure, along with some theatrical affectations of insolence typical of the Roman aristocracy. Life has acted regressively in him: he was a precocious child just as much as he is today a retarded twenty-year-old, a failed student at scholastic institutions that allow you to make up three or four years in one. He doesn't have girlfriends. He blushes in front of girls. He is clumsy, always out of place. When he speaks his voice is too loud; similarly, he can't control the movements of his hands, his arms, his head. It's as if he had progressively lost control over his body: so now he seems divided into a thousand different jurisdictions. The central government of his brain has, over the years, in battle after battle, lost control over the distant provinces of his limbs, which have begun to act autonomously, in a dangerous anarchy. It's as if his body had been sacked by barbarians. The most evident manifestation of these civil wars is his skin, which is spotted all over by an irritating psoriasis. And yet I still can't understand if Giacomo has chosen to send that tormented, neurotic body on a mission of reconnaissance out of some sinister form of exhibitionism or, rather, as a sign of détente: *Look at the state I'm in, don't hurt me, haven't I already done enough myself?* And this is the great mystery, or his strategy: the oscillation between bellicose intentions and sudden cowardly appeasements.

He is continually lighting cigarettes. His daily cocktail of alcohol, hash, tranquilizers, and anti-depressants seems to have altered his features. Although his face is distended, its edges are sharp. Most of the time he is silent, but when he speaks (this is truly miraculous) his speech is lucid, sometimes even refined. In less than five years his violent insolence has become its opposite: a kind of polished, verbose irony with which he keeps you at bay: "Oh, thanks, Daniel, you're adorable!" he says, in the fatuous tone of a Jane Austen character, after refusing an invitation for coffee or a hamburger. Who but a deranged person would express himself like this these days? He seems to want to make fun of you. Even though Gaia is sure that this is only a façade. That the show of affability, the public bashfulness, is offset by devastating tantrums at home, during which the Hydra shows its horrifying face: furniture punched, glass shattered, doors broken, curses, death threats—once he even threatened his grandfather with a knife. All because of alcohol. Alcohol's what fuels that tremendous aggression. "But why don't you call someone? Why don't you call the police?" I once asked Gaia. "Well, because . . . because . . . you know, Grandpa loves him too much!" Both Gaia and I know that the reason Nanni has decided not to call the police, even in the face of his grandson's homicidal fury, is decorum. That's it: decorum—the true god of Nanni Cittadini. He will not expose his family, his very respectable name, which he has worked so hard for, to scandal—even at the cost of being murdered by that little bastard! He won't let people say: "Did you see? They've locked up that psychopathic grandson of Nanni's! High time! He was so dangerous to others and to himself. Poor Nanni." He isn't the type who wants to evoke compassion in others. He was born to be envied, not pitied. That should be clear. This is the source of that crazy kid's excessive impunity.

I've been asked to prevent him, when we're together, from starting on his "little beers," or his "tiny little grappas" (as he calls them, in this disgusting way). But more than that I can't do. He seems submissive, but actually he's stubborn about his perverse depravity. If he wants to drink you can't do anything about it. It's clear that alcohol has a devastatingly liberating effect on him. It's as if after a couple of "little beers" and "tiny little grappas" Giacomo had suddenly discovered not so much the horror of the Universe as, rather, the outrage of his own individual condition. In those moments of frenzy and desperation it's as if the happiness of others (completely presumed) hurt him so badly that it drove him to shield himself behind all that bellicosity.

Most of the time Giacomo is silent. You have the impression that for him life—which for most people his age is, if not welcoming, certainly pregnant with infinite possibilities—is a penitentiary. Contact with daily reality paralyzes him, or, to be more accurate, circumscribes him in a cramped space. It's as if he felt the eyes of the world on him. As if he felt in the air a universal disdain that is about to crush him. It's as if every time he stuck his nose outside that nucleus of domestic illness the world stopped for the sole purpose of judging him . . . If the world is a Court of Assizes he is the Perennial Accused.

One time, at Gaia's request (*Dani, you're the only one he feels comfortable with!* She never stopped seducing me, my adorable blackmailer), I go with him to buy records. (Giacomo is a collector of rare first editions of the late sixties. He has a real talent for sniffing out hard-to-find records by Led Zeppelin, Deep Purple, etc., and perhaps the only time his face lights up with emotion, with some pleasure in living, is when he's holding some album cover from that era, grayish and slightly faded.) Suddenly we are approached by two girls belonging to the category of indistinguishable blondes whom North Rome has been churning out for decades. They ask me for some extremely banal information, which I have no difficulty in providing. But when I turn to Giacomo I realize that his face is ashen, that he's distraught. "What's the matter? Are you sick?" "Didn't you see how they looked at me?" And I am so astonished by his reaction that I fail to tell him not only that the girls didn't even notice him but that, if you think about it, their only talent lies in a fatal self-absorption. Is this the reason, the paralyzing sensation of always being in the spotlight, under the shameless gaze of the TV camera, that he can't control himself? Is this why he can't hold a bottle without its slipping out of his fingers? Why everything, even his hands, acts against him? Is this why he can't control his vocal cords and so can't adjust his tone of voice? Why he has the impression that every gesture is watched by the bold mockery of a billion female eyes?

In order to complete the picture, I have to confess what it cost me to be with Giacomo. Basically I didn't like him.

Because—unless one has a strong inclination for altruism, which most of the time is compromised by a grandiose superiority complex, anyway—it's difficult to like such ravaged individuals. In spite of that, I saw the sinister commonality that bound our destinies. Maybe, compared to him, I was saved. From what? From the temptation of not-living-in-order-not-to-suffer that leads to the bitter longing for life that we normally attribute to zombies or ghosts. Let's say that the sickness—while having touched me deeply enough to pervert my character, while having excited my gaze, leading it to the threshold of self-persecuting visions—hadn't managed to dig a definitive ditch between me and existence, between me and the duties of a good bourgeois boy, between me and my aspiration to emerge from that morass of pregenital anguish. As if something had protected me. There are those who banally call it "irony." I like to think of Bepy, of my mother, of my brother, of their involuntary seminars devoted to demystification.

Giacomo was a thoroughbred with an impeccable pedigree who one day had decided to stop jumping the hurdles that thousands of trainers (grandparents, teachers, scholastic institutions, suffragettes of adolescent love) had placed before him. And no one better than I knew the effect of that inclination to refuse, to shy. That's why going out with Giacomo Cittadini was like going around the city with the worst part of myself. There was something frightening about him, and yet so familiar.

I knew that Giacomo had been reduced to such a state because of his modest height. Anyone would have had trouble believing that between his height of five feet four inches and the destruction of his character there existed a cause and effect relationship. And yet it was so. For Giacomo his stature was the problem of problems, more than his father's death, more than his mother's indifference, more than his grandmother's snobbishness, more than his grandfather's preference for Gaia.

At a certain point, around fifth grade, a few years before I met him at Positano, Giacomo realized that his friends had begun to grow. Yes, almost from one day to the next he had seen them shoot up like daisies: he had been frightened by the observation that suddenly his gaze had to travel upward to face the same kids he had always looked in the eye. This had made him hypothesize his own differentness, and had imbued him on the one hand with a tremendous shame, and on the other with the opinion that life was a training ground for injustices. Why did they all grow so easily? What was there in him that didn't work? Why was there a treatment for almost every illness or infirmity except stature? He would have undergone any torture just to gain inches. Because for Giacomo inches were certificates of human dignity. God, how many times had Nanni's speeches harassed him! "Think of Napoleon," that shit would say to console him. "Paul Newman is short," he would say a moment later, laying it on. These phrases, uttered—perhaps—with good intentions, had the power of further emphasizing the slightness of his stature. They were the proof Giacomo needed to make up his mind to let it all go to hell. Because that was a *thing* from which he would never be able to recover. That *thing* you couldn't hide. That was the first *thing* that people looked at, the first *thing* that women judged . . . That's how it began: Giacomo had taken up smoking, drinking, numbing himself with drugs, to keep from looking in the mirror. Then he had decided to forget his own existence. And all too quickly he had realized that the more he tried not to think about it the more he thought about it.

Well, now it's easier to understand what a sweet and formative experience it must have been to show up almost every afternoon of his adolescence at the Parnaso with the sole purpose of feeling that he was a pygmy among giants. To sit and watch those privileged ones live: to have to witness their lasting struggle for reproduction. I repeat: no one understood better than me. We were brothers in that sort of masochistic voyeurism: who but the one who had formulated the paranoid idea that his nose and his eyeglasses together weighed more than his whole body could better understand the sorrows of young Cittadini?

And now?

Now the only saving joy for Giacomo consists in throwing his abulia in your face. Here's the new strategy for boycotting the Great Happiness and Redemption Project promoted by the firm of Cittadini & Altavilla. He doesn't yell anymore, he doesn't say what he thinks, he doesn't rebel. He follows a path that he judges to be nonviolent but that in reality is frighteningly aggressive: the violence of silence, the violence of failed enthusiasm, the violence of his life thrown in the mud. Here is the only violence that parents suffer. Here is his intoxicating revenge. His grandfather, his formerly severe grandfather would now be willing to give him anything, to offer him the sky, just to see him change, but he doesn't need anything. He is no longer for sale, he is stoically incorruptible, he has learned to endure privation like a Tibetan monk. And now his violence, the infinite capacity for insult, is expressed in his talent for renunciation, for not falling into line.

"If you want, Grandpa will buy you a Porsche!" Nanni said, exasperated by yet another school failure, by his abuse of cigarettes and food, on his eighteenth birthday. "In fact, you know what? I have a vacant apartment in the center of the city. A real treasure, completely renovated, with a lot of wood and lofts . . . What do you say we go and see it together? So finally you'll be free of your oppressive grandfather and your troublesome sister!"

"What's the matter, Nanni, you can't bear to have me around anymore? Are you ashamed of me in front of your friends?"

"No, come on, don't be like that. I just meant to say that . . . You know you're my dear little boy!"

"Don't call me 'little.' It infuriates me when you call me 'little'!"

"I'm sorry, it was only a way of speaking affectionately. But if it bothers you, I'm sorry. But also think about my proposals . . ."

"You know, Nanni, where you can stick your Porsche and your empty apartment?" his grandson responded.

"I'm serious. Tomorrow. I'm going to the dealer. Rather, we'll go together, tomorrow evening . . . It's so long since we've done anything together."

"Up your ass, that's where you can stick them!"

"But why does he act like this? Why does he eat, smoke, and drink continuously? None of us are like that. Why doesn't he let me help him, buy him what would make any boy his age happy?" Nanni asked the therapist who sees Giacomo. The grandfather can't reconcile himself, he has already lived through the trauma of feeling he was an impotent father, and now he is reliving an analogous experience with his grandson, which if it can't be called equally tragic is certainly more exhausting, because it's spread over time.

"You see, sir," the psychoanalyst said, "Giacomo is a very gifted boy, but he suffers from what we call an addictive personality. He is a slave to certain compulsions. Once he has established a habit it is immediately transformed into an addiction. Yes, an inexorable addiction. From innocuous things like the morning cappuccino, that he couldn't give up even in the desert, to serious and invasive things like alcohol."

This man is right, Nanni says to himself, *but why, every time I come here, does he merely describe to me pedantically, so lucidly and in terminology so precise and appropriate, what I already know, what I've felt in my flesh? Why doesn't he give me some advice? Why don't I see improvements? Why is my grandson increasingly unhappy, dissipated, infantile, lost, incurable? Why does it sometimes disgust me to be around him? Why whenever I speak to him can I not perceive the least spark? Why am I so happy when he goes out, when I don't see him, when I forget about him? Lord, if only he were like my little sweetheart. If only he had a scrap of her sunniness, of her joy in life. Sometimes I am so exasperated I even wish he would disappear. Think, to be left here alone with my two princesses: yes, Sofia and I and our little sweetheart. Why do I sometimes wish the men in my family had never existed?*

"But you think that his behavior, yes, that is, that his compulsions depend on something in particular?" Nanni insists.

"Do you have some ideas?"

"Well . . . I don't know, I don't understand certain things. Shit, am I not paying you to get some answers?"

"You are not paying me for that. In fact, I would say that our conversation ends here."

"No, I'm sorry, I didn't mean that. Please . . ."

"I'm not your spy. Is that understood?"

"Understood."

"In fact, obviously I'll have to tell Giacomo that you came to see me."

"Please. I told you I'm sorry. I don't even know myself what I'm saying . . . I'm so exasperated . . . You have no idea what he's been doing lately. He always finds a new, ingenious way of poisoning my existence. So, please, I implore you: don't tell him I came."

"That is not debatable. Don't forget that Giacomo is my patient, not you. That, in some measure, in seeing you I have already violated the rules imposed by professional ethics. You will understand that I can't claim absolute trust from a patient if I'm hiding something that regards him. And then—if you want some advice, which perhaps I shouldn't give you—it's time, sir, that you forgot the hell that Giacomo makes for you and began to imagine the hell that Giacomo inhabits."

"What do you mean by that? That I don't give a damn about Giacomo? That his fate is indifferent to me? That I hate him? Well, it's not like that! It's exactly the opposite. But don't you understand that Giacomo hates me? Don't you understand that he hates us all?" Nanni complains, and has never felt so at the mercy of another human being. He is so frightened by the intransigence of this man!

"As I've explained to you, what Giacomo thinks of you is not important. Giacomo isn't here to learn to love you. He's here to understand himself and to feel a little better."

"But you didn't answer my question! What's the origin of this condition? This violence? He's been coming here for years. Lying on this couch. Is it possible that you have no answers?"

"You are forcing me to repeat what I've said, my question: do you have something in mind, sir?"

If he doesn't stop calling me "sir" I'll wring his neck, Nanni catches himself thinking.

"Well, who knows . . . But . . . Maybe what happened to Giacomo's father?"

"Why do you call him 'Giacomo's father'?"

Nanni is silent. Petrified.

And now what are you doing? Are you starting to psychoanalyze me? Do you want to embarrass me? Would you prefer that I say "my son"? Is this what you want me to say, you piece-of-shit Savonarola? But I can't say "my son." It's cruel to make me say "my son." No wonder the boy isn't making progress if this fathead is treating him, this evil shit guru.

Your only problem, Nanni, is that you insist on asking yourself obsessively if it really has something to do with the death of . . . NO! I don't want to name him. But this is the question that you shouldn't ask yourself and that nevertheless keeps coming back: is the fact that you prevented him—come on, prevented? You didn't hold a gun to his head (shit, what an unfortunate example!)—from divorcing that woman (for his own good, because divorce is undignified in a respectable, aristocratic, Catholic family) the direct cause of his death? If you had let him be free would he still be here, would he be one among many middle-aged men with a past of escapades and a future of conjugal serenity? And then that vulgar woman Ricky was bewitched by, in that way of his: frank and passionate. That woman you offered money to so she would leave him alone. Basically you paid her off. You were concerned about his happiness, or at least about his well-being. And, besides, you were right, as always: if she had loved him, as she claimed, *dis-in-ter-est-ed-ly*, she wouldn't have accepted your money. And yet the thought won't abandon you: the question returns, in the middle of the night, to burrow darkly into your conscience, choke you: if you hadn't opposed him, if you hadn't acted for *his* good, would your son—that unique son whom you can't name except by pathetic paraphrases—still be among us? My God, if only we could go back in time! If only it were possible to buy at auction a piece of the past, in order to change it. If only God would abolish the Irremediable! Meanwhile the questions won't stop piling up: if your Ricky hadn't shot himself, would Giacomo be one of the many happy boys who go to the Parnaso, graduate from university, fuck those girls with blond bangs, plan their lives, make a mistake for the sole purpose of getting back on their feet? Yes, in fact, how much is there of yours in this disaster? And how much can be attributed to fate? Is it possible that the six inches separating this boy from his yearned-for five-ten have determined our life? Is this what you don't dare ask the psychoanalyst, fearing not so much his answers as his unseemly questions. That's why you don't say "my son." You're afraid that your most frightening suspicion, the one that you can't confront even in the depths of your conscience, that you drive away angrily every time it surfaces in your mind, will show itself to be founded, real, verifiable. Maybe, Nanni, you have nothing to do with the death of your son, or with the unhappiness of your grandson. It's pointless to search for a connection between things. Maybe things happen autonomously. And yet how can you give up the luxury of torturing yourself with the thought of Ricky's last moments? How can you not think of the desperation of that poor man, of the yawning abyss before his destiny? You don't know what it means to want to kill yourself. You don't know what it means to cut yourself off from any alternative to death. You don't know. You don't know what it means to stick a gun in your mouth, feel your hands trembling and your heartbeat accelerating, your head in a sack, fate entrusted to the pressure of an index finger, the contraction of a muscle, the simple inescapability of a nervous jerk. You have never thought of killing yourself. You belong to the generation of the war. Those who have seen war do not kill themselves. Those who have truly suffered don't have time for this non-sense. This is what you think. This is what they taught you to think. This is what you tried with all your energy to instill in the mind of your son and your grandchildren. This is your colossal fiasco.

Giacomo has sat down and is looking at me.

The strip of clouds on the horizon is like a long skid mark on the asphalt. One of those early June afternoons when the square fills with kids and new cars and motorcycles, and people are there for no reason, out of the mysterious desire not to be elsewhere. Everyone knows everyone else, and has almost forever. And this seems enough to have no wish to know anyone else.

It's too bad you all aren't here, with me: that you can't see them, these young people: because they are fantastically good-looking: and also stupendously well dressed. Besides, you will have understood by now that Daniel Sonnino is inclined to adverbial abuse—a practice condemned in the first lesson in any respectable school of creative writing. Maybe it's Bepy who infected me with the germ of the adverb: from him comes my awareness that the most discredited among the grammatical forms of discourse gives color to life, character, is devoted to the nuances. Above all, it's as if the adverb were charged with preparing the grand entrance of the adjective onto the stage of the sentence. And so it's useful to repeat it one last time—*these young people are fantastically good-looking and stupendously well dressed*—if only to understand that the small round table at which Giacomo and I are sitting must appear to an impartial observer like a sort of bare desert island amid a luxuriant tropical archipelago.

And if today we can say with absolute assurance that Karl Marx with his mania for predicting the future was grossly mistaken, we are obliged, nevertheless, to grant him an astonishing grasp of human affairs: I'm afraid that he would agree with us in saying that the impudent charm of these youths—a charm disfigured here and there by some unimportant exception—depends, just like their good taste, which is so mysteriously compromised by an inclination to vulgarity, on a couple of centuries of good nourishment, on excellent education, on investment in their own genes, and on many other unqualifiable factors and historical privileges.

Immediately the Arab approaches.

"What do you want?" he asks with his usual air of irritation, as if we were annoying him, interrupting his assigned task: to keep watch over the integrity of the neighborhood.

Giacomo asks for a grappa.

The Arab turns up his nose (the Arab's face knows only extreme expressions). Christ, grappa for a kid. The Arab can't stand Giacomo. He can barely look at him, the way he can barely look at children with Down's syndrome or paraplegics (have you ever seen a paraplegic in a novel by Tolstoy? Ah-h-h, *autrefois . . .*). They make him ill. The Arab can't bear the dark side of human beauty. He shuns it. But with Giacomo it's almost worse. In his eyes that pale boy, dressed in such a slovenly fashion, is a curse. He considers him more or less a renegade. How in the world . . .? Him, the grandson of the Princess Altavilla, brother of such a sister, wearing those combat boots—and that beard, like a Communist? He looks like a cockroach. The world is upside down. The Arab is the only one who, when he looks at that boy, doesn't think of the father's suicide. The Arab abhors psychology. *Come on, the Arab says to himself, people die every day, and that doesn't authorize those who are left to put on filthy T-shirts and not comb their hair. I lost my poor father at only thirteen and I didn't let myself go, I never lost my dignity. This young man has a name, and that name should be respected. If you don't have respect for yourself, at least have respect for the name you bear. If you don't have respect for your own life, at least have respect for all the lives that are harder than yours.* (God, the Arab's moralizing is annoying.)

So, after taking the order, the Arab impatiently goes off. But what he can't know is that Giacomo, with all his elaborate neglect, is a precursor. In a few years, that same square will be full of young cubs dressed like cockroaches, with T-shirts worn inside out and military pants worn immodestly low on the waist. And then a "decently" dressed kid will seem grotesque and stupid just as today Giacomo seems provocative. And this new insect-loving generation will not be the product of another race, of other families or different anthropological groups, as the Arab will sadly realize. No, it will be only our younger brothers, convinced with the same unreasonable determination as ours that wearing a T-shirt inside out is a distinctive gesture that will cancel out everything, so that any other fashion, past or future, pales. Those who today love comfortable lives, American-style lives, tomorrow will hate comfort and America. Those who today consider a Big Mac the avant-garde of meals will find that same meal painfully polluting, symbolically pernicious. That's how things work in this neighborhood. No offense to our desperately conservative Arab.

"So tell me, are you sorry my sister didn't come?" Giacomo asks in a low voice.

I don't answer. I know this drawling voice: he has been drinking, smoking, is stuffed with tranquilizers; he's in a fog.

"So are you sorry or not?"

I'm silent.

"It's impolite not to answer. Come on, tell me: are you sorry?"

" . . . "

"Of course you're sorry! You look broken-hearted."

" . . . "

"Why don't you say something? I just wanted to chat . . ."

He, too, is silent.

"Then tell me something else. Why is everyone in your family so servile?"

" . . . "

"I mean, why are you always sucking up to people? Why do you idolize them? Does crawling come naturally to you?"

"Come on, stop it. You know when you're in this state you only talk nonsense."

"In what state?"

"Let's just say that the stink of alcohol preceded you by a couple of minutes . . ."

"Aha, he doesn't like alcoholics . . ."

"You, an alcoholic? Who do you think you are? Edgar Allan Poe? You're a smart-ass son of a bitch . . ."

"He only likes servants and girls who give blowjobs," he continues, raising his voice and pretending not to hear me.

"O.K., you're right. Whatever you say."

"You still haven't answered me, Daniel."

"What?"

"Let's put it like this, then. Are you sure this is the right strategy? Is it your own? Or your father's or mother's?"

"What strategy? Crap. Why do you have it in for my parents today? Usually you like them a lot!"

"Well, I imagine they're the ones who taught you to crawl. Isn't that why you're such friends of Nanni's? Nanni chooses his friends all the same: nice, polite, and deferential. Just like you. Nanni can only stand people like that. Nanni can't bear the truth. And I assure you that Gaia has learned the lesson. The little princess has made herself a fine court. Don't you think so? But of course, you know perfectly well: you're the chamberlain."

Giacomo's words, apart from being unpleasant, are unfounded. That's why, even though they put me in a bad mood, I don't get mad. Come on, I'm the first to admit that my father's affection for Nanni is excessive. But that emotional exaggeration isn't flattery: rather, it's the sentimental product of a personality inclined to excess and exuberance. All my father's passions are intense, often biased, and irrational. When he eats sashimi in a Japanese restaurant. Or when, opening the latest issue of *Quattroruote*, he gurgles happily at the sight of the new-model Chrysler. Or when he abandons himself to ecstatic exclamations in front of a painting by Jasper Johns or a story by Bret Easton Ellis. *Isn't it fantastic?* he asks, with eyes that, over the years, have begun to sparkle like Bepy's . . . What does servility have to do with it? Even his devotion to Nanni is one of my father's ways of telling us that he likes the world unconditionally. My father is a chronic lover: men, women, books, designer labels, cars, soccer players, food, buildings, sunsets. Everything, all of the incomparable real, just as it is or just as he thinks it is, for him is a cult object, an occasion for fanaticism.

But Giacomo—evidently surprised by my self-control—after brandishing the knife for a few minutes, sinks it in my flesh:

"Do you want to know what Nanni thinks of your family?"

"I'm not interested . . ."

"He says that your grandfather was a thief and a blowhard, who got what he deserved. He says your father is an ass-licker and your mother is frustrated and bitter. He says that if he himself, in his time, hadn't helped you, you wouldn't have a goddam cent now."

Yes, that's it—with these words—how Giacomo's sharpened knife makes its way into my guts. It's horrible to think that those judgments about Bepy, my father, my family have been uttered millions of times in front of Gaia.

And I don't know what keeps me from grabbing Giacomo by the shirt, picking him up off the chair with all the adrenaline I have in my body, and hitting him until I get over it. I'm afraid that in this peaceful era we underestimate the intrinsic beauty of a violently liberating act. Don't you think it would be great, rather than sitting here in a daze, taking absurd insults from this lunatic, to start beating him wildly? Wouldn't it be a relief, if not for all mankind, for the majority of people who see him and pretend to feel sorry for him? Who says that you always have to respond to madness with understanding? Isn't it precisely madness that rejects dialogue, makes it impossible? Why does madness deserve what wisdom doesn't insure? Where is it written that tolerance toward the mentally ill is the last horizon of human morality? Something tells me that if, interrupting the infinite series of indulgences this kid has enjoyed in recent years, I started kicking him, if I gave in to the low instinct that urges me to stop up his mouth with a fist, a lot of people would be grateful, would give me credit. Is it possible that this counts for nothing? That the likely gratitude of those people is so insignificant? I'm sure, just to take an exam-

ple, that if I were to hit Giacomo, the Arab would go into rap-
tures, just as, behind the public expressions of indignation,
Nanni himself would feel inside a primitive, healthy pleasure.
Who gives me this certainty? No one, naturally. It's something
I feel. Someone might tell me that beating up Giacomo would
be pointless, that he's lost by now. That violence is never the
right prescription. But who says I want to, or should, help
Giacomo? Why think only of his welfare and not that of the
people he insults every day? What about me, and my welfare?
Why is only his important? Haven't I suffered enough? I swear
that punching Giacomo, here, in front of everyone, not only
would give me an immediate, almost irreplaceable joy but
would resolve, in advance, a lot of the problems that afflict me
now.

Naturally this is merely internal nonsense. In reality I'm just
sitting here, annihilated, at the mercy of this bastard who can't
wait to tear me to pieces. Meanwhile he's silent, and then he
starts up again, whiny and insincere:

"You think I don't know that the only reason you see me,
the only reason you stand what nobody can stand, the only
reason you accept the humiliation of being my friend, the only
reason you're sitting here with me, embarrassed, like a thief, is
to get credit with Nanni and Gaia? You want to be part of
their life, not mine. You want them to like you, not me. Don't
deny it! You know what I am for you? The key to the royal
palace. I'm your lucky number. That's why you're so nice. You
take me for a pizza, and you take me to buy records, and to the
movies, and you tell me stories . . . Isn't that true? You know,
Daniel, you're the worst of all. You're the fake good guy who's
about to explode. Anyway, I just wanted to tell you that it's no
use. It's pointless for you to care about me. You'd just have to
hear what Nanni says about the Sonninos to know that you
don't have any hope with Gaia. That the biggest shit among
your friends would have more. Maybe even a circus midget."

And he concludes, "It's strange that someone like you, someone who's had as much as you, goes after that loser sister of
mine . . ."

Another pause. A sip of grappa.

"And yet, Dani, if I were you, with the mother you have, the
father, the brother . . ."

He didn't look at me, continuing to enumerate almost in a
trance the members of my family, toward whom, in spite of the
nasty words addressed to them a few minutes earlier, he
seemed to feel an invidious veneration. A characteristic of his
dialogue was the sudden change of perspective. Every urgent
assertion was almost immediately turned upside down. This
didn't seem to be a means of disconcerting the other person;
rather, it was a peculiar form of intolerance, a tendency to be
ambiguous. It was as if that exasperating clash that occurs
secretly in our head between a reason and its opposite,
between truth and bad faith, between authenticity and expedi-
ence, in Giacomo, on the other hand, expressed itself on the
battlefield of his fragmented conversations.

But this is all canned crap, I caught myself thinking then, as
if to break the siege of his plodding lecture: the eternal recitation of daddy's (or granddaddy's) boys who say they envy you.
There they are, nobly reaching out and unsatisfied, ready to
throw you a sop. Happy to recognize the marvels of a humble
existence. They look at you and seem to say: "You, with your
mediocre life, with no prospects, you are the incarnation of
privilege. It's you, whose life wasn't burdened with expectations, who know the genuine value of family happiness." Yes,
the timeless role I know all too well, if only because I've played
it at least a dozen times. If this is what you have to say to me,
my dear Giacomo, you are on the wrong track. There's nothing upsetting, nothing earth-shattering in what you're telling
me. There's just a little narcissism mixed with a good dose of

self-pity. An undigestible dish that I myself have served to less well-off friends.

"Do you know what it's like to have a nonexistent mother, who sends postcards from unspecified places? Or a grandmother obsessed with *bon ton*?" he asks me suddenly, with the forced smile of someone who is holding back emotion.

Giacomo loves to reduce his existence to these snapshots: definitions that possess an evocative or even amusing power but still bear witness to an unfortunate inclination to melodrama.

"And especially the main event: that lunatic Nanni. Let's see what we have. To you Nanni seems normal, to everyone he seems normal, prudent. I realize that that's how he seems to others. He's very skillful at dissimulating. But believe me, you only have to live with him day after day to realize that he's the real lunatic in the group. Not me. Him. He always wants to give the impression of being on this side of things. Only when you know him the way I do, then you realize he's the lunatic. And that his being on this side is only a pathetic lie. A PR trick. That his true inadmissible vocation is to be on the other side of things . . . But you know his real problem," Giacomo resumes after finishing the second grappa and ordering another from the increasingly intractable Arab, "is that he wasn't born an aristocrat? Does that seem like an acceptable problem, worthy of note? It's true. Otherwise why would he encourage so many mysteries about his birth? And why spend so much money on that ridiculous genealogical research? Did you know that his name, Cittadini, annoys him? He can't bear it. It's so bourgeois. Cittadini stinks of Jacobinism. God, what a horror. He should have had a name like Odescalchi or Farnese or Pallavicino or Barberini or Boncompagni Ludovisi . . . This is what he thinks. He tortures himself. Anything but Cittadini. This is his vanity, Dani. He feels cheated of a title that is due him. That's why when he's with his fancy friends he calls him-

self by Grandmother's surname. If only you knew how thrilled
he is when someone introduces him: 'May I present Prince
Altavilla!' He doesn't see how ridiculous it is. He doesn't get it.
He doesn't see that they despise him, that they live for genealogy, for their fellow bluebloods, and they certainly won't be
taken in by a parvenu. They can smell them, parvenus. They
are surrounded by parvenus. They were born and raised with
the mission of flushing them out. That's why Papa married
Mama, under the old man's goddam pressure. That old man is
a champion in the art of pressuring and the art of damning.
You know, it's not very nice to be manipulated by a maniac of
class-consciousness. It's incredible, he brought us up as if we
belonged to the royal family. You should see the shows he
organized when we were little. When he said, 'Come,
Giacomo, be good, this behavior is unworthy of a Cittadini.'
No kidding, literally. And he said it just as seriously as you
might say: 'This behavior is unworthy of a Windsor.' Were you
at the last foxhunt? That really spectacular one? Come on,
even Bepy was there! It was like in the times of Queen Victoria.
Everyone in a red jacket and everyone, holy Jesus everyone, in
a top hat . . . How many fucking dogs were there . . ."

Another sip.

"He organizes incredible parties just to invite those people.
Anyone who has a title is asked. And they all line up, the
spongers—and how. This bunch of snobs is ready to enjoy life
at Nanni's expense. That time, during the foxhunt (but do you
really not remember it?), I sneaked under the table so I could
hear what they were saying. One goes, 'Have you ever in all
your life seen such crudeness?' And they laugh, yes, they laugh
at him. You should see how they laugh . . . In fact, I thought it
was my duty to inform him that they were laughing at him.
And he slapped me. He didn't speak to me for weeks. I think
that's when he started to hate me. But it didn't seem to me so
terrible that people were laughing at him. Isn't it great to make

people laugh? I know I make them laugh, and I'm happy about it, Dani, I swear. We're a family of comics, but I seem to be the only one who fucking gets it. You have no idea how much laughter that unwitting comic Nanni caused with that statue!"

"What statue?"

"What? You don't even know about the statue?"

"No."

"The statue at the front door, you must have seen it a hundred thousand times."

"So what about it?"

"Nanni never told you about the statue?"

"No."

"That should be enough to prove to you that you don't count for shit in his eyes . . . Come on, his adored statue. An eighteenth-century bust he bought at an auction. One day he brings it home and tells us it's an ancestor of his. He's not specific—he doesn't offer details. He doesn't tell us the name or anything else. All he says is it's his ancestor. His rediscovered ancestor. That he has no doubts. That when he saw that statue he heard a voice."

"A voice?"

"Yes: the voice of blood. So he says. The voice of blood. 'Is it possible that you don't see it?' he says, and his voice trembles. 'He has my very expression, my hair! Look, Gaia, he has your nose!'"

Giacomo tells me that over time Nanni has constructed an identity for that anonymous bust. He has given it a name, a title, invented a life for it, with events, sorrows, joys, successes, griefs. And he is so in love with that invented ancestor that he has ended up believing in his historical existence. Yes, the emotion is genuine. You'd better not remind him of the day he brought it home, when all he knew for sure was that it was the portrait of a noble relative. Better not confront him with his pathetic deception. If you did, as Giacomo has a thousand times, he would get so furious the walls of the house would shake.

"This is the man I've had to live with since Mama left. It's this deluded lunatic who brought me up. Grandma might as well not have existed. She was essentially absent. For her it was important that we behaved well. The only thing my grandmother taught me is that you kiss a woman's hand only indoors and never with girls who are younger than seventeen. And guess what, I found out a few days ago that that's bullshit, too—these people are so spineless they can't even come up with strict rules. What I mean is that I was at the mercy of this improbable duo, this vaudeville team. They left us to Nanni and Fifi. They're like a pair of miniature Schnauzers!" In full Shakespearean exaltation Giacomo concludes, "And it's Gaia who closes the circle. She is the last act of this folly. She is Nanni's worthy accomplice. What do you think happened between her and Dav? Why did they break up? You really believe the story that they didn't get along? It's all so formal with her. The world collapses, people die, kill themselves, and she continues to be formal like a lady of the seventeenth century. Dav left her. He's a sincere guy. You know, I like him a lot. Dav understood her right away. He did what he had to do with her. And then he left her. After that big mess, he dropped her."

Suddenly I feel my throat assaulted by a memory.

It was one of the first times I had to wear evening clothes, and I was driven to steal from my father a brown overcoat with emerald-green velvet lapels, to be up to the party that the Arcieris had planned for the sixteenth birthday of their only daughter, Diamante, in a club called Jackie O', I suppose in homage to Jackie Kennedy, which by then was slightly out of favor. I begged my mother to let me also take a hat, but there she was immovable: "Come, you already look like a miniature gangster. Sweetie, even the grotesque has a limit!"

A taxi left me at the start of Via Boncompagni, between the massed lights of the Excelsior and the ungainly structure that is still the home of the American Embassy. Although deprived of my gangster hat, I set off in a triumph of hopes nourished by the abundance of urban details with which I filled my spirit on the way: the lights of the closed shops, the parked cars, the mysterious archipelagos formed by the dog shit on the ground and the leaves of the plane trees in the sky . . . All this seemed to have multiplied by ten my already high expectations. I'm afraid I have to confess a fatal weakness for worldly pleasures: the two hours that precede a party, completely devoted to the care of oneself—when the steam of the shower seems to mingle with the equally dense fog of the creative imagination—are among the best things life has to offer. So naturally the disappointment inspired by the dull actuality of the party derives not from an objective evaluation but from the weighty sample book of failed promises.

And of course Diamante Arcieri's party was not an exception: and reality, yet again, got the better of fantasy.

So, with the feeling of nausea induced by emotional emptiness, at a not too indecent hour I crossed the cavernous space that led to the club's exit, where I would find a taxi in which to finally swallow the poison of that innocuous discouragement. It was then that I distinctly heard a sigh. A sigh that had something both mystical and pornographic about it. I turned in the direction of that sigh. Pitch darkness. With a servile and somewhat ironic gesture, the black bouncer, dressed for the occasion like a seventeenth-century page, half opened the door for me, and a beam of yellow light made its way in to illuminate two entwined bodies. The plastic pose of those bodies made one think of some lively Baroque sculpture. But in fact the most Baroque legacy of the scene was the girl's parted lips: lips in ecstasy: lips that have just emitted a mortal sigh. And although I would have liked to believe that that mystical sigh had originated in a vision of God, it was clear that it had been generated by the knowing hand of the boy, which had been maneuvering under her skirt.

In this theatrical, succinct, and seventeenth-century way, I had discovered what everyone had known for a while: that Gaia and Dav were together. Until that moment my tranquility had been safeguarded by the somnambulistic state by which at the time I was mercifully favored. Everyone had known about Gaia and Dav for at least a year and a half and knew it to the point that the encounter of their single names had been transformed into a trademark: Gaia & Dav. *Are Gaia and Dav coming? . . . Did you see Gaia and Dav last night? . . . What do you think, should we wait for Gaia and Dav?,* how many times recently had I heard such expressions uttered! Maybe I should have gotten angry with my brain rather than with my ears. I knew I had heard that trademark, Gaia & Dav, pronounced thousands of times in my presence, just as I knew I had never wanted to wonder about its meaning.

Gaia & Dav: it wasn't an enigma, really. It was an incontrovertible fact that I had simply ignored. No, I had never suspected. Not because some compassionate creature had kept me in the dark, as people do with standard cuckolds, but only because generally no one is interested in talking about obvious things. I had avoided the evidence and followed the lie with such obtuse determination that only now did I understand how many realities I had had to transfigure to protect myself from the unbearable truths contained in that commercial logo: Gaia & Dav.

What's certain is that the taxi, which was supposed to accommodate a bitterness that wasn't essentially unpleasant, became a real inferno. Today I know that the suffering of love consists of the progressive narrowing of the entire world into a single point. It's as if a point had devoured the entire universe in a rapid mouthful. That was exactly what was happening. It's not enough to say that the exhalation of breath that defined Gaia's sigh changed my life. It's more precise to say that that sigh became my life, superimposing itself and taking its place.

Ironically, Gaia and Dav, for the reasons that Giacomo is preparing to demonstrate, broke up a few days after Diamante Arcieri's party, and I began to suffer like a dog because of that now jeopardized relationship, after living happily—during the fabulous years of Gaia & Dav—in the grip of a self-protective blindness. But I was so thoroughly pervaded by that sigh, I was so traumatized by all its implications, that I chose not to be interested in anything else for the coming decades: to decipher that sigh with masochistic passion was the purpose of my existence.

That's why, although Giacomo has just posed two unexceptionable questions (*Why do you think they broke up? Do you really believe the story that they didn't get along?*), I have no problem admitting to myself that I've never posed them to myself. At least not in those terms.

What does it matter to me why they broke up, if I still haven't learned to endure the idea that they were together?

That's how I should have answered him.

And in fact the ending of that high-school relationship concealed other thorns that surely could not escape my intellect, always in search of a scourge to flog myself with. From the little information I'd picked up, and from observing the state of mind of the parties, I had understood not only that Dav had left her but that, with the indolence that distinguished him, the young man had not felt bound to provide her with an adequate explanation.

And the worst thing that can happen to someone who is used to being pursued and yearned for—being the principal object of Collective Desire—is to find, even once, the roles reversed. So Gaia found that she had to pursue the idol incarnate of her life. And having had, over the years, no experience as a pursuer, having no training in this difficult, tormenting discipline, she had dramatically mistaken her moves. She had not been discreet. She had thrown herself into winning Dav back too impetuously. She hadn't been able to conceal her desperation. She had made herself ridiculous. She had overwhelmed him with letters, notes, even expensive presents, and humiliating telephone entreaties. "Please, love, don't hang up, just two minutes! Please . . ." "I've got things to do, come on . . ." It was so nice that he still let her call him "love." "At least tell me what happened! I have the right to know why you left me. Don't tell me because of that scene with Grandpa. That has nothing to do with it, right?" "What's the point of discussing it?" "Please, tell me that has nothing to do with it. That I have nothing to do with it. I've done everything you asked. I'll do everything you ask, but please . . . Grandpa hasn't spoken to me for days, and all because of you!" "Come on, honey, we've talked about it at least a hundred times. There's nothing else to say. If you don't get it I'm sorry." And it was a miracle that he had the magnanimity to call her "honey"! "David, my love, dear . . ." "Come on, don't cry!" "My love?" "What?" "Another minute. Don't hang up. Please. Another minute . . . even if you're quiet—you don't have to say anything." The result of this suicidal strategy was to transform Dav's indifference into pity, pity into irritation, irritation finally into contempt. The problem was that Gaia loved him. And felt, for reasons she considered incontrovertible, that she had grasped Dav's uniqueness better than anyone else. She had a full membership in the club of the Victims of David Ruben: and, unfortunately, being attached to that uniqueness she didn't know how to give it up. *There's no other David Ruben in the universe*, she whispered to herself with the emphasis of a debutante. And, in fact, did there exist another boy who could have persuaded her to get up on a Sunday morning at five—she who so loved to sleep—to go trout fishing? No, there didn't. But the sole fact that there existed another girl (not more deserving than she was) who would soon replace her (or who had already done so), another sleepy girl forced to drink a boiling-hot latte macchiato at dawn to follow her fisherman hero through fantastic adventures amid woods, streams, and lakes, made her wild with jealousy.

And maybe we should grant her more than one extenuating circumstance: in particular, the peremptory way in which Dav had got rid of her. Without offering explanations, without listening to Gaia's protests and prayers, showing an even cruel hardness, the symptom of an astonishing incapacity for empathy, and leaving the poor girl in a state of such depression as to make her question—for the first time in the course of her brief existence—herself. Wow! Could there be something about her—about Gaia Cittadini, the most pampered girl of her generation—that wasn't right? Was her voice grating? Was her company boring? Her breath bad? Maybe that was it? Why at a certain point had he stopped wanting to kiss her? Was there anything more incredibly exciting in the world than to kiss those lips, Dav's lips? Yes, maybe there was something.

And then, how could you not value a sparkling and outgoing personality like Dav Ruben's? Good God, we're talking about one of those special individuals—like Bepy, just to be clear—who have the gift of transforming everything they touch into a cult object. Dav corrupted your existence through his. He made things that had never interested you indispensable. He awoke in you a desire for hedonistic variety that ordinary life tends to crush, even if your name is Gaia Cittadini, even if you're the granddaughter of a princess and a successful Rastignac! Dav was a repository of vices, habits, eccentricities, tastes, restaurants, places, verbal expressions, sports, films, intrigues, and a lot of other things that placed whoever came into contact with him in the condition of a poor beggar who for the first time, thanks to a prize trip, experiences the Pompeian comforts of a luxury hotel in the sordid belly of Manhattan. Once you've felt the pleasure of being served in your room by a host of waiters, and become accustomed to Oriental massages, to the variety of ethnic restaurants and high-class barbers, can you go back to living in your lousy suburb?

Dav ruined you fatally.

And Gaia, my Gaia, was desperate. She was sure, even if she wouldn't have confessed it to anyone, that this was a grief more pervasive than her grief at the death of her father. Pain that offered no respite. That didn't evolve. That was always right at the point where it started, so that she couldn't imagine an alternative. A grief that had the singular quality of returning just when it had pretended to disappear forever. She was appalled that love for a living individual could be more intense than that for a dead man, blood of her blood, *my daddy* . . . And in this regard a new thought occupied her mind—one of those worms that we tend to ignore but that in certain moments of life reclaim their right to torture us. How could you underrate the fact that the two men in her life, the ones she had loved most, had, in one way or another, chosen to abandon her? All right, her father hadn't shot himself because of her. About this Nanni had been very clear. Gaia still remembered when Nanni, disfigured by grief and the grueling attempt to hide it, had called them—her and Giacomo— to his office, to say that they—she and Giacomo—had nothing to do with that tragedy, he knew absolutely that they—she and Giacomo—had no responsibility, no guilt. That Ricky loved them—her and Giacomo— "with all his heart," that if he hadn't been forced by circumstances he would never have abandoned them. That if someone was guilty it was . . . here Nanni interrupted himself between sobs. No, Gaia hadn't forgotten her composure in the face of those foolish speeches, or that of her brother, just as she had not forgotten Nanni's tearful anguish. And yet, despite all these considerations, one fact remained: she, in barely sixteen years, had been abandoned twice, and by the men in her life. And this made her reflect,

fostering that form of self-pity which can even, in some circumstances, turn out to be pleasant.

She didn't understand how Dav had so mysteriously got into
her. She felt almost at fault for this. Thus she discovered that
the sight of every place in the city she had gone with Dav in that
year and a half of their relationship (streets, shops, bars, restaurants, movie theaters . . .) was like a blow to the back of the
neck that forced her to lower her eyes. Suddenly Gaia found
her city hostile as it had never been: not to mention when, the
rare times she was in a car on the beltway with Nanni's chauffeur, she happened to see the sign "Olgiata." That sign stung
like a lash. Gaia was discovering what, sooner or later, we all
discover: how essentially vulnerable we are in love, how easy it
is to remain stuck in something so complex and how desperately difficult it is to emerge from it unscathed. She was surprised that even her own body was a cause of evocation.

For example, Dav had always loved Gaia's mouth, he had
never made a mystery of it, in fact he was a marvelously explicit guy: he never tired of repeating: "What amazing lips, love!"
(Was it possible that he had stopped desiring them point-
blank? How was it possible to stop desiring something so highly desirable? Why had he left her? And why hadn't he
explained to her why? Was it possible that he was so cruel? So
crazy? That he felt no *affection* for her?) In other words, it
happened more and more often that, looking in the mirror to
put on her lip gloss, she was struck by the sight of her own
mouth: because if that mouth wasn't loved by Dav, if it wasn't
used by him for his pleasure (and God knows in how many
salacious ways he had used it), it no longer had any meaning.
Without Dav, her lips no longer deserved to occupy a place of
honor on that face.

And so in the first days after their separation Gaia had tried
to avoid any object, any situation, any place that could remind
her of Dav. She had done this diligently, with the determina-

tion that she always put into her passions. But she soon abandoned this intention, observing its intrinsic fallacy: it was impossible to exercise any control over the countless evocations that reality produced every day. It was pointless to try to escape those scourges because they attacked like outlaws in a medieval wood. The only way to avoid the terrible moments when a sudden memory made her knees weak would have been to stop living: to take her life. But that was unthinkable, and also vaguely ridiculous.

Gaia's senses had never been so alert as during that time. She was bothered by noises that were too loud and smells that were too strong. The mysterious fact is that from the moment Dav was no longer with her everything seemed to offend her personally: a horn blaring in the street or the smell of fried food coming from the half-open door of a Chinese restaurant. This was hell. Even at home, even with her family she became intolerant. She couldn't bear, for example, the way Nanni ate soup—he was very fond of soup. Not that her grandfather slurped noisily but at the end of every spoonful Gaia seemed to perceive a faint whistle that made her shudder. That certainly couldn't be attributed to bad manners; more probably it was the new dentures that had returned Nanni's mouth to the splendor of youth. He had been showing them off for months, for months he had been trying to keep them from whistling. Was it possible that she had become aware of it only now? And with such an alarming revulsion?

Since Gaia had been in that state, since she had been an unhappy and inexplicably abandoned lover, she had dreamed only of shutting herself up in a hyperbaric chamber and cutting off any contact with the civilized and, especially, the uncivilized world.

At the same time, however, she had a painful nostalgia for certain strong odors (some of which it would be indecent to note). How could she forget the smell of Dav? That really was unforgettable. When she got up behind him on his motorcycle—the red-white-and-blue Honda NS so fashionable at the time—when she held him from behind, and felt between her fingers the promontories of that Norman giant's ribs, she had to press her nose into the hollow between his neck and shoulder. Shamelessly nuzzling his shirt collar to sniff that unmistakable odor of bitter grapes and detergent had became a habit that nearly made her faint. Well, now the memory was enough, the memory of that damn odor of Dav—an odor that couldn't be reproduced, even in a laboratory, an odor that would never belong to someone else, an odor that presumably wouldn't survive him, that odor destined for other blondes no less attractive than she, an odor that had been given to her and then taken away, that probably she would never again smell from so close, that odor of a unique time—to make her explode in convulsive nighttime sobs.

(A few minutes ago, to rest my fingertips and brain from the tour de force I've subjected them to in the past hours of flight, I picked up a copy of *Time* from the seat pocket in front of me. As I leafed distractedly through it, my eyes were caught by a rather interesting article: a team of English scholars claim to have demonstrated that love is an experience linked in particular to the sense of smell. A smile escaped me. I don't know if this discovery is yet another tribute paid by Anglo-Saxon hyper-rationalism to universal obtuseness, but, for what it's worth, I can testify that almost twenty years ago I knew a girl who would have subscribed to that scientific hypothesis. For Gaia the smell of Dav wasn't one of the many attributes of her love for him. No, quite simply, all her love was bound up in Dav's smell.)

Gaia wasn't only sighs and yearnings. Her body also secreted rage and a legitimate desire for revenge. How could it be otherwise? The memory of how Dav had approached her, just two years earlier, drove her crazy, and so the memory of how, although he liked her, she was on the whole indifferent to him, filled her with nostalgia. God, if only she had rejected him. If only she could have replayed some of the moves on the chess-board of their relationship! If only she had given him one of the unforgettable rejections that she—Gaia Cittadini—had learned so early to extend to her suitors . . . There had been a time when he was so attentive and she so confident. She cursed herself for not having treated him badly then. For getting suck-ered like that. Naturally, to be transformed into contempt, all this rage needed some hook. And she had a physiological need to despise him. If only because the path of contempt seemed to her the right way of cutting down to size the idol who seemed to have taken possession of her mind (some days she had the impression she had been thinking of him constantly for the entire fourteen hours that divided one sleep from the next, and sometimes, on waking, was sure he had slipped into her dreams to disturb them). Yes, the road of emancipation passed through contempt. And to succeed in that desperate under-taking she had to draw on all Nanni and Sofia's snobbishness, appeal to the sense of distinction that together they had instilled in her. The only weapon available to that girl was social and religious discrimination.

That dirty Jew! That nouveau-riche bourgeois with the repug-nant father, the sparkling-clean mother, and that pretentious house!

Yes, Nanni's thoughts rethought by the mind of his grand-daughter, for a noble purpose: mental hygiene and regaining an appearance of tranquility. And yet the insincerity of those invectives was so obvious that the faults she tendentiously attributed to Dav were immediately transformed in her mind into authentic qualities. Because Dav—her Dav—couldn't live in any other house. Because Dav—the Dav she loved so des-perately—couldn't have other parents. And what could David

Ruben be if not Jewish? Jew. Jew. Jew. Was it possible that that word, which for her had never meant anything, now perfectly defined her fate? That now it would be enough to come across a television reporter speaking with dismay of the Israeli-Palestinian war to fall into an enervating swoon? Could it be that she dreamed of converting?

And finally the hoariest of all questions in that school of ours, and in the rest of the universe as well: the opinion of others. Who knows why Gaia, who had never been ashamed of anything, had now begun to consider her condition an indelible disgrace. As if having been left, and continuing to love without being loved, represented a loss of style or even a serious offense. So she constantly feigned good humor: an effort that must have cost her a great deal and and did not pay off: because the slightest thing—a fleeting allusion by someone to David, to Olgiata, Jews, fishing, American movies, and so many other unpredictable things—could produce, on that usually composed face, the livid wound of her distress. As if she had lost command of herself, as if her proverbial self-control had failed. But this wasn't the only problem. As the days passed, and the news that David had left her (for another girl?) spread, Gaia had increasingly had the paranoid sensation that others were plotting against her. Even with good intentions. But that didn't console her. It was pathetic.

One day, for example, she had left her gym shoes in the classroom. (She had been so absent-minded lately.) The teacher had allowed her to come in and get them. So Gaia, after putting them on, had run back to the gym. But opening the door with breathless energy, she had had the impression that her friends, alarmed, had abruptly stopped talking. Were they talking about her? Or about David's new girlfriend? Evidently they knew who it was, that whore! Once it had been she who knew everything about Dav, who guarded his secrets, now she was the only girl who didn't have the right to know anything. And yet she would have liked to ask a lot of questions . . . But she knew that even the most compassionate answer would upset her for days. By now she had seen how it worked: better that fog of vague notions and hair-raising hypotheses with which she had been living for several weeks than the few certain facts that she had found out by chance and that had kept her from sleeping for several nights in a row. No, she would ask nothing. She would bite her tongue in order not to ask those witches anything. But a few minutes later her ears couldn't help picking up some shreds of conversation among her companions. So she had figured it all out. The next day there was to be a big party at the Rubens'. One of the many, of course. But for Gaia the most important because it was the first at which she would not be present. That was what they had wanted to hide from her!

Not to be invited to that party seemed to her a monstrous injustice. And to think that David more than once had made her feel like the mistress of the house. She recalled the time she had helped Signora Ruben and the Filipino maid set the table near the pool with green cloth placemats for an improvised supper of cold cuts, cheese, and grilled vegetables. It was early June. In that season the air had such an evocative color and such a fragrant scent! Did all that still exist, somewhere? She recalled the smiles of understanding she had exchanged with Dav's mother, the smiles between a daughter-in-law and mother-in-law who adore one another. So, remembering those smiles, Gaia found a completely new way of torturing herself. She had only to rethink that scene with a slight variation. Picture it without omitting a single detail, and then insert the modification: change the girl and the rosy dream became a nightmare. No, she wasn't the one helping Signora Ruben, she wasn't the one breathing in that lovely scent of star jasmine and chlorine, it wasn't she who felt herself a happy daughter-in-law. Those horrible Rubens had changed the lead actress; they had given the starring role to another obliging little whore.

Everyone could go to that house. Was it possible that she alone—who had been predestined—could no longer do so? Maybe this is the risk run by the sultan's favorites: the risk of being suddenly cast out. It made no sense. Gaia had never hated the others as at that moment.

So sometimes—it could happen suddenly, without any real warning—Gaia became conscious that Dav was lost, that Dav belonged to someone else, that Dav would never be hers. This burst of observations choked her, as if she were confronted by something both unjust and implacable. Those were the moments when she would have liked to see her rival. She would have liked to know everything about her, with a morbid curiosity. What was her name? Where did she live? What had she been doing until then? Was she aware of having caused such suffering to another individual? Lord, how marvelous if she were to die! What a miracle if the nameless rival were the victim of a car accident . . . Then she, Gaia, would certainly be back on the scene. She would console him, she would pour out all her pity and all her understanding and he would be unable to resist. It was so nice to think of the death of that anonymous whore! If only she had never been born! If only he had never met her! For the moment Gaia couldn't help imagining her: tall as a model, cold as a Swede, rich as Onassis, and uninhibited as a . . .

So Gaia dreamed of being a fly on a wall. She dreamed of hovering in her antagonist's room (even if it was pathetic to consider her as such: there was basically no contest, the war had already been lost!), she dreamed of seeing her without being seen, of stealing into her room. She must be a really exceptional creature to have replaced her, Gaia Cittadini, the most desirable of all desirable girls! Imagine, at certain moments Gaia felt she loved her rival, even if in a sinister way. It was clear: if Dav loved her, how could she not love her? Dav had taught Gaia to consider necessary certain things that she would never have believed it possible to love. The thought of the faceless enemy hurt more than the thought of David. And Gaia was simply terrified by it.

And I'm afraid that Gaia deserves our respect: she is learning the hardest lesson: she is learning that no one is irreplaceable. Not even she, Gaia Cittadini—not even she, who has always felt that she was so precious, not even she, who has always believed that she was above any other woman, is irreplaceable. So Gaia has come to understand that you shouldn't believe men who say "There's no one like you." You shouldn't believe them when they say they'll never leave you. Not that they don't believe it. Maybe sometimes they do. But then? Then, from one instant to the next, they stop believing it: even the most stable of situations can be turned upside down. Don't fret over it. You have to accept it, as one accepts the death of a father and the madness of a brother. Some things sting because they don't make sense, and because you can't change them.

Dav isn't there anymore. Just try to start over. The future: well, that at least never stops existing! Ah yes, this really made her cry.

Naturally, among the countless components of that hostile universe that Gaia, out of pure expressive convenience, called "the others," there was also me.

It took me a while to grasp the sinister reason that Gaia had suddenly started hanging out with me with such suspicious constancy: evidently, apart from all her precautions, she wanted to stay close to someone who could claim a steady friendship with Dav, even at the cost of great suffering. And in that devotion of hers there was something I find it easy to call heroic. It was obvious that she was betting everything on my friendship with Dav (that manly alliance that modestly preferred to skip over every detail of our respective intimate lives, to the point that he didn't feel bound to inform me about Gaia and him, and I had never told him that Gaia was my whole life). She considered me on a level with that gray sweatshirt Dav had once left at her house and she hadn't wanted to give back: at a certain point, exasperated, she had to hide it, in order not to suffer more. Or like that gold ring with the diamond, made for the occasion by the Atelier Ruben with the blessing of a radiant Karen, which Dav had given her one evening (God, did that evening really happen?). Still, with respect to these inanimate objects that served to anesthetize her grief or intensify it, I at least had the virtue of being alive and kind and able to bring her first-hand news of Dav.

Basically why should I complain? More than I had ever dared to desire had happened. Hadn't I dreamed innumerable times of Gaia's unhappiness? Not out of meanness. Or at least I don't think so. What could I do about it if—as I had many times observed—that girl's happiness seemed to harmonize perfectly with my desperation? How could I not see that between her joys and my sufferings there seemed to have been established over time a relationship of cause and effect? So if her joy hurt me so much, if it was so intolerable, it was reasonable to believe that if she were sick or had been struck a heavy blow, or suffered a serious loss, my mood would suddenly lighten.

How wrong I was! I didn't like seeing her sad.

And not out of a sudden burst of philanthropy, which at the time I was too desperate to allow myself, or sympathy for her, which, moreover, I would never feel. How could I feel pity for her? Pity is essentially a luxury that we permit ourselves to feel only for individuals we arrogantly consider inferior. And then it has to be said that the *pain of love*—although each of us has felt it, and felt how exhausting it is for our body and for our psyche—hardly inspires pity: the most we can grant a friend in a sentimental crisis is a little well-concealed disapproval: as if he were wasting time on some foolishness. "With all the children dying of hunger . . . with all the wars devastating the world . . . you're poisoning your life for that." No, there is nothing more incommunicable than the pain of love.

More than anything else it was as if Gaia—with her display of melancholy and moodiness—were violating a commercial contract that required her to always be at the peak of the emotional curve. The fact that she took such liberties with respect to the idea that I had treacherously constructed of her, from the first time I saw her, at Bepy's funeral—an idea reinforced by the sight of the sun-drenched sailor girl who jumped out of the motorboat Riva—put my faith in my love to a hard test. It was as if my love had been nourished on expectations. Not coincidentally it had blazed up fiercely just in those days when I was staying in Positano at the magnificent villa dedicated to Gaia. And from then on my love had received from that magnificence only encouraging confirmation. And Gaia, at least until that moment, had never betrayed me. She had given me the illusion that there existed in the world a race of individuals for whom things always went well. Individuals whose lives were never poisoned by unexpected frustrations. But suddenly here I was, confronted by this new, improbable plaintive Gaia. No, it didn't make me sorry for her; it made me shudder. I, who had accepted with such stoic elation her presumed contempt for me, did not feel ready to be contemptuous of her in turn. I really didn't know what to do with my contempt.

Besides, the sole fact that she had been rejected by David— who although immeasurably superior to me was still a human being—placed her in a different perspective. Did this mean that she was not the most to which a man could aspire? Was there someone on the planet who, having enjoyed her favors for a while, had ended up being bored and getting rid of her? If from a rational point of view this was completely intelligible to me, from an emotional point of view it was insane. And yet that's how things were. My uneasiness was increased by the fact that the one who had felt that unthinkable boredom was not an abstract being whose inclinations I could transfigure and perhaps deify but, on the contrary, Dav, my friend Dav, a splendid individual, as I never tired of observing, but too real to be genuinely idolized by me. Shit, I wasn't Giorgio Sevi. I knew who Dav was. I knew his limitations better than he knew mine. And the fact that he had allowed himself the luxury of disdainfully rejecting the girl I loved so madly placed me in a position of clear inferiority in the cruel food chain. Yes, I was the small fish daily devoured by Gaia, who in turn was torn to pieces by Dav.

And maybe it was just to redress what seemed to me a Darwinian imbalance, to close the circle of that chain on which I was the last link in a cycle of death, that I resolved to stop speaking to Dav. I did it suddenly, with a self-control that seemed to everyone (but above all to him) the ultimate crazy act of that raving madman Daniel Sonnino, but which instead was, if you think about it, the product of a cold rationality and the tormented desire to restore a semblance of earthly justice.

You should have seen Dav! He couldn't believe his eyes. He followed me, asking for an explanation: what had he done to me? Had he offended me in some way? If so he was sorry! If only I'd talk to him. If I would just say something, damn it. A single word. And I remained silent, as unshakable as those heroic novices who, after making a vow not to utter a sound for the rest of their life, forget the verdant seductions of language. Not that I expected him to suffer as I had suffered for Gaia or as Gaia had suffered for him. I knew that it's not so difficult to lose a friend. But I amused myself with the idea that my having offered no explanations would keep him agitated for quite some time.

Years passed before I would speak to Dav again. But that's another story.

*

Sure enough, a few days before Gaia's birthday, she seemed to have completely gotten rid of the shadow of the only boy who had ever rejected her. To the point where the two had grown close again. They often talked on the phone as friends do (is that how love stories end, in paradise?). I had gone back to being for Gaia the best uninteresting friend she had ever had and, further, I had lost Dav. I couldn't say, besides, if in the final reckoning any of us had gained; as for myself I'm convinced— I already was then, basically—not only that I wasted a lot of time that could have been better spent in countless more gratifying ways but that, in spite of everything, I wouldn't have known how to behave differently.

One fact, however, was certain, learned from experience: Gaia's suffering insulted me personally no less than her happiness.

Come on, my boy, what do you want from this damn girl? Let's try to recapitulate: you can't bear it if she's happy. You can't bear it if she's unhappy. You can't bear her to seem indifferent. On the other hand, you can't bear her friendship. You don't want to be with her. And yet you can't accept that she doesn't want to be with you. You don't want to sleep with her. But if it were up to you, you wouldn't allow anyone else to, either . . . In short, can you tell us what the hell you want?

That's really not so hard to answer: I'd prefer that she had never existed. I'd prefer never to have known her. But at this point, having already met her, all I can do is to wish ardently for her death!

"Like a movie!" Giacomo shrieks at the height of excitement. I make a gesture with my hand to push him to lower his voice. And then, still in an exaggerated way, he starts to whisper.

"It's only been two and a half years," he says, "or not much more."

So what Giacomo called "like a movie" happened in the days after Diamante Arcieri's party, days that went down in the history of my tortured body as "the time of the mystical pornographic sigh."

"And Nanni never forgot it," Giacomo suddenly becomes explicit. "I'm telling you, it's not that long since he started speaking to Gaia again . . . Imagine, he was thinking of canceling her big party. He absolutely didn't want Dav to come. And all because of that really splendid story!"

"But what fucking story are you talking about?" I say to him, out of patience by this time.

"On Thursdays the Filipinos go out. And Nanni usually isn't there, either. He goes with Grandma to bridge, then they go to the movies. So every Thursday Gaia has David come over. They pretend to study. But then they play around . . . Shit, I can hear the moans from my room. What a marathon. They really go for it . . . One Thursday Nanni doesn't feel well and he comes home early, while the two lovebirds are in full swing. They count on Nanni's precision. Nanni is a man of habit. He always does things the same way. You know that if he goes out on Thursday, he won't be back before midnight. You know that as soon as he gets home he'll go immediately to see his little princess and give her a good night kiss with a cup of milk and honey in his hand, and he'll have her tell him about the day and all that other bullshit he likes so much . . . But this time he comes home early. No movie: he sends Grandma off on her own with her friends. He has a little headache. But he doesn't know that at home there's a show a hundred times more exciting. The show put on by his favorite little virgin. His fifteen-year-old innocent. A fine unscheduled program: because this time he doesn't find her in the giraffe-print pajamas he gave her. He doesn't find her on her bed studying, with her legs crossed and a pencil in her mouth. It's a splendid scene, Daniel. You're going to die . . .

"Nanni opens the door and sees his little princess completely naked, on her knees, and this time it's not the pencil she has in her mouth, it's Dav's dick. And you know what the really splendid part is? You can't imagine. It's that they're not alone. It's not only David and Gaia on the bed, there's another guy, too. They've invited him to watch. And he's not just watching. He's naked, too, and he also wants his nice share of . . . Get the picture, Dani? Isn't it incredibly marvelous? Isn't it something out of the movies? Gaia, before Nanni's shocked eyes, is awarded the prestigious title of Miss Orgiast of the Year. And you should have seen Nanni. He practically had a heart attack. He shrieks. He's beside himself. Or rather, no, he cries: 'What are you doing? What the hell are you doing to my little girl?' He grabs David, who's still naked, and still got a hard-on. But the other guy, Nanni's never seen him before and he can't get a hand on him. Dav doesn't react. Nor does the other guy. They're all petrified. And Nanni chases them out, wailing, 'Get out of here, you shit Jews!' Now Gaia is crying, too: 'No, Grandpa, I'm sorry, you don't understand.' So I come out of my room—out of curiosity, I've never seen them cry together, and yet they're both sentimental and they cry often, but I've never seen them together—so I come out and that shit Nanni shouts at me, 'Go, Giacomo, back to your room . . .' 'What's happening?' I ask him. 'Can't you see what's happening, you stupid lunatic? In your room, now, don't make me angry . . .' And meanwhile I see those two poor guys, half naked in their shirts, underpants in hand, going down the stairs and sneaking out the front door . . . Do you know what he called me, that shit? Lunatic."

It's what Giacomo has defined, with a certain approximation, as "a splendid story, like a movie" that triggered the disaster. In a single instant there takes shape in my mind—who knows, maybe under the influence of that innocent the Arab—the image of my Tolstoyan Natasha, my Christmas shopping companion, my vital aspiration, transformed into a feline porn actress, a champion cocksucker, a girl—according to the professional opinion of her brother—so skilled in the art of pleasure that she can no longer give it up, a whore so insatiable that she desires two men at once.

What did I do? What *was* I while this scene was taking place? How many times, during the years I spent in my little reading corner at home, engrossed in some nineteenth-century romantic novel, had I been naïvely serene, while, a few blocks away, the two most loved and envied individuals of my adolescence were playing around with a stranger? And what effect did all this produce on me now? Indignation. Pain, certainly.

But above all superhuman envy. An envy I would call transcendent.

And the really crazy thing is that I sent that letter, that terrible letter, filled with insults and threats of death, I proclaimed that ridiculous fatwa that literally ruined my life, cutting me off from the people with whom I would have liked to spend the rest of my days, that letter which made me a reject, which caused an entire neighborhood to stop speaking to my mother and father, that letter based on the ravings of a madman who had a thousand reasons to wish me harm and at least a million to ruin the birthday party so skillfully organized by his hated sister.

The rest is all consequential. Inevitable escalation. As I put on my evening jacket, faithfully helped by my father, who sticks the white handkerchief in my pocket and the monogrammed cufflinks in the buttonholes of the shirt, as I've done a thousand times with him, I think of Nanni. For once I think of him as an ally in defeat. I think of how his endemic anti-Semitism now has irreproachable pretexts. I think of the two women in his life, the two princesses, coupled by an exterior so modest and chaste and by an insatiable desire for sex . . . I think of the two Jews he had to temporarily give them to. I think of Bepy and David playing around behind Nanni's back and mine. I think of what idea the Catholic, pseudo-aristocratic, ultra-puritan Nanni Cittadini-Altavilla must have of the Jews. Nothing but satyrs. Satyrs with hard-ons. Satyrs without scruples. Without the least respect for what is high and untouchable. Satyrs always ready to attack beauty. Iconoclastic satyrs. That's what the Jews are. And I think that to this Jewish binomial (Bepy and David) poor Nanni will soon, sooner than he imagines, have to add the third musketeer of shamelessness. I'm talking about myself, naturally. Because as I tie my tie, while my father's eyes light up and my mother snaps a picture to immortalize her handsome younger son (a nice snapshot now sitting on a shelf of the bookcase in my funereal Roman apartment), I'm not so much thinking of how crazy it is to go to the party of a girl I sent a letter to, a couple of days ago, for which you could be reported to the police; nor am I thinking of a further plan for revenge—what do I know? ruin the party, behave indecently, hit Nanni, commit the threatened homicide of the just turned eighteen-year-old under the frightened eyes of her guests. No: it's the burning desire to see Gaia's room. To see the sacred precincts that hosted the marvelous sacrilege. Let's say that that mission might furnish an essential contribution to the archeology of my pain and new cues for my future sufferings.

Because this is my new obsession. The crazy letter has been written and sent. I haven't had an answer, it's logical to imagine that Gaia was upset and frightened by it. Meanwhile, in the grip of the same hysteria—squandering an adolescent's small savings, meant for something else—I bought her a ring at Bulgari. And immediately afterward I thought I had the duty and the right to see that room. I would go to the party, I would exploit the last possible occasion to enter that house undis-

turbed, at the risk of facing Gaia's astonishment and the indignation of her grandparents or of being thrown out by a security guard. I'd go to that party and at all costs visit that room, the
room upstairs that in these years of friendship with Gaia—
because of my usual boring idiosyncrasies—I'd never wanted
to see. Something compels me to this final pilgrimage!

The light is everywhere. The light is visible from a distance.
A hundred meters away the ochre house on Via Aldrovandi
sparkles like an incandescent flying saucer that is about to take
off into the sky. A metallic jam of gray luxury cars has blocked
traffic. So much polarized energy has never been seen: or
maybe only at certain night soccer matches, some movie sets,
in television studios. Neon lights, floodlights, torches: a futur-
ist triumph. Two spotlights at the corner of the gate have transformed a bougainvillea into a gigantic octopus with fuchsia
tentacles crushing a phosphorescent pine. Over the roof of the
main gate a wisteria cascades like foaming champagne overflowing from a newly uncorked bottle. And then all those kids,
the best you can find in Rome in the summer of '89. Kids
whose histories sing the praises of comfort and well-being.
Kids with a thousand prospects. Kids who will become lawyers
or who will dissipate their inheritances. Kids who aren't afraid
of the future. Who aren't afraid of ending up badly. Who
aren't afraid of disease. Kids who aren't afraid. Who won't
grow old. Among these kids there is also you, who have plenty of fears. Fear of dying at this exact instant. Fear of not being
able to get rid of this perpetual incurable virginity. Fear of not
liberating yourself from all this. Of getting stuck in it
ineluctably. Fear of never seeing David and Gaia and the others again. Fear of what will happen tonight. Yes, among them,
the cream of the crop of '89, there is also this frightened
intruder, this imposter with no talent for imposture, so grimly
determined to get to the room of the woman he has threatened

with death that it doesn't even cross his mind that the only mistake is being here. His determination is so absolute you could read it in his eyes, if only he had the courage to look up.

No one is missing. Why should anyone be? Crowded around the buffet table, elbowing in for the last truffled bruschetta or salmon mousse tart . . . Elegant, amorphous, effeminate, soporific, like a costume drama. All there in full regalia, all at the peak of their human adventure.

Pose, folks! Come on! For the last family photo before the decline sets in. Now, when you still have golden skin, a flat stomach, and fresh breath. Now, when you can run a hundred kilometers without getting tired. Now, when you have the most sweet-smelling sweat in the universe, a marvelous balm to be bottled, this resin of youthful freshness. Take your places, folks. Come on! For the last family photo.

David doesn't look good in a tux. It's something I've always thought with satisfaction. His face is too handsome for him not to seem a mannequin or a soap actor. His body seems made for casual clothes: his long arms, his six-foot-plus height, his sculpted muscles: all this in a tux looks awkward, almost. And his big feet, shod in long, narrow black shoes, make him look like a penguin. *I'm more elegant than Dav tonight*, I catch myself thinking, overcome by a roaring wave of worldly euphoria. I'm gratified to observe that the advice I've given the party girl in recent months has been followed, and especially that nothing has been altered, even though in the meantime the *adviser* has fallen into disgrace. What magnanimity, my girl! Or what indifference! And it feels almost natural, as I conceive the plan that, as quickly as possible, will bring me to the room of the birthday girl, to swoop down on the bottles of red wine left unguarded on the round tables. I chose that wine, in fact, playing the sommelier to impress my little Gaia. Impulsively I also grab one of the serrated knives scattered on the tables. I see my hand cutting Gaia's jugular, I see purple rivers of blood running down her neck . . . And meanwhile I drink without restraint, violently. I gulp down as much as I can, until the galvanizing suspicion advances in me that I've become invisible. I see you but you can't see me. My vision is fogged. I have the vision of a micro-organism that sees but isn't seen. It's the miracle caused by this gasoline I have in my body. The miracle of my invisibility. No one notices me. No one has ever noticed me. That's the point. Shit, not even the birthday girl: only three days ago I confessed to her my ardent desire to stab her, and even she hasn't seen me. It's not that she's pretending not to see me. (How could she pretend? Come on, no one can be that cynical!) It's obvious that she hasn't seen me.

And thanks to the wonder of that invisibility, thanks to the red wine poured into an empty stomach, thanks to the alcoholic mixture rushing torrentially through my veins, thanks to the fact that the attention of the guests has been suddenly catalyzed by the black platform set up at the center of the garden, where Nanni Cittadini and his eighteen-year-old granddaughter in the pale dress with rosy highlights, at exactly midnight, have begun to dance the usual goddam Strauss waltz, while the troupe of waiters distributes the flutes of champagne and the lights are dimmed and a crude luminous cone follows the clumsy pirouetting of the two dancers . . . thanks to all this simultaneous confusion, I finally find the courage and the opportunity to go into the house.

So Nanni's living room, his big, ostentatious Empire-style living room, photographed countless times by the glossy magazines, sparkles for the last time under the gaze of this unwanted guest. I'm afraid that my chance encounter with the statue of his presumed ancestor is destined to remain if not the most engaging certainly the most cordial exchange in the course of this epoch of diplomatic frictions and emotional outbursts. Maybe someone could say it's the contrast with the indifference of the young people in evening dress and the treacle of the music spreading through the grounds that makes the bust's fleeting smile so lovable. Maybe someone could add that it's the statue's unexpected expansiveness that urges me to repay its courtesy with a bow. An inattentive spectator might dismiss this as the insane gesture of a drunk toward an inanimate object: in fact my gesture is an homage to the only polite creature to be encountered at a soirée where even the summer warmth seems one of the many special effects provided by this million-dollar movie production.

And who knows why I'm happy—and I say it without irony—to observe the actual resemblance between Nanni and the bust of his ancestor. If I were to be malicious I could attribute it to the talent for plagiarism and involuntary parody that Nanni has already displayed many times.

Is that it? Is it this attitude—the passion to make one's tastes match those of one's myths—that has driven old Nanni to adopt the pageboy hair style of his supposed ancestor? Is this why I suddenly seem to see an affinity between Nanni's ironic formality and the smile the statue insists on giving me? But then is it really so odd that Nanni, seduced by the insolent Brando-esque charm of this eighteenth-century statue, has tried to revive it, or at least its most obvious features, three hundred years later, on nothing less than his own face?

These are reflections that I manage to cultivate with an amused rather than a diabolical lucidity. I feel almost at ease. Only when I realize that the Brigitte Bardot-like line of the statue's nose seems to replicate the pert outline of my Gaia's do I feel so heavy-hearted that I have to stop looking.

In the meantime, on the walls of the cream-colored marble staircase that leads to the upper floors, as if symbolically marking the point of departure of my Via Crucis, the two copies of the Caravaggios are waiting for me. There's a half-dressed Madonna who seems to be smiling scornfully. I find these paintings so insulting and unseemly. They are pure ostentation, like the gold faucets on an emir's yacht, like a platinum cow-boy hat in the office of a Texas oilman. And who knows why, but it gives me great comfort to feel in my right jacket pocket the weight of the serrated knife.

The muffled sound of the waltz leads me, light-footed, upstairs, where I've never been.

You realize immediately that in that room is everything you've ever wanted, mixed up with everything you've always wanted to forget. Like an album of memories and a jungle gym of obsessions. You have never been in that room. You find it smaller and much messier than you imagined. It's as if Gaia had wanted to break the solemnity of the museum she was com-pelled to live in with a little healthy, unadorned modernity. You start at seeing your letter—your terrible letter—open on the desk, creased and unguarded. So this letter, which everyone will soon be talking about, really exists? How many times has she read it? Was once enough? Or was she content with the first five lines, at the end of which the festival of insults had already reached a peak of madness and intolerability? It occurs to you that your greatest torment, as you composed that mas-terwork of indecency, was the fear that she wouldn't read it to the end. That was all that mattered: that she not stop reading. You were like a beginning writer, eager not so much for approval as for opportunity. Yes, you wanted to enjoy your opportunity completely, aware that it would be the last grant-ed you by Gaia, by her family, and by her entire buttery, high-class world. That's why you pick up the letter, to see if the last page has been handled, like the preceding ones. And merely touching it makes you feel something alien about it, as if you couldn't be the author of that obscenity. You have the clear impression that it's a door opened onto madness. You feel dizzy. As though on the edge of a precipice.

Yes, this room is much smaller, much more modest than

you imagined. And although at a first, distracted glance it may seem to be filled with a lot of different things, a room of plenty, in fact it says little about its inhabitant. Maybe—you think spitefully (all you have left is spite!)—because there is little to know about her. It is cluttered with all the various items you would expect to find in the room of an empty-headed eighteen-year-old from a wealthy family in 1989: stuffed animals, pens of different colors, hair clips, a green-and-white striped couch, an indefinite number of photographs with backgrounds of foreign countries or the Dolomites, a pile of schoolbooks, clothes scattered everywhere, gaudy crumpled birthday cards, sneakers, little red candles, even a half-full glass of milk whose rim is still opalescent with the imprint of those magnificent lips.

Could there be a better theater for an orgy? Nanni came through that door and saw his granddaughter completely naked and David also completely naked and the other kid also completely naked . . . You are the excited novice detective at the scene of the crime. So, let's see: according to what Giacomo said, for months the two had been meeting here. You're short of breath. You would like to cry. But the tears won't come. You are astonished by how hard it is to breathe: it's as if a red-hot flame had attacked your vital organs; but of tears not a hint.

So you find yourself in the bathroom. The tub where Gaia loves to soak. The toilet where she pees. The bidet where she washes. The wastebasket where she throws her sanitary napkins. The laundry basket where she dumps her dirty underwear. What, didn't it occur to you, until now, that this place could exist? Why did you have so little imagination? Why, on the eve of the twenty-first century, did you believe in that sappy fable? How were you able to reconcile the erotic calvary of fetishes, of classroom wanks, of countless stolen relics with the idea that Gaia wasn't a woman? What nonsense is this?

What relationship is there between this frustrated-seminarian crap and the story of your family, so secular, so Jewish, so disillusioned, so libertine? This was your real folly, Dani. Your anachronism is your folly. Your repudiation of Bepy is your folly. Not the threatening letter, not in the least. The letter is only a faint emanation of it.

But the delirium ended there, in that bathroom, at the sight of stockings and underpants, evidently abandoned by Gaia before putting on her white debutante's dress, which instantly swept any superfluous thought from my mind.

Perhaps if only Gaia had been a little neater, if she hadn't left those sensually crumpled garments next to the tub, at the mercy of the first pervert to come along, things would have unfolded differently. But those tights and those underpants provided a spontaneous outlet for my excitement.

I picked up the underpants with religious caution. They were veiled at the right point by a shading of an ineffable color. Any Japanese would have paid thousands of yen to have them in his collection. To look at them and bring them to my nose was a single act. And that ammonia-like stench took me back: the grand London night when my brother, overwhelmed, had made me smell his stiffened fingers, a few days before my life changed. That same odor now brought to an end a period that had lasted five years. That same odor created a sort of subterranean continuity: a long bridge that seemed to reach toward my puberty. How did that overrated genius Henry Miller put it? *Cunt is international!* Nothing truer. They all have—to varying degrees—the same odor, which erases every metaphor and outlaws metaphysics.

Until I was stung from behind:

"What are you doing, you slime?"

I recognized Nanni's voice. Then I felt myself being grabbed and thrown out of the room. I must have reached that point of inebriation where the body disappears. It was as if Nanni had picked up a sack and were about to throw it down the stairs:

"Get out of here . . . Out . . . You shit . . . I've had it . . . All of you with my granddaughter . . . Out . . . God, my paintings! Who touched them? And the nose of the statue? Was it you, you goddam psychopath? Was it you? I'll report you, I'll report you . . . I should have done it to your grandfather . . . Now I'll do it to you . . . I'll have you locked up!"

No diplomacy in Nanni. Only a lot of exasperation: legitimate, sacrosanct, thirty-year-old exasperation. And in fact the balance sheet of Nanni's last three decades—in spite of appearances—wasn't among the rosiest: a whore of a wife, a suicide son, a psychotic grandson, a porn-star granddaughter . . . And now his beautiful copies of Caravaggio stabbed by who knows who and his adored statue with its little Brigitte Bardot nose cut off. And that's why he was chasing me out of his house, shouting like a man possessed, to the dismay of his four hundred and ninety-nine guests. He was doing what his granddaughter didn't want, and what she hadn't done: shifting the attention onto something different from her party and her self-celebration. That's why Gaia had pretended not to see me. In order not to cause a scandal, in order to safeguard the honor of her party, not to give up the longed-for happiness, she had run the risk of being murdered by that self-styled psychopath Daniel Sonnino. But, poor Gaia, she hadn't considered that the danger could come from the least suspect individual: that magnificent generous benefactor who, at the height of exasperation, infuriated by yet another violation of his granddaughter's privacy, hadn't had the composure to calculate the risk to which he was exposing the entire party. At this point it was clear that it would be stamped on the collective memory of an entire neighborhood (of an entire city? Come on, let's not exaggerate) for that scene and not for all the rest: farewell attention to detail! Farewell to all the refinements that Gaia had done her best to provide so that the party—her party—should not be forgotten! Giacomo had won: the spoiler had triumphed. I was only the instrument he had used for his nefarious purposes.

Now everyone would remember Gaia Cittadini's eighteenth-birthday party only as the luxurious backdrop for a highly exhilarating scene. The class intellectual—with his Danny Kaye face, his romantic airs, his public whacking off, his affectations, his mania for mysteriously breaking off friendships, his lack of control, his paranoid habit of transforming reality, turning it upside down—shows up at the party of the girl he had threatened with death a few hours earlier, and, midway through the party, completely drunk, is thrown out by the party girl's grandfather, who accuses him publicly of going into his granddaughter's bedroom to sniff her underpants and panty hose. That's the scene they'll all remember. That's the scene they'll be talking about for a long time, they'll be regaling the world with, to its great delight.

But why, Nanni, are you angry with me? I'm telling you that this time you won't make me feel guilty. I'm only the obscure instrument of history: if Bepy is the anarchic regicide who ignites the conflict, I'm the bomb that puts an end to the hostilities. Basically, if you think about it, the fight between the Sonninos and the Cittadinis coincided, ironically, with the Cold War. Could that be why—in the middle of that goddam year 1989—we both feel confused and useless as rubble from the Berlin Wall? For once we're allies. We're the dupes. Come on, Nanni, it's not my fault if Bepy fucked your wife. And it's not your fault if Bepy didn't want to buy the Caravaggios and if my father idolizes you and my mother detests you. It's hardly my fault if your son killed himself like that and if Bepy predicted it. Or if your grandson is an alcoholic psychopath with a chronic need to seem poor. Or if already at the age of fifteen your dear little girl was bestowing certain heavenly favors on Dav & company. And of course, I admit it, it's not your fault if I'm a fetishizing masturbator with a lot of initiative. No, Nanni, we have nothing to do with it. The Sonninos have nothing to do with it. The Cittadinis have nothing to do with it. The Jews have nothing to do with it. The Catholics have nothing to do with it. Bepy is dead and you are definitely getting old. It happened like this, it could have happened some other way. I'm the first to admit it. But it happened exactly like this.

What to say about it all, then?

I think it's intolerable to end one's adolescence with this scene. And yet it's with this scene that my adolescence ends. It's this scene—not the thousand other scenes involving my moderately happy or honestly unhappy friends—with which I have accounts to settle. But is it possible that only now, on hearing Nanni's curses again, do I suddenly understand my mistake? The great mistake of those years. Wanting to compete with people I couldn't compete with. Ingenuously believing that all men were equal. Not paying attention to that classic moralist Grandfather Alfio when he told me that all men are different. And that their differentness is the bitter fruit of all suffering and all overflowing joy. That joy is the direct manifestation of someone else's suffering. That the inequality of our conditions is our delight. That coming in first implies that someone has come in second and third and fourth or hasn't even finished. That our happiness can't exist except to the detriment of everyone else's. Only now do I understand that there's nothing interesting in me, but only, if anything, in the beguiling conformation of my mythomania.

Let's say that during that moment (and by "moment" I mean the long period that followed the surreal experience at the Cittadini house) I wasn't lucid enough to be totally desperate, or desperate enough to understand that that pain had no purpose. Maybe I should have found comfort in the knowledge that everyone—every last one of them, no exceptions—would grow old badly. That time would render justice: yes, *time*, the notorious enemy of poets, at that moment was my only ally, my only hope of serenity: *time*, so ill-treated, would be charged with vindicating me: torturing the bodies of those copper-colored, aristocratic, flourishing eighteen-year-olds, so quick to show their solidarity with the vilified and death-threatened party girl, and to affect an equally cold reproach for that unbalanced, potential murderer—not to mention slasher of works of art and family treasures—Daniel Sonnino. Good Lord, it would be a relief to be capable of such a perverse wisdom: how amusing to be intoxicated by such inexorably and ecumenically apocalyptic scenarios! But yet again, alas, I must report my inability to be useful to myself in the fundamental moments of existence. Ah yes, because instead of fantasizing about the future varicose veins of Diamante Arcieri or Dav's decrepitude or the apoplectic stroke that would (who knows?) murder Nanni and all his race, I was drowning in the sea of sentimentality where the impotent or the heartsick flounder. I couldn't help it: I found it really amusing to torture myself with the melodramatic idea that I wouldn't recover. That all this would condition my life fatally. That I had had my chance (yes, I had consumed it but had forgotten to digest). And blah blah blah . . . behind the *voix du coeur:* the wailing bass drum of late adolescence!

But, putting aside these trite sentimentalities that dishonor the one who conceived them at the time and has the audacity to transcribe them today, I don't want to be silent on the question that has suddenly begun to gnaw at me: can someone explain to me why, as this plane is about to land, after the light of dawn has suddenly crept in through the windows, mixing with the aroma of warmed-up brioches, after I've written for an entire night, tormenting my fingertips, as Nanni's insults

dissolve into this narrow, pressurized space, and I am still flee-
ing, after so long, the looks of the party guests, among whom I
so rashly wanted to mingle; can someone explain to me why,
fostering the impression that the intervening years have never
existed or have counted for little or nothing, as I get myself
ready to see my father and mother, who certainly will come to
pick up their prodigal son, to dissuade him from going to
Nanni's funeral, a few hours from the moment when, after
almost fifteen years, I will see Gaia, will observe her metamorphosis from a debutante dressed in pink and white to a young
woman in mourning; can someone explain to me why, in this
grave moment, rather than concentrating my emotional attention on the period of my life so filled with things irremediably
lost—Bepy's broad smile, dancing with my mother to the notes
of "A Place in the Sun," the white beard of my forty-year-old
father, the exhausting nights beside that indomitable vitalist
Teo, the Rubens' turkey, the Pontormo Madonna suddenly
appearing on the dock at Positano, the optimistic roar of the
end of the twentieth century, my century—why, rather than letting myself be occupied by all this, do I think with melancholy
of the splendid opportunity thrown to the winds on that terrible night—the chance to get my hands on Gaia's tights and
underpants, which would have adorned the sanctuary of
depravity I have so laboriously erected in the course of this lifetime?

ABOUT THE AUTHOR

Alessandro Piperno was born in Rome in 1972. He is a professor of French literature at Rome's Tor Vergata University. He is the author of *Proust: Anti-Jew*.

www.europaeditions.com

The Days of Abandonment
Elena Ferrante
Fiction - 192 pp - $14.95 - isbn 978-1-933372-00-6

"Stunning . . . The raging, torrential voice of the author is something rare."—*The New York Times*

"I could not put this novel down. Elena Ferrante will blow you away."
—ALICE SEBOLD, author of *The Lovely Bones*

The gripping story of a woman's descent into devastating emptiness after being abandoned by her husband with two young children to care for.

Troubling Love
Elena Ferrante
Fiction - 144 pp - $14.95 - isbn 978-1-933372-16-7

"In tactile, beautifully restrained prose, Ferrante makes the domestic violence that tore [the protagonist's] household apart evident."—*Publishers Weekly*

"Ferrante has written the 'Great Neapolitan Novel.'"
—*Corriere della Sera*

Delia's voyage of discovery through the chaotic streets and claustrophobic sitting rooms of contemporary Naples in search of the truth about her mother's untimely death.

www.europaeditions.com

Cooking with Fernet Branca
James Hamilton-Paterson
Fiction - 288 pp - $14.95 - isbn 978-1-933372-01-3

"Provokes the sort of indecorous involuntary laughter that has more in common with sneezing than chuckling. Imagine a British John Waters crossed with David Sedaris."—*The New York Times*

Gerald Samper has his own private Tuscan hilltop where he wiles away his time working as a ghostwriter for celebrities and inventing wholly original culinary concoctions. His idyll is shattered by the arrival of Marta. A series of hilarious misunderstandings brings this odd couple into ever-closer proximity.

Old Filth
Jane Gardam
Fiction - 256 pp - $14.95 - isbn 978-1-933372-13-6

"This remarkable novel [...] will bring immense pleasure to readers who treasure fiction that is intelligent, witty, sophisticated and— a quality encountered all too rarely in contemporary culture— adult."—*The Washington Post*

The engrossing and moving account of the life of Sir Edward Feathers, from birth in colonial Malaya, to Wales, where he is sent as a "Raj orphan," to Oxford, his career and marriage, parallels much of the twentieth century's dramatic history.

www.europaeditions.com

Total Chaos
Jean-Claude Izzo
Fiction/Noir - 256 pp - $14.95 - isbn 978-1-933372-04-4

"Rich, ambitious and passionate . . . his sad, loving portrait of his native city is amazing."—*The Washington Post*

"Full of fascinating characters, tersely brought to life in a prose style that is (thanks to Howard Curtis's shrewd translation) traditionally dark and completely original."—*The Chicago Tribune*

The first installment in the Marseilles Trilogy.

Chourmo
Jean-Claude Izzo
Fiction/Noir - 256 pp - $14.95 - isbn 978-1-933372-17-4

"Like the best noir writers—and he is among the best—Izzo not only has a keen eye for detail but also digs deep into what makes men weep."—*Time Out New York*

Fabio Montale is dragged back into the mean streets of a violent, crime-infested Marseilles after the disappearance of his long-lost cousin's teenage son.

The Goodbye Kiss
Massimo Carlotto
Fiction/Noir - 192 pp - $14.95 - isbn 978-1-933372-05-1

"A nasty, explosive little tome warmly recommended to fans of James M. Cain for its casual amorality and truly astonishing speed."—*Kirkus Reviews*

An unscrupulous womanizer, as devoid of morals now as he once was full of idealistic fervor, returns to Italy, where he is wanted for a series of crimes. To avoid prison he sells out his old friends, turns his back on his former ideals, and cuts deals with crooked cops. To earn himself the guise of respectability he is willing to go even further, maybe even as far as murder.

Death's Dark Abyss
Massimo Carlotto
Fiction/Noir - 192 pp - $14.95 - isbn 978-1-933372-18-1

"A narrative voice that in Lawrence Venuti's translation is cold and heartless—but, in a creepy way, fascinating."—*The New York Times*

A riveting drama of guilt, revenge, and justice, Massimo Carlotto's *Death's Dark Abyss* tells the story of two men and the savage crime that binds them. During a robbery, Raffaello Beggiato takes a young woman and her child hostage and later murders them. Beggiato is arrested, tried, and sentenced to life. The victims' father and husband, Silvano, plunges into a deepening abyss until the day the murderer seeks his pardon and he begins to plot his revenge.

www.europaeditions.com

Hangover Square
Patrick Hamilton
Fiction/Noir - 280 pp - $14.95 - isbn 978-1-933372-06-8

"Hamilton is a sort of urban Thomas Hardy: always a pleasure to read, and as social historian he is unparalleled."—NICK HORNBY

Adrift in the grimy pubs of London at the outbreak of World War II, George Harvey Bone is hopelessly infatuated with Netta, a cold, contemptuous small-time actress. George also suffers from occasional blackouts. During these moments one thing is horribly clear: he must murder Netta.

Boot Tracks
Matthew F. Jones
Fiction/Noir - 208 pp - $14.95 - isbn 978-1-933372-11-2

"More than just a very good crime thriller, this dark but illuminating novel shows us the psychopathology of the criminal mind . . . A nightmare thriller with the power to haunt."
—*Kirkus Reviews* (starred)

A commanding, stylishly written novel that tells the harrowing story of an assassination gone terribly wrong and the man and woman who are taking their last chance to find a safe place in a hostile world.

www.europaeditions.com

Love Burns
Edna Mazya
Fiction/Noir - 192 pp - $14.95 - isbn 978-1-933372-08-2

"This book, which has Woody Allen overtones, should be of great interest to readers of black humor and psychological thrillers."
—*Library Journal* (starred)

Ilan, a middle-aged professor of astrophysics, discovers that his young wife is having an affair. Terrified of losing her, he decides to confront her lover instead. Their meeting ends in the latter's murder—the unlikely murder weapon being Ilan's pipe—and in desperation, Ilan disposes of the body in the fresh grave of his kindergarten teacher. But when the body is discovered, the mayhem begins.

Departure Lounge
Chad Taylor
Fiction/Noir - 176 pp - $14.95 - isbn 978-1-933372-09-9

"Smart, original, surprising and just about as cool as a novel can get . . . Taylor can flat out write."—*The Washington Post*

A young woman mysteriously disappears. The lives of those she has left behind—family, acquaintances, and strangers intrigued by her disappearance—intersect to form a captivating latticework of coincidences and surprising twists of fate. Urban noir at its stylish and intelligent best.

www.europaeditions.com

Carte Blanche
Carlo Lucarelli
Fiction/Noir - 120 pp - $14.95 - isbn 978-1-933372-15-0

"This is Alan Furst country, to be sure."—*Booklist*

The house of cards built by Mussolini in the last months of World War II is collapsing and Commissario De Luca faces a world mired in sadistic sex, dirty money, drugs and murder.

Dog Day
Alicia Giménez-Bartlett
Fiction/Noir - 208 pp - $14.95 - isbn 978-1-933372-14-3

"In Nicholas Caistor's smooth translation from the Spanish, Giménez-Bartlett evokes pity, horror and laughter with equal adeptness. No wonder she won the Femenino Lumen prize in 1997 as the best female writer in Spain."—*The Washington Post*

Delicado and her maladroit sidekick, Garzón, investigate the murder of a tramp whose only friend is a mongrel dog named Freaky.

www.europaeditions.com

The Big Question
Wolf Erlbruch
Children's Illustrated Fiction - 52 pp - $14.95 - isbn 978-1-933372-03-7

Named Best Book at the 2004 Children's Book Fair in Bologna.

"[*The Big Question*] offers more open-ended answers than the likes of Shel Silverstein's *Giving Tree* (1964) and is certain to leave even younger readers in a reflective mood."—*Kirkus Reviews*

A stunningly beautiful and poetic illustrated book for children that poses the biggest of all big questions: Why am I here?

The Butterfly Workshop
Wolf Erlbruch
Children's Illustrated Fiction - 48 pp - $14.95 - isbn 978-1-933372-12-9

Illustrated by the winner of the 2006 Hans Christian Andersen Award.

For children and adults alike: Odair, one of the Designers of All Things and grandson of the esteemed inventor of the rainbow, has been banished to the insect laboratory as punishment for his over-active imagination. But he still dreams of one day creating a cross between a bird and a flower.